Demons are Forever

What Reviewers Say About The Elite Operatives series:

"Baldwin and Alexiou have written a barn burner of a thriller [in *Dying to Live*]. The reader is taken in from the first page to the last. The tension is maintained throughout the book with rare exception. Baldwin and Alexiou are defining the genre of romantic suspense within the lesbian genre with this series. You'll find yourself rushing to purchase the first three books in the series if you haven't already read them, or, if you have read them, wishing the authors would write the fifth in the series faster."—*Lambda Literary*

"Kim Baldwin & Xenia Alexiou just get better and better at coming up with tightly written thrillers with plenty of 'seat of the pants' action. *Missing Lynx* is a roller coaster ride into the seamier side of life and the bonds which bind humans into trying to better the world. This is a book which grips the reader until the final page!"—*Just About Write*

"Unexpected twists and turns, deadly action, complex characters and multiple subplots converge to make this book a gripping page turner. *Lethal Affairs* mixes political intrigue with romance, giving the reader an easy flowing and fast-moving story that never lets up. A must-read, even though it has been out for a while. *Thief of Always*, the duo's second, and equally good book in the Elite Operatives series, came out earlier this year."—*Curve Magazine*

Praise for *Dubbel Doelwit*, the Dutch translation of *Lethal Affairs*:

"[Lethal Affairs] is a smoothly written action thriller which draws the reader into the life of special agent Domino. The plot surrounding Domino's secret mission is well constructed...the tension and emotional charge is built up to great heights, which makes it hard to put the book down. Equally admirable is the way in which the characters are given dimension. In most action-oriented (intrigue) fiction you won't find in-depth psychological portraits, but because of striking details, the characters become very real. As a cherry on top, the authors gift you a few sensual scenes which will leave you breathless. It's nice to know that [Lethal Affairs] is but the first entry in the Elite Operative Series."—The Flemish Magazine *ZIZO*

"The first entry in this new series shows a lot of promise. ...The plot is very well constructed. And the developments between the two women, makes all of it even more exciting. When you read books in this genre, you know you will run into things that are unlikely. Thankfully it doesn't get out of control in [Lethal Affairs] and doesn't spoil the fun you will have reading it. Bring on the next book in the series!"—*Lesbischlezen.nl*

"I loved [Lethal Affairs]: a very exciting story about a 'special agent' or actually a killer for hire. In this book you are simultaneously following the journalist who is looking for a good story and the story of a woman who wants to remain invisible and will go to almost any length to accomplish that. [Lethal Affairs] is therefore doubly exciting. It's a smooth read."—*VrowenThrillers.nl*

By the Authors

The Elite Operatives Series

Lethal Affairs

Thief of Always

Missing Lynx

Dying to Live

Demons are Forever

By Kim Baldwin

Hunter's Pursuit

Force of Nature

Whitewater Rendezvous

Flight Risk

Focus of Desire

Breaking the Ice

High Impact

Demons are Forever

by

Kim Baldwin
and Xenia Alexiou

2012

DEMONS ARE FOREVER

ISBN 10: 1-60282-648-X
ISBN 13: 978-1-60282-648-9

This Trade Paperback Original Is Published By
Bold Strokes Books, Inc.
P.O. Box 249
Valley Falls, NY 12185

First Edition: March 2012

Credits
Editor: Shelley Thrasher
Production Design: Susan Ramundo
Cover Design By Sheri (graphicartist2020@hotmail.com)

Acknowledgments

The authors wish to thank all the talented women at Bold Strokes Books for making this book possible. Radclyffe, for her vision, faith in us, and example. Editor Shelley Thrasher, your insightful editing of this book is deeply appreciated. Jennifer Knight, for invaluable insights into how to craft a series. Graphic artist Sheri for another amazing cover. Connie Ward, BSB publicist and first-reader extraordinaire, and all of the other support staff who work behind the scenes to make each BSB book an exceptional read.

We'd also like to thank our dear friend and first-reader Jenny Harmon, for your invaluable feedback and insights. And finally, to the readers who encourage us by buying our books, showing up for personal appearances, and for taking the time to e-mail us. Thank you so much.

Xenia, with only two Elite Ops books left to write I'm already missing the joyous task of co-authoring your stories. Working with you on the series has been one of the most fun endeavors I've ever undertaken, and I'll long cherish the countless happy memories of writing, reading, and signing together.

For Marty, for forty plus years of friendship and so much more. Your encouragement started me on this path, and I'm forever grateful.

Mom and Dad, I miss you both so much and know you're watching out for me. And for my brother Tom, for always saying yes when I need a ride to the airport.

I also have to thank a wonderful bunch of friends who provide unwavering support for all my endeavors. Claudia and Esther, Pattie, Linda, Kat, Felicity. You are family, and near or far, I hold you always close to my heart.

Kim Baldwin, February 2012

My eternal gratitude and respect to my invaluable friend Kim. Thank you for pointing me in this direction and for being there every step of the way. I am always there for you, no matter what…and so what if the series has two books left. I've got more stories in me and I want my wingman there.

Mom, Dad, and Sis. You are my biggest support and comfort. Thank you for everything.

May, you have made my world a richer place to write in and about.

And as always a very big thank you to my wonderfully supportive friends. Claudia, Esther, Nicki, Dennis, Steven, Georgia, thank you for putting up with my dark moods and for your constant encouragement.

Last but never least, a big bow of appreciation to all the readers who enjoy the stories and make writing one of the most rewarding things I've ever done. YOU ALL ROCK.

Xenia Alexiou, February 2012

Dedication

To May

It took me more than two decades to realize the one who could love me unconditionally, give herself to me completely, and confront my demons fearlessly was the shy sixteen-year-old girl I once ran from.

I'm eternally grateful you never gave up on me.

I gave you my first kiss and I will give you my last.

I love you.

Xenia

PROLOGUE

Near Teaneck, New Jersey
October 28

"You're hurting me!" Gigi struggled against the tight grip on her arms and fought to find her footing, but the two men flanking her dragged her up the stairs like her mother used to when she had to see the dentist.

The two johns had picked her up on a Manhattan street corner, but instead of taking her to a hotel, they'd brought her to a house in New Jersey without any furnishings. The half-hour journey itself was odd, too. Neither of the men said much or wanted to get down to business with her in the dark sedan.

"I'm a pro, I know the deal," she told the men as they pulled her along. "You don't have to fucking force me." She heard the tones of someone punching numbers into a cell phone.

"Put me through to Dario," a man behind her said. "I can deliver your order in forty minutes."

"What order?" Gigi craned to see him. A bald, buff, middle-aged man—looked like Mr. Clean. "Where's the other girl?"

When they'd arrived at the house, she hadn't noticed him among the several men present, many also in business suits. Another working girl was there, too, an unfamiliar blonde. They'd had some drinks, but the party had barely started when the two guys who'd picked her up grabbed her and hauled her upstairs.

The bald guy ignored her and continued his conversation.

"Yo, Mr. Clean! I asked you something," she yelled.

The man paused and turned his attention on her for the first time. She couldn't remember ever having seen a look like that but was sure she'd never forget it. His dark eyes looked as empty as those of a dead fish. She'd been in scary, uncertain situations before; it was part of the job, especially when she was after a fast buck and the johns were dubious at best. But she'd never felt so terrified and helpless. God, were they going to kill her? She'd heard plenty of stories about working girls disappearing or found dead, but those tragedies happened to others, not her. Had she been too arrogant? Was this a warning to change her life? Would she get that chance now?

"I want to go home. Where are you taking me?" She clawed at the walls as they dragged her down a long hallway with closed doors on either side. "Where's the other girl?" she asked again.

None of them responded. Being ignored scared her almost as much as the lifeless eyes of the man behind her.

They reached a door at the end of the corridor and the man on her left opened it. Without a word, they threw her forward, and she slid over the parquet like a bowling ball, hitting her head on the wall. "Please, let me go," she said as she got to her knees and whirled toward them. But the door was already closing. Gigi ran to it and tried the knob. Locked. "Let me out, you assholes!" She pounded on the thick wood with her fists, but their steps already sounded faint.

When she was sure they wouldn't return immediately, she studied her small, empty prison. The walls looked newly painted but didn't smell like it. Windows along one wall drew her and she tried to open one. "Goddamn it," she yelled when a fake nail broke off. She couldn't force any of them open. Not that it would have helped. She was on the second floor, too far up to drop without breaking something or killing herself. And the place was isolated—the nearest sign of civilization was too far away for anyone to hear her scream. She could see only a distant light, illuminating a rooftop that might be a house and, beyond that, a cell tower. The rest was dark woods, save for an abandoned swing set and kiddie pool below her window.

She had only one possible way to get out of there safely. They'd taken her purse and cell, but she always hid a spare phone for emergencies. She pulled it from her boot and hazily hit the first number on her speed dial. Damn, why had she drunk so much? Usually booze helped numb her, but now she couldn't think clearly.

When the line picked up, she gripped the phone tighter and a seed of hope sprouted against her panic. "Thank Jesus. You gotta help me, I'm fucked," she whispered loudly, in a rush. "Some guys picked me up and they've locked me in a room and I think they're gonna kill me."

The reassuring voice of her friend replied. "Gigi? Where are you? What are you talking about?"

"I'm in bumfuck Jersey somewhere. Near Teaneck, I think." She kept an ear attuned to the hallway in case the men returned. "Some big white house with empty rooms. It's just all creepy-ass wrong. I don't think they brought me here for sex, and they got some other girl here, too. One guy was talking to someone on the phone about making a delivery. I think they meant me."

"Are you drunk?"

"Are you even listening? I'm not drunk and I'm not crazy. Something's very wrong here."

"If you really think you're in danger, hang up right now and call 911. Even if you don't know where you are, they can trace your cell and find you."

"Yeah, right. Okay." She would rarely even consider calling the police, but this time she didn't hesitate. She mashed the disconnect button with shaking hands and dialed the number.

"911. What is the nature of your emergency?"

"Some guys have me locked up in a room and I think they're gonna kill me." She slurred her words.

"What is your name and location, ma'am?"

"I don't know where the fuck I am. A big white house. Near Teaneck, I think. There are trees and a swing set outside, and one of those blue kiddie pools, upside down. And I can see a cell tower."

"What is your name, ma'am?" the dispatcher repeated in a monotone.

"Gigi. Uh, no…uh, Francine Shelhorn. Look, that's not important, just get the cops out here. These guys are gonna do something to me, I know it. I think they're gonna kill me and deliver me to some guy named Dario."

"What makes you think your life is in danger, ma'am? Have they hurt you or threatened you?"

"I just *know*, okay? They've fucking locked me up, I said!"

"Have you been drinking, ma'am?"

Before she could reply, footsteps rang in the hall. They were coming back. In a panic, she shut the cell, disconnecting the call, and hurriedly tossed it toward a dark corner of the room. It slid across the smooth parquet floor and disappeared beneath the edge of the long curtain that ran along the far wall.

Seconds later, the door opened, and Mr. Clean and the two guys who'd picked her up came back into the room. While the two goons held her down, the bald guy pulled out a syringe.

"What the fuck! No! Stop!" she screamed, as she tried unsuccessfully to pull free.

But they were far too strong, and Mr. Clean injected the contents of the syringe into her arm. Once he did, they released her and left without saying a word. This time, she clearly heard the sound of the lock being thrown.

She started to crawl toward the curtain to get her phone, but almost immediately her arms and legs began to go leaden, her muscles unresponsive. Whatever the hell they'd shot her up with was paralyzing her. Before she could go six feet, she lay prone on the floor, head to the side and unable to move, but still fully awake.

Gigi couldn't speak or feel anything but the faint, rapid pounding of her heart. She could only see and hear. Her total and complete helplessness terrified her more than anything she'd ever experienced.

After fifteen or twenty excruciating minutes, the two men returned. They carried her back to the sedan, dumped her in the rear seat, and took her for a short ride. Since she couldn't move her head, she stared at the sedan's floor mat during the journey, then saw a smattering of images that told her they were taking her into a medical clinic or doctor's office. The dark outer rooms they passed through gave way to their well-illuminated destination, where she saw a cabinet full of medicines, a tray of surgical instruments, and a plastic IV container on a stand before they laid her flat on her back on a bed or table of some sort. She heard them leave.

What in God's name were they planning? The sterile tray held neat rows of scalpels, clamps, and other shiny medical tools. She'd barely begun to imagine the possibilities when two new people entered her field of vision: a man and woman dressed in surgical gowns and matching caps. White masks concealed their faces and gloves covered their hands.

"Which first?" the woman asked.

"The blonde," the man answered as he moved farther away from Gigi until she could see only his head. The woman followed, and from the sound of it, she was wheeling over the tray of instruments. The pair faced each other now, looking down at something. It was likely the platinum-haired girl she'd seen at the house.

"We'll take the kidneys first," the man said in a matter-of-fact tone. "Then the liver, corneas. The heart last. Same with the other." He glanced at a clock on the wall. "Let's begin. Scalpel."

Gigi screamed but no sound left her mouth.

CHAPTER ONE

Boston
November 16

"Don't hesitate to ask for me again next time you're in need of...company." The beautiful brunette traced Landis Coolidge's bottom lip with her finger.

"There won't be a next time, Jade." Landis smiled and bit the finger playfully.

"I was under the impression you enjoyed my services." The call girl pouted in disappointment. "You're not the type to fake orgasms."

"I pay so I don't have to fake anything." Landis grabbed the envelope on the table near the door. "It has nothing to do with your performance. You were great, most of you are, but...repetition bores." She smiled sweetly and handed Jade the payment.

"Repetition also makes perfect." Jade caressed Landis's hand as she took the envelope.

"Unless you used the Lord's name in vain all evening. Then striving for better is redundant."

"Well, should you—"

"Thank you, Jade." Landis was already tired of this conversation, and a glance at her watch confirmed their interaction was running two minutes beyond its allotted time. "Good night," she added, and shut the door.

She stared at her PEZ collection in its custom glass case next to the door and smiled contentedly. "Why can't they all be beautiful and silent like you guys?" she asked the plastic faces.

Her prized three-hundred-plus collection was methodically organized according to date of issue, the first slot occupied by a rare 1958 bunny and the last by a 2011 Thor. Her favorite was the full set of 1965 candy shooters—nine small handguns in a variety of colors. She routinely spent a half hour on eBay every morning over coffee, searching for new acquisitions. Price was not an issue. She looked for quirky releases that spoke to her and only went after those in pristine condition.

The rest of her spacious loft condo was as neat and obsessively arranged as her PEZ figures, and the unconventional open layout suited her personality. The three levels spread out in a fan-like arrangement, each separated by a few wide stairs. This largest bottom level held a corner kitchen with stainless-steel appliances and a granite-topped island, and a comfortable modern seating area that faced the floor-to-ceiling windows on one wall. The black-leather couch held a pair of red pillows for color, but the matching chairs were devoid of adornment. The chrome-and-glass coffee and end tables and matching chrome lamps sparkled from obsessive polishing, as did the hardwood floors throughout.

Visitors often remarked about the sparse furnishings and lack of personal items, which suggested the loft's occupant was a recent arrival still settling in. But Landis had moved here directly from the Elite Operative Organization's Colorado campus more than two decades earlier, and she'd simply never abandoned the clean, uncluttered lifestyle that had comforted her during her adolescence in the dorms.

Scaling the wide steps, she walked past her work level to the third-level bedroom and with one swoop pulled the sheets off the bed. She could have waited for the cleaning lady in the morning, but she couldn't bear to sleep on sweaty, creased sheets. Once she'd changed the bedding with the kind of meticulous care that would put the best hotel to shame, Landis stripped off her rumpled button-down shirt and slacks and tossed those into the hamper as well.

After a quick shower—two minutes shorter than usual to make up for the lost time with the call girl—she donned her work clothes: comfortable torn jeans and one of many T-shirts depicting Landor the Demon, the anti-hero protagonist of her popular graphic novels. On her way to her drawing board, she inspected her surroundings to make sure nothing was out of place.

The second-floor workspace was as tidy as the rest of the loft. Her drawing table and stool faced the windows, giving her a panoramic view of Boston Harbor. Her pens and mechanical pencils lay arranged in a tray according to line width and color, and custom cabinets concealed her published work, files, and original drawings from view. The single back wall, covered with a massive mural she'd done herself, was the only artwork in the loft. An homage to Emily, her other main character, it depicted a beautiful golden-brown-haired woman in a long white dress, her expression one of longing and regret.

Landis settled onto her padded stool. From here she could see all three of her digital clocks—the large wall display in the bedroom, the small one on her drawing board, and the glowing red numbers on the coffee table in the darkened living area below. She made sure all three were synched to the correct time before she picked up the remote to her music player and completed her routine. Shuffling through a myriad of jazz selections, she selected a remixed assortment of John Coltrane classics and put the volume low.

Staring out at the twinkling lights of boats in the harbor from her thirty-second-floor perch, she absentmindedly plucked her posable Landor action figure from its Velcroed base atop her drawing table and bent it into a variety of positions as she searched for inspiration.

Her loyal friend and colleague Gianna Truman frequently made fun of her obsessive need to be meticulous about every aspect of her life and often said Landis was constantly trying to perfect perfection. Landis believed that the world and life in general were wrought with chaos and unnecessary emotional debris, and no one could change that. But if she could control and direct her personal environment, her own world, then it would sure as hell be perfect. Her idea of perfect, anyway.

Her need for faultlessness had initially inspired her stories and drawings thirty years earlier. In Landor, she'd created an exceptionally flawed hero: a demon forever doomed to struggle between what he *had* to do and what he *wanted* to do—a conundrum familiar to all Elite Operatives.

Landor wanted a world free of pain and corruption, and one fateful day he fell from Lucifer's grace when, fed up, he decided to forego orders and stop hurting innocent people. In retaliation, Lucifer doomed him to a life of unrest and internal struggle. He told Landor he would free him of his hold only if, when the time came, he made an unspecified "ultimate sacrifice" that would prove how badly he wanted his freedom.

Landor spent centuries doing Satan's dirty work, waiting for that opportunity, being who he was born to be but never who he was meant to be, until one day while in human form, he met and fell in love with the very beautiful and very mortal Emily. Then Lucifer spelled out the terms of the ultimate sacrifice: *Kill her and you're free.*

Enraged, Landor refused and struck Lucifer, and Lucifer lashed back, unleashing such an uproar in hell the earth shook. He was about to kill Landor when he changed his mind.

"This is too easy. You are free, weakling," Satan declared. "Go, traitor, but should you ever speak to her, or love another mortal, I will kill them personally. Slowly, while you watch."

In the five years since, Landor roamed the earth, helping instead of hurting and finding pleasure in the arms of women he knew he could never love. He never again approached Emily, either as demon or human, but he kept watch on her from a distance, interceding when necessary to protect her from harm.

Landis, like her protagonist, was free to create her perfect, peaceful world—at least when she wasn't on assignment. But like Landor, she felt doomed to live in it alone. In order to do her job well, she had to free herself from any emotional attachments. Commitments of any sort only clouded her judgment and got others hurt. The only time she had let anyone in her heart was years ago, and the woman ended up dying in her arms. Sighing, she replaced the action figure on his perch and plucked a pencil from the tray. "Issue 53," she said out loud. "Let's see what Emily is up to."

She'd just finished the outline of Emily's face when her cell rang. The caller ID on her BlackBerry told her it was Montgomery Pierce, Chief Administrator of the Elite Operatives Organization, so she answered with her code name and identification number. "Chase 200967."

"I know it's late but—"

"Platitudes. What do you need?"

"Be here ASAP." Pierce waited for confirmation.

Here always meant the sixty-three-acre EOO facility, tucked into the Rocky Mountains in Colorado. Since she never wore a timepiece when she drew, Landis glanced up at each clock in turn. All read 3:12 a.m. "ASAP can put me there at thirteen hundred hours," she replied, and hung up.

❖

Southwestern Colorado

Jaclyn Harding woke up feeling drowsy, albeit surprisingly rested for the first time in months. She scanned the room and slowly rose from the narrow, white-sheeted cot. The security camera mounted in the far corner followed her as she walked over to the plastic chair where her jacket rested. She knew these cold, sparse rooms only too well. In another life, she'd been treated for cuts and concussions in the EOO infirmary. Nothing about the sterile, depressing rooms had changed.

She searched the inside jacket pocket for her Marlboros. She'd started smoking since Cassady's death; it seemed the only thing that could stop her hands from shaking. Though it was unhealthy and disgusting, she couldn't find the strength to care. Frustrated the pack wasn't there, she looked up at the cam. "Why the fuck am I here?"

Moments later, EOO Chief Administrator Montgomery Pierce entered with two cups of coffee and wordlessly offered her one.

"I want my cigarettes," she said as she accepted the steaming cup.

"You don't need them."

"Not in the mood to discuss my needs. Now, can I have my damn smokes?"

Pierce glanced up at the cam and nodded.

Director of Training David Arthur, another member of the EOO's governing trio, came in and tossed the pack to Jack. "Those'll kill you."

Jack snapped her fingers. "Damn, I knew I was forgetting something," she said with mock surprise. "In case you hadn't noticed, I was doing a stellar job at exactly that before you interfered. Now, toss me the lighter, genius."

Arthur threw her the Bic and Jack immediately lit a cigarette. She sat on the bed and sipped her coffee. Both men remained silent while they observed her.

"So, what's with the silent movie?" She flicked her ashes onto the floor. "You didn't have to bring me all the way here to off me. Even Arthur isn't that dense."

Arthur took a step toward Jack and was about to say something when Pierce lifted his hand. "Don't let her push your buttons, David," he said without looking at his colleague.

Arthur's face and neck went beet red, clashing with his copper-colored crew cut. "Ungrateful…" He clenched his fists. "If it wasn't for us—"

"If it wasn't for you, I'd be better off and Cass would be alive," Jack replied.

"Wait outside, David," Pierce ordered him. "I'll call you if necessary."

Arthur mumbled something and left the room.

"Why am I here?" Jack stared down at her burning cigarette.

"Do you remember anything?"

"Be more specific. I generally remember more than I'd like."

"We came to your house…or the remains of it," Pierce said, disgust evident in his voice.

"Yeah, I remember," Jack replied. "The three of you decided on an impromptu visit. Forgive me for not being the perfect hostess and neglecting my domestic chores. Had I known you were coming…" She shrugged. "I'd at least have burned the place down."

Pierce dismissed her remark with a wave of his hand. "Do you remember why we were there?"

"Get to the point, Pierce." Jack stood to face him. "I clearly have gaps or I'd know why I'm here and how the fuck I got back to this hell. Oh, and by the way, thank you very fucking much for shooting me up." She rubbed the sore spot on her neck where the tranquilizer dart had hit her. "Slept like a baby."

"I'm sorry about that, but you didn't give us a choice. You were about to—"

"I know damn well what I was about to do." Despite her drunken condition, she did remember going for her gun, determined to end her misery. "What I don't know is, why the fuck you care." Jack smiled and took a step closer to Pierce. "You'd think I'd be doing you a favor." She sucked on her cigarette.

Pierce never moved. "That's not the case." He looked directly in her eyes.

"What is?" Jack inched nearer until they were a foot apart. She took another deep drag on her cigarette and exhaled the smoke in his face.

He never flinched. "I…we don't want you dead, Jaclyn."

"What *do* you want?"

"We want your help."

"With?"

"Finding Lynx…Cassady."

Jack's vision swam and for a moment she was dizzy on her feet as she replayed his words in her mind. She must have looked shocked because Pierce reached for her shoulder, but withdrew his hand when she flinched. "What the hell are you talking about? Cass is dead."

"She's alive. That's why we came to see you, but you didn't give me a chance to—"

"Cass is what?"

"Alive."

"Alive?" Jack hugged herself to steady her hands.

"Yes."

It couldn't be true. Either they had staged her death and lied to everyone at Cassady's memorial service, or they were lying now about her being alive. Irrational thoughts swamped her mind. None made sense. Furious, she lunged at Pierce, shoving him hard in the chest. He rocked on his heels but remained upright and didn't strike back.

"You planned this all along. Let me believe she was dead. What kind of a sick fuck are you?" she shouted.

"We hadn't planned any of this. Turns out Andor Rózsa kidnapped Cassady. He wants the money we took from his accounts in exchange for her. The moment we found out, we came to you."

Jack didn't know if she should cry from happiness or scream in frustration. It took all of her energy not to collapse. Even the cigarette couldn't stop her from shaking, so she dropped it in Pierce's coffee. "Where is she?"

"We don't know."

Jack started for the door. "I have to find her."

He blocked her way. "I know, but—"

"Out of my way, Pierce."

He didn't move. "You're going to need our help, Jaclyn."

"Thanks but no the fuck way."

"Work with us."

"I don't need you to find her."

"Yes, you do." He replied with the same calm, placid demeanor that always infuriated her. "We have the means."

"I'll find the means."

"You can't. He could be anywhere, and finding him will mean using all of our resources. Even then…"

Jack willed herself not to push the old man aside. "I told you I—"

"Jaclyn, we're going after her with or without you. But I don't know anyone better suited for this mission."

"Don't talk to me about *missions*," she spat. "That's none of my business and I'm sure as hell not going to work for you. My priority is Cass. I don't give a shit about you or your organization. It's your fault she's in this mess to begin with."

"I'm not asking you to work *for* us. I want you to work *with* us. Help us. We already have enough intel to get us started."

"Let me guess. Unless I agree to join your puppet show you won't share the goods."

"Correct."

Jack stepped closer until their noses almost touched. "That's blackmail, you bastard."

His face remained expressionless, his tone professional. "You're emotionally involved in this one, Jaclyn. You know what that means."

"It means it's none of your business."

"It means you'll be irrational. You'll jeopardize yourself."

"You send men and women out there daily to do exactly that," she said. "You've trained them to believe that dying for this organization is honorable. How is my dying for the woman I love less worthy?"

"It's not. But I'm saying you won't be able to think clearly. If you get yourself killed, you won't be any good to Cassady."

"And how will working for you lessen my odds of getting killed?"

"Special op Chase," he replied.

"Landis...Coolidge?" Jack mumbled. She was surprised to hear that name after so many years.

"Just you and her, with all the resources we can offer and money can buy."

"You want to assign me a babysitter?"

"A partner and friend. You've worked with her before. You used to be close and you know she's one of our best."

Jack took a step back and ran her hands through her hair. "I don't think I can accept these terms. I..."

Pierce started to reach for her again but stopped. "Jaclyn, listen to me. I know how you feel about us...about me. You feel betrayed and you have every right to. What we did to you was wrong, and I've never regretted anything more. If I could take it all back I would, but—"

"Don't push it, Pierce. I'm not buying a word of your heartfelt remorse. Nothing you say about what happened then will make a difference."

Pierce looked away. "I know," he said with an uncharacteristic tone, his voice breaking. "I know. But…" He looked at her. "This isn't about me or the organization. This is about Cassady, and I know how much you love her. I'm not asking you to do this for me. I'm asking you to do it for her. Do it because you want her back alive."

Jack flinched when Pierce suddenly put his hand on her shoulder.

"Do it because you know what it'll do to her if you get yourself killed," he said.

Jack pulled away and walked to the opposite side of the room. With her back to him, she stared down at the familiar campus where she'd spent the first half of her life. The last time she'd been here was for Cassady's memorial service.

Damn. Pierce was right. She would need his help to find Cass sooner rather than later. Her own resources would take time and an exchange of favors with people she'd vowed never to contact again. She'd left that life behind and doubted her less-than-honorable "friends" would help her, anyway. Unless she owed them, which she didn't, they conveniently forgot any previous favors or contracts she might have done for them. "Get Coolidge."

"We have a general meeting in an hour, and Coolidge will be there." Pierce frowned. She was in the same clothes they'd found her in after a three-day drinking binge. "Get yourself cleaned up. I'll have someone bring you something to wear. You'll want to be there for this one."

"You mean sit with your puppets?"

"My ops."

"As what? Phantom's ghost? They all think I'm dead. Cass told me you never informed them about my resurrection."

"That's correct. You're about to do that yourself."

Jack wasn't sure she was up to this revelation. She knew how most ops regarded treason or running away. Although many had considered it, none ever actually did. Call it misplaced loyalty or plain cowardice. No one ever left.

"Fine. Now get the hell out of here."

Chapter Two

New York City

Heather Snyder leafed through the sketches for the upcoming juniors' line and sighed. After three years at Cesare Chelline Fashions, a small design house in the Garment District, she was still just a patternmaker, consigned to one of five large workspaces in a factory-like room without a window. The new line played it safe: trendy colors, conservative lines, everyday fabrics. She longed for the day when someone important in the firm seriously considered some of the dozens of more innovative designs she'd come up with in her spare time. Her inspiration was Coco Chanel, the legend behind the timeless little black dress. Heather, too, favored simple but sophisticated outfits geared toward comfortable elegance.

Like most in her industry, Heather dressed to impress, regardless of her current low-level status at Chelline. Her work wardrobe was classic, refined, and professional, consisting mostly of well-tailored suits with feminine blouses, understated jewelry, and matching pumps. Today's dark-olive suit and crème silk blouse—good colors for her gold-brown hair and hazel eyes—were guaranteed to turn heads and elicit compliments.

She had an hour left in her shift when her cell phone chimed, alerting her to a text message that read **Dario at 7**.

The text reminded her she hadn't heard from Gigi since her friend's bizarre and disturbing phone call three weeks earlier.

Normally they met for coffee or breakfast at least once a week to catch up, and she often got three or four texts as well, chronicling Gigi's latest escapades. As her worry grew, Heather left several messages, all unreturned.

When the clock hit five, she hurried home to change for her appointment. Her one-bedroom apartment on the fourth floor of a Greenwich Village walk-up was clean and comfortable, if cramped, and the view unspectacular. But the rent was reasonable for Manhattan, and she loved the eclectic mix of artists, writers, musicians, actors, and other creative types who comprised a good portion of her neighbors.

After a quick shower, she perused her closet for a sexy but stylish dress for the evening, settling on a clingy, ink-blue number that showed off her legs and dipped low in front to expose a tasteful amount of cleavage. High heels, musky perfume, and a bit more makeup than she wore to her day job, and she was ready.

She hailed a taxi and told the driver to take her to Bemelmans. Ensconced within the prestigious Carlyle hotel, the art-deco bar was her favorite of the half-dozen upscale watering holes she frequented and never failed to provide a good selection of possibilities for an evening's entertainment.

Selecting a seat near one end of the impressive black-granite bar, she ordered a Diet Coke and sipped it slowly. Within the first half hour, three men approached and tried to chat her up or buy her a drink, but none were suitable, so she deflected their come-ons with polite but firm excuses. The fourth, a handsome thirty-something businessman in a crisp blue suit, was more promising and, in light of the advancing hour, worth her attention.

"Good evening. Are you waiting for someone or can I buy you a drink?" the dark-haired stranger asked.

She smiled at him and removed her purse and coat from the adjacent bar stool, inviting him to sit. "I was rather hoping you'd notice me," she replied, eyeing him appreciatively. "I'm Amber."

"Mike." With a pleased grin, he took the stool and hailed the bartender. "Chivas 25, neat," he told the man, "and whatever my stunning friend would like."

"I'm good for now."

"Are you a native?" Mike asked as the bartender poured his drink.

Heather nodded. "I live in the Village. You?"

"In town for a medical conference. I'm a pharmaceutical rep."

"Lucky me." Heather raised her glass. "Here's to whatever fates brought us together. I'm in the mood for some fun tonight, and I was beginning to think I'd have to go home without company."

Mike's eyes lit up as they clinked glasses. "I can't believe you don't have your pick. Are you an actress? Model?"

"That's very sweet of you, Mike. But, no. You could say I'm in the fantasy-fulfillment industry," she replied coyly. "Perhaps you'd care to discover more?"

Surprise registered briefly on his face, then his eyes glinted in lustful anticipation. "Most definitely. I have a suite here. Shall we continue this party in private?"

"I prefer my place, if you don't mind. It's not far, and it's…well stocked with everything we might need. Full bar…fun accessories. One small catch, though. My boyfriend likes to watch, and he'll orchestrate the festivities. Does that work for you?"

Mike's eyes narrowed as he considered her proposal. He downed the remains of his Chivas and smiled. "Lead the way."

They caught a cab, and as Heather gave the driver the address of the brownstone owned by the Direct Connect escort agency, she stroked Mike's thigh provocatively. She was growing weary of her part-time work as a high-class call girl, but at least she only had to work one or two nights a week to make enough to meet her obligations. The money she got from the men she picked up was significant, but it was Dario, her regular and enigmatic client, who provided the bulk of her additional income.

❖

Mouchamps, France

Doctor Andor Rózsa closed the kitchen shutters of his two-bedroom stone cottage, which did little to keep out the chill wind seeping through the ancient windowpane. All the windows needed upgrading and the fireplace required maintenance, too; it didn't draw right, and now and then a backdraft of smoke would waft through the room. He hadn't been here in many years and the place suffered from lack of attention, but he didn't dare allow a workman inside as long as his prisoner remained chained in the basement.

Andor had nowhere else to go, and this small village in France was as good a place as any to lie low for a while. He'd bought it under another name, in cash, and nothing in his records or computer hard drives could lead anyone here. Interpol and who knows how many other entities were trying to hunt him down for unleashing the Charon virus, a lethal chimera of the H1N1 virus and bubonic plague bacteria. His plan to infect millions had gone exactly as anticipated, but just as he was about to cash in on his scheme with the release of the antidote, his woman prisoner and her associates had ruined everything. He'd lost his home in Budapest, his job at a prestigious pharmaceutical lab, all his virus formulas, the millions in his Grand Cayman account, and he'd even had to blow up the secret lab where he developed his lethal contagions and harvested organs for sale on the black market—the side business that had financed his scheme.

His best option for getting out of this mess was his prisoner. Though he still knew nothing about her or who she was working for, he'd managed to obtain her cell phone when he Tasered her in his office at the lab. He called back the number she had dialed twice while searching his facility and was able to reach one of her associates with his demands. She had to be a precious commodity to her employer, given her incredible ability to find the lab and break into his office to retrieve all his records and lethal virus formulas.

He'd scored some necessary operating cash by squeezing Dario Imperi—the man he'd been selling black-market organs to in the US. Imperi had millions, and everything to lose if Andor exposed him to authorities. He had kicked off his plan to collect on what Imperi owed him two weeks earlier, not long after the explosion in the lab, by mailing a greeting card to the man's PO box marked Personal. Contained within was a postcard of downtown Budapest, with the words *I'll be in touch*, along with a fine dust that would ensure compliance with his demands.

He'd followed up with a call to Imperi's private number a week later, using a cell phone outfitted with a scrambler.

"Yes?"

"It's your Hungarian associate."

"You're putting both of us in danger by contacting me," Imperi replied angrily.

"Calm down, my friend. I'll not bother you further if you cooperate. I merely want what you still owe me."

"Cooperate? Are you mad? There's far too much heat on you for us to ever do business again."

"You received my postcard?" Andor asked.

"What was that all about? What game are you playing?"

"How are you feeling? Having headaches? Getting a nagging cough that medicines are doing nothing to help?"

There was silence on the other end for several seconds. When Imperi spoke again, Andor could hear the fear in his voice. "What have you done?"

"I dusted the card with one of my formulas to ensure your quick cooperation. As soon as you give me the fifty thousand US you owe me for my last shipment, the antidote will be delivered to you."

"You're insane! I can't—"

"You can and you will, if you want to live more than a few days."

More silence. "It'll take time for me to—"

"No. You're going to transfer the funds right now. I want to see the money in my account before we hang up. No negotiations." He recited the name of the bank and his new account number, certain that Imperi was busily scribbling down the information.

"How do I know you'll hold up your end of the bargain and won't be trying this again?"

"You have my word. I'm a scientist, not a criminal."

"You're a deranged idiot," he heard Imperi mutter as he waited, watching his online bank account for the deposit to be completed. As soon as it was, he transferred the money to a second Grand Cayman account, so Imperi couldn't recover it or trace him. "Always a pleasure doing business with you, Dario. And by the way, you won't need an antidote. You have a slightly altered strain of the common cold and your symptoms should go away on their own in a few more days." Imperi was cursing as he hung up the phone.

The fifty grand would sustain him while he awaited the big payoff from his prisoner's associates. Andor glanced at his watch. Time to feed the captive. He hated having to deal with her himself—the stench down there was unbearable, and he'd always had staff to deal with the wretched human animals he'd held captive for his virus trials in the lab.

CHAPTER THREE

Cassady Monroe scrutinized the bare room yet again as she paced the few steps the length of heavy chain allowed, though she'd already memorized every detail of the space. She was weak and dehydrated, and her right wrist was raw and sore from the thick shackle that bound her to the chain.

Andor Rózsa had kidnapped her and kept her alive for reasons she couldn't understand, and every time she asked him questions he ignored her. He never talked to her at all, for that matter. She vaguely remembered him hovering over her very early in this nightmare, asking her questions, but she'd been so heavily drugged she couldn't recall anything specific.

Since then, he came only briefly once a day, his heavy descending steps announcing dinnertime. He would open the door and signal her to sit, and only then place a cup of water and a bowl of soggy oatmeal on the floor far enough away that she'd have to fully extend her body to reach them. His ascending steps always precipitated another loss of the hope she clung to, hope that he'd free her or tell her why she was here.

She'd ascertained only that she was in a basement. The walls were bare concrete blocks, devoid of windows. Constant humidity hung in the air, the place reeked of mold, and the pendulous bulb in the center of the room gave a depressing sepia color to an already wretched environment. She didn't know how she got here, where *here* was, and at this point had even started to lose track of how long she'd been captive. Besides drugging her for however long, he'd taken her watch and cell phone, so time had blurred.

Most distressing of all was her knowledge of what Rózsa was capable of. He'd had no qualms about killing millions with his virus or experimenting on how many untold unfortunates in his lab. Was he keeping her for some kind of new experiment? And if so, what further hell might she have to endure?

Her EOO training had drilled in her to never give up, but what did that mean under these circumstances? She would never go down without a fight, but she had no one, nothing to fight against. Her only option to end this madness seemed to be to stop eating and drinking and let nature take its course, but choosing that way out went against her nature.

Her only source for solace was Jack and the memory of their brief time together. The dimple on Jack's cheek when she smiled, and, God, how Cassady loved to make her smile, sustained her now. As long as she concentrated on Jack's image, recalling every freckle and scar, her mind should remain intact.

She licked her chapped lips and sat back down on the dirty blanket, a rag that clearly once belonged to a dog. Just as well, she thought, since her own odor had become unbearable. She hadn't been allowed to wash since her arrival to *nowhere*, and her clothes never seemed to dry from the extreme humidity. Aside from the blanket, the only item in the room was the bucket he'd supplied for her bodily needs.

As she leaned against the cold brick wall, her stomach rumbled and she placed her hand on it. As with any part of her body that hurt, she would pretend her own touch was Jack's hand. She shut her eyes and dozed until the sound of boots awakened her. By now, she knew exactly how many steps before he entered the room. Seven. She counted down and sat up as the familiar noise of a heavy bar and the clanging sound of his keys echoed through the small space.

Rózsa entered and Cassady, as usual, remained very still. She didn't want to startle or anger him and lose any opportunity to make him talk. He avoided eye contact at all times, but always stood at the door to inspect the room and her bucket.

The stench in the basement was so overpowering Rózsa wrinkled his nose in disgust and kept his mouth slightly open to avoid breathing through his nose. He stared at the bucket for several seconds before apparently deciding he could no longer avoid the loathsome task of emptying it. He set down the oatmeal and water by the door, picked up the bucket while watching her warily, and left briefly to complete his task. He repeated this pattern every few days. Once he'd come back with the bucket, he would give her the food and water, then depart again.

She needed to make him see her as a human being, so today, after he'd emptied the waste and as he approached with her food, she spoke to him in a soft, pleading voice. "Please, Andor. Look at me. Please."

Instead, he paused where he was and raised his head to stare at the ceiling above her.

"Please tell me why I'm here," she said calmly.

He didn't answer, but she was heartened when he didn't move or immediately place her bowl and cup on the ground. It was the first break in the routine—the one time he'd prolonged his visit beyond mere seconds. Maybe he was ready to talk, or at least nod. Maybe he'd started to trust she wouldn't get up or attack him.

"Do you want something from me?" She spoke softly. "Just tell me why I'm here and if I can help you."

He didn't acknowledge her, but at least he didn't leave. He stared at the ceiling like a statue. Maybe she needed to try a new line of questioning. Something to at least get her out of this room and give her some idea where she was. For the first time she felt like she'd found the key to that heavy metal door.

"Can I please wash myself?" She tried not to sound demanding. "I promise I won't try anything. You can trust me. I've never tried to hurt you. Just a few minutes to wash up."

Although he remained motionless, his gaze shifted to the right—a good sign he was considering her proposition.

"I'll be very fast," she assured him.

Without a word, Rózsa left, still carrying her oatmeal and water. She stared at the closed door as she heard him lock but not bolt the door. What was he up to? He ascended the stairs, then returned. When he came back, he had only another bucket in his hand, full of water and with a sponge floating on the surface.

The meager hope the break in routine had given her evaporated as he set the bucket down, leaving her more disappointed than she'd been since she arrived. "What about food?"

He turned and departed without acknowledging her in any way. The sound of the lock and bolt had never resonated louder.

❖

Southwestern Colorado
Earlier that day

Jack pulled on the jeans and navy-blue T-shirt the nurse had delivered and left the infirmary with trepidation. Unhurriedly, she made her way to the administration building. Although she couldn't wait to get her hands on whatever intel the EOO had and be on her way with Coolidge, she wasn't in the mood for reunions and explanations. She had no doubt her presence would shock or appall the other ops, and she abhorred having to confront their disdain or discomfort. Stepping back into a world she had largely managed to forget disquieted her, to say the least.

Though she'd returned to the remote campus for Cassady's memorial service two weeks earlier, she'd avoided any interaction with other ops. While they were upstairs eulogizing her lover, she'd remained isolated outside on the swing set. She needed to grieve in drunken solitude, and the swing set was where she felt closest to Cassady. When they were both living at the school—Jack about to graduate and Cassady still barely into her teens—she'd often watched her blond angel swinging back and forth, laughing and carefree, still blissfully unaware of what she would be called to do when she became an operative.

Now, as she walked the grounds, she couldn't help but reflect on her own formative years at the Rocky Mountain campus, which operated under the guise of a private boarding school. Since 1952, the complex of dorms, classrooms, and training facilities contained within the razor-wire-tipped fence had housed and trained an elite fighting force virtually unknown to the world at large. Hand-selected from orphanages worldwide and raised within the compound, the best of the ops became ETFs—agents of the Elite Tactical Force, assigned to missions outside the reach of normal law enforcement.

To her knowledge, she'd been the only agent who'd gotten out before her sanctioned retirement. Except for Cassady's memorial service, she hadn't been back since faking her death ten years earlier. Not only would most of the ops waiting inside view her as a traitor, at least one had justifiable reasons to want her dead because of her intervening work as a mercenary.

She was buzzed in as soon as she reached the entrance to the neo-Gothic administration building. Normally, one needed a hand and retina ID to get in, but Pierce was apparently keeping an eye out for her arrival. *Great, big brother is already watching.*

Jack took the stairs to the second-floor conference room. Four ops—two young men and two women—lingered in the hallway outside. Pierce and the other two EOO administrators were nowhere in sight.

One of the ops, a tall brunette, turned as she approached. "I don't think I've seen you before," the woman said. Jack remembered her. Mishael Taylor—Agent Allegro—was an adrenaline junkie who specialized in breaking and entering. Always a troublemaker with a big mouth, but mostly harmless.

"I'm Jack Norris."

"Should I know you?" Allegro asked.

Great. Now all of them were looking at her. "No, you shouldn't," she replied. "But you probably do."

Allegro smirked. "Riddles before my fourth cup of coffee make me—"

"Don't play with her, Norris," one of the men interjected. "She'll get hyper and make us all regret getting out of bed this morning." The rest laughed.

"You seem familiar," the other woman said, an agent with short, dark hair and olive skin. She didn't ring any of Jack's bells, and neither did the men, but that was probably because of the age difference. They were all thirty at most, at least ten years younger than she was. "I'm Gianna."

"I doubt you would remember me," Jack replied. "I haven't been around for years."

"But I'd remember," Allegro said, peering at her suspiciously. She turned toward the doorway to the conference room a few steps away. "Yo! Luka, come out here a sec."

Luka Madison, aka Domino, emerged stirring a cup of coffee. "What now, lunatic?" she asked, rolling her eyes at Allegro.

"She seem familiar?" Allegro nodded her head in Jack's direction.

In that split second before Domino noticed her, their last interactions three years earlier flashed through Jack's mind. Jack had been working for Terrence Burrows then, a corrupt politician who wanted to bring down the EOO. Under his direction, she'd not only tried to kill Domino, she'd also kidnapped the op's partner—journalist Hayley Ward. Only Domino's quick reflexes and resourcefulness had saved them both.

"What the—" Domino froze and her eyes widened in stunned recognition. The coffee cup recently in her hand shattered on the floor. She clenched her fists and started toward Jack, fury blazing in her blue-gray eyes. "What the hell are you doing here?"

Jack wasn't surprised Domino recognized her. Her hair was much shorter now than when they'd last met, but the distinctive scar, an inch and a half long, that ran from beneath her left cheekbone to the corner of her mouth, gave her away. "I didn't know it was you," Jack quietly replied. "I had no idea you were in the room with Burrows, or that Ward was with you."

"Who the hell are you?" Domino got right in her face, challenging her to make the first move. Jack had a good three inches height advantage over her, and Domino didn't look to be in top physical condition. She had dark circles under her eyes and was thinner than she remembered. But Jack remained silent and unmoving. She knew she deserved whatever was coming.

Her lack of reaction only infuriated Domino more. "How dare you walk in here and—"

Allegro came up behind the op and put a hand on her shoulder. "Luka, what's going on here?"

"This bitch used to work for Burrows," Domino said, her voice so loud the agents gathered in the conference room were beginning to spill out into the hallway to find out what the commotion was about. "She tried to kill me and kidnapped Hayley."

"What? How?" Allegro stuttered. She glared at Jack, her own rising anger evident in the sudden twitch of her jaw muscles. "Is this true?"

"Yes, it's true," Domino shouted, still toe-to-toe with Jack. "Operation Eclipse. Tell her."

"It's true." Jack quietly said.

All the ops surrounded them, watching the unfolding drama with interest.

"Why?" Allegro asked between gritted teeth, clearly trying to contain herself.

"I was doing my job."

"Working for Burrows?" Allegro asked. "Everyone knew he was corrupt as hell. He was trying to bring us all down."

"I didn't know Domino was involved," Jack replied in the same calm tone. "I just needed the money and—"

"You bitch. You almost killed Hayley because of money? Who the fuck do you think you are?" Domino lunged at Jack and would have landed a solid punch across her jaw but for the quick intervention of one of the other ops.

"Why'd you stop her, Landis?" Allegro sounded disappointed. "It was just about to get good."

"Long time no see, Jack." Landis Coolidge's stone-gray eyes revealed nothing about how she felt seeing her former best friend again after so many years.

For a moment, time stood still as Jack recalled their history. Even though as kids they would try to best each other, they'd always stood up for one another. Agent Chase hadn't changed much in the intervening years. Her blond hair was shorter and she'd gained a few tiny lines around her eyes, but she was still a fit and trim ETF who looked much younger than her forty years.

Domino looked at Chase. "You know her?" she asked, surprise evident in her eyes.

"I thought I did," Chase said, her eyes still on Jack.

"You were at Cassady's memorial service," Gianna remarked. "You sat outside by the swings. I saw you crying."

"That was me."

The hallway filled with deafening whispers as all the ops moved closer to get a better look at the stranger. Jack had never felt more like a circus freak.

"Who the hell gave you the right to mourn one of us?" Domino asked.

Just then, Montgomery Pierce, David Arthur, and the third member of the EOO governing trio, Director of Academics Joanne Grant, emerged from Pierce's office farther down the hall. "Enough introductions," Pierce said, taking in the crowd gathered around Jack. "We can take our places now."

Domino glared at Jack. "This isn't over."

"I know. So go ahead. Finish what you started."

"I feel sorry for you." Domino turned to walk away.

"Do it for Ward." Jack provoked her because she wanted Domino to react.

Domino spun around, her body rigid with contained fury. "Don't you ever mention her name again."

"That's enough." Chase clamped a hand on Jack's arm and started to pull her away.

"Let her," Jack whispered.

The next thing she knew, her head was spinning and she was on the floor grasping her chin. The punch had been fast and solid.

Domino walked away, rubbing her hand.

"Did it hurt?" Chase asked.

"Yeah."

Chase flashed her trademark lopsided smile. "Good."

"I had it coming." Jack got to her feet and they headed into the conference room.

CHAPTER FOUR

1 p.m.

Montgomery Pierce was about to risk his reputation by including a runaway op in this briefing, and he regretted how difficult the gathering would be for Jaclyn as well. But if they were to have any chance at finding Lynx, Jaclyn would have to face the consequences of her actions.

The room was restless and loud with whispered speculation about Jaclyn and her identity. Monty walked to the windows and let down the blinds, a habit whenever they discussed anything important. "Take a seat, everyone. We're ready to start."

As he took his customary chair at the head of the long table, flanked by Grant and Arthur, the room quieted and the ops took seats as well.

Still rubbing her chin, Jaclyn stood by the door.

"Please, shut the door and join us," he told her. He nodded at the empty chair by Landis Coolidge. "Why don't you sit next to Chase?" Everyone in the room turned to look at him. "Jaclyn is here to help us with our next mission."

"Why do we need her?" one of the ops asked.

"Because she's the best person for the job," Joanne Grant replied with an uncharacteristically stern tone.

"Since when do we employ criminals?" Domino asked her.

Jaclyn didn't react.

"I realize this is unconventional, to say the least," Monty said, "but this is also an exceptional mission."

"But—"

Monty lifted his hand. "Let me finish. Jaclyn is not new to the organization."

"Sleeper?" one of the men asked.

"No. Her name is Jaclyn Harding. ETF op Phantom."

Some looked puzzled. Others gasped. Only two didn't react. One was Reno, their computer whiz. During Operation Face a year earlier, his photo-manipulation skills had helped them identify the mercenary Jack Norris as their rogue operative Phantom. The other op who took the revelation in stride was Chase. While the rest turned to stare at Jaclyn, Chase absentmindedly caressed her coffee cup.

"Jaclyn Harding died in Israel," Allegro said.

"She doesn't look like Harding," Domino added. "I worked a couple of jobs with her. This is not Harding."

"I knew her pretty well, too," one of the male ops said. "This can't be her. I mean, we were present at Harding's memorial service." Monty remembered the two had been in the same hand-to-hand combat classes, and Jaclyn always won.

Chase spoke up for the first time, her eyes still on her cup. "It's Harding."

"What?" someone asked.

"It's Harding. Different face, same person."

More gasps. Reno said nothing, but he nodded in agreement.

"Disappeared ten years and two months ago. Probably faked her death and got a new face. Ended up taking jobs from whoever could afford her services. No one better at not asking for credentials than scum who want someone offed or scared." Chase sat back in her chair and looked at Jaclyn. "How am I doing so far…Jack?"

"Predictably accurate," Jaclyn replied wryly.

"Did you know about this?" Domino asked Monty.

He looked around the room. All eyes were on him. "We found out a year ago."

"And why were we not told?" Fetch asked.

"Why is she still alive, for that matter?" Allegro asked.

"For reasons that do not concern you," Grant replied.

"How is that fair? We all know what the consequences for treason are," Domino said.

"We have made this one exception," Grant replied.

"But—"

"End of discussion," Monty said forcefully.

"I'd rather chew my arm off than be here, which means my reasons are thoroughly selfish," Jaclyn said.

"No surprise there," Chase added.

Jaclyn seemed to ignore the jab. "I didn't show up to chew the fat or discuss my past."

"Why the hell *are* you here?" Domino asked.

Monty held up his hand. "And this brings us to Operation Phoenix."

"Oh, can I? Can I?" Allegro started waving her hand. "I wanna tell them."

Monty sighed heavily. "Allegro, let's hear what you have."

"Okay, guys. I received this phone call early yesterday." Allegro set her cell phone on the table. "Caller ID said unknown caller. I answered without saying anything. When a man with a heavy Hungarian accent came on and said, 'You have something of mine, and I have something of yours,' I started recording. It picks up from there."

Allegro: Who is this? How did you get this number?

Male voice: From your associate's cell phone. The blonde who called you twice as she was breaking into my lab?

Allegro, after a slight hesitation: You've got a lot of nerve, asshole. You'll pay for what you did to her.

Male voice: You're more than associates, yes? I assure you, your friend is very much alive, and currently my guest. That's why I'm calling.

Allegro: What did you just say?

Male voice: Your friend will be returned safely to you, as soon as you transfer the money you stole from me into my new bank account.

Allegro: I want proof you have her. Put her on the phone. Now.

Male voice: Very well. But I'm afraid she's very...tired. She may not be entirely coherent.

Another brief silence, then Agent Lynx's voice rang through the room. Instantly recognizable, though from the cadence and slurring of her words she'd obviously been drugged.

Lynx: Why are you...(groan) Why are you doing this? What's...

Monty watched Jaclyn as Cassady's voice played back. A spectrum of emotions raced across her face, from fear and anger to love and impatience, as she started to pace.

Lynx: What is this place? (groan) What do you want?

A brief silence.

Lynx: My head hurts...my mouth is so dry...

Male voice: I will call you back in a few days with the account information.

Allegro: We don't have your money. Interpol does.

Male voice: How you acquire it is not my concern.

The line went dead.

Allegro pressed the Stop button and the room remained silent for several seconds.

"So crazy-ass scientist has Cassady. She's not dead."

"What do we have to go on?" Domino asked Monty.

"Reno will give us an update."

Reno, a brute of a man with slick black hair, looked like he hadn't slept in a long while. "After the explosion that presumably killed Lynx, we sent the material we had of Rózsa's—his home hard drive and the data from his lab office—to Interpol. But I guess it slipped my mind to delete the copies I made like I was supposed to."

Many of the ops laughed, knowing Reno's tendency to meticulously catalogue every bit of information that crossed his desk. "Anyway, I started going through it once Allegro got the call.

Most is encrypted, and Rózsa deleted a lot of files, so it's going to take time to recover everything. But I did find he had another active Grand Cayman bank account we knew nothing about, which logged a deposit of fifty thousand a week ago. The money was immediately transferred to still another account I've yet to access, but I was able to track the IP of whoever sent him the money. It's an address in Manhattan."

Monty recapped. "So Rózsa has a US associate who's providing him the resources to stay hidden. Hopefully that contact can put us on the right track."

"So what does any of this have to do with Harding?" Allegro asked.

Monty could feel his blood pressure rising. "I was about to get to that when you interrupted."

"Can't wait to hear this one," Allegro replied.

"This mission goes to Chase and Phantom."

Several of the ops immediately reacted with "What?" or "Why?"

Monty ignored them. "They will be working together with all the assistance they can get from us to bring Cassady back alive."

"What is Harding's involvement in all this?" Domino asked.

"Cass is my girlfriend," Jaclyn replied.

"She's what?"

"We've been together about a year."

"You're kidding me," Allegro said. "This is like a bad soap opera."

Domino turned to Jaclyn. "Monty, Joanne, David, Cassady, Reno, and who knows who else, all knew about you. Why the hell have the rest of us been kept in the dark?"

Jaclyn shrugged. "If it was up to me no one but Cass would know."

"Of course," Chase said, without looking at Jaclyn. "Why bother with a triviality such as friendship?"

"Harding is going after her with or without us," Monty told the group. "I'd much rather have her on our side. No one wants Cassady back here and safe more than she."

He stood and looked from Chase to Jaclyn. "Operation Phoenix is yours." When Jaclyn met his eyes, he added, "Your code name and number are effective as of now. Your flight to New York leaves in two-and-a-half hours."

❖

New York
8:30 p.m.

As soon as Mike exited the room, Heather put on a robe and poured herself a Diet Coke from the well-stocked bar. Dario waited until she settled comfortably into an armchair facing the mirror before he spoke. "Thank you, Amber."

She knew his voice—a soothing tenor, with a hint of an accent—almost as well as she knew her own. After nearly two years as her sole, once- or twice-a-week client, she was also well familiar with what turned him on, yet she still had no idea what he looked like. Dario took extraordinary precautions to safeguard his privacy, perhaps because his face was too recognizable.

Ordinarily, clients who visited Direct Connect's Manhattan brownstone were admitted through the rear entrance by Massimo, the brooding hulk employed to protect the girls. But Dario had a special arrangement with the agency. Massimo would prop open the rear door when Dario's cab arrived and wait in the front until he had entered and was upstairs. Dario also had exclusive use of the second-floor watcher's room on those nights.

Direct Connect had other voyeurs among their regulars, so the owner had renovated one suite to enable optimal, discreet viewing of the bedroom through a two-way mirror. As part of her arrangement with Dario, Heather was never to open the door to the watcher's room while he was there, and she was to linger so he could chat with her through a two-way intercom after the john had departed.

"Was tonight to your satisfaction?" Heather asked.

"You are always a pleasure to work with."

"I'm glad you think so." Heather did her best to sound seductive.

"You are very good at what you do."

"Thank you."

"I have a rather personal question, if you don't mind."

This is new, Heather thought. His usual repertoire rarely contained more than sycophantic compliments, *thank you,* and *see you next week.*

"I doubt I am the first or last to ask you, but what are your reasons for doing this? I would prefer an honest answer rather than the generic *I love to please.*"

"So I'm not the first to pique your curiosity."

"But you are the first I don't expect a cliché from."

"Why is that?" she asked.

"You are different. Please answer why you have chosen this avenue."

"If I had better options, I would have chosen differently."

"And the choices we make when we haven't better options, do they define us?" he asked.

What did her choices really say about her? Was her self-worth of much lesser importance than her brother's health and her own ambitions? She refused to give up her fashion career, though it barely covered her own expenses. She needed another six grand a month for Adam's medical bills, and she got that much working an average of one or two nights a week, thanks to Dario's largesse. Sure, she could have gotten the money working a second full-time job somewhere and maintained her self-esteem, but the long hours would eventually take their toll and she'd have no time to work on her own designs. Some would say her dignity had fallen victim to her needs, but for Heather it was a matter of priorities.

"You choose to watch," Heather finally replied. "Like me, you have your reasons. Actions merely reflect our current needs or circumstances. I want to believe our dreams are what define us."

"Like I said, you are different." The silence that followed was so prolonged Heather thought Dario had departed. She was about to take her robe off and get dressed when the voice came back, startling her. "Does it bother you? What you do here, for me?"

"I can't deny it took some getting used to."

"And now?"

"It's less strange, I suppose."

"But you do not enjoy it."

"I should probably be going," Heather said.

"Of course. It was a silly question."

"I've learned to accept it."

"Very well, I won't take any more of your time, Amber. Thank you again for tonight."

"Good night, Dario." Heather turned her back to the two-way mirror. "I'll see you soon?"

"Yes."

She heard the click of the intercom being turned off.

On impulse, Heather decided to swing by Gigi's apartment on her way home. She didn't really expect to find her there at nine p.m., but Gigi had given her a key, so she could at least leave a note and maybe reassure herself if she found evidence her friend had been there recently. Gigi trolled for clients around the 8th Avenue porn and sex-toy establishments and had been robbed a few times, so perhaps her lack of contact was merely because a john had stolen her cell and she hadn't replaced it yet.

When no one answered her knock, Heather let herself in to the darkened studio apartment and switched on the overhead light. The first thing she noticed was the paper that had been slipped under the door—a notice from the landlord, dated a week earlier, that the rent was overdue. Frowning, Heather surveyed the rest of the apartment.

Nothing looked unusual or alarming, though the place was always so messy it was hard to tell if anything had been moved or stolen. Everything of obvious value—television, stereo, laptop—remained undisturbed.

But a foul smell emanated from the corner kitchen, and Heather's concern escalated when she discovered the source. Two cartons of half-eaten Chinese food had been left in the sink, and from the look of them, they'd been there several days at least. An inspection of the fridge—sour milk, mold-fuzzy cheese, rotten lettuce—reinforced the conclusion that Gigi hadn't been home in a long while.

Heather bagged up the foul Chinese food to dispose of on her way home. She was torn over whether to file a missing-person report. Certainly, no one else would. Gigi had cut all ties with her family long ago and had no other close friends. But Heather had no record with the cops and was anxious to keep it that way. Because she wasn't a relative, they'd likely question her about how she and Gigi knew each other. Not only would that put her on law enforcement's radar, it could also jeopardize her fashion career if her boss at Chelline got wind of it. She also doubted authorities would pursue the matter, given Gigi's numerous arrests for prostitution.

After long consideration, Heather decided to make the call, but with minimal risk to herself. She used a pay phone near her apartment to file the report and refused to give her name. It was all she could do.

❖

New York
11:30 p.m.

Chase avoided conversation with Jack beyond the bare minimum during their flight to LaGuardia, still brooding about the abrupt severance of their long friendship. By the time they picked up their rental car and headed into the city, the tension between them was palpable. As Jack pulled out a pack of Marlboros and started to light one, Chase said, "No smoking in my presence."

Jack put the cigarettes away. "So, you knew it was me?" she asked after a long silence.

"Yes." Chase turned on the radio and tuned to a jazz station.

"Coltrane," Jack said.

"Yes." Chase drummed her fingers on the steering wheel, keeping cadence with the beat.

Jack kept time as well, brushing her palm against her knee. "So, what's new?"

Her nonchalant effort to resume their easy camaraderie grated on Chase. If Jack expected her to throw her a welcome-home party, she was seriously deluded. "Plenty."

Jack took the hint and went back to staring out the window for several blocks. "Are you really going to play the pissed housewife?" she finally asked. "Somehow, I can't picture you in an apron."

"And I can't see you collecting on hits."

"Life makes you do things."

"I disagree. But then again, I've never been a fan of blaming my decisions on the universe."

"I'm not blaming anyone."

"Make up your mind," Chase said. "I have a strong distaste for contradictions."

"And I'm not crazy about having to defend my actions."

"Probably due to the fact that you're not very good at it."

Jack didn't answer and turned back to the view out her window. Another long silence ensued before she spoke again. "I'm not saying what I did was right. If I could do it all over, I would. The things I've done—"

"I don't want to hear about your regrets or how rough times have been for you. I don't want to hear anything, for that matter."

"What the hell do you want, Landis? You want me to say I'm sorry? You want to hear why I made the choices I did? Do you even care? "

"Ten years and two months, Jack. That's how long ago you lost the right to ask me if I care. You up and disappeared one day and never looked back."

"I had to."

"Maybe you did. I don't know the details. But you could have told me."

"It wasn't planned."

"You could have contacted me."

"I wanted to, but I couldn't." Jack's voice was subdued. "I needed to start over."

"You could have told *me*. You knew you could trust me."

"I needed to put my previous life behind me."

"I don't know if you succeeded in forgetting your previous life, but I can tell you for a fact that *it* completely erased you."

"Landis, my not telling you isn't because I—"

"He who excuses himself accuses himself. I'd rather return my attention to Coltrane."

Jack sighed. "You're still the same control freak. Still deciding whether or not a conversation or situation has ended. Let me guess. Your existence is still calculated and divided into time slots. Have you even taken off your watch since 2002?"

"You'd have known the answer to that if you hadn't gone, Houdini."

Jack laughed and Chase did her best to keep a straight face. Despite her justified acrimony with Jack, she missed their banter and easy familiarity. No one used to know her better. "And the answer is no," Chase added.

Jack laughed harder and Chase allowed herself a smile.

"I need to swing by my place at some point to pick up a few things. I have an apartment in the city. We can stay there if we're here long," Jack said.

"I'm going to ignore that proposition." Recalling the messiness of Jack's room at the EOO dorms made her shudder.

"Okay, so I need to tidy up."

"How long since someone cleaned in there?"

"About a month."

"Hotel it is."

"But I can—"

"One more word and I'm calling the WHO."

They both laughed.

"Are we okay now?" Jack asked.

"No, Jack. We'll never be *okay* again." They had to be civil if they were going to work together, but Chase didn't intend to make this easy on Jack. She turned up the radio.

CHAPTER FIVE

Washington, DC

Andrew Schuster anxiously caressed the roll of quarters in his palm as he waited for the dual parking slots beside the Pennsylvania Avenue gas station to empty. When they did, he straddled both spaces with his Lincoln Continental to reduce the chances anyone would overhear his conversation.

He dialed the number he'd memorized into the lone pay phone outside the building and dropped the requisite change into the slot.

After two rings, the line picked up. "How can I help you?"

Andrew cupped his palm over one ear to minimize the noise of the street traffic. "I'm calling for…the Broker."

"Speaking."

"I was informed you could help me."

"Start by telling me what you need."

"My son's liver is failing," Andrew said. "Familial amyloidosis. We've been on a waiting list for almost three years. His health started to rapidly decline a month ago and the situation turned critical last week. We can't afford the luxury of waiting any longer. He's fading by the day." His voice cracked. "I'm afraid he's given up."

"I understand. It's a tragedy to have a child in pain."

"Neither my wife or I is a viable candidate." Andrew would never be able to let go of the guilt. His son was going to die and it was his fault.

"How unfortunate."

"I'll do anything to save his life."

"Of course."

"Anything," Andrew repeated. "It has to be immediately."

"We deal only with direct and full amount electronic payments. Is that a problem?" the Broker asked.

"No."

"The price is two hundred thousand."

"No problem."

"The receptor's age?"

"Seven." Andrew could hear the clicking of a computer keyboard in the background.

"His blood type?"

"A positive."

"Let me see if I can help you."

More clicks. Andrew broke out in a sweat waiting for the answer.

A minute that seemed to last a decade passed before he got a reply. "Congratulations, I have a part for you."

Andrew sagged against the brick wall of the station and blew out a loud breath. "Thank you, God." If he weren't in public, he'd have let the tears of relief fall.

"God is the one who gave you a sick son. I'm the one who's going to give you a healthy one. You should reconsider who the *real* Almighty is."

"I…" Andrew didn't know how to respond to such incredible arrogance.

"Now, let's talk about the money transfer," the Broker said. "The payment is processed in advance and the delivery will occur within the same week. The procedure will take place in a Mexican hospital of our choice, and we will appoint an escort for you who will be with you throughout the trip and procedure. You should know—"

"Wait! You don't understand." Andrew pulled his hair. "We can't wait a week and my son won't survive the trip."

"It's unfortunate you waited this long, then. I'm afraid this is the best I can do."

"No, you don't understand. My son is dying. Right now, as we speak. Do you understand what I'm telling you?"

"I'm sorry your negligence is going to cost you your son."

"My what?" Andrew exploded. "I've done everything possible."

"Clearly too late," came the cold reply. "I'm sorry I can't help you any further."

"Wait. Please, wait," he pleaded as he felt his only hope slip away. "Help me in twenty-four hours and I'll double the money."

"This isn't about money. It's about time."

"Surely you can do something for four hundred thousand dollars."

This time the Broker didn't answer immediately. He heard more clicking. *Please let something show up.*

"Not possible."

The finality of the words hit him like a tornado. He sat down on the pavement, defeated. He was about to disconnect when a couple and their young son passed by.

"Are you okay, mister?" the boy, roughly his son's age, asked before his parents pulled him away.

"I'm going to hang up now," the Broker said.

"Six hundred thousand." When no reply came, he repeated the amount. "In twenty-four hours. You can't possibly turn that—"

"I'm going to need your name and your son's to complete the purchase."

"Yes!" he shouted. Now all he had to do was reveal his identity. He knew the risk he was taking, but he'd gotten this far and wasn't about to second-think his decision.

"My son is Matthew Schuster." He wiped the sweat from his forehead. "I'm Andrew Schuster."

"Noted."

"For obvious reasons, maximum discretion is necessary."

"I am discreet with all my customers, regardless of their social status or…employer. Give me a moment, please." The silence that ensued was so lengthy Andrew feared they'd been disconnected. By the time the cold voice returned he was near panic. "Please note the account number for the transfer."

Andrew fumbled in his jacket for a pen and paper. "I'm listening." He scratched down the number.

"The deal will close only after we receive your payment."

"You'll have the money within the hour."

"Should it not be there in the full agreed amount by midnight, the consequences are obvious."

"It'll be there."

"Your son is at home, correct?"

"Yes."

"The delivery and procedure will take place tonight, assuming of course the transaction is complete. Be ready to transport him to Forrest General Hospital in Brooklyn as soon as you get the call."

"Thank you for—" Andrew said, but the line was already dead.

❖

The Broker perused the four matches that came up on the computer: a thirty-seven-year-old woman from Queens, a forty-nine-year-old Brooklyn man, a twenty-four-year-old Chinatown busboy, and a twenty-year-old student who lived on the Lower East Side. Schuster's status and the price they'd agreed on ensured delivery of the highest quality merchandise possible, so the two young men were the best candidates. But since they'd be least likely to be home at ten p.m., the delivery team would get all four addresses, prioritized by the age and health of the prospective donor.

The computer genius on the payroll kept their donor list current with semi-annual hacking forays into the patient records of several area hospitals. Those included on the list had to be single and living alone, in good health, under age fifty, and a registered organ donor.

The Broker ordinarily resisted utilizing the kidnap-and-murder method of donor procurement, but the kind of money that Schuster had offered made it worth the risks involved.

After dispatching the three-man delivery team, the Broker dialed the director of Forrest General to begin preparations.

❖

Eddie Cochran's cell rang as he emerged from the Delancey Street subway station, two blocks from his studio apartment.

"Where are you, dude?" his friend Jason shouted with annoyance over the din of thumping club music and laughter. "The place is crawling with new blood. I need my wingman."

"I'll be there in twenty," Eddie promised him. "Got hung up at the library."

"You really need to chill about the chemistry final. You know you'll ace it. Now get the hell down here and let's get this party started."

"Save me a cute blonde." Eddie shrugged off his backpack as he scaled the steps of his building and fished through it for his keys. He'd just closed his hand over them when a voice from behind startled him.

"Hey, man. Got a delivery here for an Edward Cochran. You know him?"

He turned to find not one, but two guys standing behind him, both six feet tall or better. One was holding a manila envelope bearing his name and address in large letters. Eddie had no idea what the delivery could be, unless it was some new prank Jason had engineered or something from the university. "I'm Cochran."

Before he knew what was happening, the two guys grabbed him, one clamping a beefy hand over his mouth to keep him from screaming. As they hurriedly carried him toward a car parked at the curb, panic exploded in his chest and he struggled unsuccessfully to free himself, but they shoved him into the back where a third man was waiting.

One of his abductors pushed in as well and slammed the door, preventing escape, while the other hurriedly got behind the wheel. The windows of the nondescript sedan were tinted, but Eddie couldn't see anyone on the street who might have witnessed what happened. "Who are you? Did Jason send you?" His friend had pulled some monumental gags, but never something like this.

None of the men responded. All three were well beyond college age, and Eddie couldn't imagine how Jason might know them. His alarm grew. "This isn't funny. What the hell do you guys want with me?"

More silence as the car navigated side streets until it reached the ramp for the Brooklyn Bridge. "Where are you taking me?" he asked, his voice an octave higher than normal, as they left the lights of Manhattan behind. "What's going on, man?"

After exiting from the bridge, they stopped at a well-lit intersection behind a delivery truck and waited for the light to change. Eddie tensed and glanced around in growing desperation. A pickup with two men inside was in the lane to their left, and a convenience store, still busy with customers, stood on the corner. Just as he made up his mind to risk a scream for help, the man to his left pulled a handgun from beneath his jacket and pressed the tip of the barrel hard against his ribs. Eddie slumped back against the seat, fighting the urge to piss himself, as the light changed and they turned onto a dark side street.

This was certainly no prank. "What the hell do you want from me?" he asked again. "I'll give you anything you want. I can get you money."

Still the men said nothing, but the guy to his right retrieved Eddie's backpack from the floor between his feet and began to rifle through its contents.

When the man pulled out his wallet, Eddie felt a glimmer of hope that this was indeed a kidnapping for profit and he might still come out of it in one piece. But that hope faded when the man ignored his cash and credit card and focused solely on his driver's license, scanning it briefly under the illumination of the overhead light. Apparently satisfied, the man stuck the license back into its slot, then inexplicably zipped the wallet into the side pocket of the jacket Eddie was wearing.

Before he could ask more, the car pulled to a stop in front of a dark alley. The location couldn't be more foreboding. The graffiti-riddled neighborhood was run-down, with no other traffic or pedestrians—just closed shops, condemned buildings, and a couple of vacant lots littered with junked cars and trash.

"Let's go." The man to his right opened the curbside door and clamped one hand over Eddie's right wrist to pull him from the vehicle. He tried to jerk free and kicked at the brute in a last desperate struggle to escape, but with the other guy's help, they had him in the alley in seconds. The driver remained behind the wheel, the car idling.

"Listen, guys," Eddie pleaded, his voice almost girl-like as his words came out in a rush. "Whatever you want, I'll get it for you. Just tell me what it is. Don't do this. Please, don't hurt me."

The men wrenched his arms behind him and pushed him to his knees, then one held him there while the other stepped in front. Eddie watched in horror as the goon facing him pulled out his gun and slowly screwed on a silencer. He pointed the weapon at Eddie, then pulled out his cell phone with the other hand and called 911.

"I'd like to report a shooting," the man said. "Alley in the five-hundred block of Standish Avenue, Brooklyn. I think the guy's dead."

Tears streaming down his face, Eddie pleaded, "Please don't. Please don't do thi—"

❖

Andrew Schuster snatched the phone before it rang a second time. "Yes?"

"This is Doctor Elliot Griffith, with Forrest General Hospital in Brooklyn. I'm calling for Andrew Schuster."

"Speaking."

"Mister Schuster, your son is at the top of our list for a liver transplant, and we have just admitted a matching donor. How soon can you have Matthew at our facility?"

"A half hour, at most." Despite the possible risk involved, Andrew had contracted a private transport company because of his son's deteriorating condition, and two attendants with a fully equipped medical van were parked in his driveway. He motioned them inside from the window.

"Good. We'll see you then. Come right to the ER entrance."

The van made the trip in twenty-two minutes, unimpeded by traffic at that hour. When they pulled up at the entrance, a dour-faced man in a blue suit tossed his cigarette and intercepted Andrew as he exited the back.

"All is in readiness, Mister Schuster," the man said, without introducing himself. "The donor is a perfect match. Just behave normally, and your son will get the best care possible. No one you'll come in contact with will have any reason to suspect your son was moved up the list tonight."

"Who's the donor?" Andrew asked as the two attendants unloaded the gurney.

"No questions," the man answered. "I'll be nearby until it's over to make sure you get your money's worth." He stepped away as two nurses in surgical scrubs emerged from the hospital and headed toward the van.

"Matthew Schuster?" one of the nurses asked.

"Yes, that's my son," Andrew told her.

"We're taking him straight to the OR," she said. "If you follow us, there's a lounge nearby where you can wait."

Andrew walked beside the gurney, holding his son's hand as they wheeled him inside and into an elevator. As they ascended two floors, he leaned over and kissed Matt's forehead. "Be strong, pal. Pretty soon, we'll be in the backyard breaking in that new catcher's mitt."

"Daddy, I'm scared," Matt whispered.

"I'll be right here when you wake up. There's nothing to be afraid of. You're just going to sleep for a while."

The doors opened and they hurried down a long hallway, bypassing two other operating rooms, headed for the one on the end.

"I'm sorry, Mister Schuster. This is as far as you can go." The nurse pointed to a room farther on. "There's the lounge. You'll be kept apprised."

With a sick heart, he let go of Matt's hand and called out, "I love you, son," as they wheeled him inside.

During the next hour, Andrew paced the hall. He noticed early on the adjacent operating room was also occupied, but it wasn't until he saw a nurse move from one to the other, carrying a silver pan, that he realized his son's donor was in the second OR.

When the nurse re-emerged, tiredly stripping off her mask, Andrew caught up with her. "Excuse me. But I have to know. Is that the organ donor?" He gestured toward the second room.

The woman nodded solemnly. "A pity. Such a young man. He was shot in the head just a few blocks away. Brain-dead when he got here." She put a comforting hand on Andrew's arm. "But a blessing for your son and several others that he was an organ donor. So far, Matthew's doing just fine. It should be over in another half hour or so."

"Thank you." Andrew tried to remain composed, but the news made him unsteady on his feet. He didn't know exactly what he'd expected when he'd offered triple price for a black-market organ to save his son, but he hadn't thought it would require the cold-blooded murder of an innocent young man.

How could he live with what he'd done? Would the sight of Matt, healthy and strong, be enough for him to overcome this crushing guilt?

Needing fresh air and a chance to clear his head, Andrew headed back downstairs. Only when he spotted two Brooklyn police officers by the admissions desk did the possible repercussions of his actions fully hit him. Not only would his illustrious career be over, he could face serious criminal charges for conspiracy and who knew what else.

The mysterious man in the blue suit reappeared without warning as he stared at the cops. "Keep calm, Mister Schuster. We've taken care of every contingency. How's your son? Was our service satisfactory?"

Andrew bit his tongue to keep from lashing out at the man and drawing attention to himself. "You can leave now," he replied, then turned and headed back to Matt.

CHAPTER SIX

New York

Chase and Jack were still several miles from their Manhattan destination when Chase's cell rang. The caller ID told her it was Reno, so she put him on speakerphone. "We're listening."

"It turns out the IP we tracked belongs to a building, that in turn belongs to a company."

"Okay. So?" Jack replied.

"Thing is…" Reno stopped and sucked on what had to be a straw. "The company is a front for an escort service called Direct Connect, owned and run by a Margaret Lewis." He sucked again and swallowed loudly.

"Can you put your beverage down for the duration of this phone call? It's highly annoying," Chase said.

"Cola. Sorry about that." Reno sounded embarrassed. "I've been working on this all day without a break. I need the sugar."

"Talk," Jack said.

"I don't have much more at the moment, but somebody who was there that night had to make the money transfer."

"How many working girls do you know who can make a fifty-thousand-dollar transaction?" Jack asked.

"Could be a wealthy client. Or the owner of the agency?" Chase mused.

"Maybe. Give me the agency's digits," Jack said, and wrote them down.

"Anything else, Reno?" Chase asked.

"Nope."

Chase disconnected.

"I'd forgotten how easy you guys have it," Jack said.

"Easy?"

"Guys like Reno do all the homework and send you on your way."

"Is that why you faked your death? Was working for the organization not challenging enough?" Chase asked.

"You're hilarious."

"Anyway," Chase said, "I say we call the agency and see where that gets us."

Jack started to dial the number.

"What are you doing?" Chase asked, surprised.

"Calling Direct Connect. I doubt they're closed. Night time is the right time for this kind of business."

"Have you done this before?"

"I've never had to pay for it and never would, so no."

"Because that would have interfered with your otherwise noble existence," Chase shot back.

Jack put the call on speakerphone. "Hi. I'd like to make an appointment with you to talk about—"

"I'm sorry that's not the way we work," the woman on the other end said.

"I see. Well, then, can we—"

"Oh, for Christ's sake. Give me that, Neanderthal," Chase muttered in a low voice as she grabbed the cell from Jack's hand. "Please, excuse my friend," she said into the phone. "She's new at this. An acquaintance gave me your number. He happens to be a very satisfied customer."

"We do aim to please all sorts," the woman said. "What are you looking for?"

"He recommended the woman he saw last Tuesday, but he wasn't certain your employee met with same-sex customers."

"Tuesday," the madam repeated. "And what is your friend's name?"

"I doubt he uses his real name, and I was remiss in asking his alias," Chase replied, oozing charm. "He was with her at an address on West 76th around seven o'clock."

"Aha. Hold on, please."

"Of course. Take your time."

The madam came back on. "It was either Amber or Priscilla. Priscilla does girl-on-girl and is available tonight."

"And Amber?"

"Her availability is limited, I'm afraid."

"Then I'd like to make an appointment with Priscilla," Chase said. "Half an hour from now?"

"Your name?"

"Jaclyn." Chase smiled when Jack shot her a look of death.

"That won't be a problem. Payment is made beforehand. Two hundred and fifty dollars for an hour."

"Very reasonable."

"Please go to the rear entrance."

"I will. Thank you." Chase hung up.

"That went smoothly," Jack said. "Now let's hope Priscilla's our girl."

They drove in silence until they reached the brownstone, arriving fifteen minutes before the appointment. Chase had to circle the block a few times before a parking spot opened up in front.

Jack stared up at the building. "Not too shabby for a brothel."

"House of pleasure."

"Yeah, right. I don't see how anyone can get pleasure out of screwing a woman who's pretending to enjoy it."

"It happens every day in most households."

"Too true. But at least within the privacy of their own sad marriage they don't enable the skin trade."

The remark hit a sore spot with Chase. She was certainly aware her own habits had consequences, but she'd managed to neatly justify those feelings, at least in her own mind. Prostitution would continue to exist with or without her contribution, and she figured selling one's body was better than turning to theft and drugs. "Besides, not all customers are filthy, selfish pigs."

"Yeah, I bet most are gentle, charming princes," Jack said. "I seriously doubt any woman who gets paid to fuck enjoys it."

"Don't be so sure."

"Don't be so naïve. It's their job to tell you you're the fuck of the century. They'll say anything to guarantee a return customer."

"Anyway…" Chase was tired of the turn the conversation had taken. "Let's hope our girl is here tonight."

"Haven't done surveillance in years." Jack sat back and studied the brownstone.

"I'm sure you have, only your people use the term *clock*," Chase said, referring to mafia terminology.

"I didn't work exclusively for the mob and I was never one of them." Jack was clearly aggravated.

"It's reassuring to know you seek variation at the bottom of the barrel."

"I'm not going to defend myself."

"Good, because I doubt whatever you have to say is a page-turner."

"Screw you, Land—" Jack looked past her. "Two o'clock."

A well-dressed woman was walking up the driveway, headed toward the rear of the brownstone.

"You're on," Chase said. "And go for subtle."

"If you don't think I can handle it, do it yourself."

"I want to sit back and bask in the regaling of your first time."

"Oh, my God. You are *so* witty."

"Your sarcasm is a bit stale, but I appreciate the effort." Chase had reasons for not taking this one. She'd used various agencies for her own pleasure and knew all too well that most girls liked to move around. Although she'd never ordered from Direct Connect, she wouldn't be surprised to come across someone she knew.

"Maybe later I can show you where you can stick my effort." As she left the car, Jack tried not to imagine what Cassady would think of what she was doing, even though it was a necessary step in their efforts to find her. With a sigh, she walked to the rear entrance of the brownstone and rang the buzzer.

A seven-foot closet of a guy answered. "Come in. I'm Massimo."

Jack mentally added him to their list of possible suspects. "I have an appointment with Priscilla."

He smiled. "Second floor, second room to the right."

"Thanks." Jack took the stairs and knocked.

A brunette, probably in her early twenties, opened the door. "Hi, Jaclyn." She gave Jack an appreciative once-over. "Come on in and get comfortable." The call girl wore a sheer black teddy that barely covered her ass and displayed more cleavage than would be tolerated in public.

Jack tried not to stare at her breasts. "A friend of mine visited you last Tuesday." She tossed the agreed amount on the dresser. "He said you were amazing."

The young woman giggled. "Tuesday…" She pursed her lips in thought. "Ah, the Cleveland Mattress King. He's a sweetheart, and a generous tipper. I've been seeing him for three years. Are you in the same business?"

Do I look like I sell mattresses? "No. I know him from the local bar."

"Well, any friend of Bill's is a friend of mine." The girl snickered.

"He also talked about an Amber?" Jack wondered if she was being subtle enough. Damn Landis for not taking this one.

"Did he?" Priscilla sounded surprised. "He's never…been with Amber. Amber doesn't take clients here except for Dario. Frankly I don't know why she continues to see that creep." She reached over and slowly unbuttoned Jack's shirt.

"What do you mean?" Jack froze. She looked down at the girl's busy fingers like they were pesky flies and grabbed her hand to stop her. "Why don't we slow down?"

The girl laughed. "Your time, your money."

"So, Amber and the creep?" Jack asked.

"Well, she never has to please the guy, but she has to put up with him watching while she has sex with whoever she picks up or he asks her to do."

"You mean, he never screw…participates?"

"Nope." Priscilla licked Jack's neck. "You know, a watcher."

Jack took a step back. "Huh? Yeah, sure." She tried to sound like she'd heard the term before.

Priscilla guffawed. "A creep. Plus, he's like some big man of mystery. Comes and goes by special arrangement so no one ever sees his face. Not even Amber." She clearly had no qualms about discussing her colleague's affairs.

"No kidding," Jack replied. A guy with secrets. Could be their man, she surmised, 'cause Bill the Mattress King sure didn't fit the profile. "Do you think I could hook up with Amber?"

"What's wrong with me?"

"Uh…nothing. But Amber sounds like she might be good for a different kind of…weird. You know, if the mood strikes me."

Priscilla giggled. "Yeah, I don't do kinky."

"But you're…beautiful." Jack tried to sound interested and charming.

"Can we get started?" The call girl started to pull off her teddy, exposing her bare breasts.

Jack swallowed hard and stopped her. "Uhm…hold on."

Priscilla smiled. "Oh, you want to undress me? That's cool, too."

"I was actually wondering…where can I find Amber?"

"I don't know. Through the agency, I guess. Like I said, she's not here much, just for the one guy. And she usually doesn't hang around after."

"Is she cute?" Jack asked, hoping for a description.

"I guess, if you like the gorgeous type," the girl replied. "I'm kinda glad she won't put her face in the catalogue. It'd leave the rest of us in cardboard boxes, eating out of Dumpsters."

"Can you give me her number?"

"What? No. Besides, she doesn't do girls." She giggled again, her annoying trill beginning to grate on Jack's nerves.

"I can be very persuasive."

"Look, are we going to get busy?" The girl suddenly got serious, annoyance creeping into her tone. "Or are you going to drool over Amber?"

"Okay, here's the deal." Jack pulled out her wallet. "I'm giving you another two fifty for Amber's phone number, and this whole conversation never happened." She threw the money on the bed.

The call girl ogled the cash. "I don't have her number."

"What *do* you have?"

"She mentioned she's going to the Cave tomorrow night. It's a club, near—"

"I can find it. What does she look like?"

Priscilla fished a few pictures from her purse. "This is us last Christmas."

The photo was a little blurry, but Jack could make her out. She put the picture in the pocket of her jacket.

"Hey, it's not for keeps."

"It better be, for two hundred and fifty bucks."

Priscilla giggled yet again. "I guess you can have it."

Jack buttoned up her shirt. "Thanks for the…good times, Priscilla." She strode to the door.

"You're welcome, I guess."

"There's a certain glow about you," Landis said as soon as Jack got in the car.

Jack ignored the comment. "If I hear the words *I guess* or a giggle one more time, I'll implode. Aside from that, I don't think she's our girl. But we should check her anyway."

"Why do you think it's not her?"

"Because her elevator doesn't go all the way up, and a few hundred bucks were enough to make her spill on her friend. For a few more, I could've bought her mother. Not the type Rózsa would trust his laundry to, never mind keep his cash and secrets. Her Tuesday client doesn't sound likely, either."

"How about the other girl—Amber?"

"My bets are on her for now. Or her john—he fits the profile. Very secretive, doesn't want anyone, including the call girl, to see him."

"A watcher," Landis said.

"I knew that."

"Knew what?"

"Nothing. We also need to check out the muscle at the door. Name's Massimo."

"Massimo what?"

"He didn't exactly give me his business card."

"Looks like we'll have to follow him home. Get an address."

Jack nodded and sat back. "Get comfortable."

Landis smiled. "You didn't know what a watcher was."

"For all I know he likes to screw with a bag over his head."

"I don't know how to process your obtuse conclusion."

"What are you babbling about?"

"He's a watcher, and very careful to hide his identity," Landis concluded.

"My point. Sounds like someone we should meet."

"And I do not babble."

"Whatever you say," Jack said smugly.

"After we get an address on this guy, I say we go to that place you try to pass as a home to pick up some clothes, and then to a hotel."

"There's nothing wrong with my—"

"I'm sure pigs feel the same way about their sty."

"Babble, babble, babble," Jack whispered.

Priscilla left the building a few minutes later. Another hour passed and a businessman in a suit came out, then another call girl. One by one, the lights in the brownstone clicked off.

Jack sat up. "Closing time." She was so focused on the front door Landis saw the light come on upstairs before she did.

"Fourth floor. Think he lives there?" Landis asked.

Jack trained her binoculars on the window. She could make out a picture hanging on the wall, but little else—until Massimo walked by in his wifebeater T-shirt, drinking a beer. "Looks like it. I say we bag it for tonight, come back tomorrow. He's got to leave sometime. Give us a chance to get in and look around."

Landis called Reno and, after updating him on what they'd learned, asked him to find out anything he could about Massimo and the others who'd been in the brownstone that night. Though it was unlikely he could get anything on most of them with only first names to work with, some of which were probably aliases, he'd worked miracles before. When she hung up, she checked her watch and started the rental. "Now, which way to Sty Central?"

CHAPTER SEVEN

Shanghai, China

Simon huddled in the corner of the bleak cell, furiously seeking a plan to get himself out of this nightmare. A month ago, he'd been apprehended at the airport with a half kilo of opium, and every development since then had been increasingly horrific.

Deprived of any contact with either the US Embassy or family, he'd been taken immediately to a local jail, where soldiers wielding electric batons coerced him into signing a statement in Chinese he presumed was a confession. Not long after, a man who said he was Simon's attorney told him in broken English he'd been given the death penalty for his crimes.

Four days ago, he'd been transferred to the Qing Pu Prison, a squalid and massive complex, and placed into a cell block dominated by Westerners. His cellmate Rollo, a freelance Aussie journalist, was being detained without trial on suspicion of industrial espionage, a charge he vehemently denied.

A sudden chaos of noise in the hallway broke Simon from his reverie. Several soldier-guards marched past his cell in a tight formation and began pulling inmates from their cots farther down the hall. The inmates apparently knew more than he did about the purpose of the exercise, because many of them screamed or fought back until they were subdued with electric batons.

"What's going on?" he asked Rollo as they watched.

"Doesn't look good for them," Rollo replied somberly. "I saw the doctor down there a couple of days ago."

"What does that mean?"

"They're next. Their number's up, man."

"What are you saying? They're all going to be executed?"

Rollo nodded. "They're coming faster. Some of those guys haven't even been here half a year."

Simon fought a sudden urge to vomit. "You're kidding, right? What about appeals?"

Rollo's laugh was devoid of humor. "This isn't the bloody States. Haven't you caught on there's no such thing as justice here, or even basic human rights? Once you're in, they do what they want to you."

The soldiers marched past them again, dragging a half-dozen inmates, including one young woman.

"Marcia," Rollo said solemnly. "Catholic nun from Canada, arrested in a raid on an underground church. She's made it a year, poor girl, but they finally got her to sign the donor card."

"Donor card?"

Rollo looked at him incredulously. "Where you been, man? Don't you ever read the fucking newspapers? We're a precious commodity to the Chinese."

"What the hell are you talking about?"

"This country's like ground zero for black-market organs. It executes more prisoners than any other country so it can sell our kidneys and livers to the highest bidder. Why do you think they give the death penalty for virtually any kind of crime?"

"So the doctors…when they visit…"

"Are running blood tests, to make sure you're healthy and a match for whatever fucking orders they have to fill."

Another surge of nausea roiled in his stomach, and Simon dry-heaved into the bucket that served as their toilet. As he wiped his mouth on the back of his sleeve, screams erupted from the courtyard outside their window. He and Rollo peered out through the bars.

The six prisoners who'd been marched past them were lined up against a brick wall on their knees, their hands tied behind their backs. A soldier on either side held each one in place. Many were screaming or yelling. At a barked order from a man with gold braid on his uniform, six soldiers armed with rifles approached each prisoner from behind and aimed his weapon at his target's head.

Another barked an order and shots rang out in the courtyard, silencing the screams. With chilling efficiency, the dead prisoners were hoisted onto stretchers and put by pairs into three ambulances parked near the gate.

"Jesus Christ," Simon muttered, as he watched a pair of soldiers rake over the bloodstains in the sand to obliterate all evidence of what had just happened.

❖

The director of the Qing Pu Prison, a heavyset man with a large appetite, frowned when the clanging of his telephone interrupted his lunch. He wiped the noodles from his chin before reaching for the receiver.

"Good morning, Xia Jia," the familiar voice said.

Xia had never met the Broker in person but had wondered many times what face belonged to such an icy voice. "To what do I owe the honor?"

"To our mutual friends," the Broker replied. "Supply and demand."

He quickly pushed the soup aside. "Is there trouble with the supply?"

"On the contrary," the reptilian voice said. "Your services have been most satisfying. The product is not the problem. It's the delivery time I would like to discuss."

"What do you have in mind?"

"I have an order here that needs to be filled by the end of the week."

Normally, Xia had a month to fill the Broker's latest list of black-market organs, which gave him plenty of time to make the necessary arrangements. Blood tests had to be conducted on the death-row inmates to ensure they were good matches and had not become infected with HIV or other diseases, guards had to be given adequate time to coerce a signed donation release, officials had to be bribed to speed the process and eliminate necessary paperwork and review, and the hospital nearest the prison had to be notified to begin preparations. Most of the time, the organs harvested for the Broker went to rich clients from the US and Europe, who resorted to "transplant tourism" because their prospects through legitimate channels looked bleak.

Reducing the turnaround to less than a week would be extremely difficult, but he was not about to hesitate in trying to meet the Broker's demands. "Tell me what you need." Xia Jia noted the list of organs, with their respective blood types, on the napkin before him. "Big order for me to fill in a matter of days."

"And you will be rewarded accordingly. Does a twenty-percent raise sound interesting?"

"Per product or total shipment?"

"Product. If you fill the order on time."

Xia stared at the ticking clock on the wall as he calculated the hefty bonus being offered. The list was a lengthy one and would require another mass execution of prisoners. "The time is not enough. I—"

"Are you saying you can't accommodate my demands?" The Broker's cold and ominous tone gave him goose bumps.

Xia didn't know how he was going to pull this off with all the recent restrictions that had been imposed on organ donations, but disappointing the Broker would mean the end of his luxurious life. There were plenty of other penitentiary directors to turn to who would be more than willing to do whatever was necessary for that price. "I can do it. You will have your order filled on time."

"If this goes well, it could be the beginning of a permanent arrangement. A very lucrative one. How do you feel about that?"

"I would like for our business to grow," Xia replied, "but other people will have to be notified."

"He can expect a phone call from me today."

"No problem then. Everyone satisfied."

"Satisfied indeed," the Broker said slowly. Xia could picture a smile on those reptilian lips.

Once they'd disconnected, Xia summoned his second in command to begin expedited blood tests on at least forty death-row inmates, to ensure they'd have the proper number of matches. Then he called the hospital director. Holding two rounds of executions the same week was unprecedented, but it would no doubt have the unintended benefit of keeping the rest of the prisoners at the enormous complex docile and compliant for a long while.

❖

Simon shrank back against the cold brick wall of his cell when two soldiers armed with electric batons entered, followed by a man in a white medical jacket. Still edgy and anxious from the shock of seeing the executions, he panicked.

The guards pinned him roughly against the wall, and when he struggled, one discharged his baton against Simon's ear. His body jerked involuntarily and he cried out as an excruciating roar filled his ears and obliterated all other sound. Limbs tingling with pain, he saw but didn't feel the prick of the needle as the man in white drew a vial of blood from his right arm. Without a word, the men departed, leaving him gasping for breath.

Rollo watched it all from the cot but didn't move until the soldiers had gone. "Tough luck, mate," he said as he helped Simon unsteadily to his feet.

Simon fought to calm his runaway heart. This couldn't be happening. He'd just tried to smuggle a small amount of opium, for God's sake; it wasn't like he'd killed somebody. "How can I get out of this, Rollo? Isn't there somebody I can bribe or something?"

"Not unless you're rich, man. Your organs are worth a hundred grand or so, I hear. And you'd have to have it on you, 'cause they damn sure won't let you talk to anybody on the outside. My mum still doesn't even know I was arrested."

Simon stared out at the blue sky through the bars and wept.

CHAPTER EIGHT

New York
Next day, November 17

Chase and Jack returned to the brownstone at eight thirty a.m., figuring Massimo would probably allow himself at minimum a good six hours' sleep before he ventured out. By the time he finally emerged from the building shortly before noon, both of them were wired from too much coffee. A small shoulder bag containing surveillance cams and listening devices rested on the console between them.

"He knows you," Chase said as she fit an earpiece into her ear so they could communicate. "I'll take him while you go inside."

"I think I can manage to shadow someone without being seen, thus the name Phantom."

"Don't you mean Silent Death?" Chase used the nickname Jack was known by in the underworld.

Jack's head turned so fast Chase thought she'd hurt herself. "Don't look at me like you've seen a unicorn."

"What?"

"I know you heard me." Chase looked at her watch.

"Why did you call me that?"

"It wasn't random, if that's what you want to discern."

"How do you know?" Jack whispered, never taking her gaze off Chase.

"Your question isn't interesting and the answer not very remarkable." Chase opened the car door. "If you want me to really daze you, ask me the right question." She grabbed the bag and got out of the car.

Few pedestrians were in view. Chase picked the lock on the door in a few seconds and slipped inside, pausing to listen for signs of activity. All quiet, but for the low hum of the furnace. After planting cams to cover the front and back doors, she quickly checked the rooms on the ground floor. A waiting area with couches to her right, three rooms converted to bedrooms, a small kitchen in the back, and a storage room with bedding, towels, alcohol, and other supplies.

The second floor contained what she was looking for—a bedroom with a two-way mirror and attached watcher's room. She planted cams in the vents and hid listening devices, then checked the rooms on the third floor to make sure no other rooms had been modified as watchers' suites.

Massimo's door on the fourth floor was locked, but no challenge. Wrinkling her nose in disgust at the man's cluttered living room and kitchen, she stepped over dirty clothes and headed toward his desk. A stack of mail yielded the bouncer's full name: Massimo Umberto.

After planting cams and a listening device, Chase fired up his laptop. She was copying files onto her flash drive when Jack's voice came over her earpiece. "How's it going?"

"Quite productive. Got his name and I'm in his computer. Where is he?" Chase asked.

"Swallowing burgers at a dive around the corner. You'd think the guy hadn't eaten in a decade. He asked for the bill. If he's going straight back, you don't have more than seven."

"I'll be out in five. Delay him if you have to."

"I'll stall him."

"Go for the virginal, corn-fed, country-girl tourist scenario."

Chase finished and got to the car about a minute before the bouncer rounded the corner and came into view. Jack waited until he went inside to hoof it back to the rental.

Chase handed her the flash drive. "Massimo Umberto. Upload the files to Reno and see what he can dig up." She started the car as

Jack turned on their laptop. “Not much else we can do until the club gets going tonight.”

“Where to?” Jack asked, her discomfort about Chase’s earlier comment still obvious.

“I’m starving.”

“Bacon and eggs sound pretty damn good.”

“Not the bacon part,” Chase said.

“Since when? You used to live on bacon.”

“I haven’t touched meat for ten years.”

“Oh, one of those.”

“A vegetarian.”

“Almost right,” Jack said. “You love sex and vegetables. That makes you a vagetarian.”

Chase laughed. “Corny.”

Jack, still very serious, turned to face her. “So how do you know?”

“Still not the right question, but I’ll answer anyway. Because our paths crossed.”

❖

The enormous Cave’s dark ambience and décor suitably reflected its moniker. The central dance floor was lit by a frenzy of rainbow spots, digitally programmed to flicker in patterns timed to the pounding beat blasting from the speakers. Around the dark perimeter, booths and couches provided couples the opportunity for semi-private trysts in cushy comfort.

Chase led Jack into the club at the stroke of midnight—early prime time for the pickup crowd—and paused at the edge of the dance floor. Though she hadn’t visited the Cave in years, it was still so familiar she felt she’d hardly been away.

Men and women hungrily rubbed up against each other as they danced, or talked, or stole away toward the shadowed couches. The whole atmosphere was one of practiced foreplay or a prelude to sex, which made it hard to distinguish the working girls hoping to score a customer from the party women simply out for a night of fun.

Jack kept to her right as they eased through the packed crowd toward the bar. Every now and then they had to pause to negotiate a new way through. Jack seemed annoyed at times, and Chase had to smile every time Jack tried to turn her body away from whoever rubbed against her.

They found standing room at the end of the bar and ordered drinks—beer for Jack and a Diet Coke for Chase.

"So, this is your crowd." Jack watched two women kissing a few feet away.

"It hasn't been for five years."

"Most of the women are, what, twelve?"

"Over twenty-one, but yes, I like them young." Chase rarely dated or paid for a woman over thirty.

"They look barely legal," Jack said with distaste.

"If memory serves me well, and I know it does, Cassady can't be more than twenty-five."

"Twenty-six, and that's different. I didn't snatch her from a club, high on E, and seduce her in a bathroom stall."

Chase raised an eyebrow.

"Don't even try to deny it," Jack said.

"Oh, I won't. I'm merely impressed at your astute remark."

"Don't be. You're not that original."

"True. But when I realized every other stall was being used for the same reason, I felt so…common, I moved the romance elsewhere."

"Still sex-crazy. There's more to life, you know."

"What a profound observation. I might have to sew that into my pillow."

"Yeah, you're fucking hysterical." Jack sipped from her bottle. "Hotel, fuck pad, car. Where do you take them?"

"Living vicariously, are we?" Chase shot back.

"Forget I asked. Whatever." Jack scanned the crowd on the dance floor, while Chase covered the crush of people coming and going around the perimeter.

"All of the above, plus a few more. But constant hunting and relocation gets tedious after thirty-five. Don't you think?"

"Never been the partying type."

"Maybe not," Chase said. "But you had your needs before Cassady. You must have fulfilled them one way or another."

"None of your business."

"That either means you did and aren't too proud of it, or you didn't and feel embarrassed about it. Which one is it, Harding?"

"You'll never know." Jack shifted again to dodge another attractive woman who deliberately detoured to brush up against her. "So where do you take your meaningless sex nowadays?" she asked once the woman had continued on.

"I don't take them anywhere. They come to me," Chase said matter-of-factly. "I buy my romance."

Jack turned to stare at her. "As in whores?"

Chase tried to ignore the undercurrent of surprise and disapproval in Jack's tone. "Don't be crass. I use professionals."

"That would explain your attitude with the agency yesterday. You use call girls."

"Temporary companions."

"I see." Jack went quiet for a long while, obviously uncomfortable about Chase's revelation. They both went back to scanning the club in search of Amber. All of a sudden, Jack blurted, "I doubt you need to, so why?"

"It keeps things simple. All I owe them is cash, and satisfaction—in my case anyway—is guaranteed. We all have vices."

"That we do. Whatever it takes, right?"

"Have you ever indulged in the service of professional pleasure?"

"I told you how I feel about the topic," Jack said. "I think it's disgusting, and I refuse to participate in the trade."

Her hypocrisy was irritating. She wasn't above working for criminals who likely dealt in the skin trade but had a problem with Chase buying sex? Jack, of all people, was in no position to judge her.

"You're a hypocrite, Harding." Chase pushed away from the bar and eased into an opening in the throng of people passing by.

Jack stayed on her heels. "Just because I used to work for scum doesn't mean I liked it or adopted their habits."

Chase turned to look at her. "So you were held at gunpoint to work for them?"

"I did it because I thought I didn't have options. I was wrong, and if I could take it all back, I would. Trust me, no one feels shittier about my past than I do, so let it fucking rest." Jack pushed past Chase and into the crowd around the dance floor.

It was hard to see much of anything this close with all the bodies pressed up against each other, so Chase sought a better vantage point. She tapped Jack on the shoulder and pointed at the narrow gallery above. Jack nodded and followed. They both let out a sigh of relief once on the quiet balcony.

"I'm getting too old for this shit." Jack took another sip of beer.

"What was your vice of choice?" Chase was curious because she knew there had to be something. "Before, of course, you found… love?"

"And my time machine works. We're back in 1989 and you still can't handle that word," Jack said.

"Only now it's practically a Pavlovian reaction."

Jack smiled. "Can you at least try for an inward cringe?"

"And hide the cynic in me? Never."

"Is it because cynicism is still the only thing sustaining you?"

"That, and PEZ," Chase said.

Jack smiled. "I figured. I found your Spider-Man one in the glove compartment. Empty. They should have thrown you in rehab years ago."

"I make no apologies or excuses for my addiction. PEZ may even be what led me to discover my preference in temporary companions." Chase tried to sound serious.

"I can't wait to hear this one."

"Look at the similarities. Both can be bought, variety in faces, they're sure to please, and most importantly, both are disposable."

Jack rolled her eyes. "Screw rehab. You need a shrink."

"Been there, done that, then did her."

"And you even managed to pay for it by the hour."

Chase laughed. "I always get my money's worth. But she did help me discover one thing about myself."

"Is this going to get graphic?"

"My skin doesn't react well to polyester carpeting."

Jack laughed, nearly choking on her beer. "What an insightful moment for you. I'm all goose bumps."

Chase checked her watch. One twenty. Where was Amber? Two minutes later, she spotted their target amidst the crush of people at the edge of the dance floor. "Four o'clock."

Jack immediately followed her gaze. "About time."

The crowd around Amber thinned enough for them to get a better look. "She's...h...h...ho..." Chase stuttered. Amber certainly knew how to dress to show off her exquisite hourglass figure and long legs to best advantage. Her top was corset-like, exposing the ivory skin of her shoulders and arms while hugging her high, perfect breasts and the flat plane of her abdomen. A strip of black silk along the top and bottom outlined the white designer garment, and a matching ebony ribbon laced up the back. Black Dolce & Gabbana jeans—tight, and low-cut—accentuated Amber's firm ass and the curve of her hips, and designer heels gave her a statuesque presence. She wouldn't have looked out of place on any New York runway.

When the call girl turned toward them, Chase inhaled sharply. Amber's medium-brown hair, cut to her shoulders, shone with brilliant golden highlights and was layered to frame a perfectly balanced oval face. Her long neck and classically delicate features reminded her of a young Grace Kelly, but Amber's ready smile and easy laugh added an enticing approachability to her cool elegance. She was nothing at all what Chase expected.

She was with two other women, and all three seemed to be having fun—smiling and talking as they watched the mob gyrating on the dance floor. A man in his early thirties approached Amber and put his arm around her waist as he whispered something in her ear.

"Hot. The word you're looking for is hot. Why would a woman this beautiful have to turn tricks for a living?" Jack mused.

"They all have their reasons."

"Her friends don't look like...colleagues," Jack said, her gaze fixed on the trio. "Do you think she's picking that guy up?"

"Could be." *Lucky bastard.* "But I doubt it's work-related. She's not dressed for the occasion." Chase knew working girls always dressed to seduce, and although Amber certainly looked sexy, she wasn't in the usual working-girl attire. Besides, Priscilla had said Amber saw only one customer at the brownstone. That didn't necessarily mean she wasn't making something on the side by picking up other guys, but her behavior tonight didn't support that theory. She didn't seem interested in the man beside her, or in flirting with any of the others in the club, for that matter.

"If she leaves with him, we can follow and get her alone when she's done," Jack said. "Eyes only for now."

"Difficult, but I'm not complaining."

"True martyr."

"You never answered. Vice?" Chase asked, while they both followed Amber's every move.

"Porn."

"Still?"

"I haven't been near it since Cass."

"You'll go back. Revisit your collection. Marital bliss is nothing but a contradiction in terms."

"Seriously, what's fucked you up so bad?"

"Life. And I'm returning the favor."

"He's getting pushy." Jack leaned over the railing to get a better look.

Chase had seen it, too. The guy's hands were all over Amber, who was trying politely to push him away. She got irritated every time she saw this happen to any woman. Some assholes thought they could do whatever they wanted. Paid for or not, no jerk had the right to hurt a woman. "I'm going down."

"What are you doing?" Jack called after her as she headed for the stairs.

"Introducing myself. It's time to get some answers."

Chase stopped a few feet away and watched as the guy tried to palm Amber's ass. She shot him a nasty look, but he was undeterred.

"Come on baby, give me a chance." He slurred his words.

"I'm not interested," Amber replied. "Now, please, leave me alone."

"Just one kiss." The man pulled Amber close and tried to kiss her.

Chase quickly closed the few steps between them and jerked the guy back by his collar. "The woman asked you to disappear, yet you're still here."

The guy pivoted for a face-to-face confrontation, but soon realized he had to look up to accomplish that. "Who the hell are you, butch?"

Amber looked relieved.

"Her lover, gnome."

The man turned from her to Amber, his eyes nearly bugging out of his head. "You're kidding me."

Amber smiled and gazed provocatively at Chase with doe-soft hazel eyes. "What took you so long, honey?"

Chase released the drunk's collar and pushed him aside. "Got tied up at the office, baby," she replied, and gave Amber a slow kiss on the softest lips she'd ever encountered.

Amber didn't pull away; in fact, she put her arm around Chase's waist and cuddled up against her.

The tipsy suitor shook his head. "No fucking way," he said as he headed off in pursuit of more available companionship.

"Keep walking," Chase called after him.

Amber pulled her arm away as soon as the guy disappeared into the crowd. "Thank you."

"I didn't mean to scare you with that kiss. I'm Brett Coltrane," Chase said, using only the first name the EOO had given her to use as cover for this job. As she always did, she altered the last name to pay homage to one of her favorite musicians: this time, John Coltrane.

"Heather. And you didn't."

How ironic, Chase thought, that she was the one using a fake name tonight. The woman's answer confirmed her suspicion she wasn't working the club. Amber was her escort alias. "I haven't been here in years."

"It's my first time. The girls dragged me here."

Chase looked over to Heather's friends only to verify her original assessment. Married soccer moms with station wagons. "Can I get you a drink?"

"I'd say whatever you're having, but I don't like alcohol," Heather replied.

"You can ask for what I'm having if you don't mind Diet Coke." Chase smiled and lifted her glass. "I don't drink."

Chapter Nine

November 18, 1:40 a.m.

Heather had to look away for a moment and pretend to study the crowd. Her charming savior unnerved her in an exciting and totally unfamiliar way. *She's gorgeous, has the most penetrating blue eyes I've ever seen, and she doesn't drink.* "I think we're the only ones," she finally replied.

"Join me at the bar for a Coke?" Brett asked.

Heather gestured toward the bar and Brett led the way. The drunk was a moron for calling Brett butch, she thought. Androgynous was a better word. Yes, she had a certain swagger to her walk, and her clothes—black button-down shirt, black jeans, leather boots—encased a tall frame that was all lean athleticism. But Brett was decidedly feminine as well. Her short blond hair, cut stylishly, with long bangs, gave her face a softness that matched her low, melodic voice. And her incredibly long eyelashes and full, soft lips, along with the curves of her high, round breasts, were all woman.

Brett embodied the type of woman she found irresistible, *and* she possessed a certain arrogance and confidence that drove Heather crazy. Why had those attributes put her off-kilter so easily? She hadn't let anyone tempt her in years, and had especially steered clear of relationships once she started working for Direct Connect. No lover would support or even understand her decision and need to take that course, and she was in no mood to explain or excuse herself. The last time she'd dated or had been involved had been... She thought a moment. More than two years ago, she realized with a start. Had it really been that long?

That had also marked the last time she'd had sex with a woman. Although a lesbian, she refused to see female customers for Dario. Sex with women was too personal, too much a part of who she actually was and therefore not up for purchase. She'd dated men until she was nineteen, when she fell in love, her eyes finally open to the allure of women and her true sexuality. After that, she hadn't looked back. She'd had a total of three relationships and no one-night stands. All three partners, however, had complained about her obsessive need to take care of her brother, and for that reason, none of the unions lasted more than three years.

Heather never cried when they ended. Her brother was her priority, and if she had to make sacrifices as long as he lived, then so be it. They had only each other and she would never let him down.

As Brett closed in on the ridiculously crowded bar, Heather tight behind her, the shoving intensified as people jockeyed for space to place orders or sought opportunities for groping and caresses. Heather tried to steady herself as bodies pushed up behind her, but her high heels made it impossible, so she put her arms around Brett's waist to keep from falling against her.

The crush of the mob left little room to breathe. When Brett turned around slowly, a raised glass in each hand, every part of their bodies rubbed up against each other. As Heather tried to ignore the sudden rush of exhilaration coursing through her, Brett flashed her the sexiest smile she'd ever seen.

"I'm sorry," Heather shouted over the music and voices. "I can't help it. It's a madhouse."

Brett looked at her for a long time and finally brought her mouth to Heather's ear. "I quite like that you can't help yourself," she whispered.

Heather shivered at the sound and touch of Brett's lips against her ear. Unsettled, she pulled her head away and they edged through the crowd around the bar to an area less congested. "So what do you do, Brett?" she asked, eager to change the topic.

"Graphic novelist."

"I don't read them, but my brother's a fan. I take them over to him every week."

"What does he read?"

"Uhm, let's see. Hellraiser, Sandman, Walking Dead, Watchmen, and Landor the Demon."

Brett grinned. "We should exchange numbers, then, in case he ever wants the last one signed."

"You know the author?"

"As much as anyone can know themselves."

"No way! Landor the Demon?"

"Yes."

"It's his favorite. He'll have a fit if I tell him I met the creator. I'd love to get an autographed copy."

Brett fished her cell out of her pocket. "Why don't you give me your number? I'll call you when the next issue is released. We can get a cup of coffee and I'll personalize it however you want."

Heather thought about this. She rarely gave her number to anyone, never to strangers. The cell was exclusively for her brother, work, and friends.

Brett must have noticed her hesitation. "That's okay. You don't know me so—"

"No, it's not a problem." She gave her number before she changed her mind. "Make it out to Adam, if you would." Her brother would be thrilled, and he had so little reason to smile these days she just had to take the risk.

"And what's your last name, Heather?" Brett asked, still in the process of entering Heather's name into her phone.

Heather laughed. "This is getting personal."

"Would you like it to get personal?" Brett asked as she put the phone away.

"I don't have time for personal, I'm afraid."

"Married, career before pleasure, or both?" Brett asked.

"Career."

"What do you do?"

"I work for a small fashion house," Heather said. "Mostly running errands, but I hope to join the big boys one day."

"What do you do when you're not on the clock?"

"I take care of my brother. He has chronic kidney disease. What time I have left, I spend on my own designs."

"And all of the above prevent you from seeing anyone."

"Let's just say I'm not willing to burden another with certain aspects of my life. Nor am I prepared to change the status quo to please them."

"I don't consider taking care of a sick sibling something that should be negotiated or judged. Unless, of course, that's not the whole story." Brett raised one brow, insinuating she knew Heather wasn't being entirely straight with her.

Heather, taken aback by Brett's insight, had to look away. "You'd be surprised."

"At what people can run from, or at what the whole story is?"

Where was Brett going with these questions? Heather wasn't sure, but she felt increasingly uncomfortable. "The first," she replied nonchalantly.

"Of course. The first," Brett said with an edge of sarcasm.

"Uhm, you know what? I should really get back to my friends—round the party animals up and get going. I have to be up early and I'm done with the loud music." Heather knew she was babbling, but she didn't want to leave an opening for further conversation.

Every time anyone pushed her for personal information, her paranoia made it seem as though her escort job was somehow suddenly public knowledge. She knew she risked running into a client, but most of her johns, if not all, were married and wouldn't even acknowledge her outside the brownstone. But what if someone did, or pointed her out to a friend? Heather didn't want to think about that right now, didn't even want to entertain the thought that Brett knew what she did. As always, Heather figured if she made a quick exit, she'd be safe.

"I hope we meet again." Brett sounded sincere.

"Call me when you have the next issue," Heather said, and turned to walk away.

"I will." Chase watched Heather disappear into the crowd, surprised at her inexplicable feeling of frustration. Their interaction had yielded some useful information, but it had spurred more questions than answers. Heather was definitely more complicated than the call girls she knew, with perhaps more valid reasons for doing what she did. And her sexuality intrigued Chase. Heather was undoubtedly lesbian. Yet Priscilla had said she never did girls on the job. She knew it wasn't unusual for lesbian call girls to reserve same-sex coupling for their private lives. But if that was the case, why had Heather bolted when they were obviously attracted and were in one of the city's most notorious pick-up clubs?

No, she wasn't at all the kind of call girl Chase was used to. For a moment, she regretted she'd never gotten the chance to find Heather for an evening during the countless times she'd called agencies in New York.

Jack materialized by her side, jerking her from a vivid daydream about what an encounter with Heather might be like.

"It's about time. I thought we might be here all night," Jack said.

"I couldn't very well tell her I knew she was a call girl and ask about her client."

"So what do you have?"

"I'll tell you back at the hotel. Let's get out of here."

"Tell me now."

"It's too damn loud in here, okay?" Chase said, irritated.

"What crawled up your ass and died?"

"Nothing. I just need some fresh air." Chase wanted a moment of peace to reflect on her interaction with Heather. She couldn't put her finger on it, but the woman unsettled her. Maybe because Heather was so opposite what she expected. She was classy, graceful, well spoken. A dedicated sister and a woman with dreams. A woman whom Chase, under normal circumstances and in another life, before she swore off feelings and relationships, would have…*Would have what?* "I'll be outside. Move it or take a cab back." She pushed past Jack and headed for the door without looking back.

Jack caught up just as she reached the car, halfway down the block. "What the hell's wrong with you?"

Chase got in and started the engine. "Nothing." She pulled away from the curb and headed toward the hotel.

"And those were my thirty seconds of caring," Jack said. "Now, what happened with the prostitute?"

"Stop calling her that. Her name is Heather."

"Fine. Whatever. Do you think she had something to do with the money transfer?"

"I doubt it, but we can't exclude the possibility. She did volunteer that she's taking care of her sick brother, which has to require significant funds."

"Is that her story for turning tricks?"

"I think she was sincere, but I'll have Reno do a thorough background on her."

Jack dialed Reno's number and Chase relayed what she knew.

Once at the hotel, Jack hesitated outside her door. "I saw her give you her digits. Are you going to call her?"

"I told her I would."

"When?"

"Soon."

"How soon?"

"I said soon."

"What the hell, Landis? Are your boxers in a knot because you didn't get to hit and quit the hooker?" Jack said, a little too loud.

Chase hated the term anyway, but to hear it right now made her want to punch Jack. Her hands curled into fists. The problem was, the action would have been too complicated for even Chase to analyze. She forced herself to calm. "I'm going to bed."

Jack propped her shoulder against the door and crossed her arms over her chest. "In case you haven't been informed, I'm the one running the show. You're here to *assist* me because Pierce blackmailed me into taking you along. So drop the attitude and give me answers. Cass's life is at stake, and I'm not in the mood to put up with your shit. Understood?"

Chase took a few steps and came eye to eye with Jack. "I am nobody's assistant." She poked Jack on the chest. "This is my bus, and if you want to continue riding it, it would be wise to get off my case. I've worked solo for over ten years and there's a good reason for that."

"Let me guess. It's because you're crazy."

"It takes a certain amount of crazy to survive what we see, and that applies to all of us," Chase said, referring to her EOO colleagues.

"Then it's because you—"

"It's because no one can be trusted. No soldier, no op, no government." Chase smiled. "And especially no deserter." She barked the last.

"Fuck you," Jack shouted, and pushed Chase away roughly. Chase hit the wall across the narrow hall. "You have no idea what they did to me, so fuck you for taking their side," Jack said, and slammed the door to her room.

Chase checked her watch and went quietly toward her own room. She knew she was giving Jack a hard time for going AWOL, but if Jack thought they could pick up where they'd left off, she was mistaken. And neither was Chase going to take a backseat on this mission and let someone she couldn't trust call the shots. A fellow op was missing and she would do her best to get her back, but she was doing it because it was her duty and not for Jack. Jack had lost the right to expect any favors when she lied, deceived, and ran from the only friend she'd ever had.

She called her publisher and asked him to courier a proof copy of next month's Landor the Demon to the hotel, so she'd have something in hand if and when she needed to see Heather again. She spent the next half hour making her already tidy hotel room more to her liking. The maid had been in, but Chase stripped the bed, inspected the bedding, and remade it with military precision. Then she refolded the towels, scrubbed the bathroom, arranged the drapes, and neatly centered the items on the desk. Finally satisfied, she took a warm shower, hoping it would defuse her irritation and restlessness. When that didn't work, she grabbed her sketchpad and sat on the bed, distractedly penciling in some artwork for her next installment.

When Chase checked her watch again, she realized she'd been at it forty-five minutes and should be getting some rest. She put the pad on the nightstand and turned off the light, but sleep was elusive. Something nagged at the edge of her consciousness. It took a full ten minutes of tossing and turning before it hit her.

She fumbled for the light and reached for her pad. How could she have missed it? Emily, her Demon's dream girl, looked just like Heather.

CHAPTER TEN

Mouchamps, France
November 18

Gwenn Etienne carried the tea set onto her second-floor terrace just as her good friend Agnes emerged from her aging Citröen on the gravel drive below. "Up here," she called, waving.

"Be right up."

Gwenn had summoned Agnes to relay the latest update on her new neighbor. The best gossip in the village and she was front-row center, right where she liked to be. Among all her friends, Agnes was best positioned to help her in her quest to find out more about the mysterious newcomer, so she'd be first to hear about the overnight developments.

"Good morning." Agnes greeted her with kisses on both cheeks. "Something new on Monsieur Elusive this morning?"

Gwenn poured their Earl Grey. "Indeed. I was up late last night because Cosette was sick, poor darling." She petted the aging cat sleeping beneath her chair. "She's fine now. Must have caught another mouse in the pantry."

"And while you were up, you saw…" Agnes prompted her as she glanced across the wide rows of Gwenn's prized grapevines to the cottage in question.

Gwenn sipped her tea thoughtfully to prolong the suspense. So little happened in their village that any unpredictable element was welcome. "It was after three in the morning when Cosette became… indisposed," she said. "I happened to look out my window." She took another sip. Agnes knew she'd reach for her binoculars at virtually any opportunity to spy on her neighbor, but she had to maintain her veneer of respectability. "All of the lights over there were blazing. And he came outside to empty his trash. Who does that at that hour, except someone who must go to great lengths to avoid being seen?"

She'd been surprised when she'd noticed the first sign of occupancy at the cottage more than two weeks earlier. No one had lived there for many years and she wasn't even sure it was habitable, but after two straight nights of seeing lights turn on and off, she decided to investigate. Armed with a fresh-baked apple tart, she walked over and knocked, but the new tenant refused to come to the door. The next day, a second attempt with ratatouille met with the same result, and she was certain someone was home both times because smoke poured from the chimney.

Her curiosity piqued, she began to watch the cottage in earnest, certain that the homeowner would emerge at some point to go into the village, or do repairs, or take care of the horrific tangle of weeds and overgrowth that choked the walk and garden. The place was an eyesore.

But she had seen no sign of anyone until the day a village lad delivered groceries to the cottage on his bicycle. Gwenn trained her binoculars on the front door, holding her breath, as the boy ascended the front steps. To her disappointment, he didn't even knock; he just set down the crate of food and departed. She waited impatiently as five full minutes passed—then the door opened and she got her first fleeting glimpse of her neighbor as he retrieved the food and disappeared back inside.

A man, middle-aged, no one she recognized, and suspiciously furtive. He glanced about as he picked up the groceries, as though concerned about being seen.

She hadn't glimpsed him again until last night. "Any luck with Franco?" she asked Agnes, referring to the village's sole real-estate broker.

"I dropped by yesterday," Agnes said. "He said he didn't handle the sale of the cottage, so it must have been purchased before he came to town. That would make it six or seven years ago, at least."

"Someone at the town hall must know who owns it, from the tax records and such," Gwenn mused. "Who do we know there?" *We* implied the entirety of the eight women who made up their weekly sewing circle.

Agnes sipped her tea thoughtfully. "I'll ask around."

"I was thinking…" Gwenn offered her a cucumber sandwich. "Do you think Claude might pay him a visit?" Agnes's nephew had just been installed as the newest member of the village police department. Gwenn considered Claude too timid and malleable to do the job properly, but those qualities were to their advantage. Claude would do anything to please his aunt.

"I'll try to persuade him." Agnes gazed over at the cottage. "I'll tell him you're concerned about your safety, living alone and not knowing what kind of man your neighbor is."

Cassady listened intently as Andor Rózsa moved about in the rooms above her head. Several areas of the floor that separated them creaked as he walked over them, and by memorizing each nuance, and the sounds of water in the pipes, she'd begun to learn his routine. More important, she thought she now had an idea of where they were—an old, private home—and she had found a way to discern the rough time of day.

His bedroom must be in the corner to her left, because his steps retreated there just before the house went silent for long hours. The bathroom was next to it, judging from the brief whoosh of water through the pipes there a few times a day. The kitchen had to be near the stairs, because he lingered there just prior to her food delivery.

It wasn't much, and it got her no closer to finding a way to escape, but any bit of knowledge about her situation gave her hope.

Judging from what she now knew about his routine, she expected him any minute with her oatmeal and water. Her once-rabid hunger had abated to a hollow ache as the days passed, but her thirst was insatiable. Though she'd rehydrated herself by drinking more than half the water he'd given her to wash with, the sweat pouring off her made the reprieve all too temporary.

Rózsa's heavy steps descended the stairs, and the bolt was thrown back. As always, he avoided eye contact.

Cassady didn't move as he set down the daily ration of oatmeal and water. "Can you please empty the bucket again? The smell is making me sick."

Though he glanced toward the makeshift toilet, he was apparently not in a mood to accommodate her today, because he left again without a word and secured the door with a resounding clang of metal.

With a sigh, Cassady reached for the oatmeal and chewed each bite slowly to make it last. Her clothes fit loosely now, and her energy level was at an all-time low. Without proper nourishment soon, she'd have difficulty following through with any escape attempt, even if an opportunity presented itself.

She took a sip of water and held it in her mouth a long while before swallowing. Then she put the glass aside. By rationing herself to a small amount only when her thirst became intolerable, Cassady had learned to bridge the gap between her daily refills with the least discomfort possible.

But it was Jack who really sustained her. Whenever her spirits ebbed, she closed her eyes and relived some memory of their precious year together and, at least for a little while, was able to escape her nightmare.

❖

Southwestern Colorado

Montgomery Pierce stared out the window of his office at the campus below, so preoccupied with worry he didn't realize Joanne had joined him until he felt her caress his back.

"You tossed and turned all night," she said in a worried tone, "and you barely touched your breakfast. You can't keep going like this. You know what the doctor said."

He turned to her and put his hand against her cheek. "I love that you worry so, honey. But I'm fine. I'm taking my medication." Joanne had been monitoring him closely the last year, since the EOO doc diagnosed a sudden dizzy spell as a worrying result of high blood pressure.

A knock at the door announced David Arthur's arrival. Dressed in his customary fatigues, he looked vaguely annoyed at being summoned two hours before dawn. "I hope this is important. I was up late with the seniors." Every month, Arthur conducted night-time training maneuvers for the graduating class, in the massive Weminuche Wilderness Area adjacent to the EOO campus.

"Reno has an update for us," Monty replied. "He should be here momentarily."

Reno arrived with several printouts, which he distributed before taking his seat. The dark puffiness under his eyes from lack of sleep made him look as though he'd gone a round or two with a boxer, and Monty noticed his hands were trembling, no doubt the byproduct of too much sugar and caffeine. "I've recovered some of the files Rózsa deleted from his computer," he said. "The guy's a pro at moving money around. I found still another bank account of his—this one in Asia, under the name of a bogus furniture company. Regular deposits were going into the account right up until the lab exploded. It's empty now—Rózsa's transferred the cash somewhere else—*but*, it gives us a clue about one of his key financers. All the deposits came from a Manhattan bank account."

He had their full attention. Even David perked up. "Manhattan?"

Reno held up a hand. "No, it's not the same account that Chase and Phantom are tracking. But it *is* from the same bank, which has to be a hell of a coincidence. Now, the name on this new account is another furniture company—Dragon Imports Unlimited. Also bogus—can't find a record of it anywhere. And here's where it really gets interesting. The amounts and dates of the transfers match these invoice orders I found on another of Rózsa's deleted files." He pointed to the stapled sheets he was referencing.

Monty looked at the first page, dated 6/6/2010.

2 couches	$30,000
4 chairs	$20,000
2 credenzas	$50,000
Total due:	$100,000

The second invoice, dated 4/12/2010, was similar.

2 couches	$30,000
5 chairs	$25,000
1 credenza	$25,000
8 side tables	$56,000
Total due:	$136,000

There were several more similar pages. "So Rózsa's been supplying something regularly to this New York entity," Monty said, leafing through the manifests.

Reno nodded. "For at least two years. I would think the obvious conclusion is he's been selling his formulas."

The room went silent as they considered the dire implications. Monty flashed back to the news reports that dominated the airwaves just a month ago, chronicling the global pandemic Rózsa had unleashed. Could a secret US lab now be manufacturing another of the madman's lethal viruses? The development added even more urgency to their mission. "How long before you can track down the real account holder?" he asked.

"No telling, I'm afraid. US bank records are tough at best to access, and this account has so many protective layers, it's going to take time. The dummy furniture company is a front for a dummy LLC, and so on." Reno cleared his throat. "But I do have some positive news. Chase and Phantom reported that five people were at the brownstone the night the transfer occurred. We've already been able to eliminate three of them as suspects. That leaves one call girl and her john as possibilities."

Monty studied the next set of stapled printouts. A full-color photo of Heather Snyder's New York driver's license was stapled on top. Beneath it several pages contained her employment history, academic record, bank-account information, cell-phone records, and so on.

"She works at a fashion-design house by day and hooks at night," Reno summarized. "Has a brother who's very ill with kidney disease, and she's paying his bills while he waits for a transplant. Her legit income doesn't come close to covering it, and I can't track how much she's making as a call girl, so she could conceivably have saved up the fifty grand that got sent to Rózsa from her IP address. Phantom says her john—goes by the name Dario—is also a reasonable bet. Snyder sees him every few days, so they hope to be able to ID him soon."

"Good work, Reno," Monty said. "Keep us posted, and let me know if you need additional help. You should get some rest soon." Although it wasn't unusual for ops to go days without sleep, Reno would push himself until he dropped to find Lynx. Monty hoped Jaclyn didn't do likewise.

CHAPTER ELEVEN

Chase woke at six and, half an hour later, was ready to leave. She'd been restless all night, unable to stop rehashing her conversation with Heather and the woman's resemblance to Emily.

Chase had met plenty of call girls and never questioned their reasons or judged their decision to sell their body, simply because she didn't care. She wanted a few hours of uncomplicated entertainment, not sad stories about broken homes, illegitimate children who needed to be fed, or abusive parents. All the woman had to be was attractive and, even though she practiced safe sex, healthy.

Something about Heather, though, bothered her. Not because she was too beautiful to sell herself—plenty of stunning women did the same—but because so much about her didn't make sense. Heather possessed an air of class and undeniable innocence that didn't correspond with her lifestyle. Still not a reason she should care, though, Chase thought.

Still mystified as to why Heather was getting to her, Chase checked her watch. Reno should have sufficient information now to get them started. She was tempted to make the call immediately, but she'd never hear the end of it from Jack, who'd somehow deluded herself into thinking Operation Phoenix was her show. Not that Chase cared, but she planned to give Jack a chance.

She left her room and knocked on Jack's door. "Be at the car in five, or I leave without you," she announced, smiling inwardly as she headed for the car. She was almost there when she reached into her jacket for the keys.

"Don't bother," Jack said, rolling down the driver's window.

"When did you—"

"I'm a criminal, remember?"

"Last night in the hall."

Jack smiled and sipped from a Styrofoam cup. "Get in, Ms. Daisy, we're losing daylight."

Chase suppressed a smile as she rounded the rental. The sun was still only a faint pink glow on the horizon. She was barely in the passenger seat when Jack dialed Reno's number. Chase was surprised Jack had waited for her to make the call.

"What do you have?" Jack asked.

"Phantom?" Reno sounded surprised, no doubt expecting Chase, who had communicated with him so far.

Jack's distaste for the code name was obvious. The muscles in her jaw twitched and she gripped the steering wheel with both hands. "Call me Jack."

"That's against protocol, I can't—"

"Screw the protocol and call me Jack."

Reno hesitated. "Okay," he finally said. "Cross Massimo off. The transfer wasn't made from his computer, and his school records indicate he's marginal in the brainpower department."

"What did you find on Heather?" Chase asked. "Sans slurping sounds," she added ominously.

Reno sighed. "Boy, the two of you are a delight to work with. Maybe we can all vacation together some time." When neither replied, he said, "Okay. Heather Snyder. Parents deceased. Only sibling, Adam Snyder, chronically ill brother with kidney failure. She visits him twice a week on average at an acute-care facility in the Bronx. His bills are sky-high."

"Explains the escort service," Chase said.

"Still doesn't explain how a call girl came up with fifty grand," Jack said.

"In my opinion," Reno went on, "the call girl is a viable suspect. Her day job doesn't pay much, and she was a straight-A student. We have no proof she's not involved or oblivious to what's happened. Could be that she was holding the cash for Rózsa as a sort of emergency fund. Maybe he was her main man before he disappeared, and when the shit hit the fan and his accounts were depleted, he contacted her to send him the money."

"Why not have her arrested for conspiracy and withholding information?" Jack asked.

"We have no proof. She'd be out in twenty-four hours and could tip off Rózsa. Or her john, if *he's* the guy and she knows what's going on," Chase replied. "Arrange a surveillance van," she told Reno. "And park it as close to her residence as possible."

"Got it." He quickly briefed them on the other New York bank account he was tracking. "Anything else?"

"No," both replied.

"A thank you would be nice," Reno finally said.

"Send me Snyder's details. Residence and work," Chase replied, and Jack disconnected the call.

"Why does he always have to sound like a fresh-faced farm girl?" Jack frowned. "It's not healthy to be that happy."

"Huh?" Chase was still trying to digest Heather's possible involvement. Just then, Reno's text arrived with her home and work addresses and other pertinent information.

"What's the matter, princess?" Jack asked. "Not awake yet?"

"Drive," Chase said. "I just received the addresses."

"I say we start at her home. See if we can find anything relevant there. Her laptop, and maybe an appointment book. She should be at work till five."

"Let's go," Chase replied, as she plugged the street into the GPS. Could she really be that off about Heather? Why did she want to believe she wasn't? "We start surveilling the brownstone tonight. My money is still on the mystery man."

"Getting into her home to hook up cams and mics will take some time."

"Then drive already," Chase said through gritted teeth, eager to stop the conversation.

"Keep up that attitude and I *will* fire you." Jack pulled away from the curb.

"Or maybe you can have your people whack me."

"And let someone else have all the fun?"

Twenty minutes later, they parked in a lot a couple of blocks from the Greenwich Village address. Jack called Heather's home number before they left the rental to make sure no one was there.

Opening the doors to her building and apartment didn't take more than a couple of minutes. Chase jimmied both while Jack stayed on the lookout.

The apartment was small, but typical for New York, and cozy. Only two doors led off the main room, a combination living room and kitchen. Chase was pleased to find the place clean and uncluttered, the few pieces of furniture tasteful and functional.

"I'll take this room." Jack started toward Heather's computer.

"I'll start with the bedroom," Chase said.

"Shocker."

Chase walked slowly through the room, taking everything in. The bed was made nearly as neatly as her own. Framed photos of Heather and people who had to be her parents and brother decorated the dresser. Chase bent over to get a better look. Some pictures were from her childhood. Heather and her brother resembled their father. Same hair color, eyes, and smile. Their mother, blond with blue eyes, looked almost like a stranger amongst them. Funny how she never thought about the call girls she hired as someone's daughter or sister.

The rest of the pictures showed a middle-class family either in a middle-class house or on a middle-class vacation. Disneyland. The Grand Canyon. Nothing spectacular or outstanding, except for Heather, who seemed remarkably beautiful from the moment she could walk.

The more recent pictures were exclusively of Heather with her not-very-healthy-looking brother, who, according to Reno, was her last close relative. Chase had never belonged to a family or had siblings, but she could well understand the loneliness that accompanied the loss of someone you loved and trusted. She supposed the initial reaction was the same, regardless of why or how they were gone. Anger and sorrow.

"Find anything?" Jack called from the other room.

"Not yet." Chase opened the top dresser drawer. Scarves and belts. She felt around, trying not to disturb the contents. Nothing. Moving on to the next, she discovered an impressive collection of lacy panties and bras and stared down at them, momentarily forgetting her search. Unable to resist the temptation, she picked up one bra, then another. Victoria's Secret, Marlies Dekkers, and other expensive brands. She held up a particularly sheer red bra and tried to picture how Heather looked in it. Christ, if she didn't stop soon—

"Really, Coolidge?" Jack said. Chase turned to find her in the doorway. "Do you think her bra holds the answers?"

"I refuse to feel embarrassed. I'm too old for that particular sentiment."

"Sure you are. I bet you wouldn't be if the call girl caught you."

"Do you have anything?" Chase snapped.

"Nothing."

"Then why are you interrupting me with useless banter?"

"Are you going to look for something helpful or sniff her panties next?" Jack left the room. "Maybe then you can track her down by scent, Lassie," she added in a loud voice.

Chase placed the garment back in the drawer and moved to the closets. Sexy dresses filled half of it. The rest was classic business apparel. When she didn't find anything useful there, she moved to the nightstands on either side of the bed.

The first one she tried contained Heather's junk drawer, stuffed with the usual jumble of everyday items—tape, jackknife, batteries, scissors, ruler, hair clips, deck of cards, screwdriver, nail clipper, pens, measuring tape—and one unexpected treasure at the bottom that made Chase gasp aloud.

A rare 1972 "Make a Face" PEZ dispenser, pristine on card, with all seventeen pieces. The Mr. Potato Head-type issue, pulled from shelves not long after its release because of its choking hazard to small children, was her Holy Grail. She stared down at the long-elusive collectible, fighting an urge to stick it under her jacket. Did Heather have any idea of its value? Probably in the neighborhood of five grand by now—*if* you could find one.

She forced herself to close the drawer and moved to the other nightstand, where she found a day planner. The oversized calendar was mostly full of fashion sketches, probably Heather's, judging by the art pencils also in the drawer. The designs were roughly drawn, but unique and interesting.

Do you keep your escort appointments in here? And if you do, will they be obvious? She flipped to the date of the money transaction. The hours between seven and nine p.m. were marked with a D. *D as in dinner? I think not. D for Dario. If that's his real name.*

She found several previous *D* entries, an average of one or two a week, during the same early evening hours. They had to be the watcher Priscilla mentioned. Flipping forward, she saw no *D*'s indicating future appointments, so Heather apparently marked them only after they had taken place, or the guy made appointments shortly before they happened. Surveilling her would be difficult.

"Any luck?" Chase found Jack seated at Heather's desk by the window, typing furiously on her computer.

"It wasn't even password-protected."

"Maybe because she has nothing to hide."

"And maybe we can all live peacefully in a meadow full of daisies."

"This mystery guy Dario keeps showing up throughout her day planner as *D*. He was penciled in during the exact hour of the transaction."

"So?"

"She was entertaining Dario by screwing some guy and making a money transfer at the same time?"

"You think they're both in on it?"

Chase sighed. "I don't know, perhaps."

"Her PC isn't helping much. All pretty much mundane. I'll send a copy of the hard drive to Reno."

"Let's get her phone tapped and move on to her day job."

"What do you expect to find there?" Jack asked.

"Get a look at her routine. See if she meets anyone for lunch."

They installed a listening device in Heather's phone and surveillance cameras in the main room and bedroom and were headed back to the rental when Reno called Chase's cell. He told them the surveillance van was waiting in a lot just around the corner, and as Chase headed that way, Jack uploaded the contents of Heather's hard drive for him and updated him on what they knew.

They left the rental in the lot and took the van to the Garment District. The corner building that housed Cesare Chelline Fashions had several entrances. The main entry facing West 37th Street led into a posh reception area, where well-heeled clients could order custom designs. The building also had a back and a side entrance, so they'd have to split up to ensure they picked up Heather leaving. Chase covered the front from a window seat at the restaurant across the street, while Jack took up a position on the rear corner, where she could see the other two entrances.

At five after five, Chase's cell rang.

"Got her coming out the side," Jack reported. "She's headed toward the subway."

"Roger that." Chase threw a couple of bills on the table. "You stay with her. I'll get the van."

Heather went straight home, Jack shadowing her and keeping Chase apprised of their destination. Chase arrived a half hour later, after wrestling with rush-hour traffic, and picked up Jack down the block. When Jack spotted her, she tossed the cigarette she'd been smoking. So far, she'd heeded Chase's warning not to smoke anywhere around her, but Chase would bet good money Jack had more than a couple during her waits outside Heather's office and home.

"We're not going to find a parking spot anywhere within range," Jack said. "Every meter on this block has enough time on it to make it to six, when they stop enforcement."

"We'll have to open one up ourselves, then." Chase cruised slowly past the cars on Heather's block, looking for an older model that wouldn't have an alarm. "There. The Taurus."

The sun had set and the street wasn't well illuminated, so they had that much on their side, but at the moment too many pedestrians were still coming home from work to risk hot-wiring the car.

"Drop me and keep circling," Jack said. "I'll text you when I move in."

Ten minutes later, the street cleared enough for the exchange. Chase kept going around the block until she got Jack's SMS, and Jack waited until she spotted the van to pull the Taurus away from the curb. She ditched the stolen car in an alley a few blocks away and was back not long after Chase had all the equipment up and running.

Heather was lying on her couch watching the evening news. She'd changed into sweats and a short T-shirt and was eating some kind of noodle dish.

Chase's stomach rumbled loudly, reminding her they hadn't eaten in several hours. "I saw a Chinese place around the corner. Vegetables and noodles for me, in a garlic sauce. No MSG. And a large Diet Coke."

"Do I look like a waitress?" Jack asked. "Get your own food."

"I know you have to be hungry, too, and I called it first."

"How old are you, ten?"

"Are we going to argue about this, too?"

"I'll go, but only because I need some…fresh air."

"Use a mint when you're done."

While Jack went to get their dinner, Chase watched Heather wash dishes and go through her mail. As they ate, she tidied up the apartment. At nine, she stretched out on the couch with popcorn and a movie, and at ten forty-five, she retired to her bedroom with a book, just like thousands of other New Yorkers. Nothing unusual. No visitors. No phone calls.

After Heather switched off her light, they walked back to the rental and drove to the hotel to check out and pick up their things. Jack had booked reservations at a new place just a couple of blocks from Heather's that had space for their car. The parking issue in New York made staying within walking distance a prime consideration, especially since they would have to keep the van parked where it was until their surveillance of Heather yielded something useful.

CHAPTER TWELVE

Beijing, China
Next day, November 19

Zhang Anshun, a Grand Justice of the Second Rank in the Supreme People's Court, smiled when the caller ID on his private cell told him the Broker was on the line. For him these phone calls always meant a big payoff for minimum effort. Plus the Broker was the only person who could challenge him in greed. "How can I help you?" he asked, as he poured himself a warm cup of mijiu, a clear rice wine.

"You mean, how can we help each other. You are not in the habit of complimentary assistance."

"True." He laughed. "But I always give you priority."

"Your favoritism toward my money moves me."

Zhang laughed again. "I hear you want an express delivery."

"Correct."

"Xia Jia called me."

"Obviously," the Broker said. "I need you to clear the way."

"There will be an extra charge for this as you—"

"Five hundred thousand."

The amount was very pleasing indeed. Happy he didn't have to haggle with yet another friend asking for a favor, he took a sip of his wine. "You can expect your delivery on time."

"Should that be the case, I would like to make this an ongoing arrangement for at least six months."

Executions would have to be expedited, and that was difficult in light of recent regulations. He'd have to have prisoner records altered to make it appear as though they'd been incarcerated for a long time and had already had their sentences reviewed by the High Court. Fortunately he had the right people in his pocket and had to pay them only a tiny fraction of his share.

At least he didn't have to worry about a shortage of available organs. Death sentences were handed down for sixty-eight different crimes, including fraud and tax evasion, so a virtually limitless supply was available. And family members of the doomed were of no concern. Relatives were not allowed to visit, and most knew if they asked too many questions they would only find themselves under closer government scrutiny and possible arrest.

Whatever it took, Zhang would damn well make it possible for this kind of money. "I will be happy to assist."

"Someone will make that financial agreement in person in a few days."

"I look forward to it," he said, but the Broker had hung up.

❖

New York

Chase and Jack walked from their new hotel to the surveillance van long before dawn, sipping coffee they'd ordered from room service. Chase couldn't miss the dark circles under Jack's eyes, prominent under the streetlights' glare. She'd obviously had a rough night. "You look haggard. Did you get any sleep?"

"Some."

Although Chase had deliberately been keeping her distance and didn't hesitate to criticize Jack's decisions, she didn't like seeing her hurt. In another life, they'd been very close and would have done anything for each other. Chase was still having a hard time letting go of Jack's dismissal of her, but she felt for what Jack was going through. "We will find her."

"Yeah."

They reached the van and Chase fired up the monitor and audio while Jack stood outside and had a cigarette. The apartment was still dark and quiet at five thirty.

"Won't be long till she gets up," Chase told Jack as she got in.

"I suppose." Jack took a sip of coffee.

"What did you do all night?"

"Nothing."

"I see. I bet you spent it drinking."

"None of your business."

"Must you always get self-destructive when you can't cope?"

"Look, you harass me about smoking, you call me a criminal, you think I'm a deserter, and I take it all. But you will not tell me if and how much I can drink. It's none of your damn business."

Chase glared at her. "It is if it impairs your ability to function."

"Who the fuck said I can't function?"

"You look like death."

"Again, none of your business," Jack said.

"It doesn't solve anything is all I'm saying."

"And what exactly do tofu and prostitutes solve?"

"Nothing," Chase replied. "But they won't shorten my life span."

"Your life span was severely compromised when the EOO circus adopted you."

"Perhaps, but at least it'll be a short, sudden death instead of a long, painful one."

"Like the one I'm experiencing with you, you mean."

Frustrated, Chase turned her attention to the monitor. "Suit yourself. It's your death."

"And don't you forget it. Let me know when the call girl's ready to leave." Jack pulled something out of her small daypack and sat back to read it with her penlight.

Chase was surprised to discover it was the last issue of Landor the Demon. "You still read graphic novels?"

"That bug you, too?"

"Why that one?"

"You know it?"

"Yes."

"Then you shouldn't have to ask why," Jack replied. "For the longest time, Landor was me. Trapped in a world where he didn't belong. Destined to do what he didn't believe in and forbidden to approach the woman he loved. Landor needs to grow a pair and stand up against Satan—who loosely translates into Pierce, of course—and take charge of his own life. Go after Emily."

"Is that what you did? Go after Cassady?"

Jack hesitated. "No. Cassady came after me. Even after she found out who I was."

Chase looked back at the monitor. "Maybe Landor doesn't trust his instincts."

"Could be, but I don't get that vibe from him. I think he's just a coward."

"No, he's not." Chase almost dropped her coffee. "He's merely terrified of getting Emily killed."

"So you think he should wander forever alone, jump into bed with women who don't matter, because of what might happen?"

"There's nothing uncertain about it. Satan told him he'd kill Emily with his own hands."

"Landor's a smart guy," Jack said. "He could think of a way to keep her alive. Then again, I can see how you'd like the fact that he substitutes Emily with countless sexperiences."

The alarm clock in Heather's apartment went off.

Jack rolled up the novel. "About time."

The nightstand light came on, and they watched Heather switch off the alarm and get out of bed wearing panties and her short T-shirt. Chase stared at the monitor, mesmerized.

Heather was perfection, so provocatively proportioned her legs went on forever. After a long, lazy stretch, like a cat in the sun, she pulled on a pair of sweats and got on the exercise bike in the corner of her bedroom.

"I don't know why you're staring with such interest." Jack unrolled the novel again. "It's not like she'll pedal away."

Fifteen minutes of intense workout later, Heather started to strip as she walked out of view of the bedroom camera. The angle from the living room cam picked up her naked back in the split-screen view as she went into the bathroom wearing only her baby-blue lace panties. She closed the door before Chase could glimpse more.

"Damn." Chase sighed.

"What?" Jack asked, without looking up.

"Nothing."

Chase stared at the bathroom door until it opened ten minutes later. Jack evidently caught the movement on the monitor because she leaned forward to watch.

Heather was wrapped in a towel so small it barely reached her thighs. She made her way into the bedroom where the other camera picked her up.

"I have to admit, she is a beautiful woman," Jack said, just as Heather turned away from the camera and dropped the towel.

"Damn," Chase said again.

Heather started to dress, keeping her back to the camera. First came burgundy panties, then a matching satin bra.

"You just can't catch a break, huh?" Jack asked.

"What? Don't be ridiculous. It's not like I haven't seen a beautiful naked woman before."

"I'm sure. Need a tissue before your drool hits the control panel?"

Heather turned back around, finally, but not before she had put on a blouse. The color nearly matched her underwear and went well with the light-charcoal skirt and blazer that followed.

"You can start breathing again. She's dressed," Jack said. "Jeez, you'd think with all the action you get you'd be used to some skin."

"Stop talking and go back to Landor."

Jack sighed and opened the novel.

Heather disappeared into the bathroom for a couple of minutes to put on her makeup, then went to the kitchen to make coffee. She carried her mug back into the bedroom and sipped from it while she dried her hair in front of the big mirror over the dresser. She even combed her fingers through her hair in a slow, sexy way. Once again, Chase regretted never having happened upon her through an agency. *God, the things I would have done to that woman.*

After she finished, Heather carried her mug to the kitchen sink. She had her purse in hand and was about to put her coat on when the phone rang.

Chase and Jack stared at the monitor as Chase cranked up the audio.

"Good morning. Getting ready to leave?" a male voice asked.

"Hi, handsome. And yes."

"Will I see you tonight?"

"How badly do you want to?" Heather laughed.

"Bad," the man said. "I was wondering if you have something special for me?"

Heather sighed. "Not yet. I'm still waiting."

"Too bad."

"How about one of your other favorites?" Heather asked.

"No. It's okay. I'll see you later."

"Be good."

"Not like I have a choice," he replied.

"Later, then."

"Later."

Heather disconnected, took another quick sip of coffee, and grabbed her coat.

"It wasn't Rózsa," Jack said.

"Maybe the guy who made the transaction?" Chase mused.

"Maybe. Looks like we'll be on her heels all day."

"Get ready to move," Chase said. "She's coming out."

Jack rolled the comic book up and put it in her back pocket. "I'll keep you posted." She got out and tailed Heather as she walked toward the subway.

Chase waited until they were out of sight before she left to pick up the rental. Jack phoned to say they were headed to the Garment District as expected, so Chase parked the vehicle in the same nearby lot and met Jack in the restaurant across from Heather's building. They ate a leisurely breakfast and sat back to begin the long wait, Chase focused on the front entrance and Jack became engrossed in Landor the Demon.

Twenty minutes before Heather was due to leave work, Jack took up her position in the rear corner of the building while Chase remained watching the front, in case Heather decided to alter her routine because of the mysterious phone call.

"Got her," Jack informed Chase by cell just a few minutes past five. "She's coming your way."

"Roger that." Chase picked Heather up a minute later when she rounded the corner and passed by across the street. Jack followed a half-block behind, careful not to lose her amid the crush of rush-hour pedestrians.

Chase headed back to the rental. Traffic was gridlocked, and it didn't look like she'd be able to get out of the area any time soon. As she sat in a long line waiting to exit the lot, Jack called with an update. "She's headed into the subway at Times Square. Where are you?"

"Stuck in traffic at the lot. Keep on her. Update me when you can." She gripped the wheel in frustration. Jack was headed into a dead zone for cell phones, and Chase had no idea in which direction they were headed. To proceed without further information could just put more distance between them. She pulled off to the side to wait and checked her watch.

By the time Jack reported in again, more than a half hour later, Chase had uncharacteristically chewed off half her stubby fingernails.

"Exiting at the East 241st Street station in the Bronx." Jack paused and Chase heard the click of a lighter, followed by a long exhale. "She's on foot, headed east on Sagamore Street."

Chase pulled out of the lot and headed north. Traffic had only marginally improved—it would still take her forty minutes or better to travel the fourteen or so miles. "Headed your way."

Jack reported in again when Chase was about halfway to the Bronx. "She just went into the Saint Barnabas Acute Care Center."

"Visiting her sick brother?" Chase asked as she punched in the location on her GPS.

"That's my guess. I'll see what I can find out."

"Should be there in fifteen or so," Chase said, and disconnected. She thought back to Heather's telephone exchange. The man had asked if she had something special for him, and Heather had replied, *Not yet. I'm still waiting.* Then she'd offered to get him one of his other favorites.

He was a nut about graphic novels, Landor the Demon in particular. Were they referring to her promise to autograph a copy of her next installment for him? It seemed a reasonable possibility. Heather had clearly sounded disappointed. Surely because her brother was looking forward to it, right?

Or could it possibly be that Heather was disappointed just because she wanted to see Chase again?

CHAPTER THIRTEEN

Heather took a deep breath to steel herself before she opened the door to her brother's room. She never knew what to expect on her visits. Some days, Adam looked pretty good, all things considered. And he'd sounded strong and like his old self that morning on the phone. But too often in recent weeks she'd arrive to find him in the midst of another crisis: weak from vomiting, or with his hands, feet, and face so swollen she barely recognized him. And increasingly, she'd arrive to find him numbly incoherent because of the drugs he was taking.

However he appeared, she had to remain upbeat and positive. She forced herself to smile and went inside.

Today was a good day. Adam was sitting up in bed watching television. His color was normal, and he was devoid of the IVs that seemed a semi-permanent fixture in the room. He grinned when he saw her and flicked off the set. "Hey, H."

She kissed him and pulled up a chair. "Hey, Bro. You're looking great."

"Ate a big lunch," he reported. "And they actually agreed to let me order pizza tonight. Delivery guy will be here in a little." Adam had lost a third of his body weight in the last year because he so often had trouble keeping food down. Any time he had an appetite was welcome news.

"Extra cheese?"

"Of course. Now, fill me in. What's happening in the outside world? How did you meet my favorite author?"

Brett. Heather couldn't stop thinking about her. She'd told her brother very little, except that she'd run into the woman who created Landor the Demon, and she'd promised to give her an autographed copy of the next issue. "I met her at a club when I was out with a couple of girls from work." She told him most everything about that night, except how attracted she was to Brett and how she couldn't stop thinking about her. But her brother knew her well and evidently sensed there was more to the story than she was letting on.

"Why don't you give her a call?" Adam asked.

"First of all, I don't have her number, and second, I don't want to push. How desperate is that?"

"Desperate? You sound like I asked you to call her for a date."

Heather's cheeks warmed. "Yeah, well—"

"So she *did* ask you out."

"No, she offered a signed copy."

Adam picked up the last issue of Landor the Demon from his bedside table. She knew he'd read it many times, but it was still in pristine condition, kept in a plastic sleeve. "Funny how I assumed the author was a dude."

"That's pretty sexist."

"Come on, H, you know better. It's just that whenever I Googled the name Cooland, nothing showed up except for his…her works and an article about how the author never does public appearances or signings. No Web site, no pics, nothing. So I assumed it was some huge, pimpled-ass guy."

"Not the case. She's a very attractive woman."

He looked at her curiously. "Do you wish she'd asked you on a date?"

"What's up with all these questions about my love life?"

"It's just that…well, you never seem to go out with anyone. Last time you mentioned a girl was what, two or three years ago? I don't know, H. Can't be normal for an okay-looking woman to go without…you know."

"Sex?" If only Adam knew the only thing *not* missing from her life was sex. The wrong kind of sex—meaningless encounters with men, purely a means to support her brother's needs. And working for Direct Connect had crushed her need to get close to another woman. Not only because she feared they would find out about her secret life, but also because she'd have to eventually explain and deal with the consequences. Sex was once an exciting way to express emotions, but it had turned into an obligation, a duty that left her feeling drained and often disappointed in herself.

Heather seriously doubted she could ever get intimate with anyone again and not feel as though they could see right through her. How could they resist thinking of her without attaching a label that fit what she did? Prostitute. Hooker. Whore. What she did wasn't who she was, but how could anyone ever believe that or want to stick around long enough to find out the truth? "I'm too tired to even think about sex, Adam."

"But I'm not just talking about sex. It's like you don't hang out with anyone but me. Don't get me wrong. I love you and your company, but ever since Dad died, you've deprived yourself of a life. I know I'm to blame for the most part—"

"Stop that. I love you and I want to take care of you."

"I know, H. But you need to take care of yourself, too. Putting your life on hold is only making me feel like a complete loser. It's not what I want and it's not what you deserve. I know you need more. Unless, of course, you've decided to join some kind of freakish cult."

"I just don't have—"

"Oh, my God," Adam said with feigned shock. "You have. You've gone all—"

Heather laughed. "Cut it out. It's simply a matter of not enough time. I want a career and that has priority right now."

"Since when does one exclude the other? I'm not saying you need to get married or look into artificial insemination. I'm just talking about a date."

"And this has nothing to do with getting an autographed Landor the Demon?"

"Maybe a little." He smiled. "But you said yourself, she's a knockout."

"And very charming. And smart. And funny."

"And give me a break." Adam rolled his eyes. "Go out with her already."

"She hasn't called," Heather said.

"She will."

"Oh, really?"

"Who wouldn't? You're a catch, and not just because you're my sister."

"I'm flattered, your Greatness."

"You should be. Now where the hell is the delivery dude? It's been twenty—"

Someone knocked on Adam's door.

Heather smiled and got out her wallet. "Looks like he heard you, your Highness."

❖

Greenwich Village, N.Y.
Next day, November 20, 5:30 p.m.

Chase crept along in bumper-to-bumper traffic, her frustration growing with each yard of progress. The drive between Heather's home and workplace had become a metaphor for their mission. They were getting nowhere fast in their effort to track down Heather's mysterious john or determine whether she was involved in the transfer of money to Andor Rózsa.

Jack was even more on edge. She was chain-smoking at every opportunity—outside the acute-care facility last night, during the routine surveillance at Heather's apartment afterward, and again this morning. And while they'd sat all day at the restaurant again watching Heather's building, Jack had stepped outside for a cigarette so many times she'd lost count.

Her cell rang as she waited at a red light a block from their hotel.

"Same old, same old," Jack reported. "She's changed into her sweats and T-shirt and poured herself a glass of milk."

"I'm about to drop off the car. I'll see you in five."

When she joined Jack in the surveillance van, Heather once again reclined on her couch watching the news. Chase settled back for another night of non-productive waiting, but almost immediately, Heather's phone rang.

She and Jack leaned forward at the same time, both staring at the monitor. Because the call came on Heather's cell and not her landline, they could hear only her side of the conversation.

"I'm here, Margaret," Heather said after checking the caller ID. She listened for a few seconds. "That's…flattering, I guess. But I don't think I can do four nights a week. Did he say why the sudden increase? Dario's never wanted me more than once or twice at most."

Another silence as she listened.

"Just talking?" Heather looked confused. "Did he say what he wanted to talk about?" More listening. Then, "I guess I can't argue with that. It *is* a lot of money. Okay, I'm in. When's the first appointment?" She listened some more and frowned. "All right. I'll be there." She got up off the couch and went to get a pen and notepad from her desk. "Read me off the full schedule, will you?"

As they watched, Heather jotted down several things on the notepad, but the camera was too far and at the wrong angle for them to see what she was writing.

"Got it. Thanks, Margaret." After Heather disconnected, she stuck the notepad in a desk drawer.

"We need to get her out of the house," Jack said.

"I know," Chase replied.

"Well, what are you waiting for? You have her number."

"I am aware of that," Chase replied. If she asked Heather out, Jack would be free to get Heather's schedule for Dario. They'd been on the case for days and this was their first break. They needed to get a look at this guy and approach him one way or another.

But Chase didn't know how comfortable she felt about seeing Heather again. Not because of what she did, but because Heather made her uneasy and she couldn't understand why. Chase had been with plenty of call girls, and being around one should be second nature by now, but Heather made her feel exposed. Something in her eyes, something Chase couldn't put her finger on, made her look too untainted and untouched.

Heather was exactly the kind of woman Chase had avoided for years. The last time she'd allowed herself to become involved with one, it had cost the woman her life.

Chase had been working deep cover at the time, within an Italian mob family led by Dom Marco Stellari. Stellari himself was not her target; she was after an elusive Russian arms dealer Stellari did business with. Interpol had been unable to locate the man and had asked the EOO to find him and make him disappear.

Even with Chase's considerable skills, it took seven months to earn Stellari's trust, but once she did, she was accepted as part of the family. She practically lived at the dom's New York penthouse, waiting for her opportunity as more months passed. But the Russian arms dealer kept to the shadows, using emissaries in most of his business dealings, so nailing down his location was difficult.

What she hadn't counted on was Regina, the dom's daughter. She was seven years younger than Chase and notoriously straight, but so sweet and bewitchingly beautiful Chase had trouble keeping her mind on her mission. As they spent more and more time around each other, the chemistry between them built, until Regina confessed she wanted them to live out the fantasies she'd been having about her.

Chase did her best to stay away, virtually ignoring the girl for weeks. But Regina persisted, and eventually she succumbed to her flirtatious advances and they wound up in bed. Though she'd dated boys, Regina was still a virgin and, like many virgins, fell for the first person she had sex with.

Chase fought her feelings even after they slept together but eventually got too tired of fighting. She allowed herself to feel, and fall, and soon they were secretly inseparable. Their romance consisted of surreptitious rendezvous and stolen moments, until one day, Regina had told her she wanted them to run away together. "Just leave and live."

She was torn in the beginning, but as more weeks passed and her feelings grew, Chase began to tell herself that maybe it was possible. She could take Regina away from all the corruption and danger surrounding her father and give her the life she deserved. After long thought, she told Regina that after she completed an important job for the dom, they'd disappear together.

Not long afterward, the Russian arms dealer finally agreed to a face-to-face sit-down with the dom. Chase, as his right hand, would also be there. She contacted Montgomery Pierce to inform him the meeting was imminent and that she'd call back when she knew the time and location. Other EOO ops would move in to take care of the arms dealer so the Italian mob would never know she was involved.

On paper, their plan was a good one. But no one anticipated the lengths the Russian would take to protect himself. He gave them only ninety minutes' advance notice of the time and meeting place, and the abandoned warehouse was in Brooklyn, which gave them little time before they had to leave. Chase had no opportunity to pass the info on to the EOO.

Still, she was optimistic it was the break they'd been waiting for. Maybe she'd be able to put a tracker on the arms dealer. The guy was so elusive, getting to see his face at all was an achievement.

The Russian, a shrimp of a man, was already at the warehouse when they arrived. He had two men with him and five other associates positioned strategically throughout the warehouse, which was filled with rusted machinery and steel drums. The dom had brought an equal number. The sit-down started out fine, with the Russian and Italian mob boss facing each other across a cheap wooden table. Then all hell broke loose when federal agents burst in with guns blazing.

The Russians and Italians scattered, firing back and taking cover. As Chase dove behind a piece of heavy machinery, she glimpsed a familiar figure among the feds. The last person she expected or wanted to see. Regina.

Regina saw her, too. Though one of the feds tried to stop her, she ran straight for Chase and managed to join her without getting hit by the crossfire. Bullets whizzed around them in a deafening noise. The Italians were shooting, the feds were shooting, and the Russians evidently thought the mob had set them up, because they were firing at both the feds and Stellari's people.

Chase had few options. She couldn't shoot at the Italians because she'd blow her cover and they'd kill her, and she couldn't shoot back at the feds because that would be unethical. Her priority at the moment was to get Regina out of there. She tried to cover her with her own body, looking for an opportunity.

She spotted a door at the side of the building and decided to make a run for it. Chase grabbed Regina's hand and told her to stay low. They were almost there when shots started coming from behind the huge barrels. Chase couldn't see who was firing, but she was sure it was the Russians who'd taken cover.

She started to shoot back, covering them both as Regina ran ahead, but a bullet hit Regina before she made it to the exit. She lay on the cement floor, a dark circle of red blossoming on the center of her pale-yellow blouse, as more bullets zinged by Chase's head. More Russians were hidden behind the machinery surrounding them, so Chase fired back with her Colt 1911 as she dragged Regina behind a stack of metal drums. In no time, her gun was empty.

Chase put Regina's head in her lap and caressed her dark hair away from her forehead. Regina kept whispering she was sorry, she only wanted to help. She said the feds had threatened to arrest her father and his associates—Chase included—unless she told them where the meeting with the arms dealer was going to be. If she cooperated, they promised to arrest only the Russian and his men. They'd leave the rest alone.

God, she was so innocent. As she lay dying in a puddle of her own blood, Regina was only concerned that Chase forgive her and that they be together. "Promise me you'll take me away," she'd kept saying. Chase held her close and cried out of love and fury. Cried until she heard a familiar voice, from very close.

She peered through a crack between the barrels where the shots had been coming from and stared straight into the face of a stranger who sounded exactly like Jack. *No. This can't be.* But the voice was unmistakable.

She studied the woman closer. Her facial features were different, but even in the dimly lit warehouse, Chase recognized too many other commonalities for it to be mere coincidence. Height and weight. Build. Mannerisms. The shape of her face. The color of her hair. Even her trademark black clothes and weapon of choice: a Glock 34. It had to be Jack. As Chase watched, she crouched behind another stack of barrels, her focus on the shootout.

Chase hadn't seen her earlier. She didn't know what shocked her more, the fact that Jack was alive or that she evidently worked for the Russian arms dealer. None of this surreal mess made sense. Jack was standing here before her, and Regina lay dead in her arms. Jack had killed this sweet, wonderful girl. Chase looked at the useless gun in her hand. She wanted to scream out her fury and attack Jack, but Jack would shoot without hesitation. Not because Jack wouldn't recognize her, but because the look in her eyes was that of a cold killer. The Jack she knew was gone.

"Get down. I have him," Jack said to someone Chase couldn't see, before she took down one of the feds and, a moment later, one of the Italians.

Chase remained hidden and didn't make a sound.

After another minute, the arms dealer himself crawled out from behind some cover and joined Jack. "Kill Stellari," he told her.

"That's what you paid me for, that's what I'll do."

"When did you get here?" the Russian asked, wiping the sweat from his face.

"I was here before you," Jack said.

"That's why they call you Silent Death."

"Yeah," Jack replied, and fired. The dom crumpled to the floor. The feds kept shooting in all directions except theirs.

"I pay you anything you want if you get me out of here," the arms dealer said.

"What's it worth to you? My fee was for Stellari, not for saving your ass."

"Double."

"Follow me," Jack replied. She led him safely away, through the door Chase had been headed toward with Regina.

To this day, Chase still couldn't answer why she hadn't told the EOO about Jack.

The experience had changed her. Since then, Chase had avoided any kind of intimacy, especially with women who mattered. Losing Regina had cost her too much, and as long as she lived a life of such uncertainty it was painful and pointless to drag anyone else into it. Just like Landor, she'd stick to easy and uncomplicated if she couldn't have the one she wanted. Only in this case, the woman she wanted was dead.

"You still in there?" Jack's voice startled her out of her reverie.

Chase fought an overwhelming urge to say something cruel. She wanted to confront Jack with who she was and what she knew, but that would make an already unpleasant working situation impossible. Maybe she'd let it all out once this job was done. Maybe she'd finally let Jack have what was coming to her. Maybe. "I heard you the first time," she finally replied.

"Time's wasting. Christ, what's wrong with you? Remember Cass?"

"I'm calling already," Chase said. "Just shut up."

"About damn time."

Chase reluctantly pushed Dial on her phone. She watched Heather on the monitor as she reached for her cell.

"Hello?"

"Hi, Heather. This is Brett, from the Cave."

Heather smiled. "Of course. I remember who you are."

"Are you busy? Is this a bad time?"

"No, not at all."

"Excellent. I was wondering if you had time to meet with me tonight?"

"For a signed copy?" Heather asked.

"Right. I was in Manhattan anyway, so—"

"I'd love…I mean, sure. My brother hasn't stopped talking about you ever since I told him."

"I'm flattered. So when is convenient for you?"

"Can you give me an hour? How about you pick me up?" Heather asked.

Chase checked her watch. "Of course. Just tell me where."

Heather gave Chase the address they were sitting in front of.

"I'll be there at seven," Chase said.

"Great. See you in a little."

"I look forward to it." As Chase hung up, she watched Heather head into her bedroom. She pulled several ensembles from the closet, a mix of casual and dressy, and laid them on the bed, pursing her lips while she considered which to wear.

"Now, was that so hard?" Jack asked.

Chase turned to face her as the urge to physically hurt Jack returned. "Don't push it, Harding."

They were interrupted by Heather's voice on the audio feed from her landline. She'd picked up the phone beside the bed. "Hey, it's me. Guess who called?"

"Landor?"

"Brett, you idiot." Heather laughed.

"Do you have a date?"

"We're getting together for the signed copy."

"Yes!" Adam shouted through the phone.

"Okay, gotta run. Need to get dressed."

"Wear something nice," he said.

"Don't I always?"

"I guess, but if you really impress her, maybe she'll stick around long enough for you to introduce us."

"I can't promise," Heather said.

"Which part? That you'll impress her, that she'll stick around, or that you'll introduce us?"

"All of the above. Hanging up now."

"Later."

Heather plucked an ensemble from the bed and hurried toward the bathroom.

"Call me crazy, but she's actually looking forward to your… date." Jack laughed.

"Why is that so funny?"

"Who knew she'd want to give you a freebie?"

"And that has you giggling like a schoolgirl?"

Jack nodded. “I think it’s hysterical. Can you handle it, not having to pay?”

“How can you be bright enough to keep a job and still find something that stupid, funny?”

“I’m complicated.”

“I don’t intend to sleep with her,” Chase said.

“Maybe she has other plans.”

“She doesn’t.”

“Either way,” Jack said, “do whatever it takes to keep her away from the house.”

CHAPTER FOURTEEN

Heather paced from the living room into the bedroom, pausing to check herself in the dresser mirror for the tenth time. Her hair was perfect, her makeup flawless, and the ensemble she'd selected would be appropriate attire no matter where they might end up. Black dress trousers, a bronze Neiman Marcus cardigan-shell set, and black two-inch heels, which would bring her up to Brett's height. "Get a grip," she said to her image. *It's only for a drink, and you're never going to see her again.*

When her bell rang, she jumped. Why was she so nervous? She buzzed Brett into the building and took deep breaths to calm her rapid heartbeat as she waited for her to come upstairs. But her hands still shook as she reached for the door to answer the knock. "Hi, there, come on in."

Brett Coltrane looked even better than she remembered from the dark club. Dressed in jeans, a black turtleneck and leather jacket, she exuded an almost overwhelming strength. She smiled. "Good to see you again."

"Can I get you something to drink, or…?" Heather asked.

"I didn't make any plans, but I thought you might like to go out for dinner or something."

"Oh." Heather hadn't counted on a prolonged evening with Brett. She was actually hoping to make it fast and simple. As much as she was looking forward to seeing her, she didn't need any complications in her life and wanted to avoid a situation that might invite too many personal questions.

"I'm sorry if I was being presumptuous. We don't have to, if you'd rather not." Even the way Brett talked exuded charm.

"No, please. I just didn't—" She couldn't be rude. "I'd like that," Heather finally said.

"Great. I'm ready when you are." Brett handed her a small paper bag. "This is for your brother."

Heather took out the graphic novel, wrapped in a protective plastic sleeve. She didn't read them herself, but she'd bought enough for her brother to know this looked…different, somehow. The binding. She turned it over to look at the cover. It had next month's date on it and the words ARTIST'S PROOF written in small letters on the bottom right corner.

"I had the publisher print an extra proof," Brett said. "The issue doesn't come out for another couple of weeks."

Heather's brother would be beyond thrilled. She looked up at Brett. "Thank you so much. He's going to scream when he sees it."

Brett laughed, her low tone sexy. Heather had to look away for a second to make her brain work again. If she continued to stare into those amazing blue eyes they'd spend the evening in front of her door. She left the paper bag on the table and grabbed her coat.

"Here, let me." Brett motioned for the garment.

Heather let her take it and turned her back. She could have sworn getting her coat on lasted for an hour. Like time stopped, and all she could feel were Brett's slow, deliberate movements. Brett stood right behind her, and she felt the overwhelming need to back up until their bodies touched. She didn't move until Brett put her hands on her shoulders.

"Ready?" Brett whispered into her ear.

Heather shivered. God, it had been too long since she'd felt anything but dread at someone's touch. "Yes."

When Heather trembled beneath her hands, Chase woke from the near trance she'd fallen in because of their proximity. Heather looked stunning tonight, and her perfume, an earthy-spicy blend, was intoxicating. "The cab is waiting," she said abruptly, and headed out the door, suddenly desperate for fresh air.

She held the cab door for Heather and slid in beside her.

As they pulled away from the curb, Heather turned to her. "I never asked, are you from New York?"

"Boston. But I spend a lot of time in the Apple."

"Business?"

"Mostly, but the occasional pleasure pops up." Why had she said that? Chase rarely came to New York unless completely necessary. She must, for some subliminal reason, not want Heather to think she was in any way special.

"I'm glad you could drop by." Heather smiled.

"I always keep my promises."

"But you could have mailed it."

"Yes…I could have, but I didn't."

"So is this one of those occasions where you choose to combine work with pleasure?"

Chase grinned. "That's yet to be determined. So far, so good. Of course you could turn out to be a homicidal maniac."

Heather laughed. "Something tells me you wouldn't be too intimidated if I were."

"You're right. I'm not easily overwhelmed." Chase suddenly realized she'd been toying with her jacket zipper and immediately stopped. She couldn't remember the last time she'd fidgeted with anything. She tried to force herself to relax and smile. "And I can run pretty fast if I have to."

Heather glanced down at her feet. "Don't let the heels fool you. You'd be surprised at what I'm capable of in these."

"Impress me," Chase replied, almost too seriously, before she could stop herself.

The cab pulled over and stopped and Chase handed the driver folded bills. A colorful array of shops and kiosks, lined up beneath long banners and signs painted with Asian script, cluttered the street ahead of them. Pedestrians crowded both sidewalks.

"Chinatown," Heather said.

Chase slipped from the cab and offered a hand to help Heather out. "I've always rather enjoyed it. Is it all right?"

"I love coming here." Heather smiled. "The chaos, smells, and near-panic on the streets make me feel like I'm in another country."

"I thought we'd grab a bite here and walk around."

"Sounds great."

Chase realized before they'd gone fifty feet that walking with Heather was like walking with a parrot on her shoulder. Everyone stared. Men. Women. Children. Even the street vendors paused in their efforts to push souvenir fans and other knickknacks to the camera-wearing tourists.

Heather seemed oblivious to all the attention. She focused on the scenery and on reading menus posted outside the restaurants they passed.

Fragrant enticements wafted through the street—ginger and garlic, star anise and clove. Chase's stomach growled. When Heather paused at another menu, she asked, "See anything you like?"

"I don't mean to sound picky, but I'm a vegetarian." Heather sounded embarrassed.

She almost stumbled. *Well, that's just brilliant. She doesn't drink, she owns the Holy Grail of PEZ, and she's a vegetarian. What next?* "It would appear we have that in common," Chase admitted reluctantly.

"And you don't drink, either."

"Correct."

"That's almost spooky. I know so many people and none are teetotaling vegetarians."

"I know plenty," Chase lied.

"Huh." Heather looked at her skeptically.

They continued walking, neither speaking for a while. They were in the heart of Chinatown with its enormous sensory overload: the aroma of food, the vibrant colors, the crush of people, the confusing myriad of languages spoken and shouted all around them.

"Are you married? Divorced? Children?" Chase asked when Heather paused at another menu.

"None of the above. And you?"

"Serial polygamist." There. She did it again. Said the first thing that popped into her head. *Why was she trying so hard to turn Heather off?*

Heather looked at her, her expression unreadable. "I see."

"You sound disappointed."

"Not at all. How someone chooses to live their life is up to them. We all have our reasons."

"I don't need any reasons. I simply enjoy variety."

Heather started purposefully down the street again. "Like I said, to each her own." She sounded disappointed.

Chase double-stepped to catch up. "Is something wrong?"

"Of course not. I'm just different. I like to believe in true romance and happy endings."

"That's very quixotic."

"I guess," Heather said, frowning.

"What do you do besides work to pursue that happy-ever-after?"

"Not much, I'm afraid. I meant what I said at the Cave. Between caring for my brother and trying to make it in the fashion industry, my schedule is pretty full and…dull."

"No dates?"

"Not in a long time," Heather said. "More than two years, to be exact."

Chase didn't doubt Heather's romantic drought had to do with obligations and disapproving lovers, but she knew there was more. Heather was terrified of anyone finding out about her other life as Amber. Yet another thing she and Heather had in common. Both were unable to commit due to their secret lives.

Chase's stomach rumbled again. "There's a noodle place over there." She motioned with her head. "How about it?"

"Sure." Heather replied without enthusiasm.

"We can keep walking if you—"

"No, it sounds good."

They walked to the small shop and Chase perused the posted menu. She thought Heather was doing the same, but when she turned she found Heather staring off toward the street with a faraway look. "Do veggie noodles with ginger and peanuts sound okay?"

"Yes," Heather said, still distracted. "Thank you."

"Would you like to sit here or walk?"

"Walk." Heather's mood seemed to have deteriorated and Chase couldn't risk her saying she wanted to go back home. And, if she was honest with herself, she didn't like seeing Heather upset.

The place was busy, but their take-out order was ready in a few minutes. Heather sat in a chair by the door looking out at passersby as Chase waited and paid for their food. She handed Heather her carton and chopsticks and opened the door to let her out, and they ate as they continued slowly down the street, still not speaking.

Chase started to feel awkward with the silence. Normally she didn't care about anyone else enough to be uncomfortable. She actually kind of enjoyed their discomfort oftentimes, because then she could ask them to leave. But right now, someone had turned the tables and she wasn't at all happy with the development. Why was Jack taking so long? "Did I say something to upset you?"

"Not at all," Heather said. "It's just that…" She paused to take a bite of vegetables. "I don't know, I thought we'd have more in common than our eating habits."

"Like what?"

Heather shrugged. "Although I appreciate your candor regarding your private life, I'm not sure what to think about it."

"I thought you said to each her own."

"I did. And trust me, I'm in no position to judge, but…" She sighed.

"But?"

Heather stopped at a relatively quiet spot in front of a closed storefront. "Nothing. I don't know where I'm going with this. I think I've been listening to my brother more than I should."

"Adam."

"Yes. He keeps telling me I should date. Get a life, give someone a chance, and so on."

"I see. So you thought this was a date."

"What? No. I just thought…" Heather looked down at her feet. "I don't know what I thought. Please forget I said anything because I feel really ridiculous right now."

"No need for that. I may have given the wrong impression. I like you, Heather. You're a smart, beautiful woman. But I'm not interested in anything other than—"

"Sex?" Heather sounded agitated.

Where did that come from? Chase had been careful not to display any kind of attraction or insinuate anything of the sort. On the contrary, she'd been friendly and even distant. "No, not sex," she replied calmly, though just hearing that word coming out of Heather's mouth made it unbelievably erotic. "Heather, I think you're nice, and I thought we could enjoy each other's company while I'm in town, but that's it." Did she really call Heather nice? Nice? Chase couldn't even remember a time she'd used that word to describe anything other than the weather.

"Nice," Heather repeated, between bites of her noodles.

"I can't believe I said that, either. What I mean is, I don't want anything from you."

"Well, that's good…I suppose."

"Can I get you something to drink?" Chase asked.

"I'd like that," Heather replied, seeming distracted.

"Is Diet Coke okay?"

"Yes."

"I'll be right back." Chase crossed the street to a Chinese grocery. As she waited behind a couple of other customers to pay, she sorted out the confusing twists of their conversation. Heather not only thought Chase had asked her out on a date, but was even upset to learn it wasn't the case. Heather was definitely her type in every way, but aside from the fact that Chase was sincerely not interested in dating, she would never ever even consider dating a call girl. Women like that were for disposable, replaceable entertainment, period. She didn't view their bodies as damaged, but rather their minds.

Although Heather seemed to possess certain virtues, Chase knew better than anyone how appearances could deceive, how sometimes we see things in others simply because we want to. But why did she want to see this innocence in Heather? Chase glanced out the window. Heather waited patiently, glancing about, still seemingly oblivious to the fact that every man or woman on the street looked her way.

Finally it was her turn at the cash register. She set the Cokes down and reached for her wallet.

"Anything else?" the proprietor asked.

"No, that's…" She glanced outside again. "What the hell?"

Two men had cornered Heather and she was trying to get around them and across the street to the store. One tried to block her way while the other moved behind her. Heather, clearly uncomfortable, tried to push the one in front of her away. He pushed her back, and she fell into the arms of the other. Passersby were clearly too indifferent or afraid to get involved.

Chase ran out of the shop and grabbed the one in front of Heather from behind by his hair. She pulled his head back and placed her forearm around his neck in a choke hold.

He brought his hands up and tried to pry her off, but she held fast. "Hey, relax, man," he wheezed. "We were just playin' is all."

"Remove your hands from her," Chase told the other guy, incensed by the way he had his arm possessively around Heather's waist. When he didn't instantly budge, she added, "Now," from between gritted teeth.

The man released Heather and pushed her to the side, then took a step forward to stand facing his choking friend. "What's it to you, bitch?"

Chase removed her arm from around the man's throat and simultaneously used her other hand to shove the guy's face forcefully into his friend's.

Heather got behind Chase and grabbed her arm. "Come on, let's go. They're not worth it."

The two men turned to her again, still recovering from the head butt. The one she'd had in a headlock had a bloody nose. "You're going to pay for that, bitch."

Chase pulled her jacket to the side to expose her Glock. Heather couldn't see it, but both men took notice. "Am I?" she asked.

"Hey, we don't want no problems," bloody nose said, as he and his buddy backed up a step.

"Offer your apologies to the lady." Chase reached for the Glock. Ordinarily, she would have never exposed it, but she intended to make sure they apologized.

Both men nodded. "Sorry, miss," one said.

"Sorry. We were just playin'," offered the other.

"Fine. Just go," Heather replied, her voice near panic.

Both men ran off and Chase turned to Heather.

"What just happened?" Heather asked.

"I don't know, you tell me. I was getting us some Cokes."

"I mean, what you just did. The way you hit them and scared them off."

Chase shrugged. "I don't respect that kind of attitude."

"But…what did…" Heather looked toward where the men had disappeared into the crowd, her brow furrowed in confusion.

"Do you still want that Coke?" Chase asked, to change the subject.

"I, uh…sure."

Chase smiled. "You're coming with me this time. I just can't leave you anywhere."

"It's the second time you've rescued me," Heather said after they'd gotten their drinks and resumed their walk.

"It would appear so."

"I don't normally get into these situations, you know."

"You didn't get yourself into anything. They're just idiots."

"I mean, it looks worse than it is."

"I find that hard to believe."

"Well, it's true."

"Heather, you're a very attractive woman." Chase immediately regretted the admission and scrambled to do damage control. "Most attractive woman get into trouble occasionally and you're no exception." Her phone vibrated in her pocket and she almost sighed with relief. *Please let it be Jack.* The message read, **How's your date going? I'm done.** "Jerk," she muttered, loud enough for Heather to hear.

"Everything okay?"

"Yes and no. I have to head back to my hotel soon. My agent decided on an impromptu meeting."

Heather looked at her suspiciously. "I understand."

They drank their Cokes in silence until they reached the subway entrance.

Heather turned to her. "Well, thank you for the novel and the walk."

"I'm seeing you home."

"You really don't have to. I do this every day."

"I'm sure, but I'd feel better if I did."

"I'll be fine, Brett."

"I'm seeing you home," she repeated, more forcefully. Chase could have, and *should* have, let her go. She never intended to escort her back to her apartment, but she couldn't stop herself. For some reason, she needed to know Heather got back safely. She hadn't seen a woman home in too many years to remember. She never had to; they came to her for a few hours and left alone and that suited her fine.

When they started down the stairs to the trains, Chase noticed Heather proceeding unusually slowly, favoring one foot. "Why are you limping?"

"My ankle. I misstepped on the heels when the jerk pushed me."

Chase put her arm around Heather's waist to help take the pressure off. "Is this better?"

Heather put her arm around Chase's waist as well. "Yes, much better. Thank you."

As they stood waiting for the subway, Chase was hypersensitive to the sensation of Heather's body pressed against her own. Being this close to another woman was certainly not an unusual occurrence in her life, but with Heather it felt more foreign than familiar, infused with an uncommon sweetness. She had never walked or stood in anyone's embrace.

Heather moved her hand lower on Chase's waist and Chase shivered. She pulled Heather closer, and Heather rested her cheek against her shoulder. Neither said anything while they waited or during the short ride to the Village. But Heather kept close even on the train, and as soon as they got to their stop, they resumed their supportive embrace, walking slowly.

Chase allowed herself to relish the uncommon joy infusing her. The seductive scent of Heather's perfume, her soft, flawless skin, and the vulnerability in her eyes were a potent combination. She wanted to keep holding and protecting Heather, and right now she didn't want to even try to understand why. Her heart was beating so fast she was afraid Heather could feel it. Only when they arrived at the door to Heather's building did Chase finally release her.

"I had a…*nice* time." Heather grinned.

"I'm sorry about that. It really was an unsuitable adjective."

Heather didn't move, and neither did she, as though both were equally reluctant to part. After a few seconds of awkward silence, Heather said, "I…thank you for delivering in person."

"The pleasure was all mine. Maybe next time I'm in town I can visit your brother." What in the hell possessed her to say that?

Heather brightened. "You'd really do that?"

"If he wants to."

Heather smiled. "Are you kidding? I'm not even going to tell him you said that because he'll drive me crazy."

Chase, completely rapt by her smile, had to force herself to end their evening. "I'd better get going."

Heather unlocked the door and turned to her. "Good night, then." She lingered there, looking intently into Chase's eyes.

Chase hesitated, fighting the temptation to take that one step forward and close the distance between them. Instead, she backed away. "Good night, Heather," she said before turning to go. She didn't look back until she heard the click of the door closing—and only then to make sure Heather was safely inside.

Chase headed to the van and knocked twice, her mind busily replaying the evening and her body protesting the loss of Heather's embrace.

Jack unlocked the panel door and slid it open. "You looked so…perfect, walking arm in arm."

"Shut up."

"Frustrated much?"

"No."

"Then why do you look like you just lost your best friend?"

"You weren't around ten years ago to see what that looks like." Chase pushed Jack out of the way to get in the van.

"Relax, already. I just meant you look upset."

"I'm not."

"Landis, I don't know why you're so uptight about this woman, but either pay someone to get laid, and I mean soon, or see her for who she really is."

"You don't have to keep reminding me she gets paid. I'm aware."

But Jack wasn't quite done with the topic, and all trace of flippancy was gone in her parting caution. "She protects and gets paid to screw the likes of Rózsa."

CHAPTER FIFTEEN

Vatican City

In anticipation of his most important appointment of the day, perhaps the year, Emmanuel Canali, Dean of the College of Cardinals, changed from his usual black simar to his scarlet cassock and matching silk biretta. The ornate garments, usually reserved for masses and other official functions, would add weight to his authority and perhaps smooth the way for a quick resolution of his urgent mission.

Normally, he met with outsiders in one of the many public rooms reserved for that purpose, but the need for secrecy necessitated that his most trusted attendant priest escort his visitor directly into the inner sanctum of the Vatican, to a suite off his opulent apartment. It was a rare honor, but he doubted his visitor would suitably appreciate it.

"We thank you for making the long trip," Cardinal Canali told his guest, as he extended his hand for the customary kissing of his gold ring.

"Of course," the Broker said. "But you can put the ring away. Rituals as such are best reserved for the God-fearing, and I haven't any religiously related phobias."

"Of course. It was not my intention to offend you."

"It's quite beautiful here."

"Indeed, the Holy See is humbling, is it not?"

"A sentiment for believers. I personally refrain from frivolous if not futile sentiments."

"Ah, we have an atheist amongst us," the cardinal said.

"Hardly," the Broker replied. "As a matter of fact, I'm quite positive we worship the same power."

"And what power might that be?"

"The one that requires you to build fortresses such as this in order to protect it. Money."

The cardinal caressed the ornate pectoral cross that hung from a silk cord around his neck. To endure such a rare and scathing insult, both to his person and his church, required every bit of his considerable patience. "That is blasphemy."

"Is it, your…Eminence? In my opinion, the only blasphemy is the airbrushed truth you try to convey."

"His truth is the only truth."

"I'm sure that statement is meant to sound pertinent, but you understand how hollow it is when we both know it's not He or prayer that saves lives or keeps the peace."

"You don't know what you're saying," the cardinal said.

"Perhaps you need to pay better attention to that best-selling fairy tale. Even that carpenter you commemorate was bought and sold for a bag of silver."

Appalled by the Broker's flippancy toward the Holy Book and Savior, the cardinal rose and began pacing. "How dare you," he muttered, as he sought valiantly to curb his rising temper. He couldn't risk alienating this loathsome individual, no matter what insults he was called upon to suffer.

"Don't look at it as a personal failure. It's merely a business crash due to history's cyclical nature. Interests form religion, and, like the ancient Greeks, people once again need their gods to be human."

The cardinal chose his words carefully in formulating a response. He met the Broker's eyes. "I do not agree with your—"

"Of course you don't. Nevertheless, my presence here begs to differ, don't you think?" When he didn't reply, the Broker said, "Now, let's get down to business. I didn't come all this way to argue politics. I'm sure you have something a lot less boring and a lot more important to discuss."

The cardinal sat back down but didn't look forward to having to confront those cold, lifeless eyes again. If he had ever doubted the presence of evil, he was now sure of its existence, for before him sat the devil himself. Uneasy, he clasped his hands and willed himself to look back into those eyes. "It is a very private matter, and we will need your absolute discretion."

"Indubitably." The Broker smiled and looked very satisfied having made a point.

"We need a heart transplant to take place within the Vatican," Cardinal Canali said.

"Your pleas to God haven't worked, I take it."

The cardinal thought the question rhetorical, but when his visitor didn't continue, it was clear he was expected to answer. "No. I'm afraid they haven't."

"Then perhaps it is God's will that his devoted follower… expire," the Broker suggested.

"Perhaps. But his work is not done. The world has much to benefit by his presence. God would want him to continue his work."

"Then why hasn't God listened to his prayers?"

"The Lord works in mysterious ways."

"Vague statements make bad business deals. Could it be because he hasn't made the appropriate offerings to the right power?"

"Will you help us or not?" the cardinal asked, his self-control ready to snap.

The Broker smiled. "He will receive a heart. But only because you asked the right God and…all *I* require is cash."

❖

New York
Next day, November 21

The schedule that Jack retrieved from Heather's laptop indicated she would be meeting with Dario that night, so Chase and

Jack were up early to make sure their surveillance went as smoothly as possible. To ensure the van was well positioned outside the brownstone, they were outside Heather's building before most of New York was awake.

They put the rental car in front of Heather's apartment to keep the spot they'd freed up there, and Chase headed over to the brownstone in the van to try to nab a prime location as nearby residents got up and headed to work. Jack stayed behind to tail Heather. Though they expected her to go to work as usual and return home to change, they didn't know her call-girl routine and didn't want any surprises.

Chase spent more than two hours circling the block before a spot opened up close enough for their surveillance equipment to reach. She had to cut off another car to get to it, but given the mood she was in she almost wouldn't have minded if the other driver had been confrontational.

Sleep had been elusive when she returned to the hotel last night. She didn't want to believe Heather was involved with Rózsa; it was bad enough to imagine her seeing clients to earn the money to pay her brother's bills. Chase worried she was losing her ever-reliable objectivity about her mission and becoming too personally involved, as she had with the Stellari case.

With hours to kill until Heather arrived at the brownstone, Chase took a long walk to clear her head and dispel some of her restlessness. After a bite to eat, she worked some on her novel, marveling once again at Heather's resemblance to her Emily. Jack kept her apprised of Heather's status in a series of text messages beginning shortly after five p.m.: **She's headed home. Changed clothes and caught a cab. Following her into a bar not far from you.**

Jack called Landis as she claimed a table in the corner of the bar, so she could keep her discreetly updated on developments via her Bluetooth earpiece. Her position allowed a good vantage point to watch Heather—who was perched on a stool at the bar—but was remote enough that Heather wouldn't notice her. She ordered a Scotch and sipped it slowly as she surveyed the room. The upscale watering hole catered to affluent locals and to tourists and businessmen staying at the five-star hotel next door, so she felt a little conspicuous in her jeans, black T-shirt, and bomber jacket. But on the plus side, since she was the only female in sight not dressed to the nines, no one should bother her. Or so she thought.

"Are you here alone or are you waiting for someone?" a man in his late thirties asked.

"Say what?"

"I'd like to buy you a drink."

Jack glared at him. "And I'd like to put a bullet in the guy who took my girl. What's your point?"

"I'm sorry, what?"

"Wrong tree, Romeo. Not interested."

The man walked away with a puzzled expression. Landis laughed on the other end. "Smooth, Harding."

"I thought so, too," Jack replied, as she resumed her focus on Heather.

The call girl was having no trouble attracting the attention of several of the men in the bar. Within the first ten minutes, three guys approached her in an effort to strike up a conversation or buy her a drink, but she politely sent them on their way. They were all well dressed and seemingly affluent, but two of them were over fifty, and the third had gotten a rotten deal in the looks department. Several other men who seemed more likely prospects hovered nearby, apparently working up their nerve.

"Looks like she's here to pick up a john," she told Landis. "You positioned?"

"I'm in the van," Landis replied. "Her mystery lover hasn't shown yet."

"Shouldn't be long. Dario's appointment is in thirty minutes."

"Is she still alone?"

"Yup. At the bar, and she has everyone's undivided attention. If you thought she looked good last night, wait till you see her now. I think every guy in the place has a boner."

"Thanks for the colorful visual. Just stick to what's relevant."

Jack watched as Heather lifted her glass to thank a guy across the bar for her drink. "Ironic how beauty is often a wolf in sheep's clothing."

"I needed a platitude to ground me. I told you, I'm not interested," Landis said. "Black sedan just drove into the private parking area at the back. I'll send Reno the license-plate number."

The guy who'd bought Heather a drink, a balding nerd in an ill-fitting suit, tried to parlay his gesture into something more, but he, too, was rejected. Then a new contender appeared, who seemed a more likely prospect. As soon as the guy—a thirtyish stud with a movie-star smile—claimed a seat a couple of stools away from Heather, she swiveled in his direction so he could get a good look at her.

"I think she's chosen her prey," Jack told Landis. "Let's see, he's looking at her, all anticipation. He just turned to the barman and did a whatever-the-lady-is-having. Eye contact has been made."

"What *is* she having?" Landis asked.

"White wine. And how is that relevant?"

"She doesn't drink." Landis sounded disappointed.

"Would explain why her glass is planted there like decoration."

"Good."

"Wait. She lifted her wine, smiled, and the guy's mouth dropped. He got up and he's smiling as he approaches her. She ever so slowly does the hair wave. He has the smile of someone who's just won a million orgasms, and she has the look of a woman who can make that happen in an hour. You'd never believe this is the same woman you were with last night."

"Yes, I would," Landis said sharply. "I've been with plenty of Ambers. I know the routine quite well."

"He just whispered something in her ear."

"And she grabbed his shoulder, threw her head back, and laughed seductively."

Jack laughed. "Scary. Okay, what color am I thinking of right now?"

"Sadly, he thinks he's actually funny. He knows he's paying, but somewhere in his deluded mind he's hoping he'll be the best she's ever had."

"Is that what you're hoping when you go with these women?"

Landis didn't reply for several seconds. "I'm not concerned with what pleases them," she finally said.

"You know, for someone who takes so much pleasure in judging my choices, you really should take a damn good look at yourself. What happened to you? I remember you pounding me for making fun of you for being a pathetic romantic, with all your drawings and stories of damsels in distress. Now it's like your only passion is yourself."

"Dreams are the first casualty of adulthood."

"I know what you mean. I've put in plenty of selfish years myself, but it didn't get me anywhere."

"I wouldn't say that. You earned yourself quite a reputation."

Jack stiffened. She was getting fed up with these mind games. Landis clearly knew something about her past—which was bad enough—but why did she have to be so mysterious about it? "Are you going to tell me what you know?"

"Again, not the right question. But suffice it to say, had it not been you, I would have killed you."

The last thing Jack needed right now was yet another cryptic clue she couldn't decipher. "Will you just tell me what the fuck you're talking about?" she asked, and took another sip of whisky.

"I'm not in a hurry."

Jack threw a couple of bills on the table when she saw Heather reach for her coat. "Her customer just paid the bill. Fire up the cams. They're about to come your way. I'll be there in ten."

"I can't wait."

Jack wasn't sure if the sarcasm was meant for her or because of what Landis was about to see.

CHAPTER SIXTEEN

Heather would be there soon. Chase had to quickly figure out what the problem was with the camera she'd placed where Dario was about to plant his ass. "Why is the damn picture so dark?" she complained aloud. The four-way split screen showed the two entrance camera views clearly, as well as the bedroom, but the adjoining watcher's room was black. She adjusted the brightness settings on the monitor, but that didn't help, so she slapped it on the side. "What is wrong with this piece of—" As she reached behind the monitor to check the connections, she knocked over her coffee, then jumped as the scalding liquid landed in her lap.

"Goddamn it," she said between gritted teeth as she dabbed at the wet spot with napkins left from lunch. The effort did nothing to stop the pain or reduce the now-impressive wet spot highlighting her groin. "Screw it." She flung the napkins across the van and turned back to the monitor as a cab pulled into the brownstone's driveway.

The taxi was the fourth vehicle to park in the private lot at the back within the last half hour. She'd given all the previous license plate numbers to Reno, along with pics of the guys she'd captured on the rear-entrance camera. Any of them could be their man. Tracing the taxi would probably be useless in IDing its passenger, so she focused closely on the camera view to get whatever she could on this john. When she saw him emerge, she relaxed. This guy was probably not worth tracking, anyway. He was in a wheelchair, pushed by a male escort. As they came up the back ramp, she tried to at least get a picture, but the angle of the cam wasn't set low enough to see the invalid's face.

A couple of minutes later, Chase caught more movement on the rear-entrance cam. The image was dark, but clear enough for her to recognize Heather with her client. She subconsciously moved closer to the monitor. The john had his arm around Heather's waist and seemed clueless that Heather's smile was forced. "Oblivious fool," Chase said. They were just going in when Jack knocked on the side of the van. Chase opened the door without looking, her gaze still fixed on the monitor. "She's in," she said, and sat back down.

She felt Jack's stare and turned. Though it was dark in the van, enough light spilled from the monitor that she could clearly see the huge wet spot on her crotch.

Jack grinned. "Knew a dog once that reacted the same way whenever she saw me."

"Coffee."

"I bet it's driving you crazy you can't change."

Chase realized, for the first time since the incident, that she hadn't even given her pants a second thought. "I'm coping."

"I bet you're struggling against all sorts of hell to stay calm."

"I only do that where you're involved."

"I think it's precious how I can make you feel such intense emotions."

"Four clients arrived. One of them is our man." Chase drummed her fingers impatiently on the console.

"Do you mind?"

"What?"

"The tapping."

Chase looked at her hand and with effort stopped her drumming. "I'm done." She reached for the headsets and put them on.

"Can you stop the mind games and tell me what you know about me?" Jack asked.

"I'm not in the mood to talk about you." Chase focused on the monitor windows showing the watcher's room and adjoining bedroom.

Jack leaned closer to the screen. "What's wrong with the cam in the private room?"

"I just heard the door open and close, but he apparently doesn't want the lights."

"Damn." Jack put on her headset.

"We'll get his face on the way out," Chase said. "He has to go to his car."

Heather's voice interrupted them and they turned to the monitor. "Can I get you something to drink?" Heather asked her client as he helped her with her coat.

The lighting in the bedroom was tastefully subdued, but bright enough for Chase to get her first clear look at Heather in her call-girl persona. She was dressed in a spaghetti-strap black dress with a plunging neckline, made of a shimmery fabric that clung to every curve. Four-inch spike heels and the high hem of the dress commanded adoration of her long legs. Her makeup was different, and she exuded a very powerful yet provocative aura.

"Like I said, you wouldn't recognize her," Jack remarked.

Heather was the sexiest woman Chase had ever seen.

"I'll have some Scotch if you have any," the john said as he placed some bills on the bedside table.

Heather walked to the minibar and poured him a double.

"Am I drinking alone? he asked.

Heather handed him his glass. "I never really developed a taste for whisky."

"How can anyone not like Scotch?" Jack asked.

"I don't," Chase replied.

"That's just wrong."

The man downed the drink and set the glass on the nightstand on top of the money, making sure Heather saw the cash. Then he put his hands on her waist. "Are we good to go?"

"What a douche," Jack said. "Good to go, who says that?"

"Someone who pays by the hour."

Heather looked seductively toward the two-way mirror.

"You look beautiful as always, Amber. You may begin," a deep male voice said. "And fella, no kissing."

Chase tweaked the audio settings. Dario's voice was coming in hot because it was being picked up both on the bug she'd placed in the watcher's room and a speaker in the bedroom.

Heather nodded and started to unbutton the john's shirt. Chase clenched her fist till her knuckles turned white.

"What would you like tonight?" Heather asked. The client was about to answer when she placed her finger on his mouth and looked toward the mirror again.

"I want him to slowly remove your lovely dress," the disembodied voice instructed her.

Heather turned to expose her back to the john. He slowly unzipped her and lowered the straps of her dress, then kissed her shoulder and slid his hands around to the front of Heather's body.

Chase quickly lowered her head in search of her cup. "I need more coffee." She threw the empty cup across the van.

"I suppose you could suck it off your pants," Jack replied, never looking away from the monitor.

"Turn around and let him remove your garment," Dario said.

Chase looked back at the monitor. Heather turned, now facing the camera, with the guy behind her. The john pulled the dress off her shoulders and down her body. Beneath, she wore a sheer, lace-trimmed black thong and matching bra. As she stepped out of the dress, the man ogled Heather's body, his arousal evident. Heather continued to stare at the mirror with a look of desire.

"I think the guy's about to have a coronary," Jack said.

"Take off his shirt and trousers, Amber," Dario said.

Heather turned toward her customer with a practiced smile, one Chase had seen on call girls many times before. After she removed his shirt, she unbuckled his belt and knelt to slowly pull down his pants.

"Reindeer boxers? Really, dude?" Jack laughed.

Chase threw the headphones on the console and stood up. "I don't need to see this. Besides it's not like we can see the mystery man."

"Why do I have to watch?" Jack asked.

"I thought you enjoyed porn."

"I can't say porn is on my mind when I'd rather be doing everything possible to get my girl back. Besides, the magic's gone once you get to know them. Don't you think?"

"Then don't watch," Chase almost pleaded.

"Okay, relax. I won't." Jack sounded concerned. "You all right?"

"We both know how the movie ends. I doubt anything enlightening will take place while they…whatever." Chase couldn't bring herself to say it.

Jack turned off the cam in Heather's room but kept her headphones on. "I'm keeping the audio just in case something comes up. I mean—"

"I know what you mean." Chase sat back down and looked at the other camera views. She checked her watch.

"Another forty-five minutes," Jack said.

Chase ran her fingers through her hair. "At least we're getting Dario's voice recorded."

"That's for sure. The guy won't stop talking." Jack listened for another couple of minutes. "He's damn…verbal about what he wants."

"I bet." Chase tried to sound nonchalant while she fought the urge to leave the van and pace up and down the street.

Jack leaned back in her chair, hands supporting her head. Her expression was neutral as she listened in and glanced occasionally at what the other cameras were picking up.

Chase was glad she didn't have to hear or see Heather, but she couldn't help stealing glances at Jack now and then. Chase cringed when Jack lifted one eyebrow. "Is something wrong?"

"Nothing wrong." Jack tried to sound disinterested. "Just the usual stuff."

"Are you sure?"

"He's not hurting her, if that's what you're worried about."

"To each her own."

"What's that?" Jack looked at her.

Chase sighed. "I said I'm not worried. It's her life. If this is how she chooses to live it, then so be it."

"You don't need to feign indifference for my sake."

"I'm not."

"Could have fooled me." Jack sounded sincere. "Bet you never viewed them as real people before."

"I've always treated them with respect."

"What's different about this one?"

"I'm not sure. Something's just not right about her doing this."

"She seems damn proficient at it."

"She's miserable about having to sell herself. I can see the fear in her eyes. She's terrified someone will make her. She can't trust that anyone might be interested in anything but sex with her."

"Aren't they all?" Jack asked.

"I…I don't know. There's something very pure about this one."

"If that's true, then she's unfortunately just as apt at hiding her real nature as you are."

"Meaning?"

"Both of you treat sex as a means to a goal, without taking the consequences into consideration."

"What consequences?" Chase asked.

"How much your genuine nature gets obscured in your pursuit to justify what you do."

Chase wanted to give Jack points for not giving her a hard time about refusing to participate in the bedroom surveillance. And she knew Jack probably meant well with her pronouncements about Chase burying her real needs. But she was in no mood to get analyzed. Not right now. "Which is your true nature, Jack?" she asked. "The deserter, the liar, or the paid assassin?"

Jack shrugged. "Why ask, when you've already made up your mind I'm all three?"

"Because I'm curious if you're as much of an expert with self-analysis."

"Maybe someday when you're done judging me, I'll tell you what happened," Jack said.

"I'm sure it'll be a touching story, but frankly, there's no excuse for hurting innocent people."

"Don't you think I know that? Not a day goes by I don't regret the things I've done. But I refuse to apologize for leaving the EOO. Not after how that shit of a human treated me."

"I don't give a damn about the organization or Pierce," Chase said, too loud. "It's the path of destruction you left behind since you disappeared I can't forgive."

Jack turned back to the monitor. "Neither can I."

Chase saw sincere regret on Jack's face, but she was too agitated to care.

"They're done." Jack looked tired as she fished in her jacket for her cigarettes. "Our guy should be leaving soon."

Chase checked the time and moved closer to the monitor. She put her headphones back in place and turned on the bedroom monitor. Heather was wearing a short black robe and her client was almost dressed. She was facing away from both the mystery man and her client.

"You were amazing," the john said as he buttoned his shirt.

"Thank you." Heather's voice was artificially upbeat, her face devoid of any emotion as she stared vacantly into space. It was as though she had shut down completely.

"You may leave now," Dario said.

Heather turned to escort her client to the door. He tried to kiss her, but Heather turned her face away.

"Can I see you again?" the john asked.

Dario answered for her. "No, you may not."

"Too bad." The man winked at Heather. "If you change your mind, I'll be at the hotel until next week."

Heather opened the door for him without saying a word. He left and she went to sit at the foot of the bed. "Was everything to your satisfaction?" she asked Dario.

"You were splendid."

"I'm pleased you think so."

Chase heard the man sigh. "I look forward to your company, Amber. So much, as a matter of fact, I sometimes wish I could take you with me."

"Take me where?" Heather asked.

"On my draining business trips. I've gotten tired of travelling and negotiating with self-proclaimed important individuals. Your presence would surely make these affairs considerably more pleasant. You're very special, Amber."

"Thank you," Heather replied, the same empty smile on her face.

"I take it you were informed of my new schedule."

"I was."

"I shall see you again the day after tomorrow," he said.

"To talk."

"Correct."

"Why?"

"I find your companionship pleasing."

"Thank you."

Chase cringed when she thanked him again.

The rear-exit camera showed one customer leaving. "We can scratch him off our list," Jack said.

"See you then, sweet Amber," Dario said.

Chase and Jack both fixed on the camera view of the watcher's room and groaned simultaneously when he didn't turn on the light on his way out.

"We'll catch him at the door," Jack said.

Chase looked back at the view showing Heather. She remained on the edge of the bed, her expression unreadable.

Moments later, a man in his early forties departed the back entrance.

"That's right, look at the camera," Jack said as he glanced up, almost straight into the lens. "I think we have our man. Let's see what Reno gets on him."

Chase turned her attention back to Heather, who still hadn't moved. After another couple of minutes, Heather abruptly rose and went into the watcher's room and turned on the lights. The armchair was vacant, and a stack of bills had been left on the small table set before the two-way mirror.

To Chase's surprise, Heather didn't immediately take the money. Instead, she sat in the armchair and stared at the cash, then looked beyond it through the mirror at the bedroom. Even from a distance, it was clear her hands were shaking. She placed them between her thighs.

"I'm going out for a stretch," Jack said.

Chase didn't reply or take her attention off Heather, but she heard the door shut behind Jack.

Heather brought her knees up to her chest and laid her head there. Her shoulders began to shake; she was crying, but holding it in. The audio feed was silent.

Chase felt helpless and miserable. She placed her hand on the monitor and caressed Heather's hair. "I'm so sorry." Her voice broke as she whispered the words.

CHAPTER SEVENTEEN

Southwestern Colorado

Montgomery Pierce closed the blinds in his office and joined Joanne and David at the conference table, where Reno was passing out his latest set of briefing papers on Operation Phoenix.

"You look like hell, Reno," Joanne Grant said.

Reno took a long, noisy sip of his economy-sized soda and set it to one side. "Sleep is overrated. I'm fine." He pointed to the top paper on the neat stack before each of them. "First off, I finally cracked one of the large encrypted files that Rózsa had on his hard drive. Turns out he was into more than just brewing viruses at his lab. He was selling organs, probably from some of his human guinea pigs."

"He was in the organ trade? You're sure?" David Arthur asked.

"In a big way. Those furniture manifests we found were codes for organs, not viruses. That dummy firm in New York I've been trying to trace? Dragon Imports Unlimited? He's been dealing with them regularly for at least a couple of years. It's likely that whoever sent him the payment our ops are tracking, works for that company. Could be where he got the money to build his lab and fund his research."

"Have you had any luck tracing the ownership of this Dragon company?" Monty asked.

"Not yet, unfortunately. Whoever's behind it has gone to great lengths to shield their identity. It's like peeling an onion. Dragon is owned by a shell real-estate company in Turkmenistan, which is a front for a fake delivery service registered in Nauru—an island in Micronesia with a history of illegal money laundering. I haven't gotten further than that because a lot of their databases aren't online."

"I'll see if I can call in some favors to get you a contact on Nauru," Monty said. "The Russian mob funneled billions through there in the '90s, and the island was selling thousands of passports around the time of 9/11, so I'm sure the feds have a good deal of intelligence from there."

"That'd be a big help," Reno said. "On another front, I've been trying to ID this guy Dario that Chase and Jack think may be responsible for the transfer to Rózsa."

Monty corrected him. "Phantom."

"She hates it when I call her that."

"Stick to protocol, Reno."

"Sure, Boss. Anyway, since Dario's kind of an unusual name, I ran it through every database I could think of, concentrating, of course, on the New York metropolitan area. Came up with a couple of low-level drug dealers, a wife-abuser, a gang member..." He set a small portable tape recorder on the desk. "And this 911 call to emergency services in Teaneck, placed just a couple of weeks before the money transfer." He hit the Play button.

"911. What is the nature of your emergency?"

"Some guys have me locked up in a room and I think they're gonna kill me," a woman's panicky voice replied. The words were slurred, as though she'd been drinking.

"What is your name and location, ma'am?"

"I don't know where the fuck I am. A big white house. Near Teaneck, I think. There are trees and a swing set outside, and one of those blue kiddie pools, upside down. And I can see a cell tower."

"What is your name, ma'am?" the dispatcher repeated.

"Gigi. Uh, no...uh, Francine Shelhorn. Look, that's not important, just get the cops out here. These guys are gonna do something to me, I know it. I think they're gonna kill me and deliver me to some guy named Dario."

"What makes you think your life is in danger, ma'am? Have they hurt you or threatened you?"

"I just know, okay? They've fucking locked me up, I said!"

"Have you been drinking, ma'am?"

At that point, the line disconnected and a dial tone sounded.

Reno switched off the recorder. "The cops did follow up, but it took a couple of hours to find the house because of the sketchy info. The house she referred to was vacant and up for sale. Since the owner checked out—he was out of the state at the time and readily allowed them to go in and look around—the whole thing was dropped. I suspect it also wasn't pursued because of the unreliability of the caller. Francine Shelhorn has a long arrest record for prostitution and drunk-and-disorderly conduct."

"So we have two prostitutes with a Dario connection," Monty said.

"It gets better," Reno said. "Francine Shelhorn was reported missing a few days ago to NYPD. The caller who phoned it in was a woman who refused to give her name. And she used a pay phone just a couple blocks from Heather Snyder's apartment."

"Have you passed this on to Chase and Phantom?" David asked.

"Going to as soon as I leave." Reno took another long swig of his soda. "I got the missing-persons info just a little while ago."

"Any further news from them, by the way?" Monty asked.

"Yes. They sent me photos and license plates last night of three guys they think might be this Dario. My software's matching them as we speak."

❖

New York

Chase tried to work on her novel once she got back to the hotel, but she couldn't stop thinking about Heather. She supposed it wasn't the first time a working girl broke down in tears after seeing a customer, and according to Jack—who had heard everything—

the john hadn't hurt her. But Heather's reaction had thrown her off-kilter. All Chase had wanted right then was to hold her and tell her everything would be okay.

A knock interrupted her thoughts. "It's me," Jack said.

Chase quickly covered her sketches before she opened the door.

"You all right?" Jack asked.

"Yes, why?"

"You seemed to be…out of sorts."

"I'm fine."

Jack lingered in the doorway, obviously in no hurry to leave. "Want to join me for a drink? Or, in your case, a refreshing beverage?"

Chase checked the time. "Thanks, but no."

"Okay." Jack took a step into the room and looked around. "Have you heard from Reno?"

"Not yet."

Uninvited, Jack sat on one of the armchairs by the window. Was she looking for a distraction or waiting for Chase to reveal what she knew about her past? Chase wasn't sure, but something told her Jack simply wanted company. She looked tired and lost, like she was holding on by a thread.

"What's going on, Harding?" Chase asked.

Jack blew out a long breath. "I can't imagine what Cass is going through, and I feel so Goddamn useless. I don't know what I'll do if I lose her. It almost killed me the first time."

"Self-destruction is not the answer."

"But it's my go-to reaction. Always has been."

"Just focus on getting her back and you'll be fine."

Jack shook her head. "I'm not a half-full kinda person like Cass."

"You never were."

"I'm tired." Jack sat back and shut her eyes. "Tired of having to struggle for everything, including a bit of happiness. Tired of feeling tired."

"It never gets easy, Jack," Chase said. "Life is made up of brief moments of happiness. The rest is all either shades of gray or downright miserable."

Jack sat up and looked at her with surprise. "I thought you had it all figured out."

"You assumed this because you've been such a big part of my life?"

"Can you drop the sarcasm for tonight?" Jack asked without rancor. "What I meant is, you always kept it together, always made the right decisions, and even managed to reason shit away with time slots. Even now, you live like nothing touches you or matters. I envy that ability."

"There's nothing to envy." Chase sat opposite Jack on the other chair. "When you go through life like nothing matters, you wake up one day surrounded by exactly that." She looked away from Jack's intense stare. "At least you have someone to look forward to, and you have a reason to get up in the morning. So stop feeling sorry for yourself."

"All I said was I'm tired of having to try so hard to be happy."

"Who the hell isn't?" Chase asked. "But you found someone who can tolerate your dysfunctional ass."

"I did." Jack walked to the minibar and came back with a minibottle of Scotch, which she downed in one long pull.

"Why do you try so hard to numb what others have been deprived of?"

"Because feelings aren't all they're cracked up to be."

Neither spoke for a while.

Jack finally broke the silence, her voice etched with pain. "What I did ten years ago…leaving the organization. I didn't have a choice."

"Only you can be the judge of that."

Jack stared out the window. "After what happened to me in Israel, I couldn't go back."

"What did they do to you?"

"A woman I was involved with betrayed me. Turned out she actually worked for the arms dealer I was hired to kill. She handed me over to them and they tortured, raped, and beat me to near death. It lasted for weeks. By the time I managed to escape, they'd damaged my face beyond repair and pulled most of my teeth." Jack absentmindedly ran her finger over the scar that marred her left cheek.

Chase cringed at the images of Jack's suffering that were running through her head. She knew something had prompted her disappearance, but she hadn't expected this. It was difficult to picture her friend in such agony. Her *friend.* "I don't know what to say."

"Don't say anything," Jack said tiredly. "I'm not looking for sympathy. I need you to understand why I had to fake my death, change my face, and leave that life behind."

"Did you contact the EOO when you got away?"

"If I thought weeks of torture were the worst pain I'd ever feel, I was severely mistaken. When I contacted Pierce and told him what happened he…he shrugged it off. Told me I should know our job involves certain risks." Jack's voice broke and she looked at Chase with red eyes. "He said I needed to get back to base ASAP for the next assignment."

Chase sighed. "Jesus."

"I couldn't go back." Jack stood up and went to the minibar again.

"I wouldn't have gone back, either."

Jack unscrewed another minibottle and downed it. "And this is why I drink. I'm afraid without Cass to stop me, I'm going to do something crazy."

"Like what?"

"Kill Pierce."

"Jack, don't."

Jack started pacing. "Can't you see what he's doing? He's using Cass to lure me back. Get me where he wants me. No one escapes the EOO, and he's just proven that to everyone by bringing me back from the dead. I won't let him own me again."

Chase got up. "Listen, we're going to get Cass back and you're going back to your life. He will not stop you."

Jack stopped and looked at her. "How are you so sure?"

"Because I won't let him."

"I thought you didn't give a shit about me."

"Damn it, Jack." Chase ran her hand through her hair. "You… you…"

"What do you know about me? You said you would have killed me if it hadn't been me. What does that mean?"

"I don't want to get into that right now, but our paths crossed."

"When?"

"When I took a deep-cover job." Chase's cell rang. It was Reno. "Let me put you on speaker."

"Okay, so this is what I have." Reno briefed them on the 911 call he'd retrieved that mentioned a Dario and gave them all the info he had on the woman who'd made the call and the vacant house the police had checked out.

Chase frowned when he told them the girl was a known prostitute and had been reported missing by an anonymous woman who'd used a pay phone near Heather's apartment. The implication was clear.

"I'm sending you what I have, along with what I've been able to find out about the guys you wanted me to check out," he told them. "Can't exclude any of them yet. I'm still working on it."

"Anything else?" Jack asked.

"Yeah. I've cracked some of Rózsa's encrypted files. That other New York account I'm tracking that was paying him? They weren't buying viruses. He was selling them human organs. Haven't tracked the account ownership yet."

"Human organs?" Chase repeated. Heather's brother needed a kidney. Could there be a connection? Every bit of new evidence they got seemed to suggest Heather had to be involved somehow, but she still couldn't believe it.

Heather stared at the ceiling over her bed, her mind churning with too many questions for her to sleep. The evening had been treacherously long after her appointment with Dario and left her feeling emptier than normal. When she'd first started two years ago, she'd cried after these appointments, but it had been a long time since she'd broken down like she had tonight, and she couldn't understand why it had happened. Her customer hadn't done anything unusual to prompt her reaction. Maybe she was getting too tired of this work. Maybe her head was telling her it was time to stop. But why now, and what would happen to her brother if she did? What would happen to her dreams if she had to look for a second full-time job to support both of them?

How long would she have to continue this lifestyle? Could she go on until someone noticed her work in the fashion industry, or would she have to continue until her brother finally…*God. Get a grip.* Just the fact that Adam's death crossed her mind both shamed and shocked her.

She wanted her life back to where she wouldn't have to live with fear and lies. Where she could have actual dreams of dating someone like…Brett. A decent, attractive woman who made her feel safe and wanted her company because of what she could offer outside the bedroom.

Brett's response to the topic of sex was puzzling, however. Their mutual attraction seemed undeniable, yet Brett had made it clear she wasn't interested in her that way. Was it because she could see through Heather's façade? See her as someone who got paid to sleep with men? As much as Heather feared that, she doubted Brett knew. No, Brett had said she was a serial polygamist. But then why hadn't she been interested in Heather? Maybe she wasn't Brett's type. Not that Heather would have slept with her, and God knew dating was out of the question, but it bothered her just the same.

Her head spinning, she turned on the TV hoping it would distract her, but the available choices at this hour failed to do the job and she turned it back off a few minutes later. Still too restless to sleep, she got up and went into the living room to see if anything needed cleaning.

She spotted Brett's graphic novel and gingerly removed it from its plastic sleeve to examine the cover. Landor the Demon wore black, in contrast to his bright-yellow hair. His eyes looked sad. Heather took the novel with her to the couch and got comfortable.

Though she'd never read anything like it before, she was curious about what Brett had created.

Although it was issue # 96 it was easy enough to pick up on the ongoing theme. Satan forbade Landor from approaching the woman he loved, so he protected her from a distance while he sought comfort and pleasure in the arms of other women. Emily, his true love, was oblivious to Landor's constant shadowing and knew nothing about who saved her life when she got in trouble.

The artwork was amazing and something about Emily seemed familiar, but Heather couldn't put her finger on why. She lost herself in the story and didn't go to bed until she finished it, but even then, sleep was elusive. Now, in addition to her own troubled life, she'd become preoccupied with Landor's as well.

She was so lost in her thoughts she literally jumped when her cell phone rang a little after midnight. No one called her this late. Had something happened to her brother? She checked the caller ID and saw it was Direct Connect. "Hello."

"Sorry to call you this late, love," Margaret said, "but Dario rescheduled and I wanted to give you a heads-up."

"For when?"

"Tomorrow, six p.m."

"Just to talk, right?" Heather asked.

"That's right, love."

"I'll be there."

"You will if you want the cash, and I know you do."

"Good-bye." Heather hung up.

If Dario had wanted more than just conversation, she would have declined. She was still too sick to her stomach for a repeat of tonight.

Chapter Eighteen

Haarlem, Netherlands
Next day, November 22

Mishael Taylor glanced out the second-story window of the mansion she shared with her lover and watched Kris at work in the garden, pulling out the dead undergrowth around the topiary figures in readiness for winter. She couldn't help but think of Cassady and how she'd go crazy if Kris went missing and ended up in the hands of a madman like Rózsa.

She kept checking her watch and glancing at her cell phone. Rózsa had promised to call back, and she needed to stall him convincingly to keep Lynx alive. Pierce had contacted Interpol, and, as expected, they refused to release any of the twenty million dollars the EOO had diverted from Rózsa's accounts.

She had a small card to play that she hadn't expected, but she was to use it only if absolutely necessary: Pierce had offered to divert three million of his own funds and discretionary EOO money if it looked as though Rózsa was tired of waiting and determined to execute Lynx.

When her cell rang with Unknown Caller, she speed-dialed Reno on the landline before she answered–his cue to start tracing the call—and hit the Record button to capture the exchange in its entirety.

"Hello."

Rózsa got straight to the point. "Do you have my money?"

"Before we continue negotiations, I want to make sure our associate is still alive and well," she said.

"Alive, yes," Rózsa answered. "But her condition is deteriorating, I'm afraid. She's becoming an increasing liability to me, so I hope you are able to conclude our transaction quickly."

"You have to realize how difficult it is for us to regain those funds from Interpol," she said. "It's going to take more time to get the necessary approvals and set up the transfer—at least another week, perhaps two. We're optimistic we can make it happen, but you need to do your part and ensure our colleague doesn't come to harm in the interim."

"She is not my primary concern," Rózsa replied. "And I'm beginning to think you are just stalling for time."

"I assure you, that's not the case," Misha said. "We're working on several fronts to—"

"I'll give you five days to come up with, let's say, one-tenth of the funds, to keep her alive," Rózsa said. "And the remainder will be due one week after that. I'll be in touch." The line went dead.

She dialed Reno. "Anything?"

"Too quick. He's obviously savvy about how long it takes to isolate an overseas trace."

"Yeah, I didn't think so. I'm sending you the recording now." She e-mailed him the short clip and glanced out the window again. She couldn't do any more until he called back, and she had to vent her frustration. She grabbed the keys to her silver Jaguar XKR convertible and opened the window.

"I'm heading over to the track. I feel the need for speed," she called down to Kris. "Want to ride along?"

Kris looked up at her, shielding her face with one hand against the glare of the sun. "Sure, lover. As long as you promise not to break the sound barrier this time."

❖

New York

Chase was supposed to be able to get an hour's more sleep than Jack, who had to be up early to tail Heather to work, but she tossed and turned most of the night, unable to get Heather out of her mind. So by the time Jack called from the Garment District, she'd already had their new rental car delivered and was en route to pick her up.

Their constant game of musical chairs with vehicles was getting annoying. To ensure they could continue their surveillance without further parking issues, they'd left the first rental at Heather's apartment and the surveillance van at the brownstone, so they needed yet another car to check out the Teaneck house Reno had told them about.

Jack tossed her half-finished cigarette when she spotted Chase and climbed into the rental with a super-sized coffee in a Styrofoam cup. She looked as though she hadn't gotten much sleep either, no doubt a combination of worry over Cassady and the prior night's resurrection of her nightmare in Israel.

Though she still couldn't forgive Jack for her part in Regina's death, and for not contacting her after she disappeared, the story of her imprisonment, torture, and rape—and Montgomery Pierce's reaction—had softened Chase's attitude toward her.

She punched the address Reno had given them into the rental's GPS and they arrived at the New Jersey house a little after ten. Fortunately, the place was still up for sale, and no one was around.

"This is the place," Jack said. "From the looks of the lawn, no one's lived here in a long time."

"An ideal place for teens and whoever else to crash." Chase jimmied open the door.

They checked out all the rooms on the ground level first. It didn't take long; the place was vacant save for the window dressings, appliances, and a couple of cheap chairs. Chase looked out one of the windows. "The girl said she had a view of a cell tower and a swing set and kiddie pool right under the window. She must've been on the second floor to be able to see the tower. The trees obscure the view of it from down here."

They took the stairs and found themselves in a long hallway, with two doors on either side. "Only two rooms up here with that view. I'll take this one," Jack said, and disappeared into the first room on the right.

Chase took the one farther on. She checked out the view and found the swing set and plastic pool right under the windows. The tower was probably a couple of miles away. "I found the room," she yelled.

"I know," Jack said, when she joined her seconds later. "I saw the pool from the other room." She started looking around and bent to examine something near their feet. "What do we have here?" Jack held it up. "A red, fake fingernail, lodged between the floorboards."

Chase took in the big windows that ran along the length of the wall. "My guess is she broke it trying to open the window. Take a look, this one's nailed shut."

Jack pulled one side of the floor-length curtains all the way to the far wall to check the other windows, while she did the same with her side. Chase was almost to the wall when she kicked something that had been hidden beneath the drapery. "What the…?" She reached down and picked up a small cell phone. "How did the police miss this?"

Jack walked over. "Because it's the Jersey cops. They're up to their balls in gang crime and freak shows, just like the NYPD. How much effort did you think they'd put into finding a missing prostitute? At least fifty girls like her disappear every day. They probably showed up, took a look-see, and filed a missing-person's report all in the space of thirty minutes."

Chase examined the phone. "It's dead."

"It would be after three weeks."

"Do you think it belongs to the girl?"

"Don't know. We'll have to power it up and see."

They looked around the house for another fifteen minutes before returning to the hotel, where they connected the cell phone through a mini-USB to Chase's laptop. Both waited anxiously for the battery to charge enough for them to turn on the phone.

"Okay, here we go," Chase said when the display lit up. She checked the history of outgoing calls. The final one was the call to 911. The one before that was to Heather's cell, though Gigi had her listed in her contacts as Amber.

Next, Chase checked the history of missed calls. She frowned when she saw there were three, all from Heather's cell.

"Heather obviously knew Gigi's real name to report her missing, but looks like she wasn't as forthcoming in disclosing her own identity. They couldn't have been very close if Gigi didn't know Amber's real name," Jack said.

"I guess not," Chase mumbled. She dialed voice mail and hit the speakerphone button so Jack could hear as well.

Heather's voice was loud and clear. *"Hey, Gigi, what happened last night? Did you get home okay?"* Next message: *"Gi, let me know you're all right."* The final message: *"Gigi, if you don't call me back today, I'm going to come find you."*

"That was three days after she disappeared. Heather didn't phone the cops to report her missing until a few days ago. Doesn't look like she was in a hurry," Jack pointed out.

"No, it doesn't." Chase looked through the pictures on the phone, scrolling past numerous photos of men, a few women, a kitten, and…one with Heather in it. The woman with her had to be Gigi, since she was in many of the others as well. She had her arm around Heather and was smiling, oblivious to the photographer. Heather, on the other hand, was staring intently at the camera with a serious and uncomfortable expression.

"Doesn't look like a mutually fun experience, if you ask me," Jack said.

"No, it doesn't." Chase shut the phone. "She doesn't look happy about being photographed."

"I hate to say this, but it doesn't look good. As a matter of fact, it looks pretty damn bad. Heather took her time contacting the cops, and her messages sound more neutral than they do concerned."

Chase sighed and got up. "I agree."

"I want to check out Gigi's house. See if I can find anything there," Jack said.

"Reno can get you the address."

"Do you think Heather works for Dario? Lures stray working girls and sends them to him for…parts?"

Chase ran her fingers through her hair. "I don't know. It's possible." She sat back down.

"Damn," Jack muttered.

"Boy, did I misjudge her." Chase stared at the photo of Gigi and Heather.

"Makes you wonder if any of her johns have gone missing," Jack said. "I mean, if she works for Dario, she obviously doesn't have to hook for money. Maybe it's part for his pleasure and part entrapment. Potential involuntary donors."

Chase felt a headache coming on and rubbed her eyes. "It's possible," she mumbled.

"What?"

"I said it's a good Goddamn possibility."

"Come with me to Gigi's, or whatever her name is," Jack said.

"I'm sure you can cope on your own."

"It's not the same without your constant bitching."

Chase knew what Jack was doing. She didn't want Chase to be alone, and frankly she didn't want that either. "Call Reno so we can get out of here."

Jack dialed the number and got the address in seconds. After she'd disconnected, Jack said, "I'm sorry."

"What for?"

"I know you…like her."

"I just wanted to screw her. I'm over it."

Thirty minutes later they had broken into the apartment of Gigi, aka Francine Shelhorn. The place looked more like a young girl lived there than a woman. Posters of hot young actors like Zac Efron and Shia LeBeouf were tacked on the wall, and stuffed animals covered every corner of the tiny messy apartment.

"How old was she again?" Jack asked.

"Nineteen."

"Just a kid. Runaway, apparently, since no family has come looking or asking."

"Most of them are."

"At least tell me you like them older," Jack said.

Chase ignored the comment. Although the girls she paid were well over that age, she wasn't in the mood to talk about her acquired sex life. "Pull on your latex gloves. It's only a matter of hours before this turns into a proper investigation. I'm going to have Pierce call it in." She knew the police often took their time looking into missing prostitutes unless someone with pull made the call.

Jack slapped her gloves on and ran one finger over the surface of the dining table. "From the looks of it, no one's been here in weeks." She opened the fridge. "Everything in here has a pulse."

Chase went to the answering machine. The red light signaled messages. Thirty, according to the display. She pressed Play. Several of the calls were from men and, from the context, regular johns. A few women left innocuous messages about parties or other things, and her landlord reminded her the rent was overdue.

Then Heather's voice filled the room. She'd left ten messages in all, each showing increasing concern for Gigi. The final one said, *"Gigi, it's me again. I finally broke down and called the police. Are you in trouble? I know you never want to involve cops, but I'm worried. Just call me, okay?"*

"She sounds sincere," Jack said.

"She probably stopped calling the cell number after it went dead. That's why only the three calls."

"Damn. We're running around in circles here. Just when we think we have a lead."

"These messages don't clear her," Chase said.

"I know, but it doesn't sound like she sold her friend to Dario. And why report her missing if she was involved? Sure, it was anonymous, but why alert them to Gigi at all?"

"I don't know, but we need to get some answers soon." Chase checked her watch. "We should get going. She gets off in an hour."

They did their usual routine at the Garment District, with Chase watching from the restaurant across the street while Jack waited by the back corner of the building. Since Heather's next appointment with Dario wasn't until the next day, they fully expected her to go straight home, or perhaps visit her brother to deliver the novel. When she didn't emerge a few minutes after five as anticipated, they began to worry.

"Maybe she's working late," Jack said. "Think you should try her cell?"

"Let's give her a few more minutes. She could be caught up—"

"Here she comes. Hey, she's changed."

"Changed? How?"

"She ditched the pantsuit and pumps she arrived in. Must have a dress on under her coat, and now she's in high heels."

"Is she—"

"Damn. She's hailing a cab," Jack said.

"I'm going for the car. Don't lose her." Chase disconnected and hurried to the parking lot, praying Jack would be able to get her own taxi before Heather got away. The crush of rush-hour traffic should help in that regard, though it wasn't going to do her any favors in catching up to them in the rental.

As she neared the exit to the lot, she dialed Jack. "Where are you?"

"Heading north on 8th Avenue, near Central Park. I think she's going to the brownstone."

"Okay. I'm leaving the lot now and headed that way. Let me know if she goes elsewhere."

Jack called her back a few minutes later. "Yup. We're at the brownstone. I'm in the van firing up the equipment."

"Be there in a couple minutes." Chase ditched the rental in a no-parking zone, her only option unless she wanted to circle for hours, and jogged to the van.

"Dario's a day early," Jack reported once she got inside. "He was apparently already here when she pulled up."

"What'd I miss?" Chase put her headset on. The monitor showed Heather sitting on an armchair in one frame. She was wearing a short emerald cocktail dress and matching heels. The adjoining frame of the watcher's room was dark as before.

"Nothing much. He's been complimenting her on how beautiful she looks."

They both went quiet and listened in.

CHAPTER NINETEEN

Heather wished Dario would stop with the effusive praise about her appearance, which always preluded their appointments. Sure, he was more polite and civil about it than most of the johns she picked up to entertain him, but such compliments did nothing for her. She wanted him to get on with whatever this whole "talk" thing was about so she could just go home. She was still raw from the despair, guilt, and self-loathing that had put her in tears last night.

"I'm happy you could make it on such short notice," Dario said.

"I try to accommodate you if I can."

"I appreciate that, Amber. I wanted to see you tonight because there's been a change in my schedule."

"Oh?"

"I am expected to make another business trip this week."

"I see," Heather said. "Have you informed Direct Connect about the changes?"

"I have. I also asked for permission to make you an offer."

"All right," Heather said warily.

"I would like you to accompany me to China."

"I don't think I can—"

"We would leave this Friday and return Monday." Dario continued as though he hadn't heard her. "You will be generously rewarded."

"It's not about money," Heather said. "I don't feel comfortable going away with someone I don't know, let alone have never even seen."

"What are you afraid of? Don't you trust me?"

"It's simply a matter of not knowing you." Heather didn't want to offend him; he was an important client. But she was astonished he might think she could ever trust such a man. "Aside from that, it would be impossible to get the time off on such short notice."

"Your employer has already agreed."

"I don't mean Direct Connect."

"I know who you mean."

Heather was stunned speechless by the implication. She knew he could see the shock on her face.

"I talked to Robert this morning," Dario said, referring to her boss at Cesare Chelline Fashions. "He was most compliant."

"How do you know about my work?"

"I know a lot about you, *Heather*."

So he knew her name, where she worked, and what else? This was a whole new kind of violation, one she was unprepared for. She got up and walked to the two-way mirror. "How do you know?"

"Acquiring what you want is simple, if you want it enough."

"What you want?" Heather repeated. "I don't understand where you're going with this, Dario, but my personal life was never part of the deal."

"I reserve that term for business. My interest in you is purely for pleasure."

"This conversation is making me very uncomfortable" Heather turned her back to collect herself.

"What troubles you, Heather? My proposal or the fact that I know who you are?"

"You have no idea who I am." The response came out sharper than she intended, but she was having a hard time controlling her rising anger.

"Excuse my poor choice of words," Dario said with his usual unctuous politeness. "I was merely referring to the facts."

"Did you think you could blackmail me into accepting your offer?"

"Of course not. I don't want you to do anything against your will. I've been very careful to respect you."

Respect me? The guy pays to watch me have sex.

"I want you to come with me only if you wish to."

"Assuming I agreed, which I *don't,*" Heather replied, "I'd be doing it for the money, not because I wanted to."

"Which wouldn't be any different from what you do for me every week."

"Then realize what I do here has nothing to do with what I *want.*"

"I can't completely agree with that statement," Dario said. "Unless, of course, you are here against your will. Does someone force you to entertain me, or is it something you choose to do?"

"I do it because I have to."

"And why do you have to?"

"That's none of your business."

"Is it because you want to help your brother?"

"What?" she fired back, too loud. He indeed knew *everything* about her, and the realization both disgusted and frightened her.

"I'm sure it is. In which case, you do this work because you want to help him. You do it because you want to keep him alive. Do you see how necessity can make you want?"

"Who the hell do you think you are?"

"Someone who wants to help you. All I ask in return is your company."

"Why me? I'm sure you know plenty of women who'd be happy to oblige."

"You're beautiful, smart, and compassionate. The ideal woman to keep me company and make me look good. And, no, I don't associate with women of your caliber."

"What does that mean?" Though she knew how ridiculous it was to place any credence on a john's opinion, she couldn't help feeling offended.

"I don't know any other woman as painfully beautiful as well as bright."

She knew it was meant as a compliment, but the sentiment disgusted her.

If he was so clued into her life it was only fair that she ask him about his. "Is Dario your real name?"

"Yes."

"It's unusual for a client to give his actual name, especially when he's being so mysterious."

"I substitute myself for these men because I want to look like them. But I have never wanted to be anyone other than myself. They are a mere vessel—a means, if you will, to living a small portion of my life vicariously."

"Are you impotent?"

"No."

"Then why?"

"No disappointment is worse than that of yourself. I like to be surrounded by perfection. Everything in my life is ordered to give me exactly that. I can pay anyone as much as they want to give me that flawlessness, but no amount of money can make me perfect. This is why I need vessels."

"No one is perfect. No one has to be."

"That's why you're so different. Beautiful women insist on being surrounded by everything attractive."

"What kind of business are you in?"

"The purchase and distribution of furniture, worldwide."

"What do you have to do in China?"

"Pay and make…arrangements with a most irritating seller."

"What would I have to do as your escort?"

"Accompany me to business dinners and perhaps a few other formal appearances."

"Sex?"

"Maybe, but not necessarily. I would make your company worth your while, Heather. Come with me and you won't have to worry about your brother's bills for a while."

"Then why would I continue to see to your needs?" she asked sarcastically.

"If we both agree to maintain these and future travel arrangements, you will never have to worry about your brother's expenses."

"You would own me."

"Think of it as a mutually profitable arrangement, Heather. You will have plenty of time to pursue your goals, and your brother will have a very comfortable life."

"My goals?" What could he possibly know about those?

"I'm sure a smart woman like you cannot be content with creating someone else's art instead of her own."

"I can manage my ambitions without your help."

"But I can make it happen a lot faster. Think about it. I don't expect you to answer right now. I'm going to leave a number with your money. Call me when you decide."

"I already gave you my answer," she replied firmly.

"You have until tomorrow night to reconsider. Have a nice evening, Heather."

Chase leaned back in her chair and smiled at the monitor. "We can scratch Heather off the list of suspects. She clearly has no idea who Dario is or what he does."

"Do you think the irritating seller in China is Rózsa?" Jack asked.

"It's very possible. Dario's obviously the guy who made the money transfer to him from the brownstone. And he said he has a furniture company, which matches what Reno said about the other account he's been tracking."

"About the money Rózsa kept receiving for organs back in Hungary being made from an untraceable New York furniture company," Jack said.

"Which all means that Dario's furniture business is a front for his organ trade."

"We can't scare him now or he'll alert Rózsa. If he *is* in China and Dario is headed that way, he can lead us right to him and... Cass." The news had obviously given Jack a burst of renewed hope. She was suddenly all nervous energy and anticipation, sitting forward, one knee restlessly pumping up and down.

"Agreed," Chase replied. "We're going to find out where Dario lives and take it from there."

"He should be coming out any moment," Jack said as they stared at the monitor. "We're about to beat Reno at IDing our guy."

Chase grinned. "It could crush him."

"About time someone rained on Little Miss Sunshine's parade." Jack tapped her foot. "He's taking his sweet time getting out, though."

Just then a big man in a suit appeared at the rear exit. He propped open the door and disappeared back inside.

"I saw him yesterday, he was escorting a—" The man in the suit pushed a wheelchair out the door. It was the same guy from the previous night they'd summarily dismissed as a possibility, and they still couldn't get a view of his face because of the camera angle.

"Dario is in a wheelchair?" Jack asked.

"Unless the other guy is the one who's being escorted."

"Fat chance."

"Exactly."

"Explains why he considers himself flawed and all he wants is to watch," Jack said.

They waited until Dario was helped into the waiting cab, then both scrambled to get in the front of the van. Chase stayed a few cars behind Dario.

"You think Heather will take the offer?" Jack asked.

"I doubt it."

"Sounds like a lot of money."

"She may be a call girl, but she's not for sale," Chase said.

"You sound pretty confident."

"I haven't been wrong about her yet."

"You didn't seem too sure after we got a look at Gigi's cell," Jack pointed out.

"I was angry and frustrated because I don't like being wrong. Turns out I wasn't."

"Gotta hand it to Dario, he definitely did his homework on her."

Chase frowned. "He's a manipulative bastard."

The cab led them to Long Island's "Gold Coast" of luxurious mansions and elite private homes, where it turned into a fortress-like compound surrounded by a high wall. Security cameras were strategically placed near the massive iron gate and at intervals atop the wall. They paused in front of the driveway, but the cab disappeared around the side of the enormous brick home, preventing them once again from getting a look at Dario. Thanks to the massive security lights on the exterior, however, they did spot two additional goons working for the guy—one positioned by the front door and another on an upstairs balcony.

"I'm going to start thinking the guy doesn't have a face," Jack said.

"We need to update Pierce and get Reno working on IDing this guy." Chase pulled to the curb a short distance farther on and dialed headquarters. Once she had both of them on a conference call, she engaged the speakerphone. "Reno, we have Dario's address," she said, and rattled off the house number and street. "We need the full works on this guy ASAP. We also need you to run a check on all flights out of the New York metro area the day after tomorrow bound for China to see if he has a booking under his name."

"Running it now," Reno replied. "Should have it momentarily."

"Give me everything you've got," Pierce said.

Chase briefed him on all they'd learned.

Reno jumped in when she'd finished. "Okay, got it. The house ownership doesn't give us Dario's last name. The address is registered to Dragon Imports Unlimited, which at least confirms your suspicions that it's his bogus company. And unfortunately, I'm not finding any airline reservations to China with a Dario in the name."

"He could be traveling under an alias, if he has a fake passport," Chase mused. "Or maybe he lied to Heather, and Dario is his cover name."

"From the looks of this place, he could have his own plane," Jack said.

"Any way you can get inside?" Pierce asked.

"Doubtful," Chase replied. "High security, and we know he has at least three bodyguards. Probably more, from the size of the place."

"At least you have a good lead on Rózsa, finally," Pierce said. "Keep me apprised. I know you two will find a way to nail down where he's going. I'll have our people here ready to make your arrangements to follow him."

"Roger that." Chase disconnected.

"Looks like we're off to China," Jack said as Chase started the van and headed back toward Manhattan.

"The question is, where in China?"

"I have an idea."

"I was afraid you would," Chase said.

"Just hear me out and save your shit fit for the end."

"I do enjoy a grand finale."

"Dario plans to leave soon and we can't find him booked on any flight. We still don't have his last name and no clue what he looks like."

"So far, so good."

"But we do know someone we can plant inside. Someone who can get close to Dario and lead us to Rózsa. Assuming, of course, she cooperates," Jack said.

"If you're implying we use a civilian, you're crazier than I thought."

"Landis, she's our only in."

"There's got to be another way."

"Yeah, if we wait around long enough, I'm sure something will come up," Jack said. "Problem is, we don't have the luxury of time."

"She's a civilian," Chase repeated. "And this guy probably has hundreds of homicidal idiots working for him. China is the cesspool of the organ trade, and he's headed there to likely off Rózsa. Do you really think Heather needs to get caught in the middle of that?"

"We'll have her back the whole time. Send her in wired."

"What happens when she has to…perform for Dario?" Chase asked.

"Wouldn't be the first time and, besides, the room will be bugged. We'll hear if she's in trouble."

"Have you seen his entourage and security? It's only going to get worse when he's surrounded by the likes of himself."

"Heather can help us get in," Jack said.

"What makes you think she'll even agree to your master plan?"

"Hey, we got nothing to lose by asking. Think about it, Landis. She's our best shot at finding Cass."

Chase tiredly rubbed her face.

"You okay?" Jack asked.

"You're not the only one getting too old for this shit. I don't think she'll agree and I don't know if I want her to."

"Let me talk to her."

"We'll do it together."

CHAPTER TWENTY

Mouchamps, France

Cassady stared up at the ceiling of her prison, following the sound of Rózsa's footfalls on the floor above. Another ten minutes or so, she guessed, until he arrived with her water and oatmeal. Her hunger had dulled in recent days. She continued to eat only because she needed to keep up what little strength remained. But her thirst had become more acute with each passing hour. These minutes before her daily ration were unbearable, and the relief she got from her meager eight ounces was always short-lived. She sweated more than that in a couple of hours down here, or so it seemed.

She had no idea how long she'd been held captive. Long enough to become bony and thin, with only a fraction of her usual energy and strength. Certainly the EOO must think her dead by now, and she wondered how Jack was coping. Despite her fearless and formidable exterior, Jack had a gentle, fragile side, and Cassady worried that Jack might do something dangerous or self-destructive if she believed she was gone forever. To keep herself sane, she often closed her eyes and tried to send messages to Jack: *I'm still alive, sweetheart. Come find me. Please come find me.*

When Rózsa's heavy footsteps sounded on the stairs, she tried to work up some saliva so she could speak. She was going to beg him again for more water, though he'd ignored all previous requests, and she planned to ask for a proper bath. Her bucket wash, days earlier, had done little to cleanse the stench from her body. Initially she'd almost become inured to her odor, but the air in the basement had become so fetid she could scarcely breathe. She wasn't hopeful he'd agree, but the day before, she'd seen him pause as he entered and wrinkle his nose in disgust, so maybe he'd be amenable to the idea.

He entered as usual and headed toward her.

"Please," she rasped, her voice an unrecognizable croak. "Please, I need more water. I can't survive on what little you give me."

Rózsa set down her water and oatmeal and stepped back a couple of steps, but didn't leave. He looked down at her, studying her like a virus under his microscope.

"And I can't stand the smell any longer," she said while she had his attention. "Surely you can't, either. It's making me so sick I can barely eat without throwing it back up. I need a proper bath. I promise you, I won't try anything. Please. I'm begging you. Show some mercy."

Rózsa didn't answer. He stood there for a few more seconds, then turned to leave.

Cassady grabbed the water and took a long sip, holding it in her mouth for a few seconds before swallowing. It wasn't nearly enough to quench her raging thirst, but she forced herself to ration it throughout the day, so she wouldn't take another sip for at least an hour. Leaning back against the cold concrete wall, she fought the urge to weep. Not like she could summon tears, at this point, anyway, but she tried hard to resist any urge to sink further into depression.

She was so accustomed to every sound of his routine she realized as Rózsa started up the steps that he hadn't secured the bolt on the door. Was it an oversight? Or was he coming back?

Two minutes later, she got her answer when he returned with another paper cup of water. He set it down and backed away again. "Drink it," he said.

Though her instinct told her to ration it, Rózsa's odd expression made it clear he wanted her to drink the whole thing, right now.

Afraid he would take it away again if she didn't comply, she reached for the cup and downed the contents. For the first time in many days, her thirst abated to a dull roar. "Thank you," Cassady said. "Will you let me have a bath now? Please?"

He remained silent but didn't leave. What was he up to?

Before long, her head began to spin, and the Rózsa standing before her became twins. He'd put something in the water, she realized with alarm. She tried to focus, but the twins became triplets, then she passed out.

The next thing Cassady knew, Rózsa was hauling her up the stairs, one arm around her waist, her arm over his shoulder. Everything was fuzzy. She tried to keep her feet under her, but he was moving so fast and she was so weak it was impossible.

He half-carried her through a small kitchen and into a bathroom, and laid her on the cold tile floor. "Knock when you're finished," he said before departing. She heard the click of the lock, then silence.

Cassady hazily took in her surroundings as she struggled to her knees. A toilet, sink, and shower. A pile of clean clothes he'd left her to change into. And a window, big enough to fit through.

Her only chance of escape.

She mustered every ounce of strength she had and crawled toward it. The sink was just to the left of it, so she used it to pull herself up. When she did, she came face to face with herself in the mirror mounted above it and gasped. Though her vision was still fuzzy and she saw herself in triplicate, she wouldn't have recognized herself. Her once-blond hair was gray and disheveled, her cheeks were hollow, and enormous dark circles around her eyes made her seem more skeletal than human.

Shrugging off the image, she continued to the window. She saw three latches and had to fumble to find the one that was real. She twisted it and pulled at the window with all her might, but it didn't budge. She blinked several times and felt around the frame until she discovered why. It was nailed shut.

She collapsed back onto the floor, breathing hard from the exertion, and looked around again. Nothing she could use as a weapon jumped out at her. The toilet didn't have the heavy tank lid that many American ones did. The only other items in the room were toilet paper, soap, a towel, toilet brush, and shower curtain.

A shower curtain, she realized, that hung from a heavy iron bar. She crawled toward it and struggled back to her feet. The bar rested in brackets on either side, but it wasn't bolted in. She was able to lift it, though in her weakened state it seemed much heavier than it should have.

Cassady wasn't sure she had enough left in her to wield it effectively and escape, especially with her vision so compromised. But it was certainly worth a try. She might never get another chance. First, though, she'd clean herself up, just in case she didn't succeed.

She was so weak it took nearly five minutes to strip and get into the shower. Rózsa hadn't provided any shampoo, only the bar of soap, so she used it to wash her hair and her body, and as she scrubbed herself, she opened her mouth under the spray and drank until her stomach ached. She was even more emaciated than she'd thought; as she looked down at herself she wondered how she could even remain standing.

When she finished cleaning her body, she changed into the sweatpants, T-shirt, and clean socks he'd left for her. They were obviously his own clothes because they were much too large, but at least they were clean. Once she was dressed, she rested for a few minutes to catch her breath before reaching for the iron bar.

"Are you finished?" Rózsa called through the door. He'd apparently been near enough to hear her shut off the shower.

"Almost," she replied. "Please. Just another couple of minutes. I'll knock when I'm ready."

Cassady struggled unsteadily toward the door with the bar and pressed herself against the wall beside it. She took a few deep breaths and tried to focus. *Now or never. You can do this.* She reached out and knocked, then gripped the bar like a baseball bat and got ready to swing it at him.

Rózsa came in so fast he'd evidently been waiting just on the other side of the door. And he obviously suspected she'd try something or her sense of timing was off considerably in her drugged state, because when she swung the bar, he was able to dodge the blow enough that it caught him on the shoulder instead of aside his head.

It staggered him, at least, putting him off balance enough that she thought she could try again. But three of him rushed toward her, and she wasn't sure which was the real one, so she swung wildly at the triplets and prayed she connected.

She heard him groan and felt the impact of the blow in her arms as she fought to remain standing, but she'd only hit him on the arm, and he was able to tackle her before she could try again. The iron bar went flying and clattered across the tile as Rózsa got to his knees, straddling her body. He hit her, hard, across the face, and pain exploded in her jaw.

Still, she fought back, trying to throw him off with her hands and legs, renewed by a burst of adrenaline. But his fist came at her face again, and then everything went black.

When Cassady came to, she was back in her shackle in the basement. Her head was pounding, and when she put her hand to her aching jaw, she could tell it was badly bruised and her lip was split and bleeding. At least her vision was clearer. She rolled over and looked toward the door.

He'd taken away her oatmeal and water as punishment.

Chapter Twenty-one

New York

When Heather got home she practically tore off the emerald cocktail dress and heels and jumped straight into the shower, to rid herself of Dario. Soon, she was in a worn-out pair of jeans and T-shirt but still didn't feel free of him. His words kept running through her head. How dare he try to buy her? Who did he think he was?

But what power he had to find out so much: her name, her job, even about Adam. He knew *everything* about her. The revelation made her skin crawl and frightened her.

Not only was she *not* going to join him on his business trip, she would cut him off completely, and if that meant giving up the agency, then so be it. Maybe the universe was telling her it was time to stop. If she had to give up her dreams and take another three jobs to support her brother's needs, she'd do it. Having to sell her body was one thing, but having someone own her was a whole different matter. Moving on to another Dario wasn't an option, either. Who knew what the next guy would be capable of?

She hadn't realized the real danger of this work until tonight. Sure, she'd heard gruesome stories from other women, but they were all street girls like Gigi. No one she knew from her elite agency had ever been in danger. *Goes to show you there's never enough protection from obsessive freaks.*

Heather paced the room, trying to think of something to get her mind off Dario. She resorted to turning on the TV again, but it didn't help any more than it had the night before. Maybe talking to her brother would distract her. She glanced at the clock. Nearly ten, too late to call him. Normally, she would have phoned Gigi, but that wasn't an option. As far as she knew, Gigi was still missing. Though she checked the paper every day for some news about Francine Shelhorn, she hadn't seen any mention of her.

She had no one else to call, certainly not this late. Brett sprang to mind. When would she be back in town? Would she look her up again or were they just words?

She'd never met a woman quite like her. Although she always appeared calm and measured, Brett seemed rather ominous and mysterious. Heather couldn't pinpoint why, but the way she'd scared off those guys in Chinatown was unusual, to say the least. Not exactly how your average woman approaches danger. Brett not only intervened without a second thought, she did it like it was the most natural thing in the world, without even breaking a sweat. She was either very capable or very stupid. Either way, Heather realized she'd never felt safer than when in her company.

Her daydreams of Brett finally enabled her to relax, and she was just drifting off on the couch when the doorbell rang, startling her back to full awareness. The clock on the DVD player read ten fifteen. No one ever came to her door unexpected, certainly not at this time of night. Could it be Gigi?

Creeped out by her earlier meeting with Dario, she went to the intercom with an uneasy feeling. "Gi, is that you?" Heather asked cautiously.

"Hi, Heather. It's Brett."

Absolutely the last person she expected to hear from. It was almost like she'd sensed that Heather had been thinking about her and wishing for some company. "Brett? Are you okay?"

"Yes, fine. I...uhm...was wondering if I could talk with you."

"Sure...yes. Now?"

"If that's all right."

God, I look like a mess. "I'll buzz you in." She ran to the bathroom to fix her hair and was headed for the bedroom to change when the doorbell rang. "That was fast," she muttered nervously, just before opening the door.

Brett looked tired and almost reluctant to step in. "I'm not alone, I brought a friend."

Another woman stepped into view beside her. A dark-haired version of Brett, only this one had a scar down the length of her cheek and brilliant green eyes. Both were dressed in black and roughly the same age.

"Can we come in?" Brett asked.

"Yes, of course." Heather stepped aside. "Forgive my rudeness. I've had a…strange day."

"I'm Jack." The brunette extended her hand.

All of a sudden her apartment felt tiny with both women standing in it. They had a very imposing aura, and after the incident with Dario, Heather wasn't sure she liked it.

She shook Jack's hand. "Heather Snyder."

"I know." Jack smiled like she knew her.

"Do I know you?"

"I hope not."

Brett moved farther into the living room. "Heather, why don't you take a seat?"

"What's going on, Brett?" Heather felt as though she was about to hyperventilate. Nothing about this day made sense.

Jack gestured toward the couch as Brett sat down on one end of it.

"Why do I have to sit?" Heather asked. "I'm not comfortable with this at all."

Brett stood up again when Heather didn't move. Her expression was serious. "Fine. We can do this standing up."

Her alarm rising, Heather asked, "Do what?" She backed slowly toward the door but froze when she felt Jack behind her.

"We're not going to hurt you," Jack said.

"Why are you here?"

"To talk to you about Dario," Brett replied.

Heather couldn't have been more shocked. This felt like a bad dream. She stared at Brett. "How…how do you know Dario?"

"We know you…entertain him…privately," Jack replied from behind her.

Heather's stomach dropped and her head began to spin.

"Catch her," Brett said, and ran to the kitchen sink.

Heather felt strong arms around her waist. Jack helped her to the couch and then sat in the armchair opposite. Brett sat next to her and placed a glass of water in her hand, but she was shaking so much she had trouble holding it.

Brett helped her take a drink and then set the glass on the table. "I'm sorry. We didn't mean to upset you."

After a minute or two, once she'd recovered enough to speak again, she asked, "How…how do you know?"

"Let's start from the beginning," Brett said, looking at her friend. "Jack and I work for a private organization."

Jack lifted her hand. "Correction, I'm on loan. One-time deal."

Heather turned to Brett. "What organization?"

"Private contractors," Jack said.

"The government?" Heather asked. "Are you here to arrest me for—"

"No, nothing like that. It's an international company. We get hired to help any country indiscriminately, and this has nothing to do with…with…" Brett suddenly looked uncomfortable and wouldn't meet Heather's eyes.

"Prostitution," Jack filled in.

Heather felt her face burn and looked away.

"Real subtle, Jack." Brett stared at Jack with a piqued expression for a few seconds. "This doesn't involve Direct Connect. This is about your client, Dario. We have reasons to believe he works with Andor Rózsa."

"Isn't he the guy who spread the H1N6 virus?" Heather asked.

"Yup, it's that son of a bitch," Jack replied.

The papers and TV news reports had been full of little else for months—first reporting on the millions dead or dying from the virus, and then, just a few weeks ago, relaying word that the man responsible for it all had eluded capture. "Oh, my God. I had no idea. But Rózsa disappeared."

"Yes, no one can find him," Brett said. "And it's very important we do."

"The bastard has my girlfriend hostage." Jack clenched her fists.

Heather saw pain as well as fury in the woman's eyes. "I'm sorry," she said. "But I still don't understand what this has to do with me. I mean…I had no idea Dario was involved in any of this."

"We know," Brett said.

"How did you find out Dario was seeing me?"

Brett still wouldn't look at her. She kept staring at the floor. "He made an electronic payment to Rózsa from the brownstone's IP address."

"Why would he do that?"

"We don't know. We assume he panicked for some reason. When we checked out the IP address we discovered that the building belonged to Direct Connect. After that, it was just a matter of finding out who was there during the time of the transaction." Brett paused, and when she continued her voice was almost apologetic. "Everyone present that night: girls, customers, Massimo, were all suspect. You included."

"But how did you find my real name?"

"We followed you to your house," Brett said.

"And checked the registry," Jack added. "I've been shadowing you for a week. We also know about your day job."

Heather looked at Brett. "And my brother?"

Brett nodded without looking up.

"That night at the Cave, you came looking for me."

"Yes," Brett said.

"That's why you asked for my number. Why you asked me out."

Brett sighed. "Yes."

Heather reached for the coffee table and grabbed the graphic novel from under the Cosmo. "But you signed this as the author."

Brett took it from her. "Because I am. Cooland is my pseudonym," she said, and looked at Jack.

"Your day job," Heather said.

"Of sorts."

"What pseudonym?" Jack asked. "What are you talking about?" She looked from Heather to Brett.

Brett looked uncomfortable as she handed the graphic novel across the table to her.

Jack stared at the cover for several seconds, then opened it to the inscription page. "Well, fuck me."

"I was going to tell you," Brett said.

"You're Cooland?" Jack asked.

Brett nodded. "I have been for eight years."

"Well, damn." Jack shook her head in disbelief and glanced down at the novel again. "Why didn't you let me know?"

"Oh, I don't know." Brett shrugged. "Maybe because I haven't exactly been in the mood to share anything with you."

"You clearly don't have a problem sharing your opinion about me."

"Not now, Jack."

"You started it," Jack mumbled, and looked back down at the novel. "Hey, this is next month's issue."

"It's a proof," Brett said.

"It's for my brother," Heather said pointedly. Jack was clearly coveting it.

"Why does he get one?" Jack asked Brett.

"Can we do this later?" Brett turned to Heather, but once again avoided eye contact. "We've been following you because we thought you were somehow connected to Rózsa."

"And you don't think so anymore."

"Correct," Brett said.

"Why not?"

"Because it's obvious you're clueless as to who Dario is," Jack replied.

"Obvious how? I mean, I *am*…but why are you now convinced I'm not involved?"

Brett squirmed and looked down at her feet. "We had your room at the brownstone bugged and heard tonight's conversation. It's clear you—"

"Bugged? When? How?" The humiliation she'd endured in that room flooded back as images of what she'd done for Dario flashed in her mind. Heat rose to her face. "How long have you been listening in?"

"For a week," Jack said.

"You listened while I—" She couldn't look at Brett.

"Yeah," Jack said. "I know this must be very uncomfortable for you, but if it's any consolation, it's nothing we haven't heard before."

"Smooth again, Jack," Brett said, her tone tinged with reproach.

"Consolation?" Mortification began to quickly give way to anger. "That's a violation of my privacy. God, this is so embarrassing." Heather jumped to her feet, her rising fury so immense she felt as though she'd burst. She glared down at Brett. "You asked me out. We…you just stood there and watched me make a fool of myself. Why? It's not like you confronted me with any of this, so why did you ask me out?"

Brett kept her gaze glued to the floor. "I promised you the novel for your brother."

"Only to get my number. Besides, you could have mailed it."

"She asked you out because we needed to get you away from your apartment," Jack said.

Heather turned toward Jack so fast she heard her neck crack. "What?"

"While she kept you busy," Jack said, "I was in here looking through your notepad, copying the Dario dates the agency gave you."

"How do you know about those?" Heather's head began to pound.

"We tapped your phone," Jack replied.

They were listening in, even here. In her private sanctuary, the only place she'd felt truly safe. The admission stole the fight from her. Heather dropped onto the couch. "This whole clandestine show has been taking place right under my nose, and I…" She suddenly felt more lost and confused—and *violated*—than she could ever remember. "First Dario, now you. Christ, who else knows? The local news?"

Brett still avoided eye contact. "No one else knows. We're sorry we had to go to such extremes, but—"

Heather raised her hand. "Enough!" she shouted, and rubbed her temples to calm down. "It's clear I have nothing to do with Dario or Rózsa or viruses and whatever the hell else you thought I was involved in. So please remove your spy devices and stay the hell away from me. Do you hear me, Brett?"

Brett finally looked at her. "It's not that simple."

Heather felt like pulling her hair. Was her life really unraveling before her eyes?

She went to the door and opened it. "I want you both to leave. Right now."

CHAPTER TWENTY-TWO

Chase got up and walked toward the door, and Jack followed a pace behind, but both stopped when they got within reach of Heather. "We need your help," Chase said. She was standing so close to Heather she couldn't help inhaling her scent. Her hair smelled of spice and vanilla, and the enticing aroma was making it hard to keep her focus. Everything about this woman intoxicated her. "Please, just hear what we have to say," she said softly as she dropped her gaze to Heather's mouth.

In her bare feet, Heather was a couple of inches shorter than she was, and she looked down as she seemed to consider how to answer, so Chase couldn't see the expression in her eyes.

When Heather finally looked up at her, it was with such intensity that Chase's breath caught. Her heart began to pound and it took all her willpower to back up a step instead of following the overwhelming compulsion to close the inches separating them.

Heather had a quizzical look on her face, and Chase was certain she looked just as confused.

"Help you how?" Heather asked.

"Why don't we sit back down?" Chase suggested.

She and Jack both waited where they were as Heather started toward the couch. Even without makeup, in jeans and a T-shirt, this woman was incredibly beautiful. She couldn't stop staring.

"Focus, Landor. Emily is off bounds," Jack said.

Heather turned to look at Chase, and Chase saw bewilderment give way to recognition. "He looks like you," she said. "And Emily…she…"

"Looks like you," Chase said, intent on Heather.

"While this is all very cool in a creepy kinda way, can we get back to why we need her help?" Jack asked.

"I need to use the bathroom," Heather said abruptly, and shut herself away in the adjoining room.

Chase took the armchair this time. She needed to put some distance between herself and Heather, especially since Heather looked particularly uncomfortable.

"What's up with the musical chairs?" Jack asked. "You're in my spot."

"Have you lost every sense of decorum?" she mumbled. "Just sit on the couch."

"Easy, champ, this awkwardness is all you."

"The awkwardness is because you can't censor what comes out of your mouth."

"Hey, give me a break. I'm pretty surprised here, too. Who knew all those hours of doodling would lead to Landor."

"Try to deal with it mutely and sit down."

"You're in my chair," Jack repeated.

Heather came out of the bathroom, still looking uncomfortable.

"She's back," Chase said in a low voice. "Sit the fuck down or I'll hurt you."

"Oooo, I'm scared. Look at me shake." Jack sat down on the couch just as Heather did.

"So, this is the deal," Jack said. "Rózsa kidnapped an operative before he disappeared."

"I thought you said he had your girlfriend," Heather responded.

"Who happens to be an operative," Jack said.

"And you are…*what*, by the way, if you're on loan to this organization?" Heather asked.

"Long, complicated, and irrelevant story, but I check out," Jack replied. "Anyway, Rózsa has my girl, and the only way we can get to *her* is through *him*. And the only way we can get to *Rózsa* is through the only man we know who has had contact with him."

"Dario," Heather said.

"Yeah. Only problem is, if we scare Dario, he's going to alert Rózsa," Jack explained.

"And Rózsa will run," Heather said.

"You're catching on. Now, we know he's about to leave for China to see a seller he owes money to. One who's making life difficult for him. You see, Rózsa is wanted internationally, and by contacting Dario, he's jeopardizing Dario's safety. We're pretty sure Dario wants to make Rózsa disappear, and we think he's going to do it in China. So we have to get my girl out of there before Dario gets to her, because he won't leave any witnesses."

Chase had already considered that scenario but hadn't expressed her concern to Jack. She was surprised how calm Jack remained right now, knowing what Dario might be up to.

"I'm really very sorry about all this," Heather said, "and I don't mean to sound insensitive, but what do I have to do with it?"

"We need someone to get close to Dario," Jack replied. "We don't know what he looks like and haven't even been able to get a last name."

"I've never seen him, either. Can't the police help?"

"We know you've never seen him. You probably don't know he's in a wheelchair, either."

"I had no idea."

"If we involve the police, they would bring Dario in for questioning, which would lead nowhere, and we'd still be no closer to finding Cass…my girl," Jack said.

"So what do you want me to do?"

"He wants you to go with him to China," Chase said.

"So?"

Chase started squirming again, but she couldn't help it. "We want you—"

"Oh, no," Heather said, as the pieces fell into place. "No way. Forget it. I'm not going anywhere near that creep."

Though they needed her cooperation, Chase was relieved to find out she was right about Heather; she would have never accepted Dario's offer even if it meant a lot of money.

"I'm never going anywhere near him *ever again.*"

"Heather, I know the guy is scary, but we'll have your back the whole time," Chase said. "We won't let anything happen to you."

"Oh, really? Will you take my place when he wants to be entertained? Because just the thought of having to…be around him makes me sick to my stomach."

"I understand it must be difficult to—"

"Difficult? It's difficult the first ten times. After that, it's downright disgusting. I know what you both must think of me. That I'm some kind of…of…whore. But I'm not. Doing this, week after week, man after man, satisfying the needs of whoever can…afford you. Do you have any idea how revolting it is? How degrading, to have to pretend you enjoy it? How demeaning, to accept their money like they've just done you a favor? All of them, without exception, think I actually enjoy it." She laughed, almost manically. "I don't know any woman in this business who enjoys it. It's all a farce. One big joke."

Chase could feel Jack staring at her.

"I make them all feel they're special, like stallions that have just mounted the world. But when it's all said and done, the joke's on me."

Chase couldn't look at Heather, and Jack wouldn't stop staring at *her*. She hadn't deluded herself into believing the call girls she paid lived the romance of their life during those hours, but she never considered they might feel nauseated afterward. She refused to believe that.

"But I digress," Heather said bitterly.

"I won't pretend to know how it is on your end," Chase said. "But I'll do everything in my power to make sure you don't have to sleep with anyone for Dario."

"Not for Dario, not for anyone. I'm done with this. I just can't do it anymore. Not for my career, not even for my brother."

"Heather, we'll protect you at all times," Jack said.

Chase struggled to remain professional and keep to the needs of their mission. Personally, she was glad Heather wanted to stop this life, and if it was up to her, she'd keep her as far away from

Dario as she could. But she was being paid to save Lynx and stop Rózsa. "All you have to do is help us ID him."

"Catch him at the airport," Heather said.

"We've already looked into that. We can't find a Dario booked for China. He's either travelling under a false ID or privately."

"I'm not going anywhere near a creep who buys viruses and hides behind two-way mirrors. And…oh, yeah, knows everything about me."

"He doesn't deal in viruses. That's Rózsa," Jack said.

"So why does Dario owe him?"

"Because he buys organs from Rózsa. Dario's so-called furniture business is a front for a black-market organ ring," Chase replied.

Heather looked horrified. "Organs?"

"Rózsa used human guinea pigs to test the virus," Chase explained. "Once he was done with them, he sold their organs to help fund his research."

"He killed them?"

"Are you surprised?" Jack asked. "Look at how many died because of the virus. The guy's a sick son of a bitch."

"And you want me to walk into this madness eyes wide open?"

"Like I said, I won't let anything happen to you," Chase forced herself to say, though she knew all too well the risk Heather would be taking and that even the best-laid plans went wrong. Stay focused, she kept repeating to herself.

Heather shook her head. "My answer is still no."

Without warning, Jack dropped to one knee in front of Heather. "I've done a lot in my life. Good things, bad things, and things somewhere in between, but there's one thing I've never done, even when my life depended on it." Jack paused and looked down. When she looked at Heather again, Chase could see tears rolling down Jack's cheeks. "I've never begged anyone to help me. But Cassady is my everything." Her voice broke. "If I lose her, I lose everything. Please don't let me lose her." She placed her hand on Heather's and Heather didn't pull away; instead she caressed it.

"I'm so sorry, Jack," she said in a soft voice.

Jack turned to Chase. "I can't lose her again."

Chase had never seen Jack like this, and her heart broke when she saw her crying. She would give everything to take her pain away right then. She looked at Heather. "Heather, it's not just Cassady who's in danger."

Jack got back on the couch but looked miserable.

"What do you mean?" Heather asked.

Chase pulled the last trump card from her pocket. If this didn't work, they were on their own. She turned on Francine Shelhorn's cell, flipped through the pictures until she found the one she needed, and held the phone up for Heather to see.

"Gigi!" Heather covered her mouth in shock. "She's my friend."

"We found her phone at the house she called you from, the night she disappeared," Chase said.

"Where is she?"

"We don't know," Chase replied. "What we do know is that she made a 911 call that night saying Dario was going to kill her."

"Dario? She never met Dario." Heather got up. "Gigi… Francine is dead?"

"I don't know. But it's the last time she was seen and his was the only name she mentioned."

"So she could still be alive, right?" Heather looked from Jack to Chase, seeming desperate for one of them to give her hope. "Maybe he kidnapped her, the way Rózsa kidnapped your girlfriend," she said to Jack.

"I can't answer that, Heather," Jack replied.

"I mean, what else would he want with Francine? Why would he hurt her? Dario always pays. He wouldn't have to resort to violence if he wanted sex."

Chase didn't reply and Jack kept looking at the floor.

"Oh, my God. Do you think he killed her for…for organs?" Heather looked appalled.

"We don't know." Although Chase's gut knew the answer, she couldn't bring herself to tell Heather, and apparently neither could Jack.

Heather visibly paled. "Do you think he wants me to join him so he can…can…"

"No, he wouldn't take you to China for that. I think he's actually smitten with you," Chase said between gritted teeth.

"I think I'm going to be sick." Heather swayed unsteadily, and Chase ran to her side and put her arm around her waist. Heather was shaking uncontrollably and Chase feared she'd pass out.

"Maybe you should sit down," she said.

Heather let her help her to the couch, and Chase made her sip some water.

"I can't believe that bastard killed Francine," she said when she'd composed herself.

"He's hurt a lot of girls like your friend," Jack said gently. "And you can help us stop him."

Heather looked up at Chase, who was hovering over her to make sure she was okay. "I'll do it."

CHAPTER TWENTY-THREE

Mouchamps, France
Next day, November 23

Claude Theroux's evening was looking up. As the most recent hire on Mouchamps's small police force, he was assigned to work the least desirable shift—evenings and weekends—and except for the occasional bar brawl it made for a generally boring routine. The schedule had also put a crimp in his efforts to woo the new clerk at the flower shop, but Therese had worked late tonight preparing bouquets for a wedding and happily agreed to let Claude walk her home.

As they ambled slowly toward her apartment, he said, "Please tell me you've no plans for tomorrow evening as yet. I apologize for asking on such short notice, but my days off just changed so I didn't know I'd be free."

Therese frowned. "I'm afraid I've made dinner plans. I promised my parents I'd drive up to see them, and they'd be horribly disappointed if I didn't."

Claude's heart sank. A lot of other young men in the village had their eye on Therese—she wouldn't stay unattached for long. "The morning, then? I'll take you to breakfast, and we can spend the day however you like until you have to leave. Please say yes."

Therese paused and smiled up at him. "I'd love to. And perhaps if we're having too much fun, I'll have to take you with me."

"I'll do my very best to ensure that is the case," he replied. It wasn't until after he'd said good night that he realized he'd completely forgotten about his promise to his aunt Agnes. She'd been nagging him to do her a favor, and he'd told her that morning he would take care of it on his day off.

His shift ended at ten p.m., which was entirely too late to be dropping in, unannounced, on anyone. But perhaps the man she'd asked him to see might still be up and he could get the matter out of the way. If not, he could at least tell his aunt he'd stopped by and would try again.

Truth be told, he felt a little sorry for the man he was going to visit, the newcomer his aunt called Monsieur Elusive. He was Gwenn Etienne's new neighbor, and Gwenn was the village's most notorious busybody, so Claude pitied anyone within striking distance of her gossip and unrelenting scrutiny. Most likely, the man was simply a reclusive bachelor, or perhaps a foreigner still uncomfortable about interacting with locals, and that was why he was rarely seen outside his cottage.

He got into his Mini Cooper and headed toward the address his aunt had supplied. Gwenn Etienne's house was dark as he went by, but a light was still on in the back of the cottage next door, so he parked and used his flashlight to negotiate through the weed-choked walkway.

Claude knocked twice, loud enough to be heard at the back of the cottage. When a minute went by with no response, he knocked again, even louder, and called out, "Hello? Is anyone home? I'm with the village police department, and I'd like to speak with you for a moment."

He heard a distant, muted sound from within. It almost sounded like a shout of some kind, but he couldn't make it out. He tried again. "Hello? Are you all right?"

The loud click of the bolt startled him, but he regained his composure before the door opened. A man with dark hair and a beard, dressed in crumpled trousers and a work shirt, stood before him, taking in Claude's uniform with interest. "How can I help you, Officer?" the man asked in heavily accented English.

Claude responded in English. "I'm sorry to trouble you so late, sir. But your neighbors were concerned that you haven't been seen much since you arrived and wanted me to make sure everything was all right." When the man scowled in annoyance, he added, "We're a small community, and we look out for each other."

Just then, Claude heard that muted shout again. Louder, now that the door was open, and it sounded like a woman's voice. He looked curiously past the homeowner, but could see no one else inside. "Do you live alone, sir?"

"That's just my radio," the man replied. "I left it on in my workshop. I appreciate your concern, Officer, but I'm fine, I assure you. Now, if you'll excuse me, I was just about to turn in." He started to close the door, but Claude put a hand on it to stop him.

"I'd like to come in and take a look around, if you don't mind," Claude said. Something wasn't right about the man's haste to get rid of him, not to mention the odd shouts, punctuated by silence.

"Is that really necessary?" the man asked, clearly uncomfortable with the idea.

"It won't take long."

The man hesitated for another few seconds before he opened the door and stepped aside. "If you must."

Claude entered and took in his surroundings. The place needed maintenance badly. A draft of cool air came from the ancient windows, and a long crack marred one of the walls. Not surprising, really—he couldn't remember the last time anyone had lived here. "I can't place your accent," Claude said as he went from the living room into a bedroom, the homeowner trailing behind him. "Eastern Europe?"

"Croatia."

He next came to a bathroom and storage closet. Nothing seemed unusual. "May I have your name, sir?"

"Josip Klaric. Really, Officer, is this necessary? I'm a very private man, and I don't value—"

"I'm almost through. I appreciate your indulgence." As he headed into the kitchen, Claude heard another shout—louder now, and he could make out the word for the first time. *Help.* It was coming from the basement, and it didn't sound like any radio program he'd ever heard. "I'd like to see what's downstairs," he said as he turned toward the homeowner.

Claude registered the odd smile on the man's face a split second before he saw the flash of something large and metallic coming at his head. He had no time to react.

❖

New York

Heather spotted Brett and Jack waiting outside her apartment building while she was still a block away, returning home from a workday that had been anything but productive. She was too preoccupied with the previous night's events and her upcoming trip to China to do much more than the minimum her job required, and her exhaustion from little sleep was rapidly catching up with her.

Before they'd departed, Brett and Jack told her they'd be back the next night to prepare for her phone call to Dario, but she hadn't expected them to be waiting for her.

Brett stood at the base of the steps, a small duffel in her hand, and Jack was next to her. Both watched Heather approach.

She'd been nervous all day about having to contact Dario, and the fact that both women were anxious for her to make that call didn't help her nerves. Was she crazy to do this? Gigi was most likely beyond saving, yet she had volunteered to help two complete strangers by joining a murdering organ thief. Was her life in such a dip she'd do anything for a rush? Doubtful. Heather had never been the adventurous type, and aside from Direct Connect, her life had consisted of comfortable flat lines. So why had she agreed to help this organization? Was it revenge for what Dario did to Gigi? Maybe. Heather hoped her anger would be enough to fuel the courage she'd need to see this through.

"Hi," Heather said to both women as she passed them and headed up the stairs, avoiding eye contact with Brett as she unlocked the door. She was still very uncomfortable with the truths Brett knew about her. No wonder Brett had seemed nearly appalled at the idea of their meeting being a date. Heather's worst angst had finally become reality, and she was afraid she was just about to step into a situation that would give her a brand-new kind of horror.

Brett and Jack looked eager to get started, and their disregard for her feelings irritated her.

"No second thoughts?" Brett asked as she entered the apartment.

"Plenty, and constantly, so let's make this call before I change my mind."

"Heather, you have to be sure about this."

"I feel like I'm about to lock myself up in a cage with a lion. I'm afraid, okay?"

"Fear is a good thing," Jack said. "It means you're not stupid."

"I'm glad you noticed." Heather hung up her coat as both women stood waiting just inside the door. "I called Massimo. He found Dario's number."

"Massimo?" Brett asked.

"Yes. It was still where Dario left it." Heather wasn't sure why, but Brett was smirking like she was very satisfied with herself. "Are you going to hover all night?" she asked them.

The two women looked at each other. "Dibs on the chair," Jack said as they walked farther into the living room.

"Can I get you something to drink?" Heather asked.

"Scotch," Jack said.

Heather poured a glass of Johnny Walker Black and grabbed two cans of Diet Coke. She set the can down on the coffee table in front of Brett. "Glass?"

Brett smiled. "I'm fine. Thank you."

Heather handed Jack her Scotch and then sat crossed-legged on the floor beside the armchair. Sitting beside Brett on the couch would be too distracting right now, not to mention uncomfortable. "What do I have to do?"

"You're going to start by telling Dario you had second thoughts," Brett said. "He knows you're doing it for the money, so sound like that matters. Ask him how much he's going to pay and say you want it up front."

"Okay." Heather cringed that Brett knew how her job went.

"Let him know you'll want time to yourself to shop and do some sightseeing."

"So I have an excuse to meet you if necessary."

"Correct. And it will be necessary," Brett replied.

"Got it."

"We still have no idea where in China. See if you can get him to reveal that."

"Okay."

"Also, I know you're in no mood, but try to sound upbeat. Like he's going to get his money's worth."

Heather sighed. "Anything else?"

"That's it for now," Brett said. "Once you talk to him and we know it's a go, we'll take it from there."

"What happens then?"

"I'll show you how to contact us, how we can contact you, how to place bugs—just in case we can't get in to do it ourselves—and how to wire yourself."

"I'm going to wear a wire?"

"Only when you're out with him," Brett replied. "We can't risk you wearing it in the room just in case…"

"I don't intend to…" Heather looked away. "Entertain him."

"It's still too risky."

"I get it." Heat rose to Heather's face.

"I'm going to show you tonight how it's done and where to place it." Brett looked away. "We'll get into more details after you make the call."

Heather started to rise to get her phone, but Brett put her hand up to stop her.

"Do you have a private number?" Brett asked.

"No."

"Can I see your cell phone?"

Heather reached for her purse and gave her the cell. "What's wrong?"

"Use this to call him instead." Brett brought up one of the menus on the phone. "I'll hide your caller ID so he can't see your number. He'll see it if you use the landline. Don't give him any more info than he already has."

"I'm surprised he gave me his," Heather said, "since he's so careful about his identity."

"It's a throwaway. He'll use that number and phone once and toss it," Jack said.

Heather took a deep breath to calm her racing heart and dialed Dario's number. "Should I turn on the speaker?"

Brett shook her head. "If he's as paranoid as I know he is, he'll pick up on it. You can always hear the difference."

Dario greeted her before Heather could say a word. "Hello, Heather." Apparently Jack was right, and she was the only one he'd given that number.

"Hi, Dario."

"I was expecting your call. I take it you have agreed to my offer."

"Why are you so sure?" Heather wanted to smack the smugness out of his voice.

"I'm positive you wouldn't have called had you decided to decline."

"I'll do it, Dario, but I have one question and two conditions."

"You want to talk business. How quaint."

"First of all, how much money are we talking here?"

"You will be paid two thousand per day, for the four days."

Heather nearly gasped at the amount. "I can deal with that." She tried to sound nonchalant. "I'd like the money up front."

"Agreed. And your conditions?"

"I want time for myself to shop. Do some sightseeing. I don't plan to sit in the room all day and wait for your return or a dinner appointment."

"You will have plenty of time to do as you wish. I never intended to confine you."

"And you never said where we're staying. I want to be able to leave my brother some information, just in case he can't reach me by cell. He's my priority, as you understand, or I wouldn't be doing this in the first place."

Brett gave her a thumbs-up.

As Dario replied, Heather wrote down *Beijing at the Park Hyatt* and passed the paper to Jack, who was nearest. Jack glanced at it and gave it to Brett, while gesturing to her to make a phone call.

"I'll pass this on to my brother. It looks like we have an agreement." Heather's palms were moist and clammy. This dangerous idea had just turned real. What if she couldn't pull off this Mata Hari stunt?

"I'm thrilled," Dario said. "I will send someone to collect you at your home tomorrow morning at six."

"I'll be ready." Heather hung up, no longer able to tolerate his voice.

She must have looked as shell-shocked as she felt, because Brett's expression went from serious to sympathetic. "You'll do fine."

"Tell me what I need to know. I have to pack."

"Let me make a call first, to arrange our transport and accommodations." Brett got up and walked into the kitchen.

While Brett made her call, Jack began briefing her, first making sure Heather memorized the number where she could reach both of them.

Brett sat back on the couch a few minutes later and dug into the small duffel. She pulled out a round device about the size of a watch battery and held it up. "This is how we'll be able to locate you. Once you're there, we'll give this to you, and you'll hide it in the lining of your purse. You can't take it now, because of security if you're on a commercial flight."

"Okay."

Next, Brett retrieved a similar device from the bag. "This is a bug. In other words, a listening device, so we can hear what's going on in the room." She got to her feet and stepped away from the couch. "Let me show you how to place one."

Heather followed her to her desk and watched as Brett peeled a piece of thin plastic off the device, exposing an adhesive, then affixed it firmly to the bottom of the desk, near the back. "Now you try it." She gave another small mic to Heather. "Always plant them near places where you think conversations take place."

"Got it." Heather sighed. "I can't believe I'm doing this. At least you're not using cameras."

Brett and Jack looked at each other. From their expressions, they seemed to be actually considering it.

"That's out of the question and completely embarrassing," she said firmly.

"No cameras." Brett wouldn't meet her eyes.

It didn't occur to her until that moment that they might have used cameras already. "Have you—"

"No," Jack replied immediately, and she sighed inwardly in relief.

"Let me show you how the wiring works," Brett said.

"How am I going to take all this with me undetected?"

"You won't. We'll hand it to you in China and wire you personally, but you need to know how to, just in case of emergency."

"Okay. What do I do?"

Brett looked at the floor. "Take off your clothes."

Heather gasped. "Do *what*?"

"I can't place them otherwise."

She wanted to get angry at how easily she was expected to undress, but Brett looked so uncomfortable she didn't bother. Not just taking her clothes off, but having to do so in front of two appealing gay women, one of whom she was extremely attracted to, was awkward at best.

Jack coughed loudly and opened a magazine.

"Fine," Heather mumbled, and unbuttoned her blouse while Brett busied herself with the duffel bag.

She stood with her shirt undone, unsure what to do next. She was glad she'd at least chosen one of her nicer bras that morning, but it was too sheer for her to feel entirely comfortable. "How much do I need to take off?"

Brett turned to look at her and her gaze froze on Heather's breasts. "That's fine," she whispered.

Heather couldn't remember the last time someone's stare made her feel so exposed yet so appreciated.

Brett stood less than a foot away. "I'm going to place this, flat surface down, on your chest." Her eyes never left Heather's.

Heather nodded for her to continue.

Brett knelt and placed the small cold device high on her stomach, just beneath her bra, and held it in place with one hand while she handed Heather a small roll of tape with the other. "I'll need two pieces about an inch-and-a-half long."

Heather handed her the first piece. She felt like electricity hit her when Brett's soft fingers brushed her skin to apply the tape. She tried to control her breathing, but the rest of her body was beyond her control. "I'm cold," she lied when she saw her nipples react.

Brett took her time looking at them and then up at her. "It is chilly in here."

Heather handed her the last piece of tape.

Brett maintained eye contact with her as she placed it on top of the device. "Tape it diagonally across and it'll hold." She was so close Heather could feel Brett's breath on her chest.

Brett fished into the duffel again and pulled out a thin, square device about the size of a small iPod. "This is the receiver. I'm going to tape it to your back. If you're doing this alone, try to use a mirror and get it taped securely in roughly the same area."

Heather gave her two more pieces of tape and turned around. She felt Brett place it in the middle of her back, and when she was finished, Brett stood and faced her.

"So far, so good." Heather couldn't look away from Brett's intense gaze; it put her in a trance-like state. "But what happens if I have to wear something a bit more revealing, Brett?"

Brett placed her hands at the top of Heather's slacks. "May I?" she asked.

Heather nodded, too unsure of her voice to speak.

"Call me Landis."

Heather looked at her. "Excuse me?"

As she slowly unbuttoned the slacks and pulled them down a few inches, exposing cream-colored silk panties, she replied, "Brett is a cover for this job. My name is Landis Coolidge." She pulled another bug out of the bag and knelt again in front of Heather. "If you place it here…" Landis looked up at her. "Make sure you shave or—"

"I'm shaved. Was everything you said to me a lie...Landis?" Heather felt strange referring to her that way, but if she'd lied about everything else, maybe she'd also lied about her attraction to Heather.

Landis looked at her panties and with one finger pulled them down enough to expose the smooth flesh above her pubic bone.

She felt a little light-headed when Landis's fingers made contact with her skin, and her hands trembled as she ripped the tape in preparation.

Landis stopped what she was doing and looked at her. "Yes... everything...was a lie." Her voice was heavy with meaning.

"Will you be able to hear me with the mic down there?" Heather managed to say.

"Loud and clear." Landis smiled and got to her feet. "Button everything up so we can make sure you're comfortable and everything is concealed."

She got her pants refastened, but her hands were shaking badly as she started on her shirt.

"Let me help." Landis slowly buttoned her shirt. "The bugs... are you comfortable?"

Heather looked around at her surroundings for the first time since Landis touched her. Jack was still lost in the magazine. She took a few unsteady steps. "I think I'm good." She glanced down at her décolleté to make sure nothing was visible, then up at Landis, who had backed away a couple of steps. "Can you tell?"

"No."

"You guys finished?" Jack asked.

"Yes," she and Landis answered simultaneously, still looking at each other.

"'Bout time. Let's wrap it up. Our fun-packed weekend starts in a few hours."

CHAPTER TWENTY-FOUR

Mouchamps, France
Next day, November 24

Cassady woke groggy, her jaw still aching from Rózsa's blows. Thank God she'd had her fill of water in the shower, because he hadn't been back with food or water since. The malnutrition and dehydration she'd endured were beginning to affect her ability to think clearly, which worried her. Her dreams the night before had been so vivid she could scarcely separate them from reality. She remembered noises and seeing Rózsa down here, telling her to face the wall away from the door…the same wall she was staring at now. She rolled over.

It hadn't been a dream.

A few feet away, out of reach, lay the body of a young man, dressed in a blue policeman's uniform.

Cassady tried to shake off her mental fog as she crawled as close as possible to the man. She was no stranger to corpses in her line of work, so she was able to somewhat detach her emotions as she studied the body, but this new development sent a new thrill of fear through her.

As far as she knew, Rózsa always had others do his dirty work, but this proved he was capable of cold-blooded murder, though he was on the run and being sought by numerous law-enforcement entities. It didn't bode well for what he might do to her if she tried to escape again. And certainly killing a policeman would bring additional and immediate heat on him, so he might do something desperate.

Was the cop here looking for her? Did the EOO know she was alive?

The possibility gave her hope, but she felt partially responsible for the officer's death. No doubt he'd been the man she'd heard knocking on the door last night, the unfamiliar second set of footsteps walking around the kitchen above her head. Her screams had likely sealed the man's fate and made Rózsa take such drastic measures.

She peered at the sleeve patch on the man's uniform. Police Nationale, it read, and beneath that, the blue, white, and red colors of the French flag. So she was in France. Knowing even that tidbit made her feel better. The US had good relations with France, so if the EOO did know she was alive, they'd be able to get local authorities' assistance in searching for her.

Cassady stiffened when she heard Rózsa descend the stairs. She quickly crawled back to her usual place against the wall, putting distance between her and the body.

The sound of the bolt being thrown echoed through the basement. Rózsa came in with a grim expression and glanced from her to the body. "See what you made me do," he said. "His death is on your hands. I should kill you now and be done, all the trouble you have caused me."

"I'm sorry for trying to escape. I won't do it again."

"Lie face-down, with your hands behind you." When she hesitated, he said, "Now, if you want to live another day."

She did as she was told and, a moment later, the weight of his body crushed her, his knees immobilizing her arms. Too weak to fight back and throw him off, she felt the sting of a needle pierce her neck, and all went black.

❖

New York

The limo Dario sent took Heather over the George Washington Bridge to New Jersey and followed the signs to Teeterboro Airport.

When it pulled up to a gate away from the terminal, the driver showed the security guard at the manned booth some credentials and was waved through.

Heather's heart was pumping wildly. Landis and Jack had been right in guessing Dario was flying on a private plane. They passed several hangars, some empty and the others housing a variety of aircraft, from tiny, single-engine prop planes to large corporate and charter jets that could hold twenty or thirty passengers. Most of the buildings had corporate names or logos painted on the front or sides, but the one they stopped beside had only an identification number. The wide bay doors were closed.

The driver got out, took her suitcase out of the back, and opened the door for her. "Come with me, please, miss."

Heather took a deep breath and, on unsteady legs, followed him toward the hangar. *What the hell have I gotten myself into?* She clutched her purse tighter. Her hands shook badly, and she didn't want Dario to know how nervous and afraid she was.

The driver pressed a button beside the enormous doors of the hangar, and they parted to reveal a sleek white jet with black call letters on the tail. From the number of windows, it looked like it could seat fifteen or twenty people, but once inside she saw it had been customized to hold only eight, in two rows of large, comfy recliner chairs. The aisle between them was wider than normal, and the rear of the jet was mostly hidden behind faux-wood partitions.

Aside from the steward—who took her coat and greeted her with, "Welcome, Miss Snyder. My name is Howard. Please make yourself comfortable"—five other men were on board. It wasn't difficult to discern which was Dario.

Four look-alike goons with the build of football players occupied the second row, while a much more diminutive man, probably in his late thirties, had the front row to himself. He was watching her expectantly.

Dario was probably about her height—five six, or seven—and his expensive suit couldn't hide the fact he was unevenly proportioned. His upper arms and chest were well developed and stretched his crisp white shirt and blazer to their limits, while his legs looked bony thin in the matching loose trousers. Jack was right; Dario was dependent on the wheelchair she spotted stashed beside the forward galley. That explained the disparity in his physique.

He looked like an average Joe, neither handsome nor homely. Unremarkable, he would be hard to describe to the cops, except for two distinguishing features—his short, vivid red hair and his pale-blue eyes—the color of ice. He smiled at her, displaying perfect teeth. "Welcome, Heather. I'm Dario."

"Hello, Dario."

"The result of a childhood diving accident," he said, to satisfy her apparently visible curiosity. "I know I'm probably not what you expected. I hope you're not disappointed."

"I had no expectations about you," she replied noncommittally. Heather knew she had to be pleasant to the guy, but his cold stare made her feel naked and exposed.

"Please, make yourself comfortable," he said. When she hesitated, glancing from the seat beside him to the pair across the aisle, he added, "Wherever you like."

Taking him at his word, she chose the window seat across the aisle and buckled in. The bodyguard/steward delivered a coffee to Dario and turned in her direction. "May I get you a beverage, Miss Snyder?"

"Orange juice, please."

He returned with a crystal flute of fresh-squeezed OJ and set it on the tray table beside her.

"Thank you again for agreeing to come with me," Dario said.

"You made it impossible to refuse. Speaking of cash…"

Dario bent down and removed an envelope from his briefcase. "I can see how your reward is tempting," he said, and tossed it to her. "But I'd like to think you enjoy my company."

"You know why I'm doing this."

"Your reasons don't matter. I just hope they won't prevent you from enjoying yourself while you're there."

"I suppose that will depend on what I'm asked to do."

The pilot announced over the intercom that they'd be departing soon and told everyone to buckle up. A small vehicle came into view outside Heather's window and towed the plane out of the hangar. A few minutes later, they were in the air.

She'd give anything to be sure Dario was being truthful about their destination. Given all she now knew about him, it was conceivable he'd lied about everything just to get her to agree to all of this. What if Landis and Jack went to China and this plane ended up on some other continent? She'd have no way of knowing until they landed.

Not long into the flight, the bodyguard/steward returned with menus. "These are the available selections during the flight," he said. "Let me know what you'd like at any time, or if I can be of service in any other way. When you're ready to retire," he told Heather, "I'll show you to your cabin."

"My cabin?"

"We have two sleeping compartments in the back. I'm sure you'll be most comfortable."

Heather glanced at the menu. The impressive selection included filet mignon, chicken cordon bleu, lobster Newburg, veal scaloppini, and oysters Rockefeller. But the lone vegetarian option, a ratatouille, really meant she had no choice at all. Only one option for lunch as well—a Greek salad—and the breakfast choices weren't much better.

"I'm vegetarian," she told the steward, so I'll have the omelet later, if you can leave out the bacon."

"Of course, Miss Snyder. Let me know when you'd like it. And I'm certain I can come up with different meal alternatives for you from our available ingredients on board." The man glanced toward Dario with a look of apology, and in her peripheral vision she saw Dario give him a slight nod.

She took small comfort in the fact that Dario apparently hadn't known *that* about her.

"You look beautiful, as always, Heather," Dario said once the steward had disappeared into the galley. "Forgive me for not saying so earlier."

"I'm happy you approve." She'd been briefly angry with herself for taking so long this morning choosing her outfit. If it were entirely up to Dario, she'd be wearing something sexy—a cocktail dress or something similar, and high heels. So her first inclination had been to go entirely in the opposite direction—faded jeans, T-shirt, and sneakers—both to spite him and because they'd be the most comfortable for the long flight. In the end, she'd compromised, selecting new designer jeans, a white silk blouse, navy blazer, and navy pumps. The ensemble was more businesslike than provocative, which was the impression she wanted to make as they set off on this venture to hell.

Dario made further attempts at forced pleasantries, but she answered in polite, one-word replies. And as soon as she could do so without being rude, she plugged her MP3 headphones into her ears and closed her eyes. She wanted not only to discourage him from further attempts at conversation, she also wanted, at least for a moment, to postpone facing the reality of what she'd gotten herself into.

❖

Near Fort Dix, New Jersey

As Heather departed her Greenwich Village apartment, Chase and Jack arrived at McGuire Air Force Base, ninety minutes away. They parked the surveillance van in the public visitors' lot as Reno instructed and boarded the modified USAF C-37A jet Pierce had arranged for them. Since they could take a military plane only as far as Japan, Pierce had arranged a private jet for the last leg of the journey. Their departure was timed so they would arrive in Beijing ahead of Heather, regardless of whether Dario arranged for a commercial flight or private charter.

As they strapped themselves in, the single crewmember in their compartment, a young crew-cut airman, handed them a duffel. When she'd called headquarters the night before with an update, Chase had read off a list of the gear they might need, and everything she'd asked for was in the bag.

As though by mutual consent, Chase and Jack spoke very little during the long flight. Thoughts of Heather and the uncertainties ahead preoccupied Chase, and she knew Jack was thinking about Cassady. In less than twenty-four hours, they'd both need to put aside their personal worries and focus entirely on Operation Phoenix.

Chapter Twenty-five

Beijing, China
Next day, November 25

After they showered and changed clothes, Chase and Jack left their room and took the elevator to the hotel lobby and reception area on the 63rd floor. The five-star Park Hyatt, in the center of Beijing's Central Business District, was housed within one of the highest skyscrapers in the city, offering guests impressive views of the bustling metropolis. And Dario had obviously chosen the Hyatt for other reasons: its luxury accommodations and contemporary furnishings were more Western than Asian, and many of the staff spoke English.

They ordered espressos as they waited in comfy chairs near the check-in desk and studied the passport photo that Reno e-mailed them upon their arrival. He had searched the hotel's reservations list for a three-night stay for a "Dario" to no avail, but a D. Imperi had booked a luxury suite and two doubles for that period. When he'd cross-checked the name through the US State Department's database of current passports, he'd found a match: a Dario Imperi who resided at the Long Island mansion address registered to Dragons Unlimited. So they finally had a full name and photo of their target, not that it got them closer to Rózsa. They still needed Heather for that. But at least the information enabled Reno to book them a room away from Dario and his men, so Heather wouldn't be seen coming and going if they needed to meet with her.

Chase looked at her watch.

"It's ten minutes later than the last time you checked," Jack said.

"Eleven thirty, to be exact."

"What's your obsession with time, anyway? You've been like that for as long as I can remember. I don't think I've seen you without a watch."

Chase took a sip and turned to face Jack for the first time since they'd sat down. She'd been keeping her gaze fixed on the bank of elevators, so she'd see the moment Heather arrived. "Very small portions of my life are my own. What I do and what is demanded of me are unpredictable and the outcome…uncertain."

Jack sighed. "Yeah. I know the feeling."

"We have no guarantees of there being a tomorrow to get things right."

Jack frowned. "No, we don't."

"I've always felt time is like a shadow that follows me everywhere, reminding me it's running out. I check my watch to make sure it's still running and that I'm moving forward with it, that I'm still alive."

"Sounds like you're so grateful for the time you've been given you focus only on that, instead of what to do with it."

"True, but it is what it is."

"And the novels?"

"They're a distraction from that deafening ticking and an excuse to look forward. I'd go crazy without them." Chase glanced toward the elevators. "What's worst, the older I get, the more time I have to fill, and I simply don't know what to do with it."

"Then maybe you can see why I need Cass in my life. And why, without her…there's no point."

"That I understand. But your self-destruction puzzles me. I can see how much Cass means to you, but you can't let how you treat yourself depend on another. That is your responsibility."

"But I love her so much I can't—"

"Do you value yourself so little?"

"Maybe I do." Jack paused and seemed to consider the idea. "Maybe I need Cass to feel good about myself."

"You need her because you need someone to forgive you."

"Hell knows *I* can't do it."

"Then find a way to cope with your past."

"Gee, Landis, thanks. Why didn't I think of that?"

"Maybe therapy isn't a bad idea."

Jack laughed without humor. "Why would you suggest therapy when the only thing you got out of it was carpet burns? Besides, I'd rather place my head in a blender than in some shrink's hands."

"Have you tried it?"

"For a month. He asked me to leave when I threatened to shoot him."

"You what?"

"I don't deal well with criticism."

"I can see that about you." Chase laughed. "So what free prize, aside from memory impairment, do you seek at the bottom of every whisky bottle?"

Jack raised one eyebrow. "What's your aloofness a disguise for?"

"You go first."

"Redemption," Jack answered.

"Fear," Chase said.

"Of?"

"Caring for someone."

Jack didn't react. Both sat back in silence with their espressos and thoughts.

Chase returned her attention to the elevators and almost jumped when she saw Heather emerge from one. "She's—"

"I know," Jack said.

Heather looked calm, but the tightness around her eyes gave away her apprehension. Beside her, Dario was being wheeled by the same guy who'd accompanied him at the brownstone, and another three men walked behind them.

The guy pushing Dario wheeled him up to the desk and then waited with the other goons, off to one side. Heather stood a few feet away at the counter with her hands in her coat pockets.

"Let's go," Chase said.

Both of them approached the reception area. Jack paused a couple of feet from the desk—strategically blocking Dario's men from seeing what they were about to do—while Chase slid up to the counter beside Heather and blocked Dario's view.

Out of the corner of her eye, Chase saw Heather look at her briefly. With Jack hovering behind them, Chase slipped a tracker and cell phone into Heather's coat pocket. Before she pulled her hand away, Chase touched Heather's hand reassuringly, and Heather squeezed hers in return.

Chase then motioned to one of the two receptionists. "Room 506, please," she said, and waited for the keycard. She glanced at Heather briefly as she turned to go, and then she and Jack remained within earshot, chatting, until the receptionist handed Dario four keycards.

"This one is for the Presidential Suite," the woman told him. "It's on the 48th floor."

Dario took his and left the other cards on the counter for his men to figure out.

"Let's go, Heather," he said. He wheeled himself toward the elevator, with Heather following, and they disappeared inside.

Chase discreetly watched them go. For a reason she couldn't understand, all she wanted to do right then was take Heather away from everything.

❖

Heather walked silently behind Dario as they entered the Presidential Suite. Though the opulence of the accommodations shocked her, she kept her face impassive to prevent Dario from gaining any satisfaction from her reaction. In addition to the magnificent views, the suite was twice as large as her apartment and offered such amenities as a fully equipped kitchen, living room, work area, flat-screen TV, and marble bathroom. She'd never seen—let alone stayed in—any place nearly this luxurious. It was a shame the situation wouldn't allow her to really enjoy it. The major selling points for her at this moment weren't the built-in espresso machine or plush Turkish cotton robes, but the two bedrooms, one on each end of the suite, so she'd have at least some privacy.

"You're very quiet, Heather. Aren't you pleased with the arrangements?" Dario asked.

"The hotel is nice, I guess."

"Maybe some rest will do you good. I have a two o'clock business lunch, and I'd like you to join me."

She knew she'd have to be seen with him sooner or later, but she hadn't counted on it being within a few hours of their arrival. She would have to inform Landis and Jack as soon as possible. "Great. I'm starved. Where are we eating?"

"At the China Grill on the 66th floor. You will find the menu most satisfying, and it has 360-degree views of the city."

"I'm going to take a walk around. I'm too restless to stay in."

"As you wish, as long as you're ready on time for me to pick you up."

"I'll be ready." She couldn't help but cringe now every time he asked her for anything. As soon as she was alone in her bedroom, she pulled out the cell Landis had left in her coat pocket. She typed **Lunch at 2 in the China Grill** and sent it. A minute later she got a reply: **Come see me ASAP**.

Heather showered first, because once Landis wired her she wouldn't be able to, then pulled on a pair of jeans, a sweater, and sneakers, and left for room 506. She didn't know where Dario's men were staying, so she took the stairs and kept looking over her shoulder to make sure no one was around.

Landis opened the door as soon as she knocked.

"How are you coping?" she asked as Heather entered.

"I'm scared."

"Just a couple more days and all this will be a bad memory."

"He has a business lunch at two on the 66th floor. But he didn't say who he's meeting."

"We'll be there watching. You have nothing to worry about. Trust me."

"Why does everyone think I should trust them? Dario keeps repeating that like a mantra. I don't trust anyone."

"Good," Jack said, as she came out of the bedroom and joined them in the sitting area. "All you need to do is trust in yourself."

"I'm not sure I do."

"*I* do," Landis said. "I know you can do this."

Heather sighed. "Up high or down low?" She spread her arms and legs to expose her body.

Landis pursed her lips in thought as she gave Heather a once-over, her gaze stopping on her chest. "Take off your sweater."

She did as she was told, but this time avoided eye contact with Landis while she taped everything in place. The fast yet gentle hands sent the same shocks through her body as the first time, but she tried to concentrate on the wall in front of her.

"Make sure you wear something appropriate," Landis said.

"What do I do with all this when I retire for the night?" she asked as she pulled on her sweater.

"Turn off the receiver after you untape everything and hide it all in a sock."

"Will panty hose do? It's all I brought."

Before Landis could answer, Jack darted back into the bedroom. "Incoming," she called, and Landis turned to catch a pair of black socks.

"This works better." Landis handed them to her, then reached into her pocket and pulled out an audio bug. "Plant this in your bedroom. We'll see you in the restaurant."

"This meeting…do you think it's with Rózsa?" she asked.

"I doubt Rózsa would show his face in public, but it could lead to finding out where he is."

"I can't bear to be around Dario. What he does makes me sick to my stomach."

"I know."

"But you'll be there the whole time, right?" she asked.

"Every single step of the way," Landis replied. "Tru…I won't let anything happen to you."

Heather didn't immediately return to the suite so Dario would think she really had gone for a walk. She took the elevator to the ground floor and went outside, allowing herself at least a few minutes to appreciate that she was halfway around the world, in a country she'd long dreamed of visiting. She walked a couple of blocks, watching passersby, many of whom openly stared at her, and took in all the exotic smells and sights of the bustling city she could absorb in such a limited time.

The distraction actually helped calm her nerves, so when Dario knocked on her bedroom door a few minutes before two, she was ready both in appearance and mental fortitude. She'd freshened her hair and makeup, and donned a tastefully sexy red dress. Matching three-inch heels completed the ensemble.

Dario examined her from top to bottom, which gave her chills. "You look absolutely breathtaking." He licked his lips.

"Thank you," she said halfheartedly, not even trying to sound flattered.

He frowned. "Have you not rested sufficiently?"

"I'm fine."

The restaurant was as magnificent as their suite. Plush booths lined the entire perimeter of the skyscraper, and the ceiling above each one, as well as the exterior wall, was made of glass, so every patron had a spectacular view of both the city and the sky.

"And where did your walk take you this afternoon?" Dario asked.

"I didn't venture far," she replied as the waiter pulled the chair for her. "Enough to get some fresh air and do some window shopping."

"If you see anything you like, let me know. I can have whatever you want delivered to the suite."

"Thank you, but that won't be necessary. I've been buying my own wardrobe since I was fifteen."

"It would be my pleasure to gift you with anything you want."

"That won't be necessary, Dario," she repeated. She tried not to sound irritated, but his insistence on making her play the role of his mistress was getting to her.

"Ah, there's my appointment."

A blond man in his late thirties stopped at their table. Heather could tell his suit cost what she made in two months. He was fairly attractive, with an air of someone who got the job done. He smiled down at her, barely acknowledging Dario.

"And who is this delightful creature?" he asked in a thick British accent as he offered his hand to her.

"This is my—"

"I'm Heather." When she held out her hand as well, the stranger bent to kiss it.

"And I'm Oliver." He half straightened until his face was close to hers. "How much is he paying you?"

Heather looked away as she tried to hide her embarrassment. Was she that obvious?

"Don't take it personally, Heather," Oliver said. "But you aren't the type of woman to voluntarily…date someone like Dario."

Damn right, she thought.

"Heather and I have been seeing each other for years," Dario said. Heather could tell he was irritated, but she was frankly almost flattered his associate thought she was too good for him.

"Of course." Oliver took a seat. "Your taste in everything has always been immaculate and no doubt…expensive," he added, looking at her. He placed his linen napkin on his lap. "I have only an hour to brief you on tomorrow's meeting, so let's order."

Dario lifted his hand slightly and two servers materialized at his side. One handed out open menus while the sommelier recited the wine list.

"Would you like me to order?" Dario asked her.

"I think I can manage."

"She's got spunk," Oliver said.

Dario placed his hand on her knee. "That's what I like about her."

She pushed it away without thinking. "I'm actually at the table."

"Forgive us," Dario said sternly.

"Well," Oliver said as the wine was being poured, "lovers' quarrel aside, I'd like to get down to business. Your meeting is tomorrow and he expects to see figures. Also, I understand your people expressed some concerns regarding the quality and delivery time. If you wish, I can escort you to our facilities to verify the process of selection and implementation."

"I wasn't aware there were trepidations," Dario replied.

"Maybe you need to consult your employer."

"That won't be necessary." Dario sounded offended. "I intended a tour on this trip, anyway."

The waiter came back for their orders and Heather wondered how long she'd have to sit through this discussion. Oliver was clearly not their man, and the content of their discussion disturbed her, considering Dario's so-called furniture company was a front for the organ trade. Was he being asked to visit a slaughterhouse? The thought made her sick to her stomach.

She placed her order first. As the two men made their selections, she looked around casually, hoping to see Landis, certain that just a glimpse of her would give her strength and reassurance. She spotted her at a corner booth with Jack, lifting a forkful of noodles to her mouth.

Landis turned her way mere seconds later, and when their eyes met, she gave Heather a discreet nod.

After a few minutes of small talk about the restaurant, she asked Oliver, "Are you here on business, too?"

"No such luck. I live here," he replied.

"Are you in the furniture business like Dario?"

"You could say that. I make sure all transactions go smoothly. The Chinese are not exactly fluent in English and their manners leave a lot to be desired. Very cutthroat, if you know what I mean." He smiled. "And how about you? What line of business are you in?" he asked provocatively.

"I design clothes for a small house," she replied as the waiter arrived with their food.

"And you have dreams of one day owning your own label?"

"Yes."

"Well, if the old man can't help you on your way, maybe I can…take his place, shall we say."

"Thank you, but that won't be necessary." She picked at her plate. Her Luóhàn zhāi, or Buddha's Delight, looked delicious, but she had no appetite.

"You're being rude, Oliver." Dario dabbed at his face with his napkin. "Heather belongs to me. It would be wise to remember that."

"I do not belong to anyone," she said, barely containing her anger.

"Forgive me," Oliver said to her. "But I've got to hand it to you, Dario. You've managed to make me jealous." He winked at her.

"There's nothing much to be jealous about." She placed her hand on Dario's wheelchair to make a point.

Oliver laughed out loud. "I don't know what arrangement you two have, but I wouldn't mind being part of the…show."

Heather couldn't win this battle. Both men either wanted to own or screw her, and the more she had to endure this discussion the closer she felt to sticking her butter knife in Dario's thigh. She ate a few mouthfuls in silence as the two men talked about the Chinese economy and other things she could care less about.

As soon as the server cleared the table, Oliver stood. "I'm afraid I have another appointment. It was a pleasure, Heather, and should you feel the need for company while Dario is away, let me know." He dropped a business card in front of her. "I'll make it worth your while." Then he pivoted to shake Dario's hand. "I'll be in touch."

"That was a most unplea—" Dario's cell phone rang. He frowned when he checked the caller ID. "What now?" he mumbled.

"Yes?" He turned away from her. "Why are you calling me?" He was obviously annoyed. "I thought we were done." He listened for a few seconds. "I can't authorize another transaction. The first one almost cost me my head." He listened some more, frowning. When he spoke again, his clipped tones indicated someone struggling not to lose his temper. "I don't care if you're in trouble, you should have thought about the risks beforehand. And don't try to send any more cards. I've cancelled that address."

Whatever the caller said next only infuriated Dario more. His tone uncharacteristically angry, he kept his voice low, but she was sitting so close she could hear every word. "Listen, you idiot, if you think you can destroy me and my business, you're a fool. You would have to expose yourself if you did, and you know what that means." More silence before Dario spoke again. "You can call me then, but my answer will still be the same."

Without even a glance in her direction, Dario disconnected and made another call.

"It's me. Our Hungarian wholesaler called and wants more money." The response from the other end made him angrier still. "How should I know?" He pounded his fist on the table.

She tried to act as though she weren't listening.

"We have to take care of this before he does something stupid, and you know the desperate ones always do," Dario said. He listened again. "What do you want me to do?" he asked with a tone of desperation. More listening. "Decide and call me back?"

Dario glanced over at her with an irritated expression. "Make it at eight," he told the person on the other end. "I have some business before that."

Chapter Twenty-six

Chase glanced toward Jack to see whether she was drawing the same conclusions about the phone conversation they'd heard through their earpieces.

"Sounds like our man," Jack said. "And it appears as though they want to make him go away permanently."

"There's supposed to be another call tonight."

"Whoever was on the other end has a plan. It's looking more and more like Dario is someone's peon."

"We have to get into his room if we want to hear the rest of that conversation and who's calling the shots."

"Damn." Jack blew out an exasperated breath. "He has two guys guarding his door."

"We could trigger the emergency alarm."

Jack shook her head. "Could make him suspicious when it turns out to be nothing. He'll have his dogs search the room before he gets back in."

Chase checked her watch. "And his call is in three hours. He'll have to make that call from elsewhere if they won't allow people back in until they figure out it was a false alarm."

Heather's voice in their ear interrupted their discussion, so they went silent to listen in.

"I don't know about you, but I could use a nap," Heather said to Dario after he hung up. He was clearly in a bad mood and she didn't feel like sticking around.

Dario exploded. “I asked you to accompany me like a proper lady. I expect you to *act* like one.”

“What do you mean?” She tried to sound innocent. Maybe a taste of his own demeaning medicine would put him in his place.

“You’ve had this superior if not downright rude attitude since you got on the plane. If I wanted to be ignored and degraded, I would have made this trip with my sister.”

“I thought I *was* being polite, considering your associate wanted to jump my bones.”

“You practically invited him to your bed.”

“I did no such thing.”

“But you didn’t stop his insinuations or decline his card. Instead, you seemed flattered. I did not bring you here to score a new client. Your place is with me, and your body only for *me*.”

“My body is my own.”

“Not for the money I’m paying you. Furthermore, you are to act like my date and not a harlot.”

“My acting abilities only go so far,” she said calmly. “I can’t pretend you didn’t pay me to be here.”

“Very well.” Dario threw his napkin on the table. “If you insist on acting like a whore, then you shall be treated like one.”

“What’s that supposed to mean?”

“Besides, you appear to be considerably more compliant and pleasant after you’ve…worked.”

“I don’t know where you’re going with—”

“I want you to pick someone up right now.”

She gasped audibly. “You can’t be serious.”

“And then I want you to bring him to the suite, so you can please me. You’ve been nothing but recalcitrant. Maybe this will remind you who calls the shots.”

“I don’t want to. We’re *staying* here. I can’t pick someone up in the same hotel.” She was desperate for an excuse to change his mind.

“I frankly don’t give a damn about what you want,” he said with a smug expression. “Courtesy apparently hasn’t worked with you. Perhaps crudeness will.”

She tried to remain calm and think of a way out of this predicament. What complicated matters was the fact she was wired. If Dario asked his men to force her back to the room to entertain, she'd be screwed.

She glanced over at Landis's booth. She and Jack seemed to be in a serious conversation, and Landis looked angry.

Heather had to do something before Dario picked someone for her and it was too late. "I need to go to the ladies' room," she said, setting her napkin on the table. She got up slowly and reached for her purse, hoping to catch Landis's attention.

The opulent restroom was empty. She went into a stall and prayed for Landis to show up, her mind working overtime on what to do. Take off the wire? She heard a soft knock on her door and jumped because she hadn't heard anyone come in.

"Heather, it's me," Landis said.

"Thank God." Heather opened the door. "I suppose you heard what he wants me to do."

Landis's jaw was tight. "I did. I heard that and a lot more."

"You mean the two calls."

"Whoever was on the phone with him sounded a lot like Rózsa, and the second call sounded like someone was directing Dario about what to do. Dario's getting a call back from them tonight at eight for more instructions so we have to bug his room."

"How?"

"I'm going to place them."

"How are you getting in? He has men at the—"

"He wants you to pick someone out to entertain him."

"I refuse to. I told you that before we ever left for China. You promised me I wouldn't have to. He can go to hell."

"Yes, I promised you wouldn't have to entertain him again, but this could work to our advantage."

Did Landis really think she would have sex with someone in order to help her mission? She didn't know what hurt more, the fact that Landis expected her to do that, or the fact that it didn't bother her.

But why *should* it bother her? Landis knew what she did. She'd even listened in while she did it. Why did she think even for a moment that Landis might be upset if she had to sleep with yet another client? "I'm not going to…to have sex just to help you out. I agreed to this crazy plan, but screwing someone wasn't part of it."

Landis met her eyes. "I'm coming in as your…client."

Heather's face flushed hot. "No way."

"Listen to me. I need to get in the room, and you have to find someone. If we combine both, no one gets hurt."

"I'm not going to have sex with you. I can't."

Landis went silent and turned to wash her hands. She looked at Heather in the mirror above the sink. "I promise you won't have to. I'll be fast, so you won't have to suffer very long." Her voice was serious, her expression indecipherable. "Just pretend to go through the motions."

"I always do."

"Then it shouldn't be a problem. It's either me, or you run and this whole operation goes to hell."

She sighed. "Fine."

"Let me help you remove the wire," Landis said.

"I can manage." She ducked back into the stall, took off the bug and transmitter, and placed them in her purse. She went to the door. "Wait for me at the bar."

"Have you picked our man yet?" Dario asked as soon as she sat down.

"No. I can't say I want to."

"I can't say I'm very interested in your disposition at the moment. Now pick someone, or I will."

"Very well." She looked around the restaurant. "I'm in the mood for a woman. I hope you don't have any objections."

He looked surprised, but pleased. He licked his lips. "Who do you have in mind?"

"The tall blonde at the bar." She indicated Landis with a tilt of her head. She was pretty sure he'd agree to the proposition. Landis did look hot, in black trousers, a crisply ironed shirt that matched the deep blue of her eyes, and a tailored black blazer.

Dario looked at Landis, then back at Heather. "She'll do."

She asked the waiter to serve the woman at the bar whatever she was drinking. Moments later, Landis looked her way and Heather lifted her glass and smiled.

Landis pretended to look surprised, then brought her glass to their table. "Thank you for the drink."

"Why don't you join us?" She smiled seductively. "I'm Heather, and this is Dario."

Landis took a seat next to her. "Brett. Nice to meet you. Are you and your husband here on business or...pleasure?"

Dario smiled, obviously satisfied with Landis's conclusion of his relationship to Heather. "A bit of both," he said.

Heather put her hand on Landis's knee and moved it slowly and provocatively upward along her muscled thigh. Dario openly stared at the interaction.

"He takes care of the business end, and I the pleasure." She looked Landis straight in the eyes. She didn't know what she expected to see there, but it wasn't the look of raw desire Landis returned. *She's either played this role before or...or what?*

Landis leaned forward until her mouth was an inch away from hers. "Any suggestions for where we can all get some pleasure?"

"My husband likes to watch," Heather said.

"Suits me fine." Landis never took her eyes off her.

"Why don't we take this to our suite?" Dario suggested.

Landis turned to him for the first time. "Yes, let's."

❖

Belesta-en-Lauragais, France

Cassady woke to birdcalls, and when she opened her eyes the brilliant, welcome sunshine after her long days of darkness was initially painful. Her head ached and she felt hung over, but she retained enough of her faculties to know immediately she'd been moved from the basement.

Her muscles cramped badly and she couldn't move. Hazily, she realized her hands and feet were tightly bound, her mouth gagged with duct tape, and she was lying in a bathtub.

She remembered Rózsa injecting her with something, and the body of the policeman. Evidently he'd gotten away before anyone came around inquiring about the cop's disappearance and had taken her with him. Where were they now?

Grunting from the exertion, she tried to maneuver herself so she could see more of the room, only then realizing he'd hog-tied her, too. She could barely see over the lip of the enormous steel tub, and only then through maximum effort.

The bathroom was tiny. A sink, tub, and toilet, the usual toilet paper and toilet brush, a couple of towels, and some soap. On a little shelf beside the tub, three small plastic bottles filled with shampoo, conditioner, and bath gel. A closed cabinet beneath the sink hinted at more resources, but she had little chance of breaking her bindings and getting to it.

The window that let the sunlight in was too high to reach and too small to fit through. The ceiling light fixture above consisted of a cheap plastic cover over a single bulb.

Where was Rózsa? She listened intently, but could hear no sounds except the birdcalls.

She tried unsuccessfully to work up some spit to loosen the duct tape. She'd been without water too long.

Water.

The faucet for the bathtub was on the end near her feet. If she could maneuver herself around, maybe she could turn one of the handles with her chin, get some water flowing, loosen the tape.

At least then she could scream for help.

Andor Rózsa sat in front of the window, the sheer curtain pulled so he could see out clearly, but anyone outside would notice only a silhouette. Not that he had much to worry about, at least for the moment. No one had walked by all morning, and as far as he could tell, they were the only guests. He was fortunate it was the off-season.

For a hastily chosen stopping point, it could be worse. The Le Moulin Pastelier Guest House lay between Toulouse and

Carcassonne, in a region filled with vineyards and farmland and dotted with small lakes. The converted sixteenth-century brick structure was remote, but only ten minutes from the A61 highway.

By the time he'd moved the policeman's car out of sight in bushes near his cottage, hastily packed his things, and moved his hostage, it had been after midnight. He'd had only eight hours of darkness to get as far away as possible and find a place to hole up where he could figure out what to do. He'd been lucky to spot the small, dark sign to the guesthouse an hour before sunrise.

The sleepy proprietor had happily agreed to let him have his pick of the rooms and see himself in without assistance. The corner room he'd picked was farthest from the owner's, on the opposite end of the converted farmhouse.

Now, he needed a plan.

They couldn't stay here long. They had to get somewhere much more private as soon as the owner retired tonight and it was safe to leave. He was too recognizable as it was, and the situation could quickly get worse. It had been weeks since his image had been plastered all over the news, but it might soon be again if they managed to connect him to the murdered policeman. Who knew whether, even now, the proprietor of the guesthouse might be seeing his face on his television? Andor had managed to keep the man from getting a good look at him in the dark, but he couldn't avoid him for long.

He had to move them to another private home, or somewhere equally suitable, and that took money. More money than he'd gotten from Dario. He couldn't rely on getting his own money back from his hostage's people.

So he'd squeezed Dario again, this time for half a million US dollars. But Dario had resisted, and he wasn't sure he would comply.

Andor glanced at his watch. He'd give Dario another few hours to think about it. While he waited, he'd catch some much-needed rest.

He lay down and was nearly asleep when he heard the sound of water running. He bolted from bed and hurried into the bathroom.

His hostage had her head under the tub faucet and was trying to remove her gag.

Alarm and fury drove him across the room. He pummeled her face with his fists until she groaned and lay still, her blood mixing with the water to form a pale-pink pool around her.

He turned off the water and went to get some sleep.

CHAPTER TWENTY-SEVEN

Beijing, China

Chase trailed Dario and Heather as they entered the Presidential Suite so she could scope out the place. Doors off to the right and left of the spacious main area of the suite no doubt led to bathrooms and bedrooms, but she didn't know which was Heather's and which was Dario's.

"Why don't you make our visitor comfortable, Heather?" Dario wheeled himself into the living area.

Heather turned to Chase. "Please, sit down. Can I get you something to drink?"

"Thank you, I'm fine." She removed her blazer and sat on the wide, plush couch, legs apart and one arm resting on the back.

"You seem quite comfortable," Dario said. "I take it this isn't your first time."

"I'm forty and chronically single. I left first times behind me a long time ago."

She hoped Heather would relax before Dario realized how much she wasn't into her. She looked so stressed and uneasy she was going to blow the whole operation and get them into serious trouble. "Why don't you join me?" She nodded subtly and reassuringly.

"Don't keep our guest waiting." Dario tried to sound polite but she caught the agitated undertone.

As soon as Heather sat beside her, Chase moved in closer and put her arm around her shoulder. God, she smelled so good.

"No kissing on the mouth," Heather said.

"As you wish," she said, looking at her lips.

"And you will do as I say." Dario turned his wheelchair to face them.

"I know the rules." She still gazed at Heather.

"You may begin," Dario said. "Remove her dress."

She got up and extended her hand. Heather took it and stood to face her. Chase could feel how uncomfortable she was; she'd even said she didn't want sex with her. She had to calm her down and relax her, so for the moment she ignored Dario's instructions and didn't turn Heather around to unzip her.

She tried for eye contact, but Heather's gaze kept moving from her eyes, to her mouth, and back again. She swallowed hard and brought her lips to within half an inch of Heather's. She didn't do it with any kind of plan; she didn't intend to kiss Heather. That irresistibly sexy mouth just drew her in.

But Heather placed her finger on Chase's lips and stopped her.

She took the finger in her mouth and sucked it softly, then placed her lips on Heather's ear and slowly traced a path with her tongue down her neck to her shoulder. When Chase heard a soft groan, a thick fog filled her head and a battle began to rage inside her. She should be focused on her mission and why she was here, but she wanted only to lose herself in the smell, the taste, and the feel of Heather's skin.

"I *said*, take her dress off," Dario repeated more forcefully.

Chase traced kisses on her shoulder as she slowly turned Heather, keeping her own face out of Dario's vision. Her mouth near Heather's ear, she whispered, "You're doing great."

With Heather turned away, Chase ran her hands up the sides of Heather's back and stopped at the zipper. Heather's head fell back against her and she heard another soft moan. She lowered the zipper of the dress until Heather was exposed down to the small of her back, then she lifted Heather's golden-brown hair and kissed the back of her neck. Slowly, she slipped the straps of Heather's dress down. Her skin was flawless and so exquisitely soft Chase couldn't stop caressing her.

She yearned to wish Dario and the rest of the world away so she could be alone with Heather. As Heather's dress fell to the floor, Chase followed it down, stooping to stroke the back of Heather's thighs and calves, but she kept one side turned away from Dario so she could surreptitiously slip the first bug from her pocket. When she reached the tangle of dress at Heather's feet, she attached the bug to the bottom of the side table, using their bodies to shield her actions from Dario's view.

She coaxed Heather to step out of the dress, gently lifting one foot, then the other, before she slowly made her way back up her body, kissing and caressing the soft, delicate skin of her legs, back, and neck. Heather shivered.

With Heather still facing away, Chase said, "I want you at the table," loud enough for Dario to hear. Pressed together, her front against Heather's back, she led them to the dining area off to the right, placed Heather's hands on the edge of the table, then drew her hips back until Heather's ass was up against her crotch.

She slowly caressed Heather's back with her right hand, while her left—the one Dario couldn't see—slipped the second bug from her pocket. To make sure Dario's attention was entirely on Heather, she traced a path with her fingers from Heather's back, to her side, to her breast.

Heather's body tensed and Chase heard a sharp intake of breath when she pinched the rigid nipple beneath her palm, then Heather moaned loudly and pushed her ass deeper into Chase's crotch.

She could see in her peripheral vision that Dario was fixated on Heather, so in a fluid motion, she slid the bug under the massive table, then brought her hand up to cup Heather's other breast. As she did, she drove her crotch hard against Heather's ass. She was dizzy with lust; although she had to concentrate on the job, her body was working against her. She wanted nothing more than to rip Heather's panties off and fuck her senseless—not because Heather was a call girl, nor because Chase was horny—but because no woman had ever wound her up this much without even touching her.

"Take her shirt off, Heather," Dario said.

Chase was already close to losing it, so the idea of removing her shirt almost did her in.

Heather slowly pivoted and, with heavy eyelids, looked up at Chase. Her breathing was ragged and her face flushed.

"Take my shirt off," Chase demanded.

Heather never stopped looking into her eyes as she slowly unbuttoned the shirt, starting at the bottom. By the time she reached the last button, Chase was beside herself. She fought to keep her hands from shaking.

Heather hesitated briefly before she peeled the shirt from her shoulders.

Chase wasn't used to women taking their time with her, especially since time was money, which left her with very little experience as to how to handle Heather's adagio tempo. Fists clenched, she willed herself not to take Heather right there and then.

"Are you enjoying this?" Heather asked, as she expertly and swiftly pulled Chase's belt loose.

"I…God, what are you doing?" she gasped. She knew Heather was putting on a show, a really convincing one, but she couldn't possibly be oblivious to what she was putting Chase through.

"Tell me what you want." Heather pulled her forward and placed her hands on Chase's breasts over her thin, black bra.

She was so aroused her heart was beating wildly. Surely Heather could feel it. Their lips were an inch apart as Heather reached down and unzipped her trousers.

Her mind fogged by desire, she momentarily forgot everything but the woman before her. Against Heather's rules and wishes, she pulled their bodies together and licked Heather's lips.

"Don't," Heather mumbled unconvincingly, and tried to pull away.

Chase grabbed her hard by the wrists. "I need to kiss you." She dug her hand into Heather's hair and forced her head forward until their lips met.

"No kissing." Heather tried to pull away, but she bit down hard on Heather's bottom lip. She couldn't stop herself.

As she pulled back, Heather winced, and a trickle of blood bloomed on the edge of her mouth. "I'm sorry."

Heather wiped the blood away with the back of her hand. "Play by the rules," she said with meaning. "You can have anything but my mouth."

"Anything?"

Heather placed her hands on Chase's breasts and slowly massaged them. "Anything."

Chase roughly lifted her, and Heather wrapped her legs around Chase's waist.

Heather dug her face in Chase's neck. "How are we doing?" she asked in a low voice.

Chase's mind was too clouded to realize what Heather was asking. "What?" she mumbled.

"The bugs," Heather whispered in her ear.

She had to force herself back to reality. "Two down, one to go," she replied fuzzily.

"Where do you want me…the last one?" Heather corrected herself.

Chase carried her across the room as Dario watched and placed Heather atop the bar. Dario turned his wheelchair slightly to enjoy the show. Heather looked at her, half dazed, half confused, obviously not knowing what to expect. She gasped out loud when Chase forcefully spread her legs and ran her hands up Heather's thighs, stopping just short of her sheer panties.

As Chase bent over, she discreetly retrieved the last bug from her pocket. So close she could smell Heather's arousal, she struggled to keep her focus. She needed to get the last bug on the underside of the bar's banister, so in order to distract Dario she placed a hand on either side of Heather and traced hungry kisses up Heather's thighs.

As she neared the inviting apex of her legs, Heather threw her head back and mumbled something unintelligible.

Chase planted the bug just as Heather grabbed her head. Whether it was to encourage or stop her, Chase would never find out.

"I'm done," she whispered, as she memorized the sensation of Heather's hands in her hair, the scent of her arousal, the softness of the skin against her lips.

Heather nodded, and not two seconds later, Chase's cell rang.

She straightened. "I have to take it," she said apologetically to Heather. "It could be work."

"Of course. Go ahead."

"This is your very serious yet very fake business call," Jack said.

"That's very upsetting," she replied, trying to sound perturbed. "I'll talk to him right away. We can't lose this deal." She hung up. "My apologies to both of you." She turned from Heather to Dario. "But I have a crisis situation. I'm afraid I have to leave."

"Can't it wait a little?" Heather pursed out her lips in a pout.

"I'm sorry." Chase walked to the dining table and picked her shirt up off the floor. "But I really must leave."

"How unfortunate, just when it was about to get good," Dario said.

She and Heather both turned to look at him. The bulge between his legs was unmistakable, and she was glad she hadn't been able to see it earlier because it would have definitely put a damper on her zealous performance. Heather looked away in distaste as well as she jumped off the bar.

She hurriedly redressed and went to the door, pausing at the threshold to look back at Heather. "It was a pleasure. Maybe we can get together some other time."

"Yes…it was." Heather looked disoriented. "But there won't be another time."

❖

When Chase got back to their suite, Jack was at the desk with earphones on. "All bugs in place," Chase told her.

"Aha. I'm picking everything up loud and clear." Jack turned to her. "How are you?"

She dropped on the bed, sweaty and dazed. "All right, I guess."

"I'd say you need a cold shower. Just the audio was enough to make me need a smoke."

"What we won't do for the organization." She tried to smile.

"After what just happened, I think you need to thank the organization."

She shrugged. "She's a beautiful woman."

"And experienced."

"So am I."

"Then why do you look so…disoriented?"

"What?"

"You look like you just lost your virginity."

She unbuttoned her shirt. "Don't be immature. It was a job."

"If you say so, but it sure didn't sound like it. Look, I frankly don't care what it was, just don't forget what she is."

She got off the bed and stood before Jack. "What *is* she?"

"It's their job to make you feel…good. It's acting, and what she just did with you was Oscar-worthy. And good for her, considering it was the most important performance of her life."

"I know damn well what she is, and what their job is. Heather is…different."

"You've been saying that all along. I just hope your hormones aren't blurring your judgment."

She was quickly tiring of Jack's inappropriate opinions. "You should be the last person to criticize or judge another for their misguided decisions. At least she never hurt anyone but herself."

Jack looked away. "You're right. I'm sorry. I just don't want to see you get hurt."

"That's my business, not yours."

"Again, you're right."

Chase took off her shirt and started toward the bathroom.

"You probably want to postpone the stripping act." Jack waved her over and pressed the headphones to her ears.

She checked her watch. Dario's call was ten minutes early. She put her shirt back on and had her headphones in place even before she sat next to Jack.

"Have you decided how you want to handle Rózsa?" Dario asked the person on the other end. He listened, and then, "Of course we have to make him disappear, but we don't know what rock that idiot is hiding under. If the authorities can't find him, how are we—" After a short pause, he said in a surprised voice, "Cooperate?"

He listened again. "Yes, I understand. But how am I going to get him to give me his location?" Another short pause. "Of course, but I haven't been exactly friendly or receptive to his contacting me. Why would he believe me now?" A long pause this time. "Of course I realize what is at stake here, and I know very well that it will be my hide and not yours, dear sister, but—"

He listened some more, and when he spoke again, he was clearly angry. "Don't patronize me. I'm not one of your lackeys. Yes, it was my idea to work with him, but you were only too eager to welcome a new supplier." Another pause. "Very well." He sighed. "I will contact you when I know more. I expect his call in ten minutes."

They heard the cell disconnect.

"Cold bitch," Dario said, either to himself or his goon.

"They want to off Rózsa," Jack said. "That means—"

"We won't let that happen."

"Dario has no idea where he is."

"It doesn't sound like he's in China." Chase sat back, trying not to feel as defeated as Jack looked.

"Fuck." Jack threw her earphones on the desk. "What the fuck now?"

"We wait for Rózsa to contact Dario. The only thing we can do is see how Dario plays it out. Maybe he'll actually manage to find out where Rózsa is hiding."

"I'm betting he will," Jack said. "Rózsa desperately wants money, which makes him predictable."

"And desperate people make desperate decisions." She motioned to Jack. "Dario's phone is ringing." She pressed the Record button.

Jack grabbed her earphones just in time to hear Dario answer.

"Hello." A brief pause. "Ah, good evening. Please let me start by apologizing for being short with you earlier. I was in the midst of a business meeting with a most unpleasant client. It was rude and unprofessional of me to take it out on you."

Dario listened, then laughed. "Yes, one of those. I see you've had your share of egomaniacal wannabes." A pause. "Of course." He laughed again. "I have. As a matter of fact, I just finished discussing the matter with my partner. We are of the same opinion. We hold your cooperation with us in high regard. We have worked together for two years and you—" He stopped short to listen. "Indeed, nearly three years. How time flies. You have always delivered, and your dependability means a lot to us. We are hopeful we can continue to work with you once you are in a better place."

Dario listened some more before continuing in the same ingratiating, almost jubilant tone. "We are willing to help you get to that better place. We will give you the money you need to make a new beginning. An advance, of sorts, for your future services." Another pause. "Of course, we know it is only a matter of time."

He listened for a while. "Yes…about that. We are going to have to handle the transaction differently this time. Electronic banking is being monitored too closely, and an amount like this would undoubtedly set off alarms." Pause. "Yes. We came up with a solution. We are going to pay cash. In person." Another pause. "We have people all over the world. You could have the money as soon as forty-eight hours from now."

Dario listened a long time before he continued. "I understand how sensitive your situation is, of course. But you will have to meet us half way. We cannot jeopardize a multimillion-dollar corporation."

Rózsa was apparently balking at the idea of a face-to-face meeting, because the rest of Dario's side of the back-and-forth conversation was obviously designed to gain Rózsa's trust.

"You are safe with us, I can guarantee you that."

"As a matter of fact, we can offer you shelter should you need somewhere to stay or…work."

"I understand your trepidation so perhaps it is wise you think about it before you decide."

"In that case we will unfortunately not be able to help each other. A pity, don't you think?"

"Andor, please. We are doing our best for you. You know you can't hurt us, because you would expose yourself. And even if you managed to get away with it, what would you gain?"

"Exactly. So consider our proposal. Like I already mentioned, you can have that money in two days."

"Very well, where can we meet you?"

"Can you be more specific?"

"Of course. I understand. I'll expect to hear from you then. We have people nearby who can connect with you."

"Thank you, the pleasure is all mine."

"Rewind and turn up the volume," Jack said as soon as Dario hung up. He hadn't repeated the location Rózsa had given him, and the drop-off was apparently in two days. They played the recording ten times, but still couldn't make out what Rózsa said.

"Goddamn it." Jack jumped up and started pacing. "Dario's people are near Rózsa and as soon as they meet him…" Her hands clenched into fists. "And you know what that means for Cass. They'll either kill her on sight, or, if she's not around, she'll die locked up somewhere before we ever find her. *If* we ever find her."

"I'm going to mail this file to Reno," Chase said. "Let's hope he can get something."

"He will. He has to. It's his job, and he's good at it." Jack stopped pacing and stared out the window.

She tried to lighten Jack's panic. "So Reno sounds like a bright summer's day just about now?"

"Oh, what a knee-slapper. Just send the damn audio file."

A half hour after they sent the phone call to headquarters, they got a call back.

"I'm in Pierce's office," Reno said. "He wants to talk to both of you after I update you on what I found. I ran the call through several filters and enhancement software and was able to get Rózsa's side of the conversation. He's meeting Dario's people somewhere in France and is demanding Dario pay him half a million dollars. He's also supposed to call back tomorrow at eleven a.m. with specifics about the meeting place. My software enabled me to isolate the sound of a boat horn and the clanging of a ship's rigging in the background, which means he's at a harbor, either on shore or on a boat."

"He wouldn't risk being at one of the more popular resorts," Chase mused. "He's too recognizable, even without a hostage."

"And he can't be on some big commercial vessel, like a cruise ship, for the same reason," Jack added. "Reno, I know it's a long shot, but see if you can find his name on any boat rental or purchase records there."

"Will do."

"This latest development has made it imperative we get one of you to France ASAP," Pierce said. "Dario's people will be headed there to eliminate him as soon as they get a fix on his exact location, and we need to get the jump on them. Also, Rózsa's got to be suspecting by now that he's not going to get his money back from us. Allegro has stalled him as best as she can, but he's not stupid. Now that he thinks he's going to get help from Dario, he has little reason to keep Lynx alive."

"I'll go," Jack said. "Chase can stay here to get the exact location and follow me over."

"Already anticipated you'd say that. There's a ticket in your name waiting for you at the airport," Pierce said. "Your flight to Paris leaves in two hours. I have Allegro on standby to help you if needed. She's in the Netherlands, so she can be there in an hour. I'd rather not involve Interpol if we don't have to."

Jack immediately got up to pack.

"Since Rózsa's supposed to call back at eleven, have me booked on a flight around one thirty," Chase said. "And we need to have a ticket booked to New York at about that same time in Heather Snyder's name. I'll find a way to get her away from Dario."

"You got it," Reno said. "Send me a recording of tomorrow's call before you leave, and I'll see if I can pick up something further."

"Roger that." Chase asked. "Anything else?"

"Not at the moment. Good luck, you two," Pierce said. "And Phantom?"

Jack stopped packing and came over to the speakerphone. "What?"

"Don't try to do this alone. Wait for backup."

"By any means necessary, Pierce, or have you forgotten?" Jack said, reciting the EOO creed that had been drilled into them as children. She disconnected and returned to throwing her clothes into her duffel.

"He's right, Jack. Wait for me, or call Allegro if you get a lead on where he is. Don't go off half-cocked," Chase said.

"I'll do whatever I have to," Jack said as she put her coat on. "Regardless of what Pierce thinks, I'm not one of his lackeys any more, and I'll do things my own way." She picked up her bag and headed toward the door. "See you in France."

CHAPTER TWENTY-EIGHT

Sainte-Maxime Harbor, France
Early next morning, November 26

Andor Rózsa went below deck to the sleeping compartment and checked on his hostage. She was still out cold and her breathing was slow and shallow. He'd had to give her a heavy dose to ensure she didn't wake while he transferred her from the car to the boat he'd rented, but perhaps he'd overestimated. Looking at her now, he could see she'd lost significant weight during her captivity, and he should have allowed for that.

He wasn't too concerned. He shouldn't have to keep her alive much longer, anyway. Her people seemed unable to get his money back, and if Dario was true to his word, he'd soon have a safe place to hide and enough money to start over. He wouldn't need her as collateral.

He went topside and glanced around the dark harbor. No other boats were near; they were anchored far from the main pier. He pulled his coat tighter and settled into the captain's chair of the cruiser to keep watch. It would be dawn in a few hours, and fishing boats from the small village would be heading out to sea soon.

He planned to remain here only another couple of hours, until he called Dario again with the location of their rendezvous—Marseille, 100 miles farther along the coast. Then he'd set to sea and remain there until shortly before the rendezvous in two days, and he'd give Dario only a few minutes' notice of the actual meeting place—a Turkish bath—to minimize the chance of a double-cross.

If all went according to plan, he'd return to the boat and dump his hostage at sea. With half-a-million dollars and Dario's connections, he could restart his organ business anywhere and use the proceeds to build a new lab. Perhaps he'd go to South America and set up near one of the myriad slums that surrounded Lima or Sao Paulo, where he'd have an ample supply of potential donors who wouldn't be missed if they disappeared.

❖

Beijing, China

Chase was in the midst of choosing her clothes for the day, her hair still wet from the shower, when she heard Dario's voice over the laptop speaker. She glanced at her watch. 7 a.m. Still a few hours until his phone call from Rózsa. She didn't expect him to do anything more noteworthy in the interim than have breakfast, so she was surprised to hear him say he'd be ready to leave in just a few minutes. As she hurriedly dressed, she listened in.

"George will drive me. I want you to stay here and make sure Heather doesn't leave," Dario said. "I want to talk to her when I get back. I'll be gone at least a couple of hours, maybe more."

Where the hell was he going? Most important, would he be back in time for Rózsa's call? If he took it away from his room, they'd have no way to find out details of the meeting in France.

She managed to get downstairs ahead of him and was parked near the entrance in her rental when he emerged in his wheelchair and got into his own car. She followed them through the narrow streets of the Changping District north of Beijing proper, until the car stopped at a restaurant in the village of Nanshao.

Chase checked her watch. Ten minutes to eight.

Dario's driver helped him into his wheelchair and took him to the entrance, but Dario went in alone while the other man returned to his vehicle. Not long after, a Chinese couple tried to enter the restaurant but was sent away, and so were the next three people.

"Looks like it's going to be breakfast for two," Chase said to herself.

At precisely eight, a sedan drove up and a Chinese man in a drab suit got out.

Chase snapped pictures as he strode from the car to the entrance and went inside. Dario's company had arrived. It certainly wasn't Rózsa, so who was he? And what was the purpose of the meeting?

She e-mailed the pictures to the EOO and her phone rang ten minutes later.

Reno. He must have found something to be calling back so quickly. "Who is he?" she asked.

"Zhang Anshun. He's a Grand Justice of the Second Rank, in the Chinese Supreme Court."

"Which begs the question, what does he want with Dario?"

"Zhang is apparently the go-to man to expedite and approve paperwork for condemned prisoners. My guess is Dario's using him to get papers signed."

"I wouldn't say he's using him. I'm sure Zhang gets paid a pretty penny to sign those papers."

"Cripes, how many are involved?" Reno mumbled.

"Too many. It would appear the organ trade is the new black," Chase said, and disconnected.

An hour later, the meeting inside the restaurant broke up. The Chinese justice emerged first and Dario followed a couple of minutes later. Chase tailed his car back toward the hotel. She kept glancing at her watch as they inched forward in the crush of traffic streaming toward the city center. At this rate, they'd barely be back before time for Rózsa's call.

She hurried up to her room. The call, a few minutes late, was brief. Once again, she could make out only Dario's side of the conversation.

"So where is the meeting to be?" Silence, then, "That will be no problem. And you'll contact us shortly beforehand with the exact location in the city?" A pause, then, "That's fine. We look forward to renewing our mutually beneficial relationship, Andor."

As before, Chase sent the recording to Reno for analysis. Once that was done, she packed, went downstairs and checked out, and put her bag in the rental. Now all she had to do was get Heather out of there, and she could join Jack in France.

She wasn't happy their ride to the airport together would likely be the last time she would see Heather, though it was probably best. Heather had stirred up too many unfamiliar emotions, and she needed to get her head back fully in the game and return to her well-ordered existence. At least the ride would give them a chance to say good-bye and hopefully move past the awkwardness of their staged and abbreviated sexual encounter last night. It still stung that the encounter could have stirred her so, while Heather clearly wanted no part of it and only went along because of their mission.

She texted Heather: **Call me if the coast is clear.**

Heather was in her bedroom flipping through the TV channels when her cell phone chimed with a text message. She'd wanted to go out this morning, stretch her legs and free her mind of the images swirling through her head from last night, but Dario's goon had told her she wasn't to leave, that Dario was out. Though he was back now, she was doing her best to avoid him.

The text was from Landis. Heather shut off the TV and put her ear to the door. She could hear Dario talking, either on the phone or to one of his men, so she called Landis's number. "Is everything okay?" she whispered.

"We got the lead we needed. Rózsa is in France and Jack left last night to get a head start."

"You stayed."

"Of course. I'm not leaving you behind. We don't have a lot of time, so I need you to do a couple of things."

"I'm listening."

"First, remove the three bugs I planted last night."

"The wire is already in my suitcase."

"Great. Now there's one by the phone, one under the dining table, and one at the bar," Landis said. "Then you need to talk to Dario. Tell him you changed your mind and want to go home."

"I'll tell him my brother got sick."

"He seems to know everything about Adam and where to find him. Don't lie to him because he can check if he wants to. Tell him you spent the night reconsidering this arrangement and can't live with it. Tell him you can't be bought, etcetera, and meet me outside in fifteen. Can you do that?"

"I can be packed in ten."

"If there's a problem, text me."

"Okay." She hung up and hurriedly threw her clothes and shoes into her suitcase. She could care less whether anything got wrinkled or even left behind. She just wanted to get the hell out of there. She left the bag by the bedroom door and, on her way out, grabbed the envelope Dario had given her from her purse.

He sat at the desk with papers in front of him, but was staring out the windows at the glorious view. It would be difficult, if not impossible, to remove the bugs as Landis had asked, since all were in view of where he was sitting.

"Dario, I need to talk to you," she said seriously.

"Oh?" He looked at her with a neutral expression. "What's this about?"

"I'm going home."

He almost smiled, but there was no humor in it. "No, you're not."

"I can't do this, Dario. I thought I could, but I honestly think it's time I made some changes."

"What kind of alterations are you thinking of?"

"They aren't just thoughts. I've decided I can't sell myself for a living anymore. Not for you, not for anyone. God knows I need the money, but not at this price. Last night I realized I'm too good for this." Heather dropped the envelope with the money Dario had given her on the coffee table. "It's all there."

Dario didn't even look at it. "It wasn't my idea for you to have sex with a woman, and you hardly…finished anyway."

"This isn't about last night or the…woman. It's about me."

"I see. And you decided to change your life over the course of ten hours." It was more a statement than a question.

"It would appear so." Heather was getting irritated with his blasé attitude.

"And how exactly do you plan to get back home?"

"I arranged a ticket early this morning."

He wheeled himself to the middle of the room. "Is there something else you're not telling me, Heather?"

Her face burned despite her efforts to remain calm. "Something else?"

He crossed his hands and smiled. "My work is very important and very profitable."

"This is *not* about money, Dario. I—"

He lifted his hand. "I am very well aware what this is essentially about. You see, with money comes power. And with power comes responsibility."

She didn't know where this conversation was leading, but she didn't like it. "Why are you telling me this?"

"People envy what I have, Heather. They want to take it away from me."

"I'm sorry to hear that," she said carefully.

"As am I." He shook his head theatrically. "So you see, I have to be cautious. Choose my friends carefully and eliminate anyone who poses a threat."

"Eliminate?" That word coming out of Dario's mouth had a different meaning when it came to friends parting ways.

"Yes. Don't you think it wise to eradicate danger?"

"Of course."

"I thought in due time we could become friends, Heather."

"I'm not looking for friends."

"And one can only be a true friend through the test of loyalty." He ignored her response. "It would appear Amber is the one I had ambitions for that friendship, and not Heather."

"I don't understand what you're saying."

"Amber was honest and her intentions clear," he explained, flicking lint off his trousers. He paused and looked up at her with eyes of ice. "Heather, on the other hand, is a liar. A fraud."

"Why are you saying this?" She glanced toward the door.

"Like I said, people I choose must be tested for their loyalty. And I regret to say you did not pass the test." He reached into his pocket. "Jules," he said, referring to the guy who tended him and wheeled him around, "has been a friend for years. Someone I trust will do what's best for me. He is a bit overprotective, but I do so appreciate that quality. Especially since he found this in your luggage." Dario pulled the transmitter and wire from his pocket and held it up.

She felt dizzy. She'd hidden the wire in a compartment of her suitcase last night before going to bed, but she was in such a hurry to pack and leave a little while ago she hadn't bothered to check whether it was still there. Jules must have snuck into her room while she was asleep and snooped in her things. "I don't know what I'm looking at. What is it?"

"I'm sure you do know." He checked his watch. "But I fortunately don't have the time or inclination to listen to your lies. Unless, of course, you want to try something new, like…the truth."

"I…I…" She honestly didn't know what to say. "I've never seen that…whatever it is, before." Her stomach churned. She knew her blush was giving away the lie.

"I'm going to ask you one question. And only once. So think carefully before you answer."

"I already told you—"

He smiled. "Or I will do with you what is done with wood in the furniture industry. Recycle."

"Recycle?" Oh, my God. Was he going to cut her open and sell her organs? She fought a sudden urge to vomit.

"Whom are you working for?"

She contemplated a suitable answer. She couldn't tell him about Landis or Jack, because who would believe her, since she didn't even know who they worked for. Jack had never mentioned her last name and Landis…well, Landis had. But was it her real name? She had already changed her first name from Brett to Landis—what if Landis was a fake name as well? Even her friend and colleague didn't know she was a novelist. Maybe all of it was just a lie and she was being framed. Besides, if she admitted to anything at this point, it would make her seem an even bigger liar. "Working for?" She tried to look shocked. "I don't work for anyone."

"You brought the listening device along for…fun. As part of your show?"

"I told you I have no idea how that—"

"Jules," he called. The big man materialized and Dario told him, "Please let the police in."

"Police?" Her heart was pounding so hard she was afraid Dario might see it. "What for? I haven't done anything wrong."

"On the contrary," he replied. "You've done everything wrong."

Two uniformed Chinese policemen stormed in before she had time to reply. One grabbed her from behind while the other stopped in front of Dario.

"Let me go. I haven't done anything," she shouted. "Why are you doing this?" she asked Dario, her panic rising.

"In her purse," he told the policeman. "It's in her room."

The cop went into Heather's bedroom and came back with her beige handbag. He rifled through it and pulled out a small white bundle wrapped in clear plastic. It looked a lot like cocaine.

"That's not mine," she screamed, and looked at Dario. "He put it there."

Dario shook his head, disgust on his face. "Take that junk away. I can't bear to look at her."

"He's lying," she yelled as the cops dragged her out the door.

They pulled her through the lobby as everyone stared. Once outside, she spotted Landis standing a few feet from the entrance, and the image gave her hope she might still get out of this. But though Landis looked straight at her, she made no effort to intercede. She just turned and walked away.

Chapter Twenty-nine

Beijing, China

Chase walked slowly away, seemingly disinterested in what had just happened. Dario's man had been watching as Heather was forced into the police car. If Chase had reacted, they would have thrown her in beside her, and getting justice in China was impossible. The judicial system here had a throw-in-jail-and-never-ask-questions policy. Heather was in a lot of trouble.

Chase negotiated her next move as she walked around the block.

The crooked Supreme Court justice—Zhang—could get Heather out in a heartbeat. Chase had enough on him to blackmail him, but she'd have to get him alone, which was problematic. If she confronted him at work, he'd have her arrested or shot on sight, and if she waited until tonight to ambush him, she'd lose precious time. Besides, even if she did scare him enough to release Heather, he could have border control all over them. He wouldn't let either of them get away, knowing what they did about his connection to the organ trade.

That left her only one option.

She returned to the hotel and snuck past reception between tourists. They'd already seen her check out and she wanted it to stay that way.

Feeling for her gun the moment the elevator door shut, she looked around, and when she didn't spot any cameras, she removed the silencer from her jacket pocket and screwed it on to the Glock, then secured the weapon back in its holster. She knocked on Dario's door and his bodyguard answered.

"Hi. Remember me from yesterday?" She wanted to shoot him right there, but two other guests farther down the hallway were exiting their rooms.

The goon nodded.

"I can't find my wallet, and I was wondering if I could look to see if it fell from my jacket." The big man nodded again and was about to shut the door when Chase stopped him. "I want to take a look for myself. Maybe say hi to Heather and Dario."

"Heather isn't here."

"Then Dario." She smiled. "I won't be long."

"Let me ask if he desires visitors," the bodyguard said, and she let him shut the door. He came back a minute later. "Your wallet isn't here and Dario's busy. Maybe another time."

She looked down the hallway and, seeing it was empty, pulled her gun and pointed it at his crotch. "There's no time like the present, if you ask me. Oh, if you had any intention of reaching for your gun, I suggest you abort the idea. Unless of course you want to spend the remains of your existence pissing through a tube."

The man slowly took a step back into the suite and she followed, never taking the gun from his junk. She shut the door behind her and reached in his jacket to remove his firearm, then led him at gunpoint into the main living area and motioned toward an armchair. "Take a seat. Where is he?"

When the man looked toward Dario's bedroom, she slammed the butt of her gun against the back of his head and he fell limp. Then she went to Dario's room and opened the door. He was alone, looking out the window. His other goons must have still been in their own suites or off conducting some business for him.

"Jules, since when do you enter—" He turned and spotted her.

"Jules is in the other room." She walked over to Dario. "Why don't we join him?" She wheeled him into the living room and positioned him where she could keep an eye on the goon. Dario didn't appear afraid or even moved.

"How can I help you?" he asked in a bored tone.

"You can start by telling me what happened to Heather."

"Ah, yes. Beautiful Heather. What a waste, don't you think?"

"A waste?"

"The poor girl has so many afflictions," he replied. "Prostitution, drugs, bad company."

"Which of the three did you use to get her arrested?"

"I have no tolerance for junkies."

"I see. So, what prompted you to plant drugs on her?"

"I don't know what you're talking about. I was shocked to find out about her abuse."

She took a seat on the couch across from him. "You don't mind, do you?"

"Please, where are my manners? Make yourself comfortable."

"Now, this bad company you mentioned…I'm guessing you weren't referring to yourself."

"I have been nothing but a gentleman to Heather." He straightened his tie. "I was referring to you. For whatever reason I can't fathom, she decided to work for you."

"How have you concluded this?"

Dario wheeled himself to the table and brought back a small plastic bag, which he placed on the coffee table. She picked it up and saw Heather's wire and the bugs she'd planted in the suite the night before.

"Jules found the wire in her bag last night, and after she was arrested, he scanned all the rooms for more devices. You imagine my lack of surprise when he found more. Heather's background is hardly one to make me suspect she did this alone or of her own initiative. But you…" He looked at her with narrowed eyes. "I am certain you hired or blackmailed the poor girl to do your dirty work. But why? I don't see how I can be of any interest to you. Let me take a moment here to congratulate you on last night's stellar performance. I don't think I have ever seen Heather that…excited. You were both a pleasure to watch. Too bad you had to leave before the grand finale."

When she smiled, Dario frowned. If he thought he was the only one who could play it calm and indifferent he was wrong, because he was facing the master of aloofness. "I'm flattered. Although credit must be given where it's due, and the show was all Heather. It's not difficult to perform with such an amazing woman."

The goon groaned and started to move, so she got up. "But that's beside the point," she said as she hit him again on the back of the head.

Dario cringed. "What is the point?"

She sat. "I know your furniture business is a cover for buying and selling organs. I know you use Chinese prisoners and have an agreement with Zhang to sign and expedite orders. And I also know you—or should I say your people—are not above killing innocent people to get organs. Like, for example, prostitutes back home."

Dario's eyes widened. "Who are you?" he said loudly, visibly reacting for the first time.

"If I were interested in your disgusting trade, I could have had you arrested weeks ago, but I'm not."

"I save lives. That's hardly disgusting. Lives that matter."

"Those who can afford you, you mean."

He flicked his hand dismissively "I am a savior for thousands."

"Ah, yes, deliver a villain and a hero emerges. I almost pity you for your mental disorder."

"I assume you're here because you want money to keep quiet?"

"I don't care for money, and if I did, you couldn't pay me enough."

"And who are you if money is not an issue? Money is important to everyone."

"I'm not going to answer that question, so don't waste my time asking again." She crossed her legs.

"Very well, then. What do you want?"

"I want you to call Zhang and have Heather released."

"That's it?"

"You seem surprised."

"She has been a call girl and struggling designer for years," he said. "I know she didn't adopt the role for my benefit."

"She hasn't been working undercover or conspiring against your plans. That's correct."

"Are you romantically involved with her?"

"No."

"Then I fail to understand why a simple prostitute has captured your attention to the point of jeopardizing your life."

"Do I look worried?"

He smiled. "Do I?"

"You'd rather swallow your tongue than admit it, but if you're as smart as I think you are, you're inwardly praying to whatever God you believe in."

"If I had put my fate in the hands of any god, I would be dead by now."

"But money has at least put you in a wheelchair."

"So you understand what god I believe in."

She got up and hovered over him, then bent to rest a hand on either side of his wheelchair. "Then pray to the mighty buck it saves you from a bullet to the head." She was running out of patience and time. Heather would probably be made to disappear like most foreign prisoners in China, and any evidence of what happened to her would be forever erased.

"You won't kill me. Not as long as you have hope I will make that call."

"No need to flatter yourself, Dario. I have more options."

"Such as?"

"Zhang. I'm sure he'll do anything to protect his position."

"You can't get close to him."

"I can have another five like me here in less than an hour. One is already stationed in room 506 waiting for my signal. We can be up Zhang's ass before he ever knew what hit him."

"Then what's stopping you?"

"International affairs. But frankly, I've never been patient with political matters, nor have they stopped me before. I can follow protocol for only so long."

"Shoot her," he said suddenly, and Chase turned just in time to see Jules aim a small gun at her. He must've had it hidden on him.

She didn't hesitate. One clean shot between his eyes, EOO style. He fell back on the chair, eyes wide open. "Where were we?" she asked blithely. "Oh, yeah. You were proving to be quite useless, and I was growing very impatient. Time for me to visit Zhang." Chase pointed the gun between his eyes.

He placed his hand lightly on the tip of the barrel. "I'll talk to him," he said in a subdued voice.

"That's step one."

"What else do you want?" He sounded irritated.

"I want you to be there when they bring Heather back."

"Why?"

"Because…number one, I want to make sure you don't change their mind and have them kill us both on sight or prevent us from leaving this lawless hell, and number two, you're coming with us to France."

"What?" He pulled himself forward.

"You heard me the first time. We have a common interest in France. You want a certain someone killed and I want him alive."

"What are you talking about?"

"I don't have time for evasive stupidity. You know I'm talking about Rózsa. The idiot who's been blackmailing you for money is the same idiot who took something that doesn't belong to him, and I want it back."

"How do you know about—"

"The fact that he used to sell you organs after he was done with his guinea pigs?"

Dario didn't answer.

"I know a lot about you and your enterprise. And the fact that you're your sister's puppet."

"I will not admit to any of this, if that's what you expect of me."

"You don't have to. Like I said, your line of work isn't my issue. What Rózsa took, however, is. I want you to help me find him."

"What makes you think I know how to?"

"He's going to call you for the drop-off location."

Dario's eyes widened even more. "That whore…" He pounded on the armrest. "That wired whore fed you everything."

"Heather isn't the issue, either." She pointed the gun at him. "So leave her the hell out of your vocabulary." She wouldn't have anybody, let alone this freak, call Heather a whore. "Now, back to our topic. You're going to give me Rózsa."

"Why would I even consider that?"

"Think about it. Your sister wants him dead and she wants you to make that happen. I know you don't want to disappoint her. Now, why involve your own people and risk something going wrong, thereby exposing yourself or your company, when I'm willing to take care of Rózsa myself, free of charge?"

"Why should I trust you? How do I know you won't kill or expose me after you have Rózsa?"

"It's a matter of taking a good look at your odds. You either accept this offer and take a fifty-fifty chance I won't hurt you or… you refuse to cooperate and turn that fifty percent chance of survival into zero." She looked down at her Glock. "I think the math is clear."

"You wouldn't kill me now, not before you have Rózsa, because I'm the only one who can give him to you."

"I don't have to kill you to destroy you, if you know what I mean. All I have to do is ask the feds to look into a certain furniture company."

"That still won't give you Rózsa."

"True. But it will give me a great deal of satisfaction to know you're going to spend the rest of your life wheeling your sorry ass from one wall to another inside a very claustrophobic cell. I wonder how your sister will take to prison."

"No one will ever find my sister," he said confidently.

"Maybe not, maybe they will. Some people are very resilient." She winked. "Either way, I'm sure she won't be thrilled to find out you were the reason the family business was shut down."

Dario didn't speak for a long time and she didn't push. She could see the worry in his eyes. He seemed more afraid of his sister than his own death.

"I'll do it," he finally said.

"Good. Let's start by making that phone call to Zhang. Tell him to drop her off at the airport entrance. After that, call your pilot and have him ready."

Dario looked perplexed.

"Yes, I've been following you."

"My pilot isn't available. He's in Japan until tomorrow. Why do we need my private jet?"

"Because I want to make sure you don't contact anyone and that none of your friends come into contact with either me or Heather."

"Again, I don't have my pilot."

"I'll take care of that. Now, make that call to Zhang. Tell him to have her there in forty-five minutes." She sat and waited as Dario dialed Zhang's number. "Turn on the speaker."

He did as she asked. "It's Dario. I'm calling about the woman your people picked up earlier. The American."

"The beautiful one," the male voice on the other end replied in heavily accented English. "Yes."

"Is she still in jail?"

"Yes. We will move her soon."

"I want you to release her."

"I can't do that."

"There's been a big misunderstanding." Tiny beads of sweat popped out on his forehead.

"But she had…cocaine."

"Listen to me," he said more forcefully. "A misunderstanding."

"But—"

"I said it was a Goddamn misunderstanding. I want her at the airport entrance in forty-five minutes," he yelled.

"I'll destroy the paperwork and release her."

Dario hung up. "Your whore will be there."

Chase rose from the couch. "She may sell her body, but you've sold your soul. Who's the real whore? Now make another call and make sure your jet is fueled to the max."

❖

Paris, France
6 a.m.

As soon as her flight touched down in Paris, Jack turned on her cell phone and found a text from Reno. **Meeting in Marseille tomorrow.** After she claimed her bag, she checked the departures board and found a flight leaving for the coastal resort in three hours with an available seat.

She bought a large coffee and settled into a seat at the gate. She was edgy and restless, despite having gotten little sleep on the eleven-hour flight from Beijing. *I'm coming, Cass. Stay strong. I'll find you.*

Strangely, she had no text or missed voice mail from Landis. She checked her watch. 6:30 a.m. Paris was six hours behind Beijing, so it was 12:30 p.m. there. Reno's message meant that Rózsa had called on schedule, so Landis should be at the airport by now. Why hadn't she given Jack her arrival info?

She sent off a text. **I'm in Paris. Have you left yet?**

Thirty minutes later, she received a reply. **Still here. Complications. Will update soon as possible.**

Complications? What kind of complications might have come up? They had the info on where the meeting was going to be. Sure, they had at least twenty-four hours until that happened, so a minor delay in Landis's departure shouldn't pose much of a problem. But if Dario's people were close and looking for Rózsa, too, the sooner she got here the better.

It had to involve Heather. Most likely, Landis hadn't been able to get her away from Dario yet. Her terse SMS could indicate she was working on doing just that.

Jack couldn't blame her. Landis was beginning to care for Heather, and it was also her duty to see that the civilian they'd recruited made it out of there safely, especially since she'd put herself in danger.

When her cell phone rang, she expected it to be Landis. But it was Reno. "Phantom…I mean, Jack…I have a great lead. Some background noise on the latest Rózsa call is a church bell. Long story short, it's a very distinctive tune, played on the village church in Sainte-Maxime. That's a small coastal village about 100 miles from Marseille. It has a harbor. I'm e-mailing you a map of the area as we speak, and a few pertinent facts about the place."

"Good job, Reno. I mean that. I'm about to catch a flight to Marseille. Have a rental car waiting. And send the info to Landis. She hasn't left Beijing yet, so she should be rebooked to Marseille."

"You got it. Good luck. You want me to contact Allegro?"

"Not yet. I'll head down there and scout around until Landis arrives. We have time until the meeting, and I doubt Dario's people know what we know about where Rózsa was calling from. Thanks." She disconnected and downloaded his e-mail, saving it to her phone so she could study it during the flight. Her plane was boarding, so she picked up her bag and got in line.

I'm coming, Cass. Don't worry. I'll find you. If I have to move heaven and earth, I'll find you.

Chapter Thirty

Sainte-Maxime, France
2 p.m.

Jack drove slowly through the Old Town section of the harbor city, scoping out the place. Though a city of less than fifteen thousand people, Sainte-Maxime relied on tourism, so this area, which faced the harbor, was busy on this mild November day. Pedestrians packed the sidewalks, visiting the numerous shops, bars, and restaurants, and the parking lot outside the casino was full. It wouldn't be easy to find Rózsa. The info Reno sent her indicated twenty-seven hotels and a dozen B&Bs here, not to mention apartment rentals and campsites. And several companies rented out sailboats and powerboats with sleeping compartments.

When she landed in Marseille, she'd had another text waiting from Reno, with her car-rental info and a confirmed booking at the Hotel Martinengo, a four-star beachfront inn with only ten rooms. When she spotted it, she checked in and quickly changed clothes. Reno had done his homework well—the place was in the busiest part of the Old Town, so she could leave the car and go everywhere on foot.

Jack jogged toward the nearest café, crowded with a wide mix of tourists in jeans and sweatshirts or expensive resort wear. A half-dozen languages assailed her as she walked to the bar, where she caught the eye of the oldest bartender—a relaxed, forty-something guy who looked like he'd been doing this a long time.

"Johnny Walker, Black Label," she said. As he poured, she pulled two pictures from her wallet. The first was Andor Rózsa's passport photo. "Seen this guy? Probably within the last couple of weeks," she asked in perfect French.

He shook his head, and she could see no hint of recognition in his eyes.

"How about her?" She held up a picture of Cass. One she herself had taken, just a week before Cassady had left for Europe to assist in tracking down Rózsa.

Again the man shook his head.

"Merci," she said.

She repeated the routine with anyone else in the bar who stuck out as a local, before moving on to the next establishment and doing the same. No one had seen him. At five p.m., she positioned herself outside the employee entrance at the Casino Barriere and caught workers coming off shift.

She was showing the pictures to a pair of blackjack dealers when a middle-aged woman emerged in a maid's uniform. She did a double take when she saw Jack and stopped where she stood to stare, her eyes wide in recognition. As soon as the two guys left, Jack approached her.

"Good afternoon, or evening," Jack said in French. "Pardon me, but you seem to know me, I wonder if—"

"I'm sorry to stare. You look so much like a dear friend of mine, I thought almost I'd seen a ghost. But of course, you are much younger. Still, it's almost uncanny, the resemblance."

"They say we all have a double somewhere," Jack said. "I wonder if you might look at some pictures for me." She took them out of her pocket. "Have you seen this man?"

Though the woman took her time studying Rózsa's face, she seemed more interested in Jack's. "I'm sorry, no."

"How about her?" Jack showed her Cassady's photo.

The woman shook her head. "Again, no, I'm afraid."

"Well, thank you for your time. I won't keep you further."

"You know," the woman said, pursing her lips, "the friend I was talking about—who looks like you—she has lived here all her life and knows everyone in town. She may be able to help you. Come with me, and I'll introduce you."

"Now? I'd appreciate the help, but I'm hesitant to walk in on someone unannounced."

"Celeste won't mind. I often stop for coffee or tea on my way home."

"If you're sure. Lead the way, ma'am."

"Call me Brigitte."

"I'm Jack."

"What a strange name for a woman."

"My given name is Jaclyn."

"Much better. A beautiful name for a beautiful woman. Celeste won't believe it." The woman took her on a fifteen-minute walk through the streets of a residential area adjacent to Old Town, making small talk about the city, her work, and her dream of visiting the US one day. Shortly before they arrived at their destination, she told Jack a little more about the woman she was taking her to meet. Celeste Bastien was retired now but had worked at a number of the establishments in town.

"We're here." The woman stopped in front of a small, humble house. The garden in the front was well trimmed, and roses and other flowers nearly covered the path to the door. Her guide didn't bother to knock; she opened the door and gestured for Jack to enter first. "Celeste, I have a visitor for you," Brigitte called out.

"Take a seat in the parlor. I'll be right down," a deep but feminine voice answered. "I'll bring the coffee."

Brigitte led Jack to the cozy parlor where they took seats on opposite ends of the couch.

Jack got out her picture of Cass and stared down at it for several seconds before shoving it back into the rear pocket of her jeans. She hoped this woman would be able to help. They were running out of time, and joining a stranger for coffee right now seemed so incredibly wrong. She heard footsteps approach and looked up as a tall, proud-looking woman in her sixties entered the room, her attention focused on the tray in her hands. She had gray hair and wore a muted floor-length caftan that clung to her slim figure.

"And who is this visitor you brought, Brigitte?" the woman asked as she approached the coffee table.

"Jaclyn is looking for a lost friend." Brigitte's eyes were intent on her friend. "I thought you might be able to help her."

"Jaclyn. What a beautiful name," Celeste said almost wistfully.

"My name's Jack Harding. Please, call me Jack."

Celeste was almost to the table when she looked at her visitor for the first time.

Jack gazed straight into the most penetrating green eyes she'd ever seen. The woman's short hair matched her own, and the smile was identical to hers. Her whole face, for that matter, was a complete replica of her own before she'd had it surgically altered. Suddenly the woman dropped the tray, sending coffee cups, spoons, milk, and sugar across the table and floor.

"Jaclyn," Celeste muttered as she grasped the table to steady herself. "It can't be."

Jack immediately shot up and went to her side. "Are you all right?" She placed her hands on the woman's back. "Are you ill?" she asked, feeling a bit off balance herself.

Celeste stood straight and simply stared at her, and she stared right back. A mixture of strange emotions ran through her head. "You look so…familiar?" Jack finally said.

"Why are you here?" the woman whispered.

"I'm looking for…"

"Who sent you?" Celeste's eyes narrowed.

"No one sent me."

"How did you find me?"

"Brigitte brought me here."

Celeste glanced about, almost as though she expected Jack hadn't arrived alone. "Does *he* know?"

"Does who know what?" Jack asked with a mixture of aggravation and confusion, still mesmerized by the strange emotions and spooky resemblance.

"I need to sit." Celeste pulled away from her.

"Let me help you." Jack started to reach for her waist, but Celeste waved her off.

"I can manage on my own."

She waited for Celeste to settle into one of the armchairs before she retook her seat on the couch across from her. The sudden tension in the room was palpable.

Brigitte broke the silence. "I thought you might want to see her for yourself. The two of you are just alike."

Celeste looked from Jack to her friend. "Brigitte, thank you for bringing Jaclyn here, but if you don't mind, could you leave us alone for a while?"

"What's going on, Celeste?" Brigitte asked, worry knotting her features. "You don't look well, and…why do you want me to leave?"

"I want to talk to Jaclyn alone."

"But you don't even know if you can help her yet," Brigitte said.

"Not now, Brigitte."

"Do you know her?"

"Yes. Now, please, leave us alone. I'll call you later."

Brigitte frowned, obviously irked she wasn't going to witness the rest of Celeste's story unfold. "Let me clean up the coffee before I go."

"Don't bother. I'll take care of it later."

Reluctantly, Brigitte got up and looked from Jack to Celeste. "She could be your—"

"Leave," Celeste said sternly, and Brigitte left without another word.

Left alone with the lookalike stranger, Jack didn't know what to say. She couldn't make sense of whatever Celeste was referring to. So she kept quiet as they studied each other, and, finally, Celeste broke the silence.

"Your French is fluent. Not a trace of an accent."

"Why would I have an accent?" She assumed everyone would think her local, since her French was indeed fluent.

"Because you are not from here."

"How do you know me?"

"You look different," Celeste replied.

"Different?"

Celeste was studying her so intently she fought the urge to squirm under the scrutiny. "Your face. You have changed it."

She actually felt her jaw drop. She sat forward and grasped the seat cushion beneath her. "How do you know about my face? Who are you?"

Celeste's expression changed to one of suspicious disbelief. "You mean you don't know?"

"I have no idea."

Celeste sighed and leaned back in her chair.

❖

Beijing, China
1:15 p.m.

The drop-off lanes outside the Beijing Capital International Airport were crowded with cars, buses, and motorbikes when Chase and Dario pulled up in their taxi some ten minutes before Heather's scheduled arrival. As much as she hated to touch him, she had to lift him from the cab into his wheelchair, because all the curbside baggage clerks and other personnel were busy.

Dario was cooperating—he'd instructed his goons to stay behind to deal with Jules's body and they'd had no problems getting safely out of the hotel—but she wouldn't relax until Heather was with them and they left China. Dario hadn't seemed concerned as to how his men would dispose of a dead man, which was probably due to his connections, but he did seem unnerved by the prospect of having to travel with a complete stranger and Heather. He'd said little during the journey here and was sweating despite the cool temperatures.

While they waited for Heather to arrive, Chase moved a few steps away from Dario to call headquarters without him overhearing. She briefed Pierce and made sure a military jet would be standing by at the Misawa Air Base in Japan to take them to France. During the excruciatingly long minutes that followed, she kept checking her watch and feeling for her concealed Glock. Though she was pretty sure Heather would be there as expected, she couldn't help worrying Dario would try to pull something.

Heather arrived five minutes later than expected, escorted from a dark sedan by a young man in a Chinese military uniform. If Chase hadn't had to appear controlled in front of Dario, she'd have bitten every single fingernail to the bone.

Heather smiled tentatively when she spotted Chase through the crowd, but her upbeat demeanor evaporated when she saw Dario there as well. "What's going on?" she asked once she'd joined them.

"I'll explain later," Chase said, "but we need him about as much as we need to get away from here."

Heather's face puckered in disgust. "I don't want him anywhere near me."

Dario snickered. "I can assure you, you are not exactly my company of choice, either."

"Heather, please." She glanced around, skimming the faces of those near them. They were far too exposed. "We need him and we need to go."

"Have you arrested him?"

"No. He's our ticket to Rózsa."

"Arrested me?" Dario looked shocked. "You're with the feds?"

"No such luck for you." Chase smiled and turned back to Heather. "We need him to find out where Rózsa is." She grabbed the handles of Dario's wheelchair and pushed him inside, with Heather following, and they hurried to the area dedicated to private business jets and charter aircraft. Once she'd handed over the necessary permits and paperwork—some of it Dario's and some provided by the EOO—Chase received a cleared departure slot for a half hour later, and the three of them rode to Dario's plane in an airport shuttle that resembled a golf cart.

One burly airport worker was busily refueling the jet, while another, clipboard in hand, waited for her to hand over her paperwork for a final perusal. Once she'd given him the documents, she dropped the staircase, then approached the two men. "English?" she asked, and the one with the clipboard nodded. "Lift him in," she said, handing the man several yuan bills. He took Dario inside while the other got his wheelchair and their bags.

"I suspect you're responsible for my freedom," Heather said as they both waited for the workers to get Dario settled.

"Are you all right?" Chase avoided eye contact, not sure she could face Heather after what had happened between them.

"They didn't hurt me, if that's what you mean."

She could feel Heather staring at her.

"But I was pretty damn scared I was about to become someone's next donor," Heather continued. "God, I just want to go home and forget all about this…abysmal experience."

"About that," she said softly. "I can't let you go back to the US yet."

"What do you mean?"

"Dario isn't the forgiving type."

"But I take it you made a deal with him."

"Do you think he'll care about our agreement after I let him go?"

"Let him go?" Heather sounded furious at the prospect, but Chase still couldn't meet her eyes.

"I can't just kill him," she said. "He's not part of my assignment."

"He's a criminal."

"He is, but I wasn't hired to go after him."

"Can't you have him arrested?"

"Again, he's not my problem."

"He became your problem when you involved me."

"I'm getting you out safe and sound, right?"

"Out, yes," Heather snapped. "But not safe and sound. Not when I can't even go back to my own country. And what's going to stop him from coming after me when you're done with him?"

"We're going to relocate you, with the help of the feds."

"Are you serious?" Heather shouted. "My life isn't for you to play with or decide what happens to me. I came here to help you, not for a life makeover. Did you conveniently forget to tell me all this before you scammed me into helping you?"

"I understand this is all too much to take in right now," Chase said, "but I didn't set out to destroy your life. If things had gone according to plan, if Dario had never found the wire, everything would have worked out differently."

"But I suppose you forgot to inform me about that particular scenario. So, instead, I get a, 'Oh, oops, Heather…things didn't go according to plan. It's too bad, but we're going to change your life now.'" Out of the corner of her eye, she saw Heather run her hand through her hair in exasperation. "I have a sick brother, or did you forget about that, too?"

"Of course not. We'll make arrangements for him to come with you," she said quietly, hoping to calm her down.

"That's just….just…"

The two airport workers emerged from the jet, interrupting their conversation. The one with her paperwork nodded at Chase as he returned the documents. "Takeoff in twenty-one minutes," he warned her sternly, as though there might be repercussions if she wasn't ready to depart precisely on time. "I still have to check the cockpit."

She nodded her approval and he went back inside. Heather stared at the jet like it was a one-way transport to Hell. "You have to get in, Heather," she said gently. "Please. It's for your own safety."

"Fuck." Heather hesitated another several seconds, but finally headed toward the narrow stairway with Chase beside her. Chase extended her hand to help her aboard.

"Don't touch me." Heather's icy tone and rigid body language spoke volumes about her state of mind, and if looks could kill, Chase would already be six feet under. It hurt to see Heather so angry with her, but this whole damn situation was beyond her control. Yet again, her job was defining her personal decisions, actions, and reactions, and silently demanding her to do whatever was necessary. She wanted only to take Heather the hell away from this mess, but, like Landor, all she could do was protect her from the danger she herself had put her in.

Chase followed her into the plane and asked both Heather and Dario to buckle up as she walked past them up the aisle toward the cockpit.

The airport worker was just coming out with his clipboard. "You're ready for takeoff," he told her.

"Thanks. I'm good to go."

As she followed him out, Heather and Dario simultaneously blurted out, "What?"

She turned to look at them as she closed and secured the door.

Heather looked dumbfounded. "You're going to fly this?"

Dario sat rubbing his thighs with his eyes shut, as though willing his legs to work long enough for him to jump off the jet.

"Relax, I've done this before. Once." She smiled. She hoped Heather would realize she was joking to break the ice, but when Heather started to unbuckle, Chase went to her and stooped to stop her hands "I used to do this for a living in the military," she whispered. "Tru…I know what I'm doing."

Heather looked at her dubiously for a few seconds, but finally relaxed back in her seat.

Once she was satisfied Heather wasn't going anywhere, she went back to Dario and withdrew a set of handcuffs from her jacket.

"Is that necessary?" he asked. "Do you think I'm going to jump?"

Heather answered before she had a chance to. "I think it's necessary."

Chase secured Dario's wrist to his armrest. "You heard the lady." She rose and headed toward the cockpit. "First stop, a US military base in Japan to change aircraft. Then on to France."

"I wish to avoid any involvement with the military." Dario still looked and sounded shell-shocked about her piloting the plane.

She shrugged. "And I wish you didn't exist. If only wishes made a difference."

CHAPTER THIRTY-ONE

Off the coast of France

Cassady groaned as she came awake, her jaw aching from Rózsa's beating when she'd tried to free herself in the bathtub of the hotel. The intervening hours or days—she wasn't sure how much time had elapsed—were a blur. He'd drugged her so heavily she had only rare and brief semi-lucid moments, but whatever he'd given her seemed to be finally wearing off enough for her to ascertain her current situation.

She was on a small motorboat of some kind, and they were at sea. The porthole near her head gave her a view of endless blue, and nothing else. She was lying on a cot in the sleeping compartment, hog-tied so tight her hands were numb. Her mouth was sandpaper, so dry she couldn't swallow, and after so many days without adequate nourishment, she was too weak to free herself. Not that she had any useful resources to help her—he'd stripped the room of everything but the bed and a blanket.

The urge to despair was strong. He'd won. She could no longer hope for any chance of escape, and if he continued to deprive her of food and water, she'd be dead in a few days at most. Thinking of Jack was her only comfort. *I'm sorry, sweetheart. I tried. I did everything I could to get back to you.* She closed her eyes and tried to block out everything but images of their happy times together.

Some minutes elapsed before a sound broke her from her reverie—kitchen noises, from close by. Rózsa was fiddling with pots and pans; the galley must be right outside the small door to the sleeping compartment. A short time later, he entered, holding a bowl and a glass of water, and though he tried to keep his face neutral, she detected a hint of relief in his eyes.

"Please," she croaked through parched lips. "I can't feel my hands."

She'd grown so accustomed to his stoic silences and indifference to her suffering she didn't expect him to answer, but he surprised her. "I'll untie you for ten minutes, but if you make any further trouble, I'll toss you overboard with an anchor and be done with you. In a few hours, I'll likely have no further use for you, anyway."

His cryptic warning sent chills through her. "What does that mean?"

"Your people are apparently unable to meet my demands, but I may not need them after all," he said as he untied her. "Enjoy your meal. It's probably your last."

❖

Sainte-Maxime, France
6 p.m.

"You never answered me," Jack said, her heart hammering with anticipation. "How do you know me?"

"I promised to never contact you," Celeste replied. "I wanted to, but…he made me promise."

"Who made you promise what?"

"Your father."

"My father? You know my father?"

"I do."

"How? And why would you contact me in the first place?"

"Look at me, Jaclyn," Celeste said quietly.

Jack couldn't get past their resemblance, but was that what this woman was referring to?

"What do you see?"

"A woman who looks a lot like me. So what?" Unnerved by the conversation, she tried to sound flippant.

"That is because you are mine."

Jack opened her mouth to speak but nothing came out.

"You are my daughter, Jaclyn."

Jack got up and paced. How was this possible? She was here to find Cass but instead found a stranger who looked freakishly like her and claimed to be her mother. This was all too weird to be true. She knew she'd been born in France, but that was all. Ops were told only their country of origin and that they'd been selected from orphanages because of their intelligence and other extraordinary abilities. As far as she knew, none had ever run into their biological parents. Why was this happening to her? What kind of joke was life playing on her this time? She raked her hand through her hair as she continued to pace, then finally stopped and turned to face the woman. "How are you sure?"

Celeste got up. "Please, wait for me here. I want to show you something." She paused in the doorway leading toward the rear of the house as if to make sure Jack wouldn't leave. "I will be right back."

Her head felt as though it would burst. It was all too much to grasp. Could this woman really be her mother? She kept pacing, this time more keenly attuned to her surroundings, curious about the stranger who had her face. The house was even smaller than it appeared from outside, but clean and orderly and warm. Homey, with crocheted afghans and embroidered pillows on the antique couch and matching armchairs, and local watercolors on the walls.

She stopped to look at a photo on the fireplace mantel. Celeste, at a much younger age, probably in her twenties. The resemblance was uncanny. Celeste's smile was forced and her eyes were worried, which made her look even more like Jack.

"It was shot shortly after you were taken away from me," Celeste said from behind her. "Please, come sit next to me."

She turned and found Celeste on the couch with a shoebox on her lap. She hesitated, not sure she wanted to see what Celeste wanted to show her, but after several seconds succumbed to her curiosity. "Who took me away?" she asked as she took a seat beside the woman.

"Your father."

"Why?"

"I didn't have the means or…lifestyle…to support you back then, so I had to tell him about your existence when I called him to ask for help."

"He didn't know he'd fathered a child?"

"No. I never told him I was pregnant, or anything about you at all until three years later, when I realized I couldn't…support you."

"So you weren't married to him."

"He was an officer in the American army. When I told him about you, he travelled here immediately. He refused to leave without you after he saw you. I wanted to keep you, Jaclyn, but I was afraid my lifestyle would affect you."

"Hold on a minute. Where did you meet him? Was he a tourist here?"

Celeste shook her head. "He was in France for six months for his work. A tall, handsome man. Always so gentle and charming." Her expression became wistful, almost sweetly melancholic. "A true gentleman, the type of man I wasn't used to back then. Even after the six months were over, he used to come back to visit me. We had been seeing each other for two years before I got pregnant."

"How did you meet?"

"I came from a very poor family, Jaclyn. I had no education and no prospects for a future. I did what I could to help support my siblings. I cleaned houses, sewed clothes, and baked to help my family."

"You gave me away because you were poor?" she said, exasperated. "That's no reason to—"

Celeste raised her hand. "The money wasn't enough to feed so many mouths, so I did the unthinkable. And that's where I met your father."

"What do you mean?"

"I was working in a brothel at the time."

"You mean you were a…a…"

"Prostitute."

Jack dropped back against the couch and ran her hands though her hair. "Jesus fucking Christ." She pulled out her pack of cigarettes and prepared to light one. "I need a smoke."

"I will not have that in my house. It's a disturbing habit, and I will not have you kill yourself in front of me. And watch your mouth, young lady." Celeste frowned.

"First of all, I'm forty, and second…really? Cursing and smoking are what bother you about all this?"

"There's no need for harsh language," Celeste said sternly, "or self-destruction." Her face quickly softened. "Your father took you away, and he was right to do so. A place like that is not where a child belongs. You deserved a better life than I could offer."

"How…how did you know he was the father? I mean, you were seeing other men then."

Celeste shrugged. "I just knew it. I was careful with other men, but not with your father. He knew there was a good chance you weren't his, but that didn't stop him from coming right over. Once he saw you, he knew. Just like I did."

"So, where is he now? What happened to him? Because I sure as hell didn't grow up with my father."

Celeste looked away. "I don't know. I was never informed."

"I grew up in an institution, adopted by a private organization in the US where they train children from all over the world to kill, steal, and die for them." She saw Celeste wince in pain at the recounting of her history. "Did my father sell me to them?"

Celeste took the lid off the shoebox. "I don't know," she replied as she busied herself with the contents.

"What was his name?"

"Jack Burnes. He named you after himself. I had given you the name Isabelle, but he insisted on changing it to Jaclyn even though you were already three years old." Celeste removed a picture from the box and held it up. "This is the day you were born. You were such a beautiful baby."

Jack took the faded Polaroid and stared at it. A much-younger and weary-looking Celeste, propped up on pillows in a bed, cradled her infant daughter with an expression of serene joy. She had never expected to see a picture of herself as a newborn in the arms of her mother; the experience was so overwhelming she had to fight back tears.

"This one was taken six months later." Celeste handed her another photo.

Jack was clutching a stuffed bunny, her eyes bright with glee as she smiled at the camera.

"And this one was taken on your first birthday." Celeste wiped her eyes.

Jack in a highchair, dressed in green overalls, caught laughing—her tiny fist gripped a remnant of cake and she had chocolate smudged all over her face. "I do like chocolate," she said, and her voice broke.

"And these are—"

"I remember those," she said, when Celeste gently lifted a mobile from the box. Five cherubs—thin, delicate sculptures about three inches long and made of braided gold wire—hung from a frame of wooden dowels. "My angels. My golden angels."

"I made them for you," Celeste said. "They used to hang over your crib. From the day you were born until you left."

Jack reached for them and couldn't fight the tears anymore. They fell freely down her cheeks. "My angels," she said again.

Celeste put her arm around her and they cried together. "I'm so sorry, Jaclyn. I want you to know if I had to do it all again, I would do it differently. I would have never let you go. Not to that kind of life."

Jack kept looking at the mobile. "They were always in my dreams. The golden angels." She held it up. "One angel is missing."

"I gave it to your father when he took you," Celeste said. "You used to look at those angels for hours. I wanted you to have something from your time with me. Something you loved, that made you smile."

"I don't know what happened to it."

"Maybe your father does."

"How did you know I changed my face?"

"I used to get pictures of you every few years." Celeste reached in the box and handed her pictures starting in her preteens up to before she left for Israel and changed her life and face. All were candid shots taken of her private life—the early ones when she was away from the Colorado EOO campus on field trips, the later photos when she was in New York between assignments. "Who sent you these?"

"I don't know. There was never a return address but I'm sure it's your father."

"Was he keeping tabs on me?"

"Maybe."

"You said he was American, so I guess it's possible he found me or knew where to find me," she mused. "Do you ever hear from him?"

"No, but he still sends me money. He has a man deliver it to me once a month. He was always very generous."

"I see."

"Do you still work for that organization?"

"No…well, I haven't for years. I faked my death to get away from them, but…they found me ten years later. I agreed to work with them this once because some fuck…jerk kidnapped the woman I love. She's an op…works for the same organization."

"I'm sorry to hear that." Celeste didn't seem the least bit surprised at her sexuality.

"This is her." She removed the picture of Cass from her back pocket and held it up. "Her name is Cassady."

"Very pretty."

"Yeah." She smiled but could also tell from the neutral look on Celeste's face that the picture didn't ring any bells. "She's in a lot of danger and I have to find her soon."

"You love her."

"More than I love myself."

"It is the only true way to love."

She smiled. "Yeah, it is the only way."

"Then you must do whatever it takes to find her."

She got up. "I have to get going."

"Will I see you again?" Celeste rose too and led the way to the door.

Jack followed her, still in disbelief but with a strange sense of euphoria. "I would like that."

Celeste opened the door. "I, too. I don't want to lose you now that I've found you," she said, tears in her eyes. "Can I hold you before you go?"

She hesitated for a moment and then practically threw herself at…her mother. She held her so tight she was afraid she'd hurt her. For the first time in her life, she felt she had a past; she belonged to someone. She dug her face into Celeste's neck and took a deep breath to savor her essence. "Did you love me? While I was with you, I mean?"

"Then and now," Celeste murmured as she hugged her back, "more than I love myself."

CHAPTER THIRTY-TWO

Misawa Air Base, Japan
4:15 p.m.

Less than three hours after leaving Beijing, Dario's plane touched down in northern Japan at a sprawling airfield busy with military aircraft and personnel in US Army, Navy, and Air Force uniforms. From her window, Heather could see a navy-suited airman waiting for them with a van. He conversed privately with Landis, then helped get Dario and their luggage into the vehicle and took them across the tarmac to a waiting US Air Force jet.

Heather went inside. The seats were similar to those on a commercial plane, but arranged along both sides of the interior, apparently so cargo could be transported in the large empty space between them. She took a seat toward the front, on the opposite side from Dario. It was as far from him as she could get, though the arrangement meant she'd have to face the jerk during the entire journey.

When she went to buckle in, Heather found a shoulder-belt harness instead of the standard lap belt, and though it looked straightforward, her hands were shaking so much from exhaustion and anger she couldn't fasten it. After several unsuccessful attempts, she tossed it aside in exasperation. "Screw it," she said out loud.

Sighing, she looked out the window at the bustling personnel and luggage trucks. Landis was talking to a senior air-force officer with a barrage of medals on his chest. When did her life get this surreal? She had never felt more lost or alone; she didn't know what to make of this situation. She hadn't spoken to her brother in days, and he hadn't contacted her at the hotel number she'd given him. She wanted to call him just to hear his voice and make sure he was okay, but she would have to wait until they reached France.

What if something had happened to Adam during this disastrous trip? She'd never be able to forgive herself. How would she ever be able to deal with having left her brother just to help a couple of strangers or a friend who was dead anyway? She'd trusted Landis would keep her promise to keep her safe, but she'd failed. At this point, Heather didn't know who had betrayed her more: Dario, the murderous organ-snatching bastard who'd had her arrested as a junkie, or Landis for using her. Either way, both were a threat to her life. The only difference was, Landis had gained and abused her trust; Landis had presented herself as a caring individual who had asked Heather to trust her. At least Dario hadn't made any phony promises or shown anything other than lust. She could have sworn up until last night that Landis sincerely liked her, which only made the betrayal harder to accept.

The object of her musings came on board and tilted her head toward the seat next to Heather. "May I join you?"

She shrugged. "If you must." She was in no mood to chat, however; she was far too angry, so she pulled her MP3 from her bag and plugged the buds in her ears. Not long after, once they were in the air, she felt Landis lean back and relax. When she ventured a glance that way a few minutes later, Landis had her eyes shut and appeared to be dozing.

She used the opportunity to study the mysterious woman who had turned her life upside down. Dark circles under her eyes and deep worry lines marred the usual calm confidence that she'd come to associate with Landis. For the first time since they'd met, she looked vulnerable and near collapse from exhaustion. Despite her own feelings of hurt, Heather wanted to erase the pain and pull Landis to her chest.

Soon, she drifted off as well, and when she awoke, she felt pressure on her left shoulder. Landis's head rested there; she could feel her slow exhalations through the thin material of her blouse. She checked her watch and found she'd been asleep for an hour and a half. Though she'd tried not to disturb Landis, the other woman stirred and groggily opened her eyes.

"I'm sorry." Landis sat up abruptly.

"Just woke up myself," she replied.

Dario laughed. He was watching them intently.

"What's there to laugh about?" Landis asked.

"You looked so perfect sleeping together." His voice oozed sarcasm.

"Jealous?" Landis asked.

"Hardly. I can get another Amber whenever I please."

"If you pay her enough."

Dario ignored Landis's comeback and turned his attention to Heather. He smiled at her with an inexplicably smug expression, considering his current circumstances. "Tell me, Amber, how long have you known your friend?"

"My name is Heather and it's none of your damn business."

"From your pouting attitude," he said, "and unpleasant exchange with her in China before you were politely abducted and made to join us, I'd say you don't know her much at all."

"What business is it of yours?" she asked.

"It's not, but I refuse to be judged about how I attain my company…sexual gratification, if you will, from someone who, in my humble opinion, is no better than I."

"What are you getting at?" She was curious.

Landis grabbed the armrests of her seat until her knuckles turned white. "You don't know anything about me."

His smile grew. "I know enough to recognize someone who isn't a stranger to the pleasures of paid sex."

She turned to Landis. "What's he talking about?"

"Ignore him." Landis glared daggers at him. "He's trying to divide and conquer."

"From my angle, there's nothing to divide. Our Heather doesn't seem very happy with the predicament you've put her in. And correct me if I'm wrong, but didn't you put her life in danger when you decided to use her?"

"Shut up," Landis said quietly.

"Tell me, Heather…the performance you two put on for my benefit last night," he went on. "Didn't it seem peculiar to you how comfortable…familiar, even, your friend was with the rules and how quickly she adapted?"

"She was acting." She didn't know why she felt the need to defend Landis, but the thought of her having to buy sex seemed too absurd and somehow made Heather feel exposed.

"Was she?"

"Mind your own business," Landis said aggressively.

"Some things cannot be acted." He kept his focus on Heather. "She didn't have a moment of hesitation or need explanations. The way she…handled you…a true pro."

"I did my homework," Landis said through gritted teeth.

She didn't understand why Landis was getting so worked up.

"If your homework includes buying sex, then you've been quite studious."

"What are you trying to do?" Landis unbuckled her belt and got up, hands curled into fists.

"Tell me I'm wrong." He smiled, clearly happy he was pushing Landis's buttons. "No reason to be ashamed for your choices…or is there?" He rubbed his hands. "You see, I may be a lot of things, but I'm not a hypocrite. I may have to pay to fuck, but I at least have the balls to admit it. How about you? Are you so ashamed of yourself, so spineless, that you can't admit you like to pay for pussy?"

Shocked, Heather stared at Dario. Though she now knew the true nature of his loathsome business, he had always rigidly maintained a veneer of polite decorum and control. She had never heard him use such language, and although he was outwardly calm, the hate was clear in his eyes.

Without warning, Landis crossed the plane in a blur and grabbed him by the throat.

"The truth too ugly to bear?" he managed to say while choking. "You thought fucking whores was fun until you fell for one?" He started to cough.

She tried to pull Landis away, afraid she would kill him right in front of her. "Let him go."

Landis relented and released her grip, but she wasn't done with him. She leaned into him with menace in her eyes, fiercely gripping his armrests. "You're right. I pay for sex. But I have the spine to show my face and do it myself. I don't need to hide behind glass and jerk off while some joker in reindeer underwear does it for me."

"Reindeer underw…" Her mind clouded with Landis's admissions. She hires call girls. And worse—there was only one way she could know what that john she had been with the other night had been wearing.

Landis let go of Dario and turned to her. It was clear from Landis's face that she didn't immediately realize what she'd just said; she was still enraged with Dario. But when she saw the expression on Heather's face she put it together pretty quickly. Her rage faded, replaced by shock and regret.

"You watched me while I…" She stuttered. "You said you never…" She didn't know where to start. "You pay for sex?" Flabbergasted by the revelations and lies, she sat back down and covered her face.

"Is there a problem?" an unfamiliar male voice asked.

She looked up. A young man in civilian clothes but with a military stance loomed over them.

Landis straightened after giving Dario a final threatening look. "We're fine now," she told the man, dismissing him.

When he'd returned to the cockpit, Landis sat beside her again but didn't look at her. "I was going to tell you."

"Which part?"

"Both, all."

"When?"

"After we—"

She waved her hand. "You know what? I actually don't give a damn about what you have to say because you clearly have a problem with the truth."

"I'm sorry, I—"

"The two of you are just a different shade of evil." She tried to keep calm, but her emotions were all over the place, and she was close to losing any trace of composure she had left. She felt so ashamed and…used. "Only difference between you is he's a greedy, murdering bastard, and you're a lying, ruthless one."

She got up and walked to the rear of the plane and sat by another window, facing away. When she was sure Landis didn't intend to follow her, she let the tears of betrayal and pain fall.

CHAPTER THIRTY-THREE

Marseille, France
10:15 p.m.

Chase dialed Jack's number as soon as they landed and asked her to meet them at the Villa Massalia Concorde, where Reno had found two available rooms one floor apart. Three miles from the city center in a quiet, residential neighborhood, the four-star hotel offered panoramic views of the Mediterranean Sea, a few blocks away, and the adjacent Borely Park. The drive getting there in the rental van was tedious and deadly quiet—Heather was still angry at the whole situation, and Dario was either pouting or scheming.

Jack was outside, her bag at her feet, when they pulled up to the curb. She pushed herself off the brick exterior when Chase emerged from behind the driver's seat. Glancing inside, she asked, "What's up with the tourist group?"

"I'll explain later, but it was necessary."

"This'll be fun."

"What have you been up to?" Chase asked as Heather got out the other side.

"No luck with tracking Rózsa," Jack replied benignly. She had a calmness about her that didn't make sense.

"Anything else?"

"Yeah. Later."

"Is someone going to help me out?" Dario asked.

Jack glanced his way. "Looks like your carry-on is getting impatient."

Chase removed the wheelchair from the back of the van and wheeled it over to the passenger side, while Jack helped Heather get her suitcase. "Welcome to the screwed-up world of intrigue," Jack said to her. "How are you enjoying it so far?"

"Let's see," Heather replied drolly. "I've been lied to and misled by you and your friend, arrested because Dario planted cocaine in my bag when he found the wire, thrown in jail, and was about to become spare parts."

"I can't vouch for the other two," Jack said, "but I never lied to you."

"You said there were no cameras in the brownstone."

"Oh. That." Jack looked down at her feet.

"Yes," Heather said. "That."

Jack fidgeted and cast a reproachful look Chase's way. "Christ, Brett, why'd you have to tell her?"

Heather didn't even blink when Jack used Chase's fake name because Dario was there. "Brett…didn't tell me, she told Dario."

"Why would you do that?" Jack asked Chase.

"Can we let it go? I'm really not in the mood for this conversation."

"Why wouldn't you be?" Heather asked. "It wasn't you who was being violated."

"If it makes any difference, she didn't watch," Jack said. "Neither of us did. We turned off the visual before anything happened and stayed with the audio. As a matter of fact, Brett didn't even listen in. I did."

Chase was helping Dario into his chair during the exchange. When she glanced at them, she saw Heather staring at Jack in surprise.

"Don't look at me like that," Jack told Heather. "Someone had to, and it's not like I hadn't heard it all before."

Heather turned to Chase with an unreadable expression. When Chase didn't react, she said, "Why didn't you just tell me?"

Chase didn't reply. She rolled Dario up on the pavement.

"Interesting question, Heather. Please, tell us, Brett." Dario was clearly enjoying the conversation.

"Butt out," Jack said. "Your voice bothers me."

"And who exactly are you?" he asked.

"My name's Bite Me and I don't like questions."

"Let's check in." Chase started to wheel Dario toward the entrance.

"You never answered the…lady," he said.

"Another word out of you and I'm going to push you into oncoming traffic. Accidentally, of course," Jack said.

"Your friend, or colleague, or whatever, wouldn't be too thrilled about that since I'm a precious commodity." Dario tried to appear unmoved, but Chase could see Jack's threat unnerved him.

She knew Jack would never hurt Dario because it was necessary to keep him alive in order to get to Cassady, but he had no idea how much Jack had riding on him. If he felt threatened enough by Jack to stay quiet and afraid, so much the better. Chase winked at Jack to encourage her.

"She's not my friend." Jack loomed over him with a feral grin. "As a matter of fact, I can barely tolerate her. I'm here because I owe her a favor, but paybacks only go so far."

"Play nice," Chase said. "I need him alive."

"Fine. But if he so much as looks at me, I'm going to remove his eyes."

"That's my job," Dario said casually.

Jack pushed Chase aside and went for her gun. "Let me at him."

Chase pretended to struggle with her and Dario looked worried for the first time.

"You owe me," she told Jack as they fought. "You can't hurt him."

Jack stopped the fake struggle and glared daggers at Dario. "One more word and all bets are off."

He looked terrified. Heather was trying hard not to smile.

Chase grabbed her rucksack. "Can we go now?" she asked them all.

"Yeah. I'm cool." Jack reached for Dario's chair to wheel him in.

"Not her," he shouted in panic. "Don't let her touch my chair. I'll do it myself."

"Then get moving." Jack kicked his chair from behind and Dario rolled through the entrance. They followed with their luggage.

Chase checked them in and, as she collected the pair of key cards, asked the receptionist to have the maids stay away from their rooms.

"I don't want to share a room with anyone," Dario said as they took the elevator up to their rooms. "I'll pay for my own."

"It's not about money, prima donna," Jack replied. "It's about leaving your sorry ass alone."

Dario looked up at Chase. "I'm not sharing with her," he said, referencing Jack.

"Aw, too bad," Jack replied. "I was really looking forward to bonding with you."

"Let me stay with Heather," Dario pleaded.

Heather wrinkled her nose in disgust. "Yeah, that's gonna happen."

"You're staying with me," Chase told Dario. "Heather, you're with her." She avoided using Jack's name in front of Dario.

"Why can't I get my own room?" Heather asked.

"I'm starting to feel unwanted," Jack said.

"I wonder why?" Dario muttered.

"Did he just talk to me?" Jack reached for her gun again.

"Brett," Dario said quickly. "I'm talking to you, Brett."

The whole situation was so comical Chase had to do her best not to laugh. God, how she'd missed Jack. "You'll be fine," she told Heather.

"You want her to babysit me."

"I want her to make sure you're safe."

"Are you implying I might hurt her?" Dario asked, trying to sound offended.

"Never, being the sweet soul you are," Jack replied. "We're just worried she might slip and fall in the shower."

"Why does *she* get to talk to *me*?" Dario asked no one in particular.

The elevator opened on the fourth floor and they got out. Chase handed Jack one of the key cards. "The three of us need to talk before we quit for the night. Your room."

"What do you want to do about the creep on wheels?"

"He's coming with. I'm not leaving him alone in case Rózsa decides to call."

"This late?" Heather asked.

"Crime knows no time." Jack glanced at Dario as she unlocked the room. "Right, creep? And don't talk, it was rhetorical."

They all entered the spacious room, which had a pair of double beds, a table and two chairs, and a balcony. Though it was clean and modern and had the usual amenities of any four-star hotel, the room lacked the opulence of Dario's suite in Beijing.

"Mediocrity is the elephant in this room," Dario said, looking around.

"Do you need to use the bathroom?" Chase asked as the others dropped their bags.

"No, why?"

"Because I'm about to cuff you to the radiator."

"That's absurd."

"So is your occupation."

"I'm a cripple, isn't that handicap enough?" Dario asked. "Why do you have to detain me?"

"Your disability hasn't been an obstacle as far as causing trouble is concerned. You seem to manage just fine." Chase secured one handcuff to Dario's left wrist, the other to the sturdy steel radiator. "I'm going to step out on the balcony. I'll be able to see your every move."

Dario tested the cuffs. "I'm not exactly in any position to escape."

"Where's your cell?"

"Why?" he asked.

"Where is it?"

"I'm not comfortable with any of this."

"I'm not concerned with your comfort level," Chase said. "Just tell me where the damn thing is."

"Want me to frisk him?" Jack asked. "I'm very thorough."

Dario pulled it out of his pocket with his free hand. "Here." He gave it to Chase. "What if Rózsa calls?"

"I'll hand you the phone."

Heather frowned. "Are you going to leave me in here with him?"

"We'll be just outside," Chase said.

"Call me if Hot Wheels bothers you." Jack gave Dario a menacing look, which he pretended not to see, staring instead at the ceiling.

Heather flipped on the television as Chase and Jack stepped out onto the balcony.

"Do you want to tell me why you seem so upbeat or should we skip to business?" Chase asked. "Although, I have to admit, your bright attitude is a bit disconcerting."

"You go first," Jack said. "I can't wait to hear why the peanut gallery is here."

Chase caught her up on Dario finding the wire and how he had Heather arrested for cocaine possession, and the deal she made with Dario to get to Rózsa.

"Of course, just because he said he'd play nice doesn't mean he will," Jack said when she'd finished. "He could still have his goons go after Rózsa and throw our hides in for good measure. I doubt his sister wants any witnesses."

"I told him to call his men in France off, and as far as I heard he did, but you know how it works."

"Yup. Say one thing to your men and mean another."

"And that's why Heather is here," Chase said. "I don't want her back in the States before this is resolved. I'm going to have Pierce get the feds to relocate her and her brother after we give them Rózsa."

"Hell, if we deliver Rózsa, the feds will do our laundry and windows."

"That's right."

"I'm gonna guess Heather didn't take it too well."

"Well…" Chase sighed.

"Yeah. I didn't think so."

"The money drop-off is tomorrow. Rózsa hasn't called yet, but I'm sure he's not going to make it easy."

"He didn't invent a virus, kill millions, and run with my girl by being stupid."

"Chances are we're going to have to deal with both Rózsa and Dario's men."

"Yeah. But come hell or high crap, I'm getting Cass back. We don't have to deliver Rózsa alive, right?"

"Pierce never said."

"Good," Jack replied. "Because the guy has the life expectancy of a bad sitcom."

❖

Heather tried to distract herself by flipping through the channels, but the few mildly interesting possibilities were in French. Now and then she'd glance over at Dario, sitting across from her. She had his undivided attention and didn't like it. It was creepy being alone in a bedroom with him now, with him *watching* her, so much so she deliberately chose a chair instead of relaxing on the bed. "Why are you staring at me?" she asked.

"Because you are like a puzzle to me, Heather."

"Whatever."

"With all due respect, I would think that someone in your line of business would be a bit quicker to see when they are being used."

"My line of business."

"Someone who's…been around." He smiled knowingly.

"You do enjoy rubbing that in, don't you?"

"Why shouldn't I? I have a lot of respect for what you do."

"Have done."

His feigned look of apology was pathetically transparent. "Of course. In any case, it takes a strong individual to decide to follow your particular path. A determined, selfless woman more concerned about the well-being of her brother than her own."

He was up to something. She just didn't know what it was. "What are you trying to do?"

"Do? Nothing. Nothing at all. I'm merely impressed and at the same time surprised by your choices. A puzzle."

Heather lowered the sound on the TV. "What are you saying?"

"While I am impressed for the reasons I just mentioned, I can't help but feel surprised at how impaired your reasoning has become as far as…" He pursed his lips. "Let's play along and call her Brett…is concerned. There's no reason why she'd give me her real name, and let's face it, she doesn't look like a Brett." He gave her a chummy conspiratorial smile, like two good friends who could see through a lie.

"Brett," she said with emphasis, "has not impaired anything."

He shook his head. "I doubt that. She is more or less a complete stranger to you, who—"

"No, she's not," she lied. "I know her well enough."

"Not well enough, or you wouldn't have been surprised at how she lied to you. She spied on you while you were with me and denied it."

She didn't respond.

"I wonder what else she's lied about. Don't you?"

"What do you care?"

"I care because I can see what they are doing to you."

"That's rich. You care so much you had me arrested."

"I felt betrayed. I trusted you. I sincerely liked you and still do, now that I realize how innocent you really are. But when I found out about the wire, I…I felt hurt. I asked you to join me in China because, like I told you then, you're different. Compassionate. I never meant to hurt you, but I reacted like any deceived lover. I lashed out. I'm sincerely sorry, but only now do I realize how stupidly compassionate you really are. So much, as a matter of fact, you can't see the game they're playing and how it's going to end."

"What do you mean?"

"You're delusional if you think they're going to let you live. You've seen too much and know too much."

Chapter Thirty-four

"I think you're officially the first operative to find their biological parent." Chase still couldn't believe Jack's revelation. Jack had relayed the amazing story of meeting her mother and what she'd learned: how her parents had met and how her mysterious father took her away but kept tabs on her.

Chase had stopped wondering about her own past and roots after her teenage years; she knew only that she came from some orphanage in Norway. But she couldn't help feeling happy and jealous that Jack had managed to discover some of her history. "I suppose I would be in good spirits, too, had I found my mother."

"What's funny is how easy it is to consider her just that," Jack said. "I don't know if it's because we look alike or because she was never replaced. It's not like the kids at the organization ever get adopted by new parents."

"No. A corporation adopts us. Hardly the same. Will you see her again?"

"Yeah." Jack smiled. "We'd both like that."

"Are you going to look for your father?"

"Wouldn't know where to start."

"Do you care?"

Jack leaned against the balcony rail and gazed out at the distant Mediterranean, a vast, black void dotted here and there with the twinkling lights of anchored or passing boats. "I'm not sure. I somehow always pictured him as a strong, heroic figure. Someone who gave me away against his will. Turns out, my mother was the heroic figure who wanted to keep me. He was just some guy who had his fun and left her, even when he found out they had a child."

"But he took you with him."

"Only to give me away again. As far as I'm concerned, he can screw himself."

"He cared enough to look you up and send her pictures."

"I don't get that part." Jack went quiet for a moment. "Either way, he never manned up enough to approach me and deal with his actions. I don't like cowards."

"I guess. But you never know what reasons people have for their actions. It's not like you haven't been there."

Jack straightened and glared at her. "Are you going to tell me how you know? If not, how long are we going to continue the insinuation game?"

"You still haven't asked the right—"

"Fuck that, Landis," Jack shouted. "Don't start getting all superior on me again about what I've done."

"It was never about any of that. Yes, you worked for scum and you were good at it because you learned from the best. And honestly, I can't blame you for leaving the organization. When it comes down to it, they only took us in because of what we can do for them, not the other way around. None of the three cares about our needs. They care about our skills."

"Pierce is worse than the rest." Jack gripped the rail with both hands. "All he cares about is himself and how much he gets if we do the job."

"Don't be naïve. They're all the same. At least he doesn't pretend to care. He acknowledges good work and rewards it accordingly."

"Rewards who?" Jack looked puzzled. "What?"

"He let you live, didn't he? Take that as a show of affection. It's as good as it gets. And in case you never noticed, you were the only one he ever showed any understanding and weakness for."

"Are you shitting me?" Jack laughed bitterly. "The guy ran me ragged, never said a good word."

"Then you clearly don't remember how you were the only kid he ever ran to when you fell, or hurt yourself, or got sick. The only one he visited in the recovery ward and slept by their side."

"I don't remember…" Jack stared off into the distance. "Why don't I remember that?"

"I do. I wished he'd have shown even a fraction of that interest in me."

Jack went silent, either because she was trying to remember or, because for the first time since their reunion, she was speechless.

Either way, Chase had had enough of her pity parade and insane ideas of how the world had conspired against her. In reality, as a kid, Jack had it better than the rest, as far as Pierce was concerned. And had it been any other op but Jack who'd deserted and deceived him, they simply wouldn't have lived to bitch about it. "The right question is…*Who did I kill?*" Chase said, aggravated.

"What?"

"Do you remember Stellari?"

Jack looked surprised. "That was a long time ago."

"I worked deep cover on that case. I was in the warehouse when everything went to hell with the Russian arms dealer and the feds."

"That was ten years ago. One of my first jobs."

"If you say so."

"You've known about me from practically the beginning." The shock was clear on Jack's face. "You made me and never told anyone?"

She ignored the question. "A lot of innocent people died that night."

Jack didn't respond right away but looked back out over the water. "I know."

"You killed some of those innocent men."

Jack nodded.

"You also killed my lover. Stellari's daughter."

Jack spun to look at her with a horrified expression. "I…I had no idea. I…was just shooting at anything that moved. I had no idea his daughter was even there. Christ. I never even saw you." She pounded her fist on the railing. "You've got to believe me, Landis, I never saw her. I was pumped on adrenaline and angry at the world. I wanted the likes of the Russians to respect and fear me. I wanted them to accept me, because no one else would. After I survived Israel and fooled the EOO, I thought I had to reinvent myself. Show everyone who Jack really was."

"And who was that?"

"Someone to be reckoned with. Taken seriously. Not some misfit who jumped when she was asked to and was ignored if she wasn't needed. I wanted someone to care if I lived or died, even if it was for the wrong reasons."

"I cared."

"I know." Jack frowned. "But I didn't want to make you a conspirator. If they ever found out you knew or that we had contact, they'd have taken you down with me."

"I would have at least gone down fighting for something. Someone I believed in. That would have been a first."

"You must've been very angry with me." Jack hung her head and shook it slowly from side to side. "Not only for lying to you, but…Stellari's daughter…I don't know how to apologize. I don't think that's even possible."

"There was a lot of shooting going on. I can't say for sure you killed her, but yes. I was furious."

"And you never told Pierce," Jack repeated in disbelief.

"Would you have told on me? Even if I never spoke to you again, and let you think I was dead. Even if you thought I had killed your lover?"

Jack considered the question only for a few seconds before answering, and when she did, there was a catch in her voice. "No."

"Then you know why."

Jack nodded ruefully. "Yeah."

❖

"They'd never hurt me," Heather insisted. "I can't say I'm happy with how all this has played out, but they'd never harm me."

Dario's eyes narrowed dubiously. "How are you so sure, Heather?"

"Why would they? I'm no threat. As a matter of fact, I'm helping them out."

"They got what they needed from you, which now makes you disposable, if not redundant. You're nothing but an extra headache for them now."

"I know what you're trying to do."

"Oh?"

"Divide and conquer, like Brett said earlier."

"What would I gain? I'm not asking you to become my friend or ever see me again, and I doubt anything I say will make you help me from this predicament. Besides, it's not like you can do anything about it, even if you wanted to."

That was true, she thought.

"I don't want to see you get killed."

"They would never."

"That you don't know them…*Brett*…has already been established. But I wonder how little you actually do know her."

"Enough. I know her enough to believe you're evil."

"I doubt you even know her name. Let's face it. We're both aware it's not Brett. It would be highly unprofessional—not to mention dense—to give me her real identity. But I wonder if the name she's given *you* is real."

Heather had the same thought in China. Truth was, she didn't know Landis or Jack at all. Who was to say they weren't hit men, or whatever they were called, after Rózsa for their own benefit, like bounty hunters. Maybe they were after Dario to steal the money he intended to give to Rózsa. Who knew what was true anymore? Maybe the whole story about Jack's girlfriend was just to make Heather feel sorry for them. And how did they conveniently happen to find Gigi's cell? Could it be that Dario had nothing to do with her death after all, and they had made her disappear to get Heather to help? God, this was all too much to take in.

"You don't have to believe me, Heather. But if you ask me, this has nothing to do with any honorable cause, if that's what they've convinced you of. They haven't told me why they want Rózsa, but I'm guessing they're bounty hunters. There must be millions on his head. Last time I checked, there was nothing honorable about their sort. They'll kill their own mother if the price is right."

Oh, my God. Dario had spoken her thoughts. Could this possibly be true? She had never asked for or seen any official credentials. Maybe she could ask for that now. She got up from the chair and took a couple of steps toward the balcony, then reconsidered. No. What if they really were criminals and killed her on the spot for asking too many questions? They had no further use for her. She sat back down. But then why were they keeping her alive if they didn't need her? Landis could have let her rot in the Chinese prison.

"They probably still need you. I wouldn't know why, but perhaps some involvement in tomorrow's arrangement. Implicate you somehow with Rózsa."

Landis had admitted she thought Heather was helping Rózsa when they started following her. Could Dario be right?

"Perhaps they want someone to take the fall for what they're about to pull off. Someone they have evidence is linked to Rózsa."

"The payment through the brownstone's IP address," she whispered, and caught Dario's look of surprise, though concern quickly replaced it.

"Do they have any kind of proof, Heather? Something they can use against you?"

She needed to get out of here, fast.

"From the look on your face, I'd say they do." Dario shook his head. "They have framed you."

She looked over at him.

"Go, Heather. Go home to your brother. Leave now, while they're busy plotting and planning how to spend my money after tomorrow."

He was right. She had to leave. She got up and checked the balcony to make sure they weren't looking.

Dario followed her gaze. "Their backs are turned. Do it now. It'll be a while before they notice you're gone. Go."

She grabbed her purse and quietly walked to the door, keeping one eye on the balcony.

"Good luck," Dario called as she slipped into the hallway and shut the door.

❖

"You like Heather a lot, don't you?" Jack asked.

Chase didn't reply. Not because she didn't know the answer, but because she didn't want to admit it. She wasn't prepared to face her feelings, especially since she knew they were futile and unrequited.

"You don't have to tell me if you don't want," Jack said, "because I already know."

She shrugged.

"Want to know how I know?"

She shrugged again.

"Because the only time you don't check the time is when she's around."

She hadn't realized it, but it was true. Time never seemed to matter with Heather. She didn't feel chased or worried time would run out when they were together. As a matter of fact, she had a hard time thinking about anything at all around Heather. Even her upcoming deadline for her next novel was trivial.

"I know I've been hard on her because of…well, you know why," Jack said gently. "But you know what? She's a wonderful woman. Look at everything she's done for us, and at the risk of her own well-being. She loves her brother to the point of selling her… you know…"

"Her occupation has never mattered."

"Then what's the problem?"

"I am. I don't have the right to burden anyone with my life. My demons."

"I used to think the same, but you know, some demons…with the help of someone who truly loves you, eventually get the hell up and leave."

"And the rest?"

"Some never do." Jack looked away. "Some demons are forever."

She put her hand on Jack's shoulder. "We'll find Lynx."

"Yeah." Jack faced her. "We will."

She pivoted to check on Dario. "He has a smug look on his face."

Jack grinned. "Want me to change that?"

"Yes." She smiled back. "In this case, you can tease the animal."

"Let's see what he's up to." Jack opened the balcony door.

"Send Heather out. I want to talk to her."

"Sure." Jack went inside, but came back almost immediately and stuck her head out the door. "Uhm, we have a problem." She sounded upset.

Chase pushed Jack aside and went in. "Where's Heather?"

"She left," Dario said calmly, smiling. "She decided she was through being used."

"What did you say to her?" Chase grabbed him by the throat.

"The truth." He choked.

She forced herself to release him. "How long has she been gone?"

"I can't remember." He smiled again.

"Not long," Jack said. "Chair's still warm." She had her hand on the fabric where Heather had been sitting.

"She can't be far." She could have killed Dario on the spot.

"You made her run to distract us. You know she cares for Heather," Jack said, tilting her head toward Chase. "And you want to throw us off, distract us for the drop-off tomorrow. What are you up to, creep?" Jack went to Dario and loomed over him menacingly.

"I don't know what you're talking about," he said benignly. "I sincerely care about the whore."

Chase shoved Jack aside and punched Dario in the face so hard she knocked him out.

"Fortunately, the Geneva convention doesn't apply to us." Jack grinned her approval. "We're free to torture him."

"Don't impair him. I'm going out." She slammed the door so hard she heard a picture on the wall inside the room fall and shatter.

Chapter Thirty-five

Heather kept running until she came to a secluded bench at the edge of the sprawling park adjacent to the hotel. She needed to stop to catch her breath and collect her thoughts. Decide where to go next. Maybe the darkness and unfamiliar setting would make it difficult for Landis or Jack to come after her. How could she have been so foolish to let Landis and the attraction she felt cloud her judgment? And to think she'd considered Landis a catch, a dream woman. The two of them must have had a good laugh at her expense.

She had to make flight arrangements and get back home, a difficult task at this hour. Her cell wasn't set up for international calls, and the area they were in was mostly residential. The few shops near the hotel were closed, the streets empty.

Maybe she could find a bar still open. Or another hotel, where she could access a phone and maybe even the Internet to find a flight. Hotel was a better option, because there would likely be no flights out until morning and she couldn't risk hanging out at the airport. She'd be too easy to find. Thank God for American Express.

She started walking down the main thoroughfare, keeping to the shadows in case Landis and Jack were out looking for her, her spirits sinking further with every block. No sign of another hotel. No pay phone. And the area she soon found herself in looked dicey—the homes more run-down, graffiti everywhere, trash in the streets. This was definitely not a tourist area.

In the distance, she spotted a building with an illuminated sign. A bar, and it was open. Without a second thought, she pushed through the door. If nothing else, it had to have a phone so she could call a cab to take her to another hotel.

The place looked as seedy as the neighborhood. Ten men were spread out through the bar, and from the looks of them, most had been there all day and night. Unshaved, unkempt, and either completely or mostly wasted. She avoided eye contact as she made her way to the bar.

The bartender said something in French.

"I'm sorry. English, please?"

She heard a murmur of voices behind her and caught the word *Américaine*, but didn't turn to look.

"What do you want?" the bartender asked with a strong accent.

"Can I use your telephone?"

"First you drink, then maybe you can call." He laughed, and so did the others.

Heather sighed, in no mood for games. "Okay. A Diet Coke, please."

The guy behind the bar shook his head. "You must drink alcohol."

"I can't." Heather sat down on the stool. She was too tired and terrified to cope with this. "I'm allergic."

"Bon. One Coca-Cola," he said. "I have the best."

Heather suddenly felt exhausted. "Look, I just want to use the phone." She wanted to add *I'm tired, lost, and being hunted*, but didn't want to alert these drunk strangers to more vulnerabilities than her gender. Her years as a call girl had taught her when it came to physical strength, there was no comparison, and men were all too eager to remind any woman of that. "I'll have a drink after I'm done. I promise." She smiled. Once she knew a cab was on the way and had a time estimate, she'd make a fast exit. Plus, she'd make sure to mention loudly that she'd called for one and that it was due any minute.

"Bon. The telephone is back there next to the toilets." The bartender grinned as he pointed the way.

Halfway there she realized she didn't have foreign money. She walked back to the bar. "Can you exchange dollars, by any chance?" She gave him her most charming smile. "I just arrived in your wonderful country."

He fished in his pocket and gave her a fifty-cent Euro coin. "The drink will be on me."

"That's so sweet. Thank you." She headed toward the back of the bar and found the phone in a hallway leading to the restrooms. As she started to slide the coin into the slot, she heard a familiar voice speaking French. No. It couldn't be. She peeked around the corner to make sure and saw Landis. She looked angry and aggressive, like she was about to attack the barman.

"Don't play games with me, idiot," Landis said in English before resuming her tirade in French.

"Fuck off," the guy replied. "I told you, I didn't see a woman come in here tonight. Ask the rest if you don't believe me."

The men still sober enough to talk jumped in but were laughing. "She want to stay with us," one guy yelled from his table. "We good company for a beautiful American woman. We teach her French fast, teach her how to drink. Coca-Cola is for children and she is not a little girl." He winked at Landis.

"Oui, we show her good times," another man said.

Landis turned back to the barman and grabbed him by the collar. "Tell me where she is. Now."

"Don't touch me," the man said defiantly, and bunched his fists. "No woman give me orders."

At this, another five men got up and approached Landis from behind. One grabbed his bottle of wine by the neck and held it upside down, ready to use as a weapon.

"I don't tell you anything, *gouine*," the barman said.

Though Heather had seen Landis work her way out of a similar scary situation in Chinatown, she had faced only two men then, neither drunk or armed. These guys were aggressive and, from the sound of it, had their own plans for Heather. No wonder they were ready to team up to get Landis out of there.

The bartender pushed Landis away and grabbed a crowbar from behind the bar. He held it up with both hands. "You ask for trouble, you get trouble. She not going anywhere with you."

Heather wanted to summon the police and cursed herself for not knowing what number to call. She'd never seen anyone look as angry as Landis. It was almost scary to see her like this.

Landis grappled for the crowbar and the two of them struggled over the weapon, knocking glasses off the bar between them. As she released one hand and punched the bartender hard in the face, the other men jumped her, two grabbing her from behind to pull her back. Landis fought to get away and had almost succeeded when the other three started to punch her.

As she tried to duck their blows, Landis struggled free of the two men holding her—getting one in the ribs with her elbow and head-butting the other. The latter guy screamed in pain as he grasped his nose, but quickly rejoined the melee, as did the bartender, who'd come around from behind the bar with his own broken nose. Now it was six against one, and no matter how hard Landis fought them off, they punched and kicked her back just as fiercely.

Heather couldn't watch any more. She had to do something. Stripping off her jacket, she pulled at the neck of her top until her shoulders were exposed, quickly applied lipstick, and entered the arena. "Hey, what's going on, guys?" she asked sweetly.

The fighting stopped abruptly and all went quiet as the men turned to look at her. One guy froze with his arm pulled back, about to throw a punch. They'd formed a circle around Landis, so Heather couldn't see her.

"Guys, it's not polite to fight in front of a lady," she said as she slowly strutted over to them. "Someone promised me a drink." She looked at the barman seductively. "I'm ready for it now, so stop this nonsense and get me one."

"I will when we are done with this…woman."

"Woman?" She pushed him aside and came face to face with Landis. Her nose was bleeding and her lip was bruised. Her eyes were aflame with aggression.

"Oh, my God, sweetie, what are you doing here?" She caressed Landis's cheek, then turned to the guy restraining her from behind. "Remove your hands from my friend."

He reluctantly pulled away and she put her arm around Landis's waist. "You have to stop these jealousy scenes, honey. I told you I was going out for a drink."

Landis stared at her, clearly spellbound. "I can't help it," she finally said. "I'm crazy about you...baby," she added behind gritted teeth.

"Let's get you back to the hotel," Heather said. "You're a mess."

"Yes...let's."

"But first, you have to offer your apologies to these sweet men. They were nothing but polite and generous to me, and you beat them up for no good reason."

Landis's eyes narrowed and flashed with renewed fury. "Are you kidd—"

"Sweetie...what did your anger-management counselor teach you?" She turned to the men with an apologetic smile. "Sorry guys, but she has a condition."

They stared first at Landis and then at her, with befuddled expressions.

She caressed Landis's hair. "Go ahead."

"I'm sorry," Landis mumbled. "I should have never hit you," she told the barman.

After taking Landis's hand, she started for the door. "We're sorry," she called over her shoulder. "Thank you for being so understanding."

They left with all six men still staring after them, as were the four guys who'd been too drunk or self-absorbed to participate in the fracas.

Neither spoke until they were well away from the bar and certain no one had followed. Landis let her take the lead, though she had no idea where she was heading.

"Thank you," Landis said.

"Now we're even," Heather said, referring to the time in the Cave when Landis had played the part of her girlfriend to get the annoying jerk away from her.

"I wasn't keeping score."

She fished in her purse for a Kleenex. "Your nose is bleeding."

Landis took the tissue and dabbed at her nose. "Why did you run?"

She had been so upset, afraid, and busy scheming her getaway that she had forgotten just how angry she was at Landis for lying. She stopped walking. "I don't even know where to start."

"What did Dario say to you?"

"Nothing I hadn't already concluded. I can't believe I was so naïve." She knew she should probably quit while she was ahead. Who knew what Landis was capable of if she got her angry or admitted she knew what Landis was up to. But her own anger got the best of her. "I let you convince me you were after Rózsa to save someone…an innocent woman, like Gigi. You did a bang-up job, by the way, of convincing me Dario had her killed."

"He did."

"And you just conveniently happened to find her phone."

"I told you how we found it."

Heather rolled her eyes. "And I stupidly believed that implausible scenario."

"Can we go back to the hotel and talk about this?" Landis took her elbow and tried to gently steer her toward a street branching off to their left.

She pulled away and kept walking. "I'm not going *anywhere* with you," she shouted. "I'm getting on the first plane back to the States."

"It's not safe for you there. Not yet."

"And it is here?" She laughed without humor. "Between you and Dario, I'm in much greater danger here."

"What do you think I'm going to do to you? Have I harmed a hair on your head?"

"What is tomorrow really about…Landis?" She stopped again to look at her.

"About rescuing another op."

"I think it's about framing me."

"Framing…where did you get that?"

"You want to connect me with Rózsa after you pull off whatever scheme you have in mind."

"Heather, listen to yourself." Landis shook her head. "You're not making sense." She seemed sincere, but Heather doubted she was capable anymore of discerning lies from truths as far as Landis was concerned. This was probably just another ploy to keep her involved in whatever they'd cooked up for tomorrow.

"Are you two bounty hunters paid to deliver Rózsa, or are you just after Dario's blackmail money?" She shouted the words so loud that a window in the apartment building they were near banged open and a woman popped her head out.

"Please, everyone can hear you. It's the middle of the night." Landis took her by the elbow again and led her farther down the block before she stopped to face her. "I don't know how you came up with these stories or if that bastard put them in your head, but Jack and I work for an organization. Private contractors, if you will. Heather, we work with governments worldwide. We're not paid assassins, nor are we after Dario's blood money. He wants you to believe we are to scare you, and he accomplished it. He wanted you to run to distract us tomorrow. I don't know what he's up to, but he's doing a good job so far."

Heather considered what she was saying, but she didn't know who or what to believe anymore.

"The only reason I want you here with me is because you're not safe yet," Landis said. "Not until I arrange relocation so Dario can't find you."

"And who the hell said I'm willing to change my damn life because of you?" She shoved Landis as hard as she could, but Landis barely budged, and her benign, unreadable expression never wavered.

"This deal could offer you a better life. The feds will find you a job and take care of your brother so you don't have to—"

"Don't have to whore myself?" She unleashed her rising fury. "Do you really think I need you to save me from a life of sin and take care of my brother? Have I given you the impression I need to be saved, or are you always this Goddamn chivalrous?"

"No, I'm just saying you have other options."

"Is that what you tell the girls you pay to fuck? Do you have them come over so you can preach about better options, or do you have them spread their legs and tell you what a fantastic fuck you are?"

Landis opened her mouth but nothing came out.

"I didn't think so," she said. "Women like me are nothing but objects to you. So why the hell do you care what happens to me?"

"Because I got you in this mess."

She laughed. "You won't even deny I'm nothing more than an object."

"I…" Landis looked genuinely hurt, which didn't make sense. "This isn't about you or your occupation, it's about—"

Landis was right about that, but Heather couldn't let go of the topic, though she wasn't sure why. "It's about you using women. How can you do that, being a woman yourself? I doubt it's hard for you to get laid, so what is it? Do you like degrading women? Does it turn you on?"

"Don't take your frustrations for the life you've chosen out on me," Landis shouted.

Heather was surprised; she'd never heard Landis raise her voice, not even when Dario provoked her.

"I'm not one of your hairy-assed clients asking you to scream my name during fake orgasms," Landis said loudly. "If you have a problem with what you do, then look for other solutions. You could have tried to find something else to support you and your brother, but this is what you came up with. You *chose* to sell sex."

"Are you saying it pleases me to have sex with strangers for money?" she shouted back, and a couple passing by paused briefly to gape at them. "Do you know what it does to me, every time I have to be with some guy?"

When Landis didn't answer and continued to look aloof, her rage deepened. How dare Landis think she enjoyed this life? That would imply she was no mere call girl, but a real whore at heart. "I know you think I'm disgusting, but that doesn't mean you can stand here and insult me."

Without thinking, she raised her hand to slap her, but Landis caught her by the wrist. She tried to pull away, but Landis wouldn't let go. "Let me—" She froze when she glanced up at Landis.

The look of indifference she'd seen there had been replaced by hurt.

Landis lifted her hand to her mouth and kissed her palm. "Yes. I know what it does to you, and I hate it," she whispered. "I hate what you do, and I hate every man who's ever touched you." She put her free arm around Heather's waist and pulled her closer. "And no, you don't disgust me." She kissed Heather's wrist. "As a matter of fact, I find you amazing."

Before she could fully register what was happening, Landis was kissing her softly on the lips. Such a sweet, brief kiss, in stark contrast to the fury raging between them seconds earlier. She should resist, but the exquisite sensation of their lips together mesmerized her.

"You are so damn beautiful it hurts to look at you." Landis bent to kiss her neck and Heather trembled. "You're giving…" Landis kissed the other side of her neck and Heather let her head fall back. "And caring…" She closed her eyes as Landis's mouth brushed the corner of her lips. "And brave…" Landis pulled her closer until their bodies touched. "And I'm going to die if you won't let me really kiss you."

She opened her eyes. Landis's lips were a breath away. Desperate to kiss her, Heather pulled their mouths together. The world melted away. Soft, tentative explorations with their lips, their ardor building until both were breathing heavily. She loved kissing women—so much so that was why she never let her johns kiss her; she didn't want to taint such profoundly personal contact. But it had been such a long time since she'd kissed a woman, and Landis was such an amazing kisser, that this moment aroused and excited her more than she would have thought possible.

Landis cupped the side of her face as they kissed, and when her thumb brushed the edge of her mouth, Heather licked it seductively with the tip of her tongue.

Landis threaded her fingers roughly through Heather's hair, pulling her closer to deepen the kiss. Her heartbeat accelerated in an instant, and she kissed Landis back with equal passion, their mouths and tongues claiming each other in a frenzied unleashing of the energy that had been building between them.

She wasn't sure whether a minute or a day had elapsed before Landis pulled away.

"Come with me?" Landis looked as aroused as Heather felt.

"Where?" she asked suspiciously.

"I don't care." Landis's voice was husky.

CHAPTER THIRTY-SIX

Chase waited, her body thrumming with desire, as Heather considered how to respond.

"Get us back to the hotel," Heather finally said, taking her hand.

She was surprised, but said nothing.

"Yes, I know what I'm doing," Heather added, as though she'd read her mind.

"I know you don't want to hear it, but you *can* trust me."

Heather squeezed her hand. "I want to."

The clock in the lobby read ten past midnight as they stepped into the elevator. Chase pressed the button for the fifth floor. "I'm going to let Jack know we're back." She dialed Jack's cell.

"Stop sighing or I'll put a pillow over your head," she heard Jack say distantly to Dario when the connection went through. Then, to her, "Find her?"

"Yes. We'll be in my room. Don't disturb us unless it's a matter of death and death."

"Why?" Jack asked. "What's going on?"

She didn't answer. Jack's quarter should drop any second.

"Are you two about to—" Jack whispered into the phone.

"Good night, Jack."

"One of us is going to have a good night and it's sure as hell not going to be me. Be good to her." Jack hung up.

She opened the door and let Heather go inside. Heather went to the middle of the room and stopped there, glancing about.

Chase remained just inside the door, looking everywhere but directly at Heather. A jittery anticipation and a totally unfamiliar nervousness infused her. She'd been in similar situations too many times to count and, until now, it had always been easy and predictable. How ironic. Here she was, a sex veteran with a beautiful woman in her room, and she didn't even dare look at her. Heather didn't say anything either, as she observed the room like it was a study in art history. And there wasn't much to see. The room was a duplicate of the one Jack and Dario were in. *Say something*. "I, uhm…can I offer you something to drink?"

"Is Landis your real name?" Heather spoke at the same time as she turned to face her.

That was awkward. "Yes. Landis Coolidge."

"And you're a graphic novelist?"

"Of course."

Heather laid her purse on the table. "What do you have?" She looked uncomfortable. "I mean, to drink."

"Nothing, but I can call the reception desk."

"No, that's okay."

Chase approached her slowly, fists clenched at her side. She was acting like a complete idiot and couldn't help herself. It was like having an out-of-body experience. She stopped a foot away from Heather. "I don't know why—"

"You feel as uncomfortable as you look?"

She smiled. "This has never happened to me before."

"That makes two of us."

"I noticed." Frustrated, she sat on the bed. "It's not like either of us lack experience."

Heather frowned. "Thank you for reminding me."

"That's not what I meant." She got up. "I mean…I don't know what I mean. God, why am I being such an idiot?" She sat back down. Could she act more like a fool?

Heather came over and squatted so they were eye to eye. "We don't have to do this."

Heather was so close again, all she had to do was reach out. She raised her hand hesitantly but stopped before she touched Heather's face. "What the hell is wrong with me?"

Heather started to touch her knee but pulled away as well.

Chase knew nothing was wrong with the chemistry. They'd had plenty of that, since just a few moments ago they were ready to do it in the middle of the street.

"I'm…I'm sorry. I don't know what's going on. I've never had this…I already said that." She sighed.

"You know, maybe we're both too tired." Heather stood. "Or maybe you reacted without thinking out there. Let's face it. I'm not exactly the type you go for."

"What type is that?"

Heather crossed her arms and scowled. "Would it help if you paid me?"

"Do you think this is about you being a call girl?" She couldn't believe Heather had just said that.

"What I think is that my worst nightmare has come true. That a beautiful, interesting woman I'd like to get to know has found out what I do and can't deal with it, even though she thought she could. Because every time she looks at me all she sees is a…a…" Heather blinked hard, obviously fighting tears. "I feel like an idiot for losing control out there and letting myself think I could get away with this." She was talking so fast, stating so many things, Chase didn't know what to react to first.

"Heather, this…my inability to be normal right now…isn't about you. I'm not sure what it is, but I know it's me."

Heather turned her back. "Whatever you say," she mumbled. "What-ever-you-say. Listen, I'm exhausted and need to get some rest. I'll take this room, if you don't mind. I'm in no mood to see his ugly face any time soon and need to get a decent night's sleep." She walked to the bathroom and never looked back. "I'll see you tomorrow, Landis." The door closed behind her.

Chase stared at the door as though it held the answer to who had abducted and taken over her body. She dropped back on the bed and stared at the ceiling. She knew Heather wanted her to leave, but she couldn't even if she wanted to. She was incapable of putting any more distance between them.

How could Heather get angry with *her*, when she appeared just as disoriented and uncertain? What if Heather's reaction was a defense mechanism? Something she did without thinking, when she felt judged because of what she did? Chase had made it clear she didn't care about all that.

But Heather clearly had problems herself fully accepting the decisions she'd made. And that probably meant she couldn't allow herself to believe that anyone else could, either. Was she looking for a reason to run and escape whomever from condemning and dumping her? It disturbed her to see how money could make such a beautiful, wonderful woman feel so insecure. And the worst part was, she'd just contributed to making Heather feel inferior by making her feel undesired.

She heard the water running in the shower. She had never wanted any woman more. Had never yearned so to protect and care for anyone, had never wanted so much to make any woman smile and take her away from everything that had ever hurt her. *All I want to do is love you.*

The sudden realization terrified her and she jumped off the bed. Damn, this wasn't supposed to happen. She paced the room and stopped in front of the bathroom door. Caressing the frame, she stopped with her hand on the handle. She tested it and it wasn't locked.

She took a deep breath and opened the door. She couldn't see Heather through the glass of the shower because of the steam.

She took another deep breath and approached the glass. "You'd really like to see me again?" was all that came out.

Heather slid the door open and stood naked before her, water cascading off her in sheets. She looked relieved and happy, but didn't reply.

Chase took her time looking from Heather's eyes, to her mouth, and then all the way down her amazing body. She swallowed hard. "I asked if you'd like…"

Heather grabbed her by the hand and pulled her under the water. Their mouths met in fury and hunger, and she didn't know whether she or Heather removed her clothes, but in seconds their naked bodies clung fiercely together under the spray.

"You feel so good," she murmured as she rubbed against Heather, nuzzling her neck, inhaling the fragrant citrus essence that lingered from her shampoo. "Smell so good…" She nipped at the delicate skin beneath her ear. "Taste so good."

Heather wrapped her arms around Landis's neck, as much for support as the thrill of touching her. The feel of Landis's body pressed against hers, the sensation of those soft lips along her skin, made her dizzy. She'd schooled herself so successfully to shut down physically and emotionally during sex that touching Landis was as though she'd been reborn with a new body, hypersensitive to the slightest brush of flesh against flesh. When Landis's hands slid slowly down her back to clench her ass, her heart fluttered like it had suddenly sprouted wings.

If she didn't slow things down, she'd come before Landis even reached her area of greatest need.

Heather gently extricated herself from their embrace. "Not so fast," she said playfully as she reached for the shower gel the hotel had provided. Landis looked at her with glazed, heavy-lidded eyes, confusion in her expression. "I'm going to explore every inch of that incredible body of yours until you beg for mercy."

Landis trembled as Heather turned her, facing away, and lathered her shoulders and the back of her neck, kneading away the tension in the soft musculature along her spine. Landis groaned and surrendered to her touch, visibly relaxing as she put her hands against the wall of the shower for support.

Soon, the therapeutic touch became more sensual, as Heather extended her caresses to fleeting, maddening brushes around Landis's sides to her breasts and down to her ass. Here and there, she touched rough places in the smooth flesh of Landis's back and hips; healed scars that made her wince and wonder at their origin.

She stooped to continue her tactile exploration of Landis's exquisitely sculpted body, smoothing the lather into her ass and legs. She could feel the muscles beneath her fingertips tense as she slid her hands up Landis's inner thighs, stopping just short of her groin.

"You're killing me," Landis said between clenched teeth.

"Turn around." Heather smiled up at her.

Landis pushed off the shower wall and slowly pivoted, looking down at Heather with such open hunger and desire that she had a hard time maintaining her slow buildup. She squeezed more gel into her hand and stroked her way up Landis's front, fingertips moving sensually over her thighs and abdomen and along the curves of her breasts. As the steamy water cascaded down off Landis's shoulders, Heather teased her with soft, circular brushes over her erect nipples.

Landis moaned again when she trailed kisses and swipes of her tongue over the soft triangle of hair.

"Come here," Landis said huskily, helping her to her feet. "It's my turn." She kissed her soundly before pulling away with an expression of lust and determination, and took the gel from her.

"But I'm already clean," she said playfully, as Landis turned her around and began to soap her back.

"I don't care." Landis pulled her close, grinding her crotch into Heather's ass as she cupped her breasts from behind. "You're amazing. So incredibly beautiful."

Heather relaxed into the embrace, her head on Landis's shoulder, her back against Landis's chest, as Landis caressed her breasts and stomach, sweeping strokes that teased her rigidly sensitive nipples and then dipped low, mere inches from her clit. Moisture pooled at the juncture of her thighs, and her pulse beat loud in her ears as her breathing became ragged with desire.

"Mmmm, I can't begin to tell you what you're doing to me," she said, as Landis slowly descended to her knees behind her, caressing her back and ass.

Landis urged her legs apart, and she complied willingly, bracing herself against the wall as another dizzying wave of arousal sent her head spinning. Landis toyed with her, driving her higher with caresses up her inner thighs and soft bites and nips into the soft flesh of her ass.

When she was about to beg for more, Landis turned her around but remained on her knees. She looked up at her with such intense longing Heather's breath caught in her throat. But something else was there, too—uncertainty—and she couldn't understand why.

"I want to taste you," Landis murmured, more request than statement.

"Oh, yes. Please."

Landis spread her legs farther, taking her time, building her to unfamiliar heights of anticipation with teasing sweeps of her tongue, closing in slowly as her clit swelled and throbbed with need.

By the time Landis's mouth claimed her, she was so hyper-sensitized she climaxed almost at once: her whole body rigid as the waves crested over her, her hands clutching Landis's scalp.

"I…I'm sorry," she said, once she'd regained her breath. "It's been so long."

Landis looked up at her, confusion in her eyes.

"I haven't been with a woman in years," she explained. "And never with one I wanted so much."

Landis smiled as she caressed her way back up Heather's body, pausing to kiss her breasts as she got to her feet. "I've never wanted anyone this much, either." She looked deeply into Heather's eyes. "I don't just *want* to make love to you. I *need* to."

Chase wanted so much to be inside Heather, but she didn't know whether she should go there on her own, considering Heather's past. She yearned to be different than anyone who had ever touched her, man or woman, and for that to happen, she'd have to let Heather take the lead in showing her what she wanted.

She'd hoped that her words would convey her need, and the hunger she saw on Heather's face, even after her orgasm, gave her hope.

Heather took Chase's hand and placed it on her breast, encouraging her.

As Chase tweaked the nipple with her thumb, she snaked her other arm around Heather's waist and pulled her close for another searing kiss. Her tongue conveyed her desire more eloquently than words could have.

Heather responded by grasping Chase's wrist, to bring her hand lower. She placed it between her legs, and when Chase slipped her fingers into Heather's slick, silky folds, Heather sighed and trembled.

Chase had never been so aroused touching someone else, and as she worked Heather again into another heightened state of excitement, her own body began to ache for release. Soon, Heather was close to climaxing again—she could tell by her firm muscles and irregular breathing, and the way Heather's clit pulsed under her hand.

"I want you inside me," Heather said urgently, and the words unleashed Chase's restraint. She pushed Heather against the shower wall and thrust two fingers inside her, penetrating her slowly, as Heather moaned and clung to her, hands locked around her neck.

"More," Heather murmured, and she pushed three fingers into her, still fucking her slowly, edging deeper with each thrust.

Heather leaned her head back against the wall, her pupils wide and dark, her face displaying her ecstasy. She was never so breathtakingly beautiful as at that moment, and Chase fought to keep from coming just from the view. Their breathing became one, jagged and fast, as Heather's hand pushed against hers, urging her even deeper.

"So good…" Heather rocked against her hand, stroke for stroke, surrendering completely to the driving sensations.

"What do you want?" Chase asked.

"Come with me," Heather replied. "I'm so close." Her hand slipped between their bodies and Chase opened her legs eagerly, so painfully ready for Heather's delivering touch she could barely breathe.

As Heather pushed into her, Chase shuddered from the joy of it as they rocked together, slowly matching strokes, gazing deep into each other's eyes.

"I want to see you come," Heather said breathily.

"I can't get enough of you," she replied, before claiming Heather in a searing kiss, their tongues matching the slow, insistent rhythm of their hands.

Chase was lost—immersed in a wellspring of overpowering stimuli—the heady scent of their mutual arousal, the passion in Heather's eyes, the excitement of her thrusts into Heather's welcoming warmth, the pulsing of her own clit. Too much. Too much.

"I'm going to come," she told Heather, unable to prevent the crest from overtaking her.

Heather nodded and let go, her eyes never leaving Chase's, and they climaxed together in a shattering crescendo that left both struggling to breathe.

Spent, they rested beneath the spray with their heads on each other's shoulder, clinging together along the lengths of their bodies. The water was still warm, but she couldn't stop shaking.

"Are you cold?" Heather asked, enfolding her even tighter.

"No. I don't know what's happening, but I'm not cold." She turned off the water and took Heather by the hand to lead her out of the shower. Snatching one of the large, plush towels from the rack, she dried Heather off first, paying extra attention to her breasts, before toweling herself off.

Chase was drying her back, with the towel wrapped around herself, when Heather grabbed the two ends of the towel and dragged her, cocoon-like, into the bedroom. Once there, Heather whisked the towel away and shoved her playfully onto the bed.

"Is it bad that I want you again?" Heather smiled, her eyes shining with desire.

She reached for her and pulled her down on top of her. "Very," she replied, as she enfolded Heather in her arms. "But I'm a big fan of bad."

An hour later, they lay spooning, Chase embracing Heather from behind. She traced her finger down Heather's shoulder to her thigh, delighting in the trembling it evoked. She was tired but wanted to savor the moment, the feeling of peace. Peace with her past, herself, and the present. She wished she'd never have to let go of the contentment, but if all she had with Heather was tonight, she wanted the memory to last forever.

She had fallen for Regina Stellari, but her feelings and intentions had been mostly about getting the girl out of her dysfunctional environment and away from her father. The young girl was infatuated with her, and the sex was shy and experimental, with Chase taking the lead to please and teach her.

Up until tonight, she hadn't known or even understood the difference between sex and making love. If Heather disappeared tomorrow in some relocation program and Chase never saw her again, she would forever be grateful for having learned to appreciate the difference, even if that meant never again being satisfied with cheap imitations of what sex could be like.

Only one thing bothered her right now. Only one obstacle remained between her and complete peace, and that was what Heather thought about her need to pay for sex. She kissed Heather's shoulder and Heather nestled closer into her.

"This feels good." Heather said. "Very good."

"Too good."

Heather rolled onto her back and looked at her. "Does that scare you?"

She sighed. "Yes."

"Me, too."

"You first." Chase kissed her.

"I'm afraid I'm going to wake up and regret tonight."

"Why?" Chase asked.

"Because…" Heather turned her head away. "I know it's only about now."

"Is that what you want?"

"I'm being realistic. You know what I've done, and my past doesn't make for romantic endings."

She tenderly turned Heather's face so she could look at her. "Is that what you'd like…with me?"

"Look at us, Landis. You buy sex and I sell it. How screwed up are we?"

She dropped back on the pillow and stared at the ceiling. Neither talked or stirred for a long time.

"I did it because I was a coward," she finally said. "I thought if I bought sex then no one would get hurt."

"Plenty of women out there want the same uncomplicated, superficial fun for an evening and nothing more. You could have turned to them. Why pay for it?"

"It's myself I didn't trust. I didn't want to risk feeling anything at all for them."

"Why is that so bad?"

"A long time ago, someone I cared for was shot and killed. It took me a long time to get over it, and after that, I promised myself to never get emotionally involved. One-night-stands imply talking with someone, getting their name, and sharing a dinner and drink. That was already more than I wanted to deal with. I started seeing call girls because it was simple, fast, and anonymous. I didn't have to share anything with them, not even our names. They were there to…"

"Please you."

"Yes."

"Was it satisfying?"

"I thought it was. Until tonight."

Heather turned to cuddle in her embrace.

"I don't know what to do now, after tonight, after…you," Chase admitted.

"This could be going nowhere." Heather kissed her fiercely and cupped her groin.

Chase grinned. "Then let's go there one more time."

CHAPTER THIRTY-SEVEN

Next morning, November 27

Chase roused to Heather's finger caressing her lips. When she opened her eyes, she found Heather gazing down at her, hair tousled and looking incredibly sexy. "Good morning." She smiled, unbelievably content.

"Hi." Heather kissed her. "Your phone vibed off the nightstand."

"Damn. What time is it?" She sat up. Jack was right. When Heather was around, she forgot to even casually check the time.

"A bit past nine thirty."

She picked up the cell and dialed Jack. "What's up?"

"I called five minutes ago, but—"

"I didn't answer, I'm aware. Any reason you called?" She didn't try to hide her irritation.

"You're in a foul mood for someone who just got some," Jack said cheerfully. "Nothing's wrong, I wanted to make sure everything was okay."

She rubbed her eyes. "Everything's fine."

"Heather?"

She turned to look at her. "She looks beautiful even in the morning."

"Can't say the same for my roomie."

"Is he still cuffed?"

"You mean *again*. Had to take him to the toilet."

"That must have been exciting."

"A genuine thrill, especially since I had to place him on the bowl."

She laughed.

"Told him I'd castrate him with a blunt knife if he ever mentioned it."

"I'll see you in a little." She laughed again and hung up.

"I guess it's almost showtime." Heather kissed her shoulder. "Are you nervous?"

"Normally, no, but I know how much this means to Jack and Cass—she's a colleague, one we already buried once. None of us want to go through that again, and Jack won't survive it a second time."

"Buried her once?"

"When Rózsa's lab blew up, Cass was in there. We thought she died in the explosion, but it turned out Rózsa had kidnapped her."

"So you gave her a proper funeral and everything?"

"The organization did. Jack was about to end her life when my bosses found her."

"Thank God they did."

"She's been self-destructive ever since. Smoking, drinking. She hardly eats or sleeps. Cass is everything to her."

"What happened to her face?"

"That's her story to tell."

"Fair enough." Heather pulled her back down on the bed with her.

"You really are painfully beautiful." Chase kissed her and was aroused in seconds.

"I love the way you touch me."

"I love the way you react when I do." She enfolded Heather in her arms and rolled them over until Heather was lying on top of her. Their mouths met in renewed passion, but just as she thrust a muscled thigh between Heather's legs, her cell went off again. She fumbled for it, frowning with annoyance. "What now?"

"Rózsa called." Jack's voice was urgent and businesslike. Her irritation vanished. "Said Dario should have his man ready in an hour at the Hammam Eden on the Boulevard Garibaldi."

"Hammam?"

"Turkish bath."

"I know what that is."

"Be here ASAP. We need to prepare."

"Give me two." She hung up. "Rózsa called," she told Heather as she got out of bed and headed into the bathroom. "We have to be there in an hour. Damn, my clothes are soaked." She grabbed the hotel robe. "Jack is going to love this."

Heather got up, too. "What do you want me to do?"

"Stay with Dario. He'll be chained the whole time so he can't hurt you, and I'll give you the key. But please—"

"Don't say it," Heather said, smiling up at her. "I won't listen to him again."

Chase kissed her. "Can you be at the room in ten?"

"Yes."

❖

After Jack hung up with Chase, she gave Dario his cell. "Make the call to your delivery man. On speakerphone, and keep it to the bare minimum. Try anything, and I'll stick that phone down your throat."

Dario watched her warily as he waited for the connection to go through. "The Hamman Eden on the Boulevard Garibaldi. 11 a.m. You're to leave the money in a small black duffel in the men's steam room."

Jack waited only until the guy confirmed the information before she took the cell from Dario and disconnected. Then she put it back into her pocket. "What's your delivery man look like?" she asked Dario.

"Big guy," he answered. "Dark hair, wears it in a ponytail."

She glanced up at the wall clock. "Heather will be here momentarily and will stay with you while we're gone." She loomed over him with a wolfish smile. "Should I spell out what body parts I'll carve out of you if you try to pull any more of your bullshit with her?"

"Not necessary." Dario tried to appear unconcerned, but he shrank back into his chair and wouldn't look at her.

"Peachy."

Thirty minutes before the scheduled drop-off, Chase and Jack sipped coffee inside a café across from the hammam, to plot their strategy as they watched people come and go from the Turkish bath. Chase had to force herself to push aside thoughts of Heather so she could focus entirely on their mission.

"This is it," Jack said, more to herself than Chase, "the day I see Cass again."

She drummed her fingers impatiently on the tabletop.

"It sure is." She hoped she sounded confident.

"How was your evening?" Jack made a sad attempt not to smile.

"It was…great." She sighed. "She's great."

"Going to see her again, when this is over?"

"I hope so."

"That's refreshing. What happened to your theory of screw 'em and dump 'em?"

"It was never a theory. It was a defense mechanism."

"One you apparently don't need with her?"

"I always thought my life was too screwed up to inflict on anyone else."

"Until you found someone with the same screwed-up life."

She smiled. "Who knew all it took was someone as broken?"

"Maybe a new angle for your novels. Perhaps it's time Emily saved Landor from the devil and his self-persecution. Emily is too perfect, and even if perfection wasn't an illusion, it would be a boring trait."

"I never wanted Emily damaged."

"It's time you threw some shit at her. Otherwise Landor will never feel confident enough to reveal who he really is. Emily will continue to love a mortal, a lie…and not the truth."

"What if she can't deal with who Landor is?"

"She won't. Not until he accepts it himself."

She turned to look outside. Jack's words made her feel transparent and vulnerable, feelings she'd put aside years ago.

"Only when you accept who you are will you get what you need…Landis."

"Emily save Landor," she mumbled to herself.

"Heather doesn't have to be perfect. She just has to be perfect for you and vice versa."

"Is that the case with you and Cass?"

Jack's expression darkened. "I doubt Cass will ever be the same after this."

"Will that be a problem?"

"Only if she ever stops loving me."

"After today, she'll never let you go."

Jack frowned and stared out the window. "And I'll never let anything happen to her again," she said, her voice breaking.

She looked down at her coffee cup. Her friend was miserable, and for the first time, she realized that Jack felt responsible for what had happened to Cass. She saw no point in trying to reason with Jack's misplaced guilt right now; she was too stubborn and this wasn't the right moment. "Please, don't try to be a hero. Wait for me before you decide to do anything."

"I'm not exactly a beginner. I know what I'm doing."

"I'm anxious to get Cass back, too, but I know you can get unpredictable when it's personal."

"I won't do anything stupid, Landis."

"Are you nervous?" she asked tentatively.

"Yeah."

"Good. It means you won't do anything stupid."

Jack smiled. "You're quoting me. I'm not nervous about the job. I am about seeing Cass again."

"I know you don't want to hear this, but there is a chance Cass is…" It had crossed her mind many times, but she'd never dared share this with Jack.

Jack's smile disappeared. "She's not dead. I know she isn't."

"Please try to take that scenario into consideration."

"I can't. Won't. She's somewhere out there, waiting for me."

Chase didn't press. She checked her watch. "So we're clear on our positions. I'll take the front."

"And I the back."

"Chances are Rózsa will be disguised."

"He'll be the one leaving with a small black duffel," Jack said.

"Or whatever he replaces it with."

"I'll follow him on foot until you pick me up by car."

"Eyes only, Jack. If you stop him or do anything to alert him, we're screwed."

Jack nodded. "I realize that. If we catch him, he knows he's a dead man walking anyway. He'll have no reason at all to tell us where Cass is."

"And by the time we find her, if we ever do, it'll be too late."

"I realize, I said." Jack was getting irritated, but Chase had to make sure she didn't act on anger.

"Time to turn on the earpieces."

Both switched on their tiny mic/audio pieces and placed them in their ears.

"Good to go." Jack got up and headed for the door as Chase threw a few Euros on the table.

Not long after, she took up her own position, casually leaning against a kiosk in front of the hammam. She was pretending to be absorbed in a French magazine when she spotted Dario's goon. "If Dario's description is right, his guy is about to enter. He's holding a small black gym bag."

"No sign of Rózsa here," Jack replied from the back entrance.

"He shouldn't be long. I don't see anyone who looks like him going in. So many are coming and going at the moment."

Andor Rózsa smiled as he checked himself one last time in the window of the antique shop, four doors down from the meeting place. He'd shaved his beard and mustache, cut his dark hair to near-stubble and dyed it blond, and added a pair of cheap reading glasses to complete the look. Dressed in plain black trousers and a T-shirt he'd bought in a harbor gift shop, he looked radically different from the photos that had appeared worldwide during the pandemic he'd unleashed. The camera around his neck completed the *I'm just another tourist* image he was going for.

He'd chosen the meeting place with care. Though he didn't know Dario well, he knew him enough to suspect he'd have some game up his sleeve. People like Dario didn't just give money away, and the man considered him a liability. But he had to take the risk. The fifty grand wouldn't last long, and he had no means to make any himself anytime soon. The payment he was about to receive from Dario would at least ensure a comfortable life. He had no other options. The people who'd promised to return his millions in exchange for his prisoner were all excuses and delays; they apparently weren't concerned enough with getting the girl back to find a way to make it happen.

Ideally, he would have sent his aide Patrik to the meeting in his stead, but he'd been arrested back in Budapest, and Andor couldn't afford the luxury of trusting anyone else. They'd either recognize him and turn him in—the price the FBI had on his head was one he'd never be able to match—or they'd take their chances with whatever was in the bag and run.

The Hammam Eden was the best place for him to get the transaction done in person. Whoever Dario sent with the money would have to undress, which would make concealing a weapon impossible. Not that he expected the emissary to recognize him, but it was better to be safe than dead. Of course they might catch him on the way out, but he'd done a very good job preparing his disguises, even if he said so himself. He would look one way coming and going from the place, and an entirely different way for the drop itself, to minimize the chances they would recognize him as he left.

He entered the toilet in the locker room and took a gray wig and mustache from his bag. He put them on and removed the fake glasses, pleased with the result. Moments later, wrapped in a towel, he entered the steam room and sat among the dozen or so men already there.

The conditions were ideal. This was the busiest time of day for the bath—which he'd learned during a phone call that morning—so it was easy to blend in. And the thick mist made it difficult to see anyone clearly.

Once seated, he removed the towel like all the other men and waited, trying to appear relaxed. He was nervous, but the prospect of getting the money kept him focused. Not long after he'd arrived, he caught movement out of the corner of his eye and a big man got up to leave. Andor waited another couple of minutes, then moved to where the man had been sitting. When he reached beneath the bench, he found the small duffel.

He glanced around casually. No one was paying him any attention, and the steam was thick as fog. He leaned over, unzipped the duffel, and rummaged through it for a closer look. It was full of hundred-Euro bills, with no sign of a tracking device. Satisfied, he closed it again and leaned back against the wall. He remained there another twenty minutes.

In the locker room, he entered the toilet stall again and placed the small duffel in his own bigger one and removed the wig and mustache. Back to his new blond self, he dressed and left through the back emergency exit, which he'd spotted the night before while scoping out the exterior.

He was home free. Dario had lived up to his word. Maybe they could do business together again, after all. Now all he had to do was return to the boat to pick up his belongings. He'd dispose of his troublesome prisoner out at sea, en route to his new life.

Jack's nerves were so on edge she jumped when a man exited through the back of the hammam. She'd been waiting behind a trash bin in the alley for forty-five minutes, and no one had used this door except a couple of employees stepping out for a smoke. "A blond guy with glasses just came out through the door."

"It doesn't sound like Rózsa, but why leave through the back?" Chase said into her ear.

"Exactly. His duffel looks damn heavy, if you ask me."

"Stay on him."

"I intend to."

"Let me know where you're headed."

Jack watched the blond stranger get farther down the alley. She was just about to step out from behind the bin to follow him when a second man came through the rear exit. He wasn't carrying a gym bag, and he strode purposefully after the first man. "Fuck. We have company. Dario's guy. Black hair in a ponytail?"

"That's him. But it doesn't make sense. He came out thirty minutes ago, and he's still parked on the bench out front. Green polo and blue jeans?"

"Yup."

"A double," they said at the same time.

"Dario's trying to pull a fast one on us," Chase said. "When did he arrange all this?"

"The goon's behind Rózsa and in front of me." Jack came out of hiding and started after them as quietly as possible, her Glock in her hand.

"Do what you have to."

"You know I will."

Ponytail was closing in fast on Rózsa, who was too intent on making a getaway and probably so confident he'd succeeded to bother looking back. It would be easy for the goon to off him in this quiet back alley, and if it were Jack in his place, she'd take him out right now.

When Ponytail reached for his chest, Jack broke into a run as silently as she could. He had the gun out and was taking aim at Rózsa when she jumped him from behind, hitting him on the back of his head with the butt of her Glock. The big man dropped like a brick wall and Jack had to use all her might to catch him so he didn't make noise. Rózsa was still in view; all he had to do was turn around and he'd see both of them.

Jack kept one eye on the fleeing figure as she let Ponytail fall quietly onto the cobblestone pavement. She didn't have time for this shit. She had to keep up with Rózsa, and he was nearing the main thoroughfare where he could lose himself in the crowd, or maybe get into a waiting car.

She stuck Ponytail's gun into her coat pocket and was about to leave when the guy came to and pulled a small automatic from the back of his jeans. Jack didn't hesitate. She raised her Glock with its silencer and shot him in the head, then ran after Rózsa.

Chapter Thirty-eight

"What's going on? Where is he headed?" Chase was restless. She'd heard a struggle in her earpiece and then Jack's fast breathing. She wanted to run in the direction Rózsa was headed, but Jack's lack of feedback made that impossible.

"I had to take down Ponytail," Jack finally whispered. "Rózsa is headed toward the cabs at the intersection of La Canebière and Rue Papiere."

Chase ran to the rental van, parked a few feet away from the bathhouse entrance, and punched the address into the GPS. "On my way."

Less than two minutes later, Jack was next to her in the van and they were tailing Rózsa's cab.

"Looks like we have company," Jack said.

Chase looked in the rearview mirror. She'd seen it, too—a small Clio with two men inside was keeping pace with them, always careful to stay a few cars back. "I noticed."

"Dario told his men to follow us if Rózsa got away," Jack surmised.

"I think they were ordered to follow us anyway. Only I'm not sure whether Dario or his sister put the request in."

"Same thing as far as I'm concerned. I'd love to get my hands on that crazy bitch."

"I know what you mean."

"When did he talk to her last?" Jack asked.

"He hasn't since the call we recorded, as far as I know. But it's possible he contacted her that last morning in Beijing. He probably had his cell when he met with Zhang, and by that time, he knew about the wire. The only person he spoke to after I got him in custody was his own guy—Dario made him get rid of Jules's body and told him he was going to take care of Rózsa himself and that the plans had been altered."

"Could be that the guy Dario talked to informed his sister and got new orders."

"But she had no way of knowing where Rózsa's meeting place was."

"She'd know if the Ponytails informed her after Dario called," Jack replied.

"I think we overestimated Dario. His sister's controlling this operation."

Chase pulled out her cell. "If she had somebody waiting at the airport to find out why Dario made the change in plans, they may have been following us ever since we got here. Which means they may know about the hotel."

She called the reception desk. "I'd like to book a room for two for…right now. My friend will check in, in a few minutes." She gave her own name and credit card number and then called Jack's room, relieved when Heather answered. "I need you to go to reception right now and pick up the keys for room 305. Then uncuff Dario and take him and your things to that room and stay there. You can leave our bags behind."

"What's going on?" Heather asked.

"I'm not sure yet," she said, gripping the phone tighter as she imagined Dario's sister sending goons to the hotel after her brother. "Just do it, and do it now."

"No problem," Heather replied calmly.

They followed the cab for another twenty minutes until it finally stopped at the quiet harbor of Montredon, a village south of Marseille. Rózsa got out and hurried toward the marina.

"Reno was right," Jack said. "He's been hiding on a boat the whole time."

Chase looked out over the crowded moorings. “At least two hundred boats are out here. If Dario’s men attack now—”

“I’ll check every single one until I find her,” Jack said.

“Not if he’s anchored somewhere out at sea, or at another harbor altogether.”

“Fuck. They’re getting out.”

Two rows behind where they were parked, Chase saw two men get out of the small Clio that had been following them. She and Jack pulled their Glocks out. “Who do you think they’ll go after first, us or Rózsa?” she asked, although she already knew the answer.

“We’re closest, but he’s about to get away with the money and his blackmailing ass.”

“Him it is, then.”

“Yup.” Jack grabbed her small rucksack. “And I’m not letting that bastard out of my sight, either.”

They got out of the rental and stayed close to the other parked cars, dodging and avoiding Dario’s men, but keeping an eye on them. The goons seemed too preoccupied with Rózsa to notice them.

“I think our hides are a bonus, not a must.”

“Rózsa’s on the dock. They’re going to move in on him.” She took off in that direction, staying back, while Jack followed Rózsa onto the pier.

The small marina was bustling with people and activity, and Rózsa seemed completely oblivious to the fact that four people were after him. He got into a small blue speedboat with an open cockpit.

Jack hung back, several slips away. She looked like she was inspecting the various watercraft anchored all around her.

At the same time, one of the goons Chase was following disappeared into the boat rental office, while the other waited outside.

“What are you doing?” Chase asked her through the mic.

“I doubt there’ll be a shoot-out here,” Jack said, “and we can’t just walk into the rental office with the other two to get a boat.”

“You can see them from there?” It was impossible from Jack’s position.

“That’s what I would do. Am I wrong?”

"No." She had to admire Jack's perceptiveness.

"Didn't think so. Be ready to jump on."

"Are you going to hijack one?"

"Of course not. I'm going to borrow it without asking."

Chase passed the boat rental and headed closer to the dock. She could feel the one goon standing lookout staring at her while they both kept an eye on Rózsa. Moments later, the other guy came out and they hurried toward a red speedboat just as Rózsa's blue one started moving.

"I hope you're almost done hotwiring," she told Jack as she closed in on the pier herself. "Rózsa and the goons are on the move."

"Walk faster. We're good to go." Jack waited behind the wheel of a small yacht, already idling, and when she jumped on they took off after the others. They cruised behind Rózsa and the other boat for fifteen minutes, headed out to sea. Like them, the goons were keeping their distance from Rózsa. On this sunny day, the Mediterranean was dotted with pleasure craft, mostly sailboats.

"Where the hell is he going?" Jack asked.

She grabbed a pair of binoculars off the console and looked toward the horizon. "I think I see something. A small, beat-up cruiser that's not moving."

Jack grabbed the binoculars to look for herself. "Cass," she said. "Let's take the goons out now."

"Still too many boats around. Be patient, you're close."

"Damn it." Jack gripped the wheel with both hands. "If he's hurt her, I'll kill him on sight."

"Rózsa's almost to it," she said, following his progress with the binoculars. The red boat pursuing him picked up speed, but before she could tell Jack to gas it, too, Jack hit the throttle and she had to hold on for balance. "He just changed boats," she said as Rózsa climbed aboard the cruiser.

They were gaining rapidly on the boat carrying Dario's goons. "Slow down, they saw us," she said when the two men turned their attention to their yacht and pulled out handguns. "Get down, Jack, they're going to—"

She pulled Jack down with her when the bullets started to fly around them. She stuck her head up during a brief lull and saw Rózsa peek out of the cruiser's cockpit, then duck back down again.

Dario's men were getting dangerously close to Rózsa's boat. She and Jack had only a minute or so to stop them before they went aboard and killed both Rózsa and Cass.

Jack pulled a grenade from her rucksack and handed it to her. "You know where this is for. I'll cover you." She revved the engine to full throttle and sped toward the men. The goons started shooting again and they shot back, Jack with one hand on her gun and the other on the wheel. They stayed low and were only a few yards from the boat when Jack yelled, "In five."

She removed the pin and held it.

"In two," Jack yelled, and slowed down.

She released the spoon, which gave them five seconds to detonation, and stood up while Jack kept firing. They were no more than four feet away when she threw the grenade into the other boat.

Jack hit the gas to get as far away as possible and they braced themselves for the impact. Seconds later, the air seemed to reverberate from the massive explosion, nearly knocking them off their feet, and bits of fiberglass and other debris rained down all around them. When she looked back, all she could see were floating plastic cushions and lawn chairs, and a swath of fire on the oily surface from spent gasoline.

Rózsa's cruiser was close enough for the waves to toss it around like a ball. Jack turned their boat around and headed for him. As they pulled alongside, he started shooting at them from a broken window of the enclosed cockpit.

Jack and Chase crouched down and waited. "How many bullets do you think the crazy scientist has?" Chase asked.

"Enough to put one in Cass."

"Not if he thinks we're here for the money," she said. "He'll use or kill Cass if he thinks she's important to us. Otherwise, she may still be his only meal ticket." She hollered over at the other boat as another bullet whizzed over their head. "Stop!"

"Who are you?" Rózsa yelled back.

"We just want the money."

"Are you with Dario?"

"Yes," Chase hollered.

"Who was on the other boat?"

"I don't know, but they looked like feds. They've been following us since the bathhouse."

"Why did you kill them?"

"Dario asked us to. If you get caught, he's screwed."

"I made a deal with that idiot," Rózsa shouted angrily. "Money in advance, for services not yet rendered."

"Look, man…" she shouted, then whispered to Jack, "Go now," before turning her attention back to Rózsa. "I don't know what your deal with Dario is. I'm just doing my job."

Jack crawled to the side of the boat away from Rózsa and slipped over and into the water.

"He wants me dead," Rózsa yelled. "He can go to hell."

"Just give me the money and we can get out of here." She tried to keep him occupied. "The police will be here soon after that explosion. I don't want to be around when that happens. Do you?"

"I made a deal with—" Rózsa stopped talking and, a few seconds later, Jack's voice rang out.

"I've got him!"

She looked up. Jack had Rózsa in a headlock from behind, his gun in her hand.

Chase jumped on the other boat and took him from Jack.

"Take the money," Rózsa pleaded. "It's in the cabin."

"Fuck you and your money. I'm going inside." Jack opened the hatch and disappeared below.

"Who are you?" Rózsa appeared confused.

"The people you stole from," Chase replied.

"But the money—"

"Stole the *woman* from."

"What?" Rózsa stared at her, obviously shocked.

CHAPTER THIRTY-NINE

Jack passed through the galley and opened the door to the tiny sleeping compartment. A petite figure wrapped in blankets lay on the floor. "Cass?" she whispered. "Cass? Baby, is that you?"

When the figure didn't stir, Jack's heart almost stopped. She knelt and slowly pushed back the blanket a bit. She saw her angel's blond hair, immediately recognizable. But still, she didn't move. Jack was close to losing her sanity. "Cass?" she said again, her voice shaking. She pulled the blanket down farther. Cassady's back was to her, and Jack gingerly touched her neck.

The skin beneath her fingertips felt cold. "Oh…fuck," Jack croaked as tears streamed down her cheeks. "Fuck. God, please, no." She touched Cass again and gently pulled her by the shoulder until she was lying on her back. Cass's eyes were shut, bruised and hollow, her lips were cracked, and her forehead had a long gash across it. Although she was dressed in an oversized sweatshirt, Jack could tell she was severely underweight. Jack touched her face and it, too, felt cold.

"God, baby, what did he do to you?" She fell back against the wall in anguish and pulled her hair. "I'm so sorry, Cass, I should have been there. I should have never let you go. I—"

"Jack, is she…?" Chase asked through her earpiece.

She couldn't bring herself to answer and admit the truth.

"I'm so sorry, Jack," Chase said when she didn't respond.

She rested her head on her knees and sobbed until she couldn't breathe.

"Jack?" The familiar voice was so faint she barely heard it.

Holding her breath, Jack scrambled to kneel beside her lover.

"Baby?" Cass opened her eyes.

"I'm here, baby." Jack caressed her hair. "I'm here, now." Her tears of grief became tears of relief, and she let them fall freely. "Landis, call for a fucking ambulance. Now!"

The rescue helicopter arrived ten minutes later, as the local police pulled up in two boats. Chase could tell Jack was doing her best not to shoot Rózsa as she watched the paramedics load Cassady onto the chopper. Every now and then, she had to remind Jack that Cass would be okay and that it was over.

Some of the local cops took Rózsa into custody and left immediately, while the rest stayed to interview them. After some discussion and a call to Interpol, Chase was given possession of the duffel bag with Dario's money. By the time they were escorted back to the harbor, the FBI and Interpol had agents there, waiting for a debriefing. One of the feds was already giving an interview to the media about how they had done their best to catch Rózsa and that all their efforts, time, and money had paid off.

"News travels fast."

"Especially where grabbing the glory is concerned. Some things never change," Jack said.

"No, they don't." Chase's phone rang and she checked the caller ID. "It's Pierce. Want to take it?"

"Yeah, right," Jack replied.

"Chase 200967."

"Is Lynx all right?" Pierce asked immediately.

"She'll be fine. They took her to the hospital."

"And Phantom?"

"She's next to me. Do you want to talk to her?"

"Yes. Great job, Chase."

"It was all Jack, Pierce. I could have never done it without her. She's the best you ever had."

Pierce cleared his throat. "I'm aware. I hope she stayed out of trouble."

"I kept her straight." She smiled. "Oh, I need you to call the feds and get the paperwork started on relocating Heather and her brother."

"Will do. Reno's already working on your transport home."

"Great. Here's Jack." She held out the phone.

Jack cringed. "I said no."

"He just wants to thank you."

Jack rolled her eyes and put the phone to her ear. "Yeah?" She tapped her finger impatiently on the cell as she listened for a few seconds. "Yeah, okay," she said, and hung up.

"I swear," Chase said, "sometimes you two are like father and daughter."

"And you would know this through all your years of experience with one?"

"Touché, but you know damn well what I mean."

"Scary thought," Jack said.

"Could be worse. By the way, I haven't smelled nicotine on your breath since we got here."

"I quit after I met Celeste."

"Did she scold you?" Chase smiled.

"Yeah, something like that." Jack chuckled. "I'm going to get my stuff from the hotel and head over to the hospital. They should be done examining Cass by then. I should have shot that medicopter bastard for not letting me go with her."

"There wasn't enough room."

"There would have been if I'd shot him." Jack laughed.

"It's good to hear you laugh again." Chase put her arm around her shoulder as they walked to the van.

Jack paused and looked at her. "We good again?"

"Yeah. We're good."

Jack insisted on driving them back to Marseille because she couldn't wait a second longer than necessary to be reunited with

Cass. The paramedic had tried to reassure her that Cassady would fully recover, but she'd looked so weak and frail Jack had to be with her to be certain. Chase didn't protest as she zipped between cars with the accelerator to the floor, and they were back at the hotel in record time.

"They're in 305," Chase told her as they scaled the steps to the lobby. She handed Jack the duffel with Dario's money. "Go ahead. I'll check us out."

"Are you flying back tonight?" Jack asked.

"I'm sure Heather can't wait to see her brother."

"And I bet you can't wait to see her."

"I won't bet against that." Chase grinned. "What are your plans?"

"I'm taking Cass back to Colorado to her place."

"And you?"

"I'm moving in and not letting her out of my sight."

"That's not going to be easy with her job," Chase said.

"Yeah, I know. But we'll figure it out."

"Are you coming back to the organization?"

Jack stared at her, mouth agape. "You're kidding, right?"

"I didn't think so. I'm sure Pierce wants you back, especially after this job. You really were born for this."

"Maybe I was," Jack replied. "But I can tell you what I *wasn't* born for. Someone controlling my life."

"It doesn't have to be that way. You could arrange something with him. With all due respect, you're too good an op to spend your life counseling runaways. Plenty of other people out there can do that, but only one can get *any* job done by any means necessary."

Jack knew that much was true, and that if she had to spend the rest of her life counseling she'd go stir-crazy. Could she really stick to counseling until Cass got out of the organization so they could retire to her dream house on the beach? Would she eventually come to envy Cass for going on a job? She didn't have those answers right now. "I'll see you upstairs." She rode the elevator to the third floor and knocked on 305.

"Come in," someone responded, but it wasn't Heather, as she expected, but Dario.

Alarmed, Jack opened the door and found Dario, uncuffed, in his wheelchair, with a smug smile. When she looked around and didn't see Heather, she pulled her gun. "Where's Heather?"

"Where is my money?"

Jack dropped the duffel on the floor at her feet. "Where is she?" she repeated.

A man came out of the bathroom, holding Heather roughly from behind. He had a 9mm semi-automatic pointed at her head. "Throw your gun on the floor."

Jack saw the look of terror in Heather's eyes and dropped her Glock.

The goon pushed Heather forward. "Both of you sit on the bed."

She sat next to Heather. "What's going on?"

"I wanted to make sure you kept your promise," Dario replied. "Where's your friend?"

"Still talking with police about Rózsa's capture." She was sure Dario had been informed.

"You are with the FBI, after all."

"Yeah," she lied.

"Then why are the police not breaking down that door for me?" Dario asked placidly.

"We made a deal. You give us Rózsa, and we let you go."

"Since when does the FBI make deals?"

"All the time," she said. "Don't be naïve. It's all we do." She hoped Chase would catch the conversation through the door before she walked into this. "Now take your goon and money and let us go," she said loudly.

"I don't think so," Dario replied. "You see, Heather and the two of you know too much. And frankly, although I thought you were with the FBI in the beginning, I have strong doubts now."

"And why is that?"

"Because one of my men had both your faces sent to someone who has access to a lot of information."

"Your sister," she said.

"And although we can't match...*Brett* to anything, we did find you. It would appear you have been very active."

"I don't have police records."

"No, you don't. But you have left quite an impression with others. The underworld, mainly."

"And of course you'd know them," she said.

"One hand rubs the other." Dario smiled.

"So what do you want, creep?"

He folded his hands in his lap. "We're going to wait for your friend to come back from her fake interview with the fake police, and then we're all going for a ride. And my sister thought I couldn't do this." He snickered.

Chase had her hand on the doorknob and was about to go in when she heard Jack from inside; she was telling Dario to leave with his goon and money and let them go. She pulled her Glock and quietly stuck her ear to the door. Dario said something, but she couldn't make out what it was.

She couldn't open the door because she had no idea where anyone was positioned, and she couldn't very well start shooting without knowing that. She'd only have one chance to fire before whoever was in there took someone down. Somehow, she needed to get a look inside before she took that shot.

Spotting the cleaning lady with her cart down the hall, she fished her cell from her pocket and dialed the reception desk. "I want two salads and a bottle of white wine in room 305."

If Jack was quick, she'd pick up on it and say she'd ordered it on her way up.

Room service arrived ten minutes later. Chase hid her gun behind her back when the young man approached with his tray. "Go ahead," she said, and stepped aside.

He knocked on the door.

"Who's there?" Dario asked loudly.

In a low voice, Chase told the delivery boy, "Tell him, Ms. Jack's order."

He nodded and called out, "Room service. Ms. Jack ordered dinner."

"She changed her mind."

Chase told the young man, "Say, 'I'm sorry, but you still have to sign for the bill. It'll get charged anyway.'"

He repeated exactly that, with enthusiasm. He seemed to be enjoying the game.

"Go away," Dario hollered.

"I will call my superior if you do not sign, sir," she instructed next, and the teenager repeated that as well.

She heard whispers and commotion inside the room, and Dario finally spoke again. "Just a moment."

The door opened a crack, and she saw Jack's hand stick out. "Let me sign," she said.

Chase took the bill before the delivery boy had a chance to give it to her. She shooed him away and wrote, *Where is he?*

Jack took the bill and her hand disappeared inside. When she thrust it back through the door a few seconds later, she held it so Chase could immediately read *to your right.*

Chase crouched, pushed the door open, and, without hesitation, shot the goon under the chin.

Jack put her arm around Heather, who instinctively screamed. "It's all right," Jack reassured her. "He's dead."

Chase ran to Heather and pulled her up. "Thank God you're okay."

"Call your sister," Jack told Dario.

"What?" Dario had a glazed expression, as though he couldn't register what had just happened.

"Call your sister," Jack repeated more forcefully, "or I'll fucking kill you."

"Why?"

"Because I want to tell her something."

"No." Dario tried to regain his composure, but he was obviously shaken. He'd gone white, and his hand trembled slightly.

Jack cocked her gun.

"Jack, what are you doing?" Chase didn't like the look in Jack's eyes. She wasn't playing.

"*Now.*" Jack pressed the Glock against his head.

Dario fumbled for his cell and dialed. When he hit the last digit, Jack grabbed the cell from his hand.

"Hi, bitch," Jack said, her voice oozing menace. "I want to introduce myself, since you seem to know a lot about me. My name is Jack." She paused to look at Dario for a moment before she shot him between the eyes. "And I just killed your fucking brother."

Two feet away from Jack, Chase could hear Dario's sister scream something in reply, but she couldn't make out what it was.

"Not if I find you first, bitch," Jack said, and hung up.

CHAPTER FORTY

The coroner's office removed the bodies of Dario and his goon while the French police tried to question Chase, Jack, and Heather about the shootings. Since they couldn't reveal much about themselves and their mission to the local cops, Chase contacted Interpol again to get the matter resolved quickly. Interpol had a direct line to Montgomery Pierce, so within an hour, the French police were ordered off the case and told to return Chase's and Jack's guns.

They all went back to Jack's room so she could retrieve her bag and head to the hospital, but as they were going in, Chase's cell rang with a call from headquarters.

She answered with her identification number, then immediately held out the phone to Jack.

Jack wasn't surprised that Pierce wanted to talk to her, since Interpol had filled him in on everything that had happened. She hated to defend herself to anyone, especially him, but considering the circumstances, she didn't have a choice.

"Was it really necessary to kill Dario?" Pierce asked.

"Yeah, it was necessary," she said, irritated. "He threatened both Heather and me with our lives."

"I understand he wasn't holding a gun."

"He planned to have his man do it,"

"Chase had eliminated him," Pierce pointed out.

"Why are you so uptight about the world being an organ trader down?" she asked angrily.

"I'm not. That's not the point."

"I killed him because it was only a matter of time before he sent someone else after Heather, probably even before we got her out of France and relocated."

Pierce sighed. "You don't know what you've started."

"I refuse to defend myself for killing that sorry excuse for a human."

"Damn it, Jaclyn. I don't give a damn about him," Pierce said. "It's you I'm worried about."

"I think my conscience can live with it," Jack replied sarcastically.

"But his sister can't. She's known as TQ—aka 'the Broker'—and, as it turns out, is one of the most dangerously influential people on the planet. She has links to everyone who's anyone, and then some. The feds have been trying to find her for years."

"I gave them her other half," she said.

"He was a halfwit they didn't care about and kept alive in the hopes of getting to her. The feds aren't thrilled about his demise."

"You're upset because I threw in a wrench for the feds? They owe us…you, for every damn job we've done for them so they can get the credit."

"It's you I'm concerned about," Pierce repeated, louder. "TQ will not rest until she avenges her brother."

"Then let her."

"Don't be stupid," Pierce shouted. "You have no idea what she's capable of."

"*You* have no idea what *I'm* capable of," she shouted back. "But aside from that, my life isn't your problem, as you've already proved. So take your concern and stick it." She hung up.

"That went well," Chase said.

"Jerk thinks he can start to care just because he feels like it today."

"He's right, you know." Chase put a hand on her shoulder. "The bitch will come after you."

"She won't find me."

"It sounds to me like she can do pretty much anything."

"So can I. I've learned from the best and worked for the worst. Let her bring it."

Chase squeezed her shoulder. "Let me know if…she starts making problems. I'll be there."

"Thanks." She smiled and looked from Chase to Heather. "When do you two leave for home?"

"In a few hours," Chase said.

"Take care of her, she's your Emily." Jack winked.

"How about you?"

"I'm going to the hospital. Cass and I will fly back as soon as she's stable. Could be a week or so." She crossed the room to get her bag.

"Will I see you when you get back?" Chase asked, her tone hopeful but uncertain.

She walked over and embraced her, and Chase hugged her back. "Yeah. You will."

❖

One week later
Marseille, France

Outside the hospital entrance, Jack opened the door for Cass to get into the rental car. She was thrilled Cass was almost back to her old self, and excited about her surprise. She hoped Cass would feel the same.

"Can you tell me now?" Cass asked impatiently. "You've been talking about this surprise for the past week."

"I'll tell you when we get there." She smiled as she got behind the wheel. She couldn't remember the last time she felt this happy. The sun was shining, they were in France, she had the world's most beautiful woman by her side, and she felt more in love than ever. She kissed Cass almost shyly on the cheek. It had been so long since she'd kissed her she wanted to swallow her whole, but Cass was still recovering and she didn't want to appear insensitive.

Cass turned to her. "Jack?"

"Yeah?" she said as she put the key in the ignition. When Cass didn't immediately respond, she looked over at her, concerned. "You okay?"

Cass grabbed her face with both hands and pulled Jack to her. They kissed so fiercely and so long, blinded by their emotions and lost time, they didn't realize a crowd was gathering outside the car. Someone yelled something in French and both of them laughed.

"We need to get a hotel soon," Cass said.

"Trust me, we will, because I'm about to pop in my pants."

They drove for nearly two hours, passing through farmland and vineyards and small towns. Jack steered and shifted with one hand, so she didn't have to let go of Cass's. Cass looked out the window, seeming absorbed in the scenery and her thoughts.

"It gets better." Jack squeezed her hand. "Someday, you'll give what happened a place."

"I know," Cass said, still looking out the passenger window. "How long did it take for you to deal after Israel?"

"Let's see." She pretended to think. "When exactly did we meet?"

Cass smiled. "Shouldn't take me long, then."

"I'm here for you, baby."

They reached the outskirts of a quaint but crowded village on the coast. Sailboats and yachts and other pleasure craft dotted the harbor.

"This is a beautiful little village," Cass said. "Where are we?"

"In Sainte-Maxime."

"Can we stay here tonight?"

"You bet."

Cass perked up, excited. "What a wonderful surprise."

"The surprise is yet to be revealed," she replied as she turned onto a narrow side street.

"You're killing me, Jack."

She pulled up to the curb outside Celeste's small house. "We're here."

"How quaint. Is this where we're staying?"

"No. Come on, I want you to meet someone." She got out and ran to the other side to open the door for her.

They walked to the door hand in hand and Jack knocked.

Celeste opened the door and smiled. "Right on time for lunch. Hello." She extended her hand to Cass. "I'm Celeste."

Cass shook hands. "Hi, I'm Cass." She looked from Jack, to Celeste, and back again. "My God. You two—"

"Cass, this is my mother." Jack put her arm around Cass's shoulder. "Celeste, this is who I love more than myself."

EPILOGUE

Boston
Two months later

Landis never imagined herself living in a house with a white picket fence and friendly neighbors, but here she was, and loving every minute of it. She'd sold her bachelor loft in the city and moved into the suburban four-bedroom only a week ago, but the split-level fit like a Glock, and she felt like she'd been here all her life.

No one who knew her well would believe the change. Her monotone, minimalistic and spotless environment had been replaced by warm, earthy colors, occasional clutter, and sentimental décor—framed photographs, mostly. Most significant, there were no clocks, aside from the one on her wrist, which she wore only when she was out.

She was in her study working on her next novel when the news came on, so she took a break to watch. The whole world was abuzz about the election of the first American woman president, and Landis had to admit she was quite psyched. Today was the day they intended to verify the result of two months of recounts that the guy who finished second had demanded.

Once she learned they would indeed have a female in the oval office, she switched off the TV and stopped at the display case with her collection. She smiled as she delicately ran her finger over the rare 1972 "Make a Face" PEZ dispenser Heather had gifted her, then returned to Landor. She was so absorbed in her work she jumped when she heard the main entry door shut.

A few seconds later, she felt hands run from her shoulders to her chest, hugging her tight. She spun in her chair and pulled Heather onto her lap. "I missed you." She kissed Heather meaningfully.

"Have you been drawing since I left this morning?"

"More or less. I have a deadline, beautiful." Landis kissed her neck. "How was your day?"

"You mean aside from the pandemonium because of the first woman president?" Heather smiled. "How cool is that?"

"Not as cool as having you come home to me. So how was it at work?"

"It was great." Heather beamed. "This design house is so progressive, and they're really interested in my ideas. I can't believe it."

"I can. You're very talented."

Heather was wearing a V-neck sweater that displayed her enticing cleavage. Landis kissed the spot between her breasts.

Heather caressed her neck and bent to kiss her. "I still can't believe we're…here," she said when they came up for air. "This isn't what I had in mind when you mentioned relocation."

"If you're not happy with the arrangement…"

Heather laughed. "I've never been more happy."

"Neither have I."

They both turned when someone knocked on the door.

"Is it safe?" Adam stood in the open doorway in his robe. "I can come back later if it's a bad time."

"The answer will still be the same." She sighed. "You are not allowed to peek at the drawings."

"Aw, *man*." Adam stuck out his lower lip in a pout, then exaggerated his frustration by dragging his feet down the hall back to his room. "You can't just tease a guy like that," he called out before he shut his door.

"Have you been teasing him?" Heather asked, ruffling her hair.

"I told him the tables were going to turn on Landor, and nothing more."

"Oh?" Heather lifted an eyebrow. "Do *I* get more?"

"Let's say…Emily will succumb to temptations and get in trouble."

"I see." Heather looked away. "And the demon saves her from the danger."

"Of course."

Heather blew out a breath. "Does Emily ever get to save the demon from danger?"

"Better yet." Landis kissed her. "Emily gets to save the demon from himself."

About the Authors

Kim Baldwin has been a writer for three decades, following up 20 years as an Emmy-winning network news executive with a second vocation penning lesbian fiction. In addition to her *Elite Operatives* collaborative efforts with Xenia Alexiou, she has published seven solo novels with Bold Strokes Books: *Hunter's Pursuit, Force of Nature, Whitewater Rendezvous, Flight Risk, Focus of Desire, Breaking the Ice,* and *High Impact*. She is a 2011 Lambda Literary Award finalist, seven-time Golden Crown Literary Society finalist—winning twice in Romantic Suspense, a 2010 Independent Publisher Book Award Silver Medalist, a 2010 Rainbow Award for Excellence recipient, six-time Lesbian Fiction Readers' Choice Award winner, and the recipient of an Alice B. Reader Appreciation Award for her body of work. In 2010, she recorded an audiobook of *Breaking the Ice*. She has also contributed short stories to six BSB anthologies: The Lambda Literary Award-winning *Stolen Moments: Erotic Interludes 2, Lessons in Love: Erotic Interludes 3,* IPPY and GCLS Award-winning *Extreme Passions: Erotic Interludes 4*, *Road Games: Erotic Interludes 5*, a 2008 Independent Publishers Award Gold Medalist, *Romantic Interludes 1: Discovery* and *Romantic Interludes 2: Secrets*. She lives in the north woods of Michigan. Her Web site is www.kimbaldwin.com and she can be reached at baldwinkim@gmail.com.

Xenia Alexiou lives in Greece. An avid reader and knowledge junkie, she likes to travel all over the globe and take pictures of the wonderful and interesting people that represent different cultures. Trying to see the world through their eyes has been her most challenging yet rewarding pursuit so far. These travels have inspired countless stories and it's these stories that she has decided to write about. *Demons are Forever* is her fifth novel, following *Dying to Live*, *Missing Lynx, Thief of Always,* and *Lethal Affairs*. She is a Lambda Literary finalist and has received Honorable Mention for the Rainbow awards, has won two Golden Crown Literary Society Awards and five Lesbian Fiction Readers' Choice Awards. Xenia is currently at work on the sixth book in the *Elite Operatives* Series. For more information, go to her Web site at www.xeniaalexiou.com, or contact her at xeniaalexiou007@gmail.com.

Lethal Affairs and *Thief of Always* have been translated into Dutch and Russian. In 2010, *Dubbel Doelwit* (Lethal Affairs) won second place among Dutch readers in their vote for best all-time Lesbian International (translated) book.

Books Available from Bold Strokes Books

Night Hunt by L.L. Raand. When dormant powers ignite, the wolf Were pack is thrown into violent upheaval, and Sylvan's pregnant mate is at the center of the turmoil. A Midnight Hunters novel. (978-1-60282-647-2)

Demons are Forever by Kim Baldwin and Xenia Alexiou. Elite Operative Landis "Chase" Coolidge enlists the help of high-class call girl Heather Snyder to track down a kidnapped colleague embroiled in a global black market organ-harvesting ring. (978-1-60282-648-9)

Runaway by Anne Laughlin. When Jan Roberts is hired to find a teenager who has run away to live with a group of anti-government survivalists, she's forced to return to the life she escaped when she was a teenager herself. (978-1-60282-649-6)

Street Dreams by Tama Wise. Tyson Rua has more than his fair share of problems growing up in New Zealand—he's gay, he's falling in love, and he's run afoul of the local hip-hop crew leader just as he's trying to make it as a graffiti artist. (978-1-60282-650-2)

Women of the Dark Streets: Lesbian Paranormal edited by Radclyffe and Stacia Seaman. Erotic tales of the supernatural—a world of vampires, werewolves, witches, ghosts, and demons—by the authors of Bold Strokes Books. (978-1-60282-651-9)

Tyger, Tyger, Burning Bright by Justine Saracen. Love does not conquer all, but when all of Europe is on fire, it's better than going to hell alone. (978-1-60282-652-6)

Words to Die By by William Holden. Sixteen answers to the question: What causes a mind to curdle? (978-1-60282-653-3)

Haunting Whispers by VK Powell. Detective Rae Butler faces two challenges: a serial attacker who targets attractive women, and Audrey Everhart, a compelling woman who knows too much about the case and offers too little—professionally and personally. (978-1-60282-593-2)

Wholehearted by Ronica Black. When therapist Madison Clark and attorney Grace Hollings are forced together to help Grace's troubled nephew at Madison's healing ranch, worlds and hearts collide. (978-1-60282-594-9)

Fugitives of Love by Lisa Girolami. Artist Sinclair Grady has an unspeakable secret, but the only chance she has for love with gallery owner Brenna Wright is to reveal the secret and face the potentially devastating consequences. (978-1-60282-595-6)

Derrick Steele: Private Dick The Case of the Hollywood Hustler by Zavo. Derrick Steele, a hard-drinking, lusty private detective, is being framed for the murder of a hustler in downtown Los Angeles. When his best friend Daniel McAllister joins the investigation, their growing attraction might prove to be more explosive than the case. (978-1-60282-596-3)

Nice Butt: Gay Anal Eroticism by Shane Allison. From toys to teasing, spanking to sporting, some of the best gay erotic scribes celebrate the hottest and most creative in new erotica. (978-1-60282-635-9)

Worth the Risk by Karis Walsh. Investment analyst Jamie Callahan and Grand Prix show jumper Kaitlyn Brown are willing to risk it all in their careers—can they face a greater challenge and take a chance on love? (978-1-60282-587-1)

Bloody Claws by Winter Pennington. In the midst of aiding the police, Preternatural Private Investigator Kassandra Lyall finally finds herself at serious odds with Sheila Morris, the local werewolf pack's Alpha female, when Sheila abuses someone Kassandra has sworn to protect. (978-1-60282-588-8)

Awake Unto Me by Kathleen Knowles. In turn of the century San Francisco, two young women fight for love in a world where women are often invisible and passion is the privilege of the powerful. (978-1-60282-589-5)

Initiation by Desire by MJ Williamz. Jaded Sue and innocent Tulley find forbidden love and passion within the inhibiting confines of a sorority house filled with nosy sisters. (978-1-60282-590-1)

Toughskins by William Masswa. John and Bret are two twenty-something athletes who find that love can begin in the most unlikely of places, including a "mom and pop shop" wrestling league. (978-1-60282-591-8)

me@you.com by K.E. Payne. Is it possible to fall in love with someone you've never met? Imogen Summers thinks so because it's happened to her. (978-1-60282-592-5)

High Impact by Kim Baldwin. Thrill seeker Emery Lawson and Adventure Outfitter Pasha Dunn learn you can never truly appreciate what's important and what you're capable of until faced with a sudden and stark reminder of your own mortality. (978-1-60282-580-2)

Snowbound by Cari Hunter. "The policewoman got shot and she's bleeding everywhere. Get someone here in one hour or I'm going to put her out of her misery." It's an ultimatum that will forever change the lives of police officer Sam Lucas and Dr. Kate Myles. (978-1-60282-581-9)

Rescue Me by Julie Cannon. Tyler Logan reluctantly agrees to pose as the girlfriend of her in-the-closet gay BFF at his company's annual retreat, but she didn't count on falling for Kristin, the boss's wife. (978-1-60282-582-6)

Murder in the Irish Channel by Greg Herren. Chanse MacLeod investigates the disappearance of a female activist fighting the Archdiocese of New Orleans and a powerful real estate syndicate. (978-1-60282-584-0)

Franky Gets Real by Mel Bossa. A four day getaway. Five childhood friends. Five shattering confessions...and a forgotten love unearthed. (978-1-60282-585-7)

Riding the Rails: Locomotive Lust and Carnal Cabooses edited by Jerry Wheeler. Some of the hottest writers of gay erotica spin tales of Riding the Rails. (978-1-60282-586-4)

Sheltering Dunes by Radclyffe. The seventh in the award-winning Provincetown Tales. The pasts, presents, and futures of three women collide in a single moment that will alter all their lives forever. (978-1-60282-573-4)

Holy Rollers by Rob Byrnes. Partners in life and crime, Grant Lambert and Chase LaMarca assemble a team of gay and lesbian criminals to steal millions from a right-wing mega-church, but the gang's plans are complicated by an "ex-gay" conference, the FBI, and a corrupt reverend with his own plans for the cash. (978-1-60282-578-9)

History's Passion: Stories of Sex Before Stonewall edited by Richard Labonté. Four acclaimed erotic authors re-imagine the past...Welcome to the hidden queer history of men loving men not so very long—and centuries—ago. (978-1-60282-576-5)